THE
CH

THE
CHOICE

JAKE CROSS

bookouture

Published by Bookouture in 2018

An imprint of StoryFire Ltd.

Carmelite House
50 Victoria Embankment
London EC4Y 0DZ

www.bookouture.com

ISBN: 978-1-78681-416-6
eBook ISBN: 978-1-78681-415-9

*I just told a hundred-thousand-word story to people
I don't know, and there's no more to say.
This is for my mum, my dad, and my uncle Frank,
who I didn't say nearly enough to at the end.*

CHAPTER ONE

KARL

Nobody wants to run someone down in the road, but for a long time afterwards Karl Seabury wondered if things might have worked out better if his van had slammed the woman into bloody oblivion.

He was piloting 3,500 lbs of Ford engineering along a road as wet as a solid river when something came at him. He didn't even see a shape, let alone a woman, just a hint of colour that extracted itself from the black wall of trees on his right. Instinct pistoned his foot hard onto the brake. There was a screech of rubber that sent birds panicking from the treetops like gravity-defying leaves. His seatbelt cut hard across his chest as he was thrown forward. Before he had time to wonder what the hell had happened, it was all over. The van sat stalled and silent, headlights illuminating the curving road ahead and a woman in a sodden summer dress.

He reached for the handle to open his door, missed it, cast his eyes away from the road to locate it, found it, started to open the door, ready to unload foul language, and let out a yelp as the door was wrenched from his grasp as if by a fierce gale.

She was right there in the doorway, a face that had been gaunt and terrified in the headlights now gaunt and terrified in the van's interior light.

'What the Jesus are—' Karl began, but froze when she grabbed his shirt in two tight fists.

'You gotta help me!' she moaned.

Autopilot kicked in. On a bright summer's day, he might have told her to calm down, might have stepped out of the van and led her to the side of the road to seek an explanation. But it was dark and eerie out there and that fired an alarm in his mind. He grabbed the woman under the arms, yanked her up and literally threw her across him into the passenger seat. Her head smacked the window but she didn't seem to care, and neither did he. He just needed to get out of there. He twisted the ignition key and stamped and pulled at all the appropriate pedals and levers until the road started to vanish beneath the vehicle. By the time he hit second gear, the woman had already slipped out of the seat and crammed herself into the footwell. She clearly didn't want to be seen in the van by whoever she was running from.

And then it happened again.

This time the shape was black, just like the night, and he didn't see a thing until it stepped into the funnels of his headlights. He recognised a human form, but the mental alarm was in full flow and this time his foot stayed away from the brake. He did not want to stop out here again, ever.

Instead, he tugged hard on the steering wheel, and the silhouette in his headlights vanished off to the side. It flashed by his door window then was gone. Only once he had passed did he realise it was a man in dark clothing and wearing a balaclava. A shiver ran down his spine at the image.

He looked in the driver's wing mirror at the shape in the road, saw twin dots of white high up in the blackness that must have been eyes, staring after him. Then the masked face turned to look the other way along the road, as if searching for something.

Karl gripped the steering wheel hard and faced forward again. Nothing ahead but the road and the trees and the headlights. He glanced at the woman.

'What the fuck's going on?'

'Is he gone?' she croaked.

The road grew bright ahead. Another vehicle. Karl hit his door lock, then cursed his paranoia – what did he expect, this new vehicle to screech to a halt and block his path? It would just be some car, just some guy heading some place. The headlights grew brighter, and then the car emerged from around the curve. The van's interior was lit up like a surgery.

In that moment he noted that her dress was patterned red and yellow, the material thin. She had manicured nails, smooth skin, and a bob haircut that was an ash blonde you couldn't get from a chemist. An indoor look, or a summer-lunch-on-the-patio look. Certainly not a cold-March-walk-in-the-woods look.

Then the car flashed by and all was dark again.

'He bloody who? Was he chasing you?' Karl realised his error even as he asked the question. Of course the guy was chasing her – he all in black, and her face coated in fear. 'What did he want? You know him? Where did you come from? What are you doing out here?' He took a breath, aware that his rapid speaking broadcast his own panicking heart. The man in black was gone, and the woman was safe, but not yet calm, and he felt some kind of male pride telling himself he needed to appear strong, as a knight in shining armour would. 'You want to tell me what's going on? The guy's gone, so you can sit up.'

She didn't sit up. She lay her head on the seat as if it were a pillow and closed her eyes.

'Do you live nearby? Did you get chased out of your house? You weren't out geocaching dressed like that, that's for sure.'

No answer. He touched her shoulder, using a fist because that felt less intrusive. She jerked but her eyes stayed closed.

'They came for us,' she said, voice low, as if talking in her sleep.

They? More than one? 'What did they want?'

'We have a house on land beyond the woods,' she murmured, a delayed answer to his previous question. 'We were going to have dinner. Our friends. I hope they're okay.'

'And what, these men came? And everyone ran away? Why are you on your own?'

'They wanted to hurt us, I think. And rob us. My husband… he…'

This was making his head spin.

'Where are you taking me?' she blurted, eyes open, a new fear imprinted on her face as if she suspected the nightmare might yet have another chapter.

'I'm sure all the others are okay,' he told her. He tried to picture a party on a rain-drenched patio. Men in tuxedos and women in flowery dresses. Expensive wines and political chat. And masked men in black rushing at them out of the trees, making them scatter. Might there be other drivers out here with scared people in their passenger seats, listening to such a tale?

'You're not going to throw me out, are you?' Her eyes were pleading.

'I'm not taking you anywhere,' he said. 'I mean, I'll take you to a police station. I'm not going to throw you out.'

She didn't speak again for a minute, and he was grateful for the silence. It gave him time to let this whole palaver sink in. He held his breath until he caught sight of the mist of orange lights oozing from around the next bend. A few seconds after streetlights appeared. Ahead were terraced houses in two neat lines. Karl felt himself relax. The proximity of the human world woke some confidence in the woman, too, because she struggled up out of the footwell and sat in the seat like someone… normal. She gazed out of the window as if enjoying the view, but then he realised his error: she was concentrating on the wing mirror. Checking behind them for pursuers.

'Burglars don't come chasing people who got away,' he said, unable to think of anything else. 'I'm sure they got spooked by everyone seeing them and just ran off.'

She looked at him. Hard. As if he had said something naive. Or just plain wrong.

'Maybe you shouldn't have stopped for me. Now you're caught up in this and in danger, and it's my fault.'

'What? Why?'

She was examining a cut on her elbow, probably from crashing through trees to escape her pursuer.

'Hey. What do you mean? Why would I be in danger?'

'It's probably fine,' she said. But she didn't sound sincere. In that moment, he wished he'd never slammed on the brakes.

CHAPTER TWO

BRAD

Brad knew something was up the moment he spotted his partners.

Set in a clearing dotted with tree stumps, the house was a stone barn conversion with an open-air porch containing all-weather sofas arranged around a large firepit. And there sat Mick, puffing away at a cigarette and seemingly oblivious to the light rain. Like a guy on holiday, no worries in the world. Dave paced nearby, agitated.

He saw them clearly in the light from the flames despite their black clothing, but they did not see his approach until he was almost upon them. Like an apparition, he appeared from out of nowhere on the porch, right next to Dave who jerked with a grunt when Brad said: 'Why are you two outside?'

'Where the hell is she?' Dave snapped. He was thirty-five, short and black and sinewy, like a track guy.

Mick jumped to his feet. He was in his late forties, tall and white and heavily built, like a gym guy. He had an iron-grey buzzcut. 'Where is she, Brad?'

Brad ignored the question, his eyes on the kitchen door, fearful of what lay beyond. He didn't like that his partners were both outside. And not wearing their balaclavas.

Dave seemed to sense Brad's concern and said: 'It went bad. Ain't a summer scene in there.'

Brad started for the door. He got the handle in his fist and was about to twist it when Mick called out: 'We can't leave her body out in the trees, Brad. Come on, let's go get her.'

Brad hesitated but didn't turn around.

Mick said: 'I mean, a body she is, right? Dead and no threat to us, for sure. Because you wouldn't stroll back all casually like this if she had escaped.'

'She escaped.'

Dave started cursing.

Mick's voice was low and calm as he said: 'Brad, how did she get past you and outside from all the way upstairs? A five-foot woman in high heels.'

He ignored that question and explained that she'd hit the road and jumped into a passing vehicle. This news increased the tempo of Dave's complaints. He'd expected rage from Mick, but there was none. The man simply shook his head like a parent disappointed in a child.

Brad said: 'She's running for her life. Scared. That's what you wanted. What's the problem?'

'Shut the screeching, Dave. Why don't I show you the problem, Brad? Open the door.'

*

Brad entered the house, his worry rising. The kitchen hummed with modern technology but retained a graceful air with bespoke cabinets, a slate floor and exposed timbers. There was a wine rack. It had been attached to the wall beside a tall freezer, but was now broken on the floor, bottles scattered or shattered everywhere, and in among them was a man in a white suit, sitting against the wall. The red soaking his torso wasn't a vintage Bordeaux.

Grafton. Dead.

Mick spoke from right behind him, like a devil on his shoulder. 'I wish you could have seen his face. He knew the end was coming.'

Brad could hear Dave further back, still moaning.

'I'm thinking the plan to put him in a wheelchair looks like a no-go now, right?' Brad asked, shocked. But was he really that surprised? He knew what Mick was capable of.

'Well, I fucking apologise, Brad. I went a bit far.'

Brad turned to him. 'You didn't go too far, Mick. You made the exact journey you planned. You were going to kill this guy all along.'

'For what he did to me, you really think it was going to be just a scare? Really?'

The silence of the house. Dave's constant moaning. The fact Dave and Mick had been waiting outside, no balaclavas. Something was horribly wrong about that picture. Brad moved through the kitchen and stopped in a hallway with a vaulted ceiling and paintings lining both walls. It was there he learned exactly what was wrong.

Another body. Another man. This guy wore jeans and a corduroy jacket. He was down on his face, and there was a chunk missing from where his shoulder and neck met, as if a giant bite had been taken out of him. The shotgun blast had taken him in the back. As he ran away.

'He had the audacity to turn his back on me, this one,' Mick said.

Brad ignored him. The vast living room was next. Three-quarters of the floor was carpeted, the rest wood and set aside for an office. Here again was a vaulted ceiling in white and exposed timbers painted black. Colour had been added with yellow and green spotlights arranged artfully around all the walls. The lounge section of the room had a corner sofa and upon it, sitting back as if relaxing in front of the TV, was a woman in a dress. A spotlight above the sofa bathed her in green, making Brad think of some bizarre art exhibit. Her death had been cleaner because she had just a single bullet hole in her forehead. No blood, strangely. His head spun.

'Jesus Christ, Mick, what the hell is this? We came here to put Grafton in a wheelchair, but he's dead. That was overkill. But this. I don't know what the hell to call this.'

Dave followed them into the room looking like he'd just lost a winning lottery ticket. 'This is a fucking escalation into a new universe, that's what this is. What do we do? And the woman's running around out there. So now we're fucked.'

'Not if we get her before she goes to the cops,' Mick said.

'She's probably in a police station right now,' Dave screamed.

Mick grabbed Dave's shoulders. He was a clear head taller than him. 'Calm down. She won't be running to the cops tonight. She'll expect this to have been a robbery, or some guys wanting to give her sweet hubby a hiding. Like you said, he always told her: if any shit kicks off, crawl under a rock and wait it out. So, she'll just hide away somewhere till morning, and then try to call him, or go to some place they pre-arranged. He'd fucking kill her if she brought the cops around. So she won't be going to any fucking police station tonight. Hell, he's Mr Invincible, remember. Maybe she thinks he killed us all. So, we have time to find her.'

'And then what?' Brad said. 'Kill her right out in the open?'

Dave was shaking his head. 'We need to sterilise this place and get rid of the bodies. Make out somehow that Grafton fled. No one was ever here. Let's think about this. No one knows about this place. Everyone thinks he's in Spain. That gives us time to get rid of the bodies. We could torch the place afterwards. It won't matter if his wife goes to the cops after that.'

Mick let him go. 'That wasn't the plan—'

'This slaughterhouse wasn't the damn plan!' Dave yelled.

Mick pulled something from his pocket, holding it out to Dave and Brad. 'This was the plan. And we're sticking to it. It will work. Understand, you two?'

Dave glared at the item in Mick's palm. 'Provided he didn't go to a party five minutes after I stopped watching him. He could be surrounded by witnesses.' That would muck up their plan entirely.

'It buys time. It gives him a damn headache. That's enough for me. So that's the plan. Right, Dave?'

'Whatever!' Dave said, throwing up his arms like a petulant child.

'Right, Brad?' Mick asked.

Brad didn't speak, and he didn't look. He was staring at the woman on the sofa. The only one who hadn't fled. When they had burst into the house, the three dead people had been in here, very much alive and sitting on the sofa and chatting. Grafton's wife had been upstairs, using the toilet. When Brad had gone up to get her, he'd left Dave and Mick holding their guns – a shotgun for Dave and a pistol for Mick – on the three captives. Brad could see now how it had gone down. At some point after Brad had climbed through the bathroom window in pursuit of Grafton's wife, Mick had shot sofa woman, and the two men had fled. No way would Dave have pulled the trigger, so Mick must have taken the shotgun from him and pursued the two men. He had probably blasted the other guy first just because he was a loose end – an obstacle between Mick and his target. Grafton must have thanked his lucky stars when he heard the explosion in the tiny hallway and the guy next to him had dropped. But there were no lucky stars a few seconds later. Grafton hadn't been shot in the back, so, trapped in the kitchen, he probably turned to face his executioner. Mick probably said something to the man before pulling the trigger. Probably smiled right at him, knowing the last laugh was his.

Two men escaping. Perhaps reason enough, in a panic, to blast away. But the woman?

'You shot this woman out of the blue,' Brad said. 'She didn't try to escape. She didn't move. She didn't do anything. There was no reason to kill her.'

'You were chasing Miss High Heels through the woods, so how would you know? Maybe she pulled a weapon.'

Last he'd seen, the dead woman had been shivering with fear, a million miles from launching a counter-attack against two masked

gunmen. 'You planned to kill them all. Not just Grafton. Not just
a scare. Kill them all. Everyone here tonight. Planned all the way.'

Mick stepped in front of him, blocking his view.

'This doesn't work if the woman who got away from you in
high heels saw a face that wasn't dark-skinned, does it? So, can
you be sure she didn't see your shiny white skin?'

'I didn't let her escape on purpose,' Brad said, shifting the focus
from the question. Because she *might* have seen white skin through
the large eyeholes in his ski mask. And that would well and truly
fuck up the plan. 'Since we're in this shit together, at least admit
you came here planning to kill everyone.'

'What did you think, we'd blast Grafton away and make the
others do pinky promises that they wouldn't tell? Besides, any
friend of his doesn't deserve to live.'

A scary thought. Brad wondered what would have happened
if this party had been for thirty or forty people. He wondered if
he had really believed Mick's assertions that the plot had been to
steal Grafton's money and smash his legs and spine to confine him
to a wheelchair. But it was what it was, and they had to deal with
it. They didn't have a choice.

'So what's next?'

Mick walked to the sofa and sat down, just feet from the dead
woman. The cushions moved under his weight, and the woman's
head lolled to one side. Mick laid his head on hers, like lovers
watching a romcom, and laughed at Brad's expression.

'We need to find the wife. Tonight; because when she finds
out her hubby's dead, she'll have no reason not to go to the cops.
Let's not panic, though. We've got all night.'

'We don't have to do that,' Dave said, shocked. 'She didn't see
our faces. She can't tell anyone. The so-called plan still works. It
could still work if we torched this joint.'

Mick stared at Brad.

Brad stared back.

And then Brad said: 'I don't know if she saw I was white.'

Dave started to complain again. Mick halted him with a raised hand.

'Don't worry, Dave, because Brad got the registration of the car she jumped in. Right, Brad?'

Brad nodded. 'I got both. Two cars out there.'

'There we go. Good news all round. Dave, you go and make sure we haven't left anything that can make Her Majesty our landlady for the next fifty years, like some of that cheap tacky jewellery dripping off you with your name all over it. Brad, you go to the shed. Then we find whoever picked up the wife and make him wish he hadn't. I'll call Król for that shit. Right up his alley. Then we go home and celebrate. That's a plan and a half. Grafton's going to spare me a bottle of Scotch. I reckon he won't mind. I'll ask him and take silence as a yes.'

'And what's in the shed that you could possibly want?' Brad said. He had a notion in mind, but dearly hoped he was being silly.

Mick's grin said he wasn't in luck. 'This is my one and only date with Grafton, and I'm not leaving the dance early.'

CHAPTER THREE

KARL

He had been on his way to a house in Wilmington, to see a client, but that plan was out the window. Once he was through the housing estate, he cut north on Leyton Cross Road because a sign pointed that way for the A2 which he could use to get back to London. As if sensing that he had changed his route, the woman in the summer dress asked him where he was going.

'To a police station,' he said, surprised. Where did she think – Alton Towers?

Since reaching lights and civilisation, she seemed to have calmed down. But suddenly she appeared agitated.

'What's wrong?' he said, his own fear rising. He checked the mirrors, just in case she'd spotted a tail. He imagined a man on a bike emerging out of the darkness like a ghost ship, but the world behind was black and blank.

'We need to go somewhere safe,' she said.

He was full of conflicting emotions. The urge to do the right thing was wrestling a cowardly craving to stop and kick her out. He didn't like hassle, and this was a big one. At the same time he was annoyed at her for dumping a shitstorm in his lap, and embarrassed that he felt that way.

'What do you mean? Police stations are safe places. You're making no sense. You want this guy caught, right?' Plural, he remembered. More than one guy.

Her hand went onto his arm, which made him jerk and almost tug the van into the oncoming lane and an insurance claim by a people carrier.

'Jesus.'

'Just take me somewhere safe. Then you can go back to your quiet life and forget about me.'

He laughed. Disbelief, not amusement. 'How about the 71st Signal Regiment?' They'd passed a sign for the barracks a minute earlier.

And then she started to cry. He thought about putting an arm on her shoulder, just for comfort, then thought better of it. If he tried to console every lost soul in London, he'd have to give up work and drink a lot more caffeine. He wasn't Florence Nightingale. He'd rescued her on a dark road, so it wasn't as if he was being unkind.

He pulled out his mobile phone and started to type, but she snatched it from him and tossed it down by her feet. Without a word. And that was when he knew: she had a problem with going to the police. And he thought he knew why.

'You know these people. That's why no police, isn't it? I see your wedding ring. Is it your husband? Is he a wife beater? Were you running from him? Him and his pals? Did they get too drunk or something? Started trouble?'

She didn't answer. He took a sharp left, and they drove west with the A2 running parallel on the right. She stared out of the side window, forehead on the cold glass. No answer from her, which was answer enough.

'Did he hurt you? What happened?' No response. 'Hey, just because this guy's your husband, it doesn't mean he's allowed to smack you around.'

No answer. He'd read about beaten wives before. About their desire to believe their violent partners were good men. He pressed his foot harder on the accelerator. He would take her to the police station and that would be his part over. If she chose to pretend to the boys in blue that nothing had happened, that she had walked into a door or fallen down the stairs, well, that was her choice. His good deed for today would be done.

But her continued silenced gnawed at him. He imagined a big man making this little woman cower in a corner. Hitting her. Begging for forgiveness afterwards, and getting it. Again and again. And that made him angry.

'You've got to tell the cops about him, before he bloody kills you next ti—'

'I don't know who they were,' she cut in. 'It's not my husband. It was my husband they came for. They came to hurt him. He...'

She fell silent. He looked at her for so long that the van drifted, and he had to jerk the wheel to retain the road. She had been about to admit something, he figured. Something she suddenly decided she didn't want him to know. Something that would explain why her husband had the sort of enemies who'd crash a party to get at him, who'd hurt his wife to hurt him. But that just made it stranger that she wouldn't go to the cops. *She wasn't think*— '—ing straight,' he said out loud. 'We should go to the police right now. Your husband might be hurt. He might need help.'

'I just need somewhere safe. I will go back to the cottage tomorrow.'

He laughed. Disbelief. 'This is stupid. You can't just hide away. Is there someone you know? We could call the cottage. Maybe he'll answer, and all will be fine.'

'Not tonight. Not until we know what's happened.'

'Is it a pissed-off ex-boyfriend or something?' Her attitude was so puzzling that it was becoming scary. 'You need to tell me why you can't go to the police.'

They passed a streetlight. Her face flashed; he saw pleading eyes, like a hungry dog's. You were supposed to go all soft, seeing eyes like that. He just got annoyed.

'Tell me why you can't tell the cops?' he snapped. 'That guy back there was trying to hurt you. He might go hurt someone else. Why wouldn't anyone with a brain tell the police? Why are you protecting him?'

She was silent again. Head on the glass.

He shook her shoulder. 'Hey, listen to—'

'I'll go tomorrow, I promise,' she snapped, and slapped his hand away. 'But not now. I just need somewhere to stay. Until tomorrow. Do you live alone?'

He really didn't like this.

CHAPTER FOUR

MAC

In a job devoid of humour, you had to get your laughs somewhere. One piece of comedy enjoyed by Bexley's Murder Investigation Team was to ring the HAT phone at end of shift. This was the Homicide Assessment Team's phone, and it only rang when there was a dead body. That meant a trip out to a scene, where the team would search for signs of foul play. No fun for the team getting ready to go home; much fun for the detective making the bogus call.

Detective Sergeant Manzoor Gondal, a British-born Pakistani copper, expected a colleague to laugh down the line when he stomped to the phone and slapped it against his ear. But it didn't happen. He gave his two other HAT pals the sign that the call was real. They groaned. At least with a bogus call you didn't have to go out in the dark and peruse some lunatic's handiwork. Half an hour later and the next shift would have got this one. Killers could be so inconsiderate.

'Three dead,' he said. 'Cottage on Tile Kiln Lane. Thank the Lord for catch-up TV. Someone call Mac. Tuesday's his gym day, isn't it? He'll have a barbell above his head, so be careful not to say, "drop everything."' Gondal was the only one who laughed at his joke.

Tile Kiln Lane was only a mile and a half south of them. They were there fifteen minutes later. The scene was already a party.

Outside the postcard-material house were three patrol cars, two crime scene vans, and two ambulances. The crime guys were suiting up in plastic outfits to prevent contaminating evidence. The paramedics stood around their vehicles like guys on strike because there was nobody to save, and the bodies couldn't go anywhere until the pathologist said so, and he wasn't here yet. The uniformed cops stood around because the remote location meant no horde of gawkers and reporters to hold back, chatting as if welcoming a break from slinking around dark streets in the hope that some hoodie would smash a window right in front of them.

A uniformed officer stepped up and introduced himself by his full name, making a big show of adding the title First Officer Attending. The HAT guys got sent out in advance to see if the dead body was a homicide, but uniforms were always dispatched prior to that to make sure there was actually a body to assess. Couldn't have important detectives mobilised for an old rolled-up carpet that some fool thought looked like a dead man. The uniform explained that an anonymous call from a phone box in Greenwich had directed the police here. That he had secured the scene. And that it was not a pretty sight inside: three in a very serious state of dead-as-doornails. He pointed out the plastic shoe covers on his feet, as if to wordlessly say he had taken care inside, touched nothing, followed the rulebook in preparation for the big boys. Gondal was happy with the man because he'd attended scenes where cops were covered in blood or holding murder weapons.

As DS Gondal was on the porch, warmed by the dying pit fire and about to head inside, he turned at the sound of a vehicle arriving. The cops blocking the woodland gateway, their fluorescent jackets glowing brightly in the approaching headlights, parted to let a car through. Bexley detectives, who'd get the case if it wasn't a homicide. This late, no doubt they were hoping for foul play so they could turn right around and vanish. Gondal, likewise, was hoping for a suicide or accident that he could dump on the local boys.

He put his hand on the door handle, ready to go inside.

Not a pretty sight, the FOA had said, but a gruesome and suspicious scene didn't always mean murder. Just three days ago the police had been called to a house to find an old man dead with a vicious head wound and a hammer lying in a pool of blood. The HAT boys got there and saw the loose and cracked light fitting above and the blood on the corner of a metal coffee table, and had a vision: a slipped foot as the guy was doing DIY, a tumble, a temple against the sharp table corner. Dead. Seconded by the coroner.

He stepped inside. So, announcing murder wasn't always straightforward, or easy. You had to walk around, read the scene, analyse the little details, and make a professional judge— There was a bloody chainsaw next to a severed leg in the kitchen. Right before him, dead centre of the room, as if carefully arranged as a welcome for visitors. This would be one for the crime encyclopaedias.

He stepped back out. The pair of local detectives were approaching the other two HAT members, and in a croaky voice Gondal called out to the newcomers: 'Waste of petrol. We're having this one.'

He walked over to all four guys, almost shaking. He'd attended many murders, but most were committed by one spouse or family member against another: crimes of explosive rage; a moment of lost control followed by a lifetime of regret. Stab or blunt-force wounds, not the work of a chainsaw. Cut throats or cracked skulls, not chopped-off body parts. They all saw his face and knew this was a big one.

He explained what he'd seen. Everyone looked at the house, as if wary of the building itself.

'Is it him, then?' one of the borough detectives said. The HAT guys looked at him in puzzlement.

'You know who owns this place, right?'

They didn't.

'It's owned by Pasticcio Food and Wine.'

One of the HAT guys said: 'Ronald Grafton's mum's joint?'

That was right, the borough detective told them. Elena Grafton owned the restaurant, a gift from her son. And the house had been bought in the name of that company.

'So, this is his hideaway?' a HAT guy said. 'I assumed he had run to Spain.'

Yeah, they all agreed. They'd heard that, too.

'So is it him? Is he inside? Is he dead?' the borough detective said.

'Someone's dead,' Gondal said.

They decided to have a quick look. They did it from the doorway before shifting off the porch and waiting on the grass.

'That's Mac,' someone said as they heard loud music heading towards them from beyond the treeline.

*

Thirty seconds later a Nissan turned into the woodland gateway. A large man got out. Late forties, brown bomber jacket and trousers in black. The trousers had a crease above both knees because they'd been folded in his car all day. His right ear was bandaged. The Mac in question: Bexley murder squad's boss, Detective Chief Inspector McDevitt.

'Is it Ronald Grafton?' Mac called over from his car as he opened his boot to get protective coveralls.

'Not sure yet,' someone said. 'Grafton's joint, but maybe he fought back against whoever came for him. Maybe Grafton and his boys painted the town red in there. It would be just like that guy to get out of this one untouched.'

'Well, he's fucked either way,' Mac said.

CHAPTER FIVE

KARL

Unsure of where to head or what to do, Karl had parked on a quiet stretch of road. They had sat in silence for what seemed a long time.

'What's your name?' he asked.

She didn't look at him, and didn't speak for a few seconds.

'Liz… Smith.' She stuck out her hand.

A pause there before giving up Britain's most popular surname. Added to her dress, and the fact that she was secretive about her husband, her use of a clearly false name dinged another alarm bell. She was obviously hiding something, and not because she was scared and didn't trust him but because it was something a person might want to keep secret. He shook her hand purely to prevent her from becoming more unsettled. Her skin was cold which made this whole shebang that little more unnerving. He checked the mirrors to make sure no vehicles were approaching.

'So what's your name?' she asked.

Those wrestling emotions again. She was wet and hurt but hiding something, and sad and scared, but lying to him. He knew he should be more sympathetic, but suspicion was blocking that response.

'Your name?' she pressed.

Wet and hurt and sad and scared, yet calmer now.

'Perhaps it's an embarrassing name like Doug Hole or Sonny Day?'

And now making jokes.

'I'll just call you white-van man, shall I?'

'Peter,' he said. It was his wife's dad's name: anonymity was his safest option here, until he knew what the hell was going on. 'Over the moon to meet you. I wish you'd jumped in front of my van years ago.'

'And you're married?'

'Happily. So, hands off.'

'Well, you got an attitude all of a sudden.'

Back there: masked men, maybe a beaten husband, and some missing silverware – and she was worried that he seemed unfriendly?

'What do you plan to do if you don't tell the police, eh?'

She didn't seem fazed by his sudden change of subject. 'I need to stay away just for the night. I can't risk running around tonight because I have no idea what's going on. I'll meet back up with my husband in the morning. He'll know what to do. He always does—'

'Always does? This chase-through-the-woods thing some kind of weird weekly role play, is it?'

She glared at him like a teacher impatient with a child interrupting her class. 'This a big joke to you?'

He met that glare with a stubborn one of his own. 'Hey, for me fear and sarcasm are lifelong soul mates. So, if I'm making wise cracks, you can be sure I'm far from having the time of my life.'

She looked away. 'Like I said, I'll meet with him in the morning. But not tonight. And if I can't stay at your house—'

He barked a laugh and showed her his wedding ring. 'See this? We'll both be running for our lives if I take you to my house. So, burn that idea and scatter the ashes, okay? Isn't there a friend's house you can stay at?'

'All in Kensington. Too risky, though.'

'A hotel?'

'Ron always told me not to trust… to stay hidden until the next morning.' She put her hand on his arm. 'It's Karl, isn't it?'

'How the hell did—' And then he saw what she held in her hand. His business card, plucked from a bunch on the centre console. For a daft moment he feared that she somehow knew who he really was.

'Karl, I know you're worried about what's happening. I understand. But please, trust me. I don't want to go to the police. I have my reasons, but I don't want to tell you any more than I have to. I *am* thinking straight. Please understand. Although it sounds a bit dodgy to you, it's the way it must be done. No police, not tonight. Tomorrow. Tonight, I just need a safe place to stay. You have a shop, don't you? It'll be closed and empty, won't it? Can I stay there? Just for tonight?'

He couldn't believe what he was hearing. What the hell was he getting into? Or, more correctly, what was he being *dragged* into?

CHAPTER SIX

MAC

'Witnesses?' Mac asked.

'Over east, 500 feet or so, are some estates,' Gondal said. 'But there's trees blocking any noise the killers might have made. Even the chainsaw. There's nothing around here. It still amazes me that you can find remote places like this in London. Great for containing the crime scene, terrible for witnesses.'

Mac nodded. It was the damn reason the killers chose this place for the hit.

Gondal said: 'I sent a guy out to fingerprint the phone the initial call to the police was made from. And a guy hunting for CCTV. Out here, no one cruising past would have seen or heard anything, so the caller might actually have been present during the carnage. It was all the way over in Greenwich, weirdly. That seems off to me. Someone feeling a sudden bout of guilt, maybe.'

Good idea. But these killers were professional. Nobody would find CCTV footage of any use, and the fingerprint man would return with the bad news that the phone box had been wiped clean. Mac asked if anyone had been inside the house yet.

'Just the FOA and the paramedics, but they were careful. We were about to head in. The pathologist isn't here y— oh, here we go.'

Two thick beams of light splashed over them as the uniforms barring the entrance to the area had admitted another vehicle. A middle-aged man got out, nice and slow for his £40 per hour. He waved, then went to the back of his vehicle to suit up.

The detectives shook hands with the pathologist. Mac explained for about the fifth time how he'd lacerated his ear: car door. The pathologist was on call tonight, like Mac's team, and moaned about having to bring his dog, which they saw in the back of his car. Mac couldn't resist a stroke of its fur – it accepted happily. The pathologist clapped his hands together when he was told that the bodies inside were probably not in whole form, like a guy getting ready for a challenge.

The borough detectives offered to hang around – akin to saying the murder squad needed them – but Mac gave them a firm no, thanks, we've got it covered, go find a stolen cat or something. The locals made their exit, somewhat reluctantly, like partygoers turned away from a nightclub door. Everyone else went indoors, except Mac, who chose to remain outside for the time being to think to his iPod music. It was how he did things sometimes.

*

Everyone spread out once inside. The bodies were the pathologist's domain, so nobody touched them. They stepped around blood and body bits as if they were pieces of furniture, taking photos and bagging and dusting things because you never knew what insignificant piece of nothingness might provide the breakthrough.

The MIT detectives on the next shift arrived shortly afterwards. One was a slimeball DC called Downey, one day from the end of his police career. Two HAT guys left to pursue enquiry avenues, but Gondal chose to stay. They filed past their boss and went inside. Mac continued to look around outside, thinking, to a backdrop of loud rock music.

When finally he entered, he was called to a body in a white suit. Or, more correctly, body parts in a white suit. Or what technically should be described as a red suit.

'I think it's him, sir,' Gondal said. He searched his superior's face for an emotion. Mac was staring down at the head, which was a good five feet from the nearest part of the rest of the body. It was impossible to recognise the face, of course, because the face had gone. Literally. And not because of the chainsaw: it had been peeled away carefully. A bloody knife, surely the surgical instrument, had already been bagged. It would go for DNA testing, and the scientists would shake with anticipation.

A typical home in this mess would have required a long face, a shake of the head, an angry or saddened tone, and the detectives stuck to the script. Every cop in London would be glad Ronald Grafton was out of the picture, but an abattoir was no place for rejoicing. Plus, cops didn't want their jobs taken away by street justice. And there were two other victims, who might turn out to be law-abiding citizens. So, there were counteracting emotions at play, which explained a host of neutral expressions.

'It might have been a trophy,' Gondal said, referring to the face. They hadn't found it.

Mac doubted they ever would.

There was a shout from the lounge. Gondal and Mac headed that way. They knew the tone of that shout. It meant one of their team had found an important clue. The hand of lawful justice might still get a role in this case.

In the living room, a detective stood by the dead woman on the sofa, holding aloft a necklace in a pair of tweezers.

'Our bad guy is Davey-boy,' the detective said with a grin, as if the case had already been solved.

Mac and Gondal closed in carefully, stepping on boards placed so that shoes wouldn't crush evidence, while the slimeball DC Downey took out his phone and sent a text about this new development to someone who had no business knowing. All three stared at the swinging pendant, and understood the detective's cry of glee. It was the sort of clue that detectives dreamed of: a military identification tag.

CHAPTER SEVEN

KARL

He'd heard the urban legend of the kidney thieves, but right now wished he hadn't. What an idea to suddenly pop into his head: that she was planning to drug him and steal his organs to sell on the black market. But the fact that this woman didn't want the police involved was making him paranoid. He almost blurted out a silly lie that he had kidney cancer.

'You would be helping me more than you know. I know this is very puzzling for you, and I'm sorry that I can't give you answers.'

Kidneys on the black market was a wild idea, but stolen goods on a flea market was not. He could imagine the plan. She pretends to be escaping from an attacker and flags down a lone guy in a vehicle, and then asks for a place to stay the night. A lot of guys would find it hard to say no to a beauty in a thin dress. Maybe there would be some sex, maybe not. But during the night she opens a window, and her supposed attacker sneaks in. Their victim wakes from a drugged sleep the next morning with, at best, a need to visit DFS for new furniture. *If* he wakes.

'Just for one night, Karl. Please.'

He knew he was being silly even considering that this was some kind of scam. Too much detail in the plan: she could have pretended to be lost, or homeless. But he still regretted saying 'Okay' even before the word dissipated in the air. Too late to back out now, especially given how buoyant his news made her. He was glad she was no longer a shivering ball of fear but still wished he'd never met her. Maybe the police would have picked her up and all her problems would have been solved by now. But it was what it was. He shut her out and drove.

The guy in Wilmington waiting for his new fancy car alarm to be fitted would soon wonder what was going on. He might call Karl's home, and then Karl would have to explain to Katie where he'd been. That was a new damn worry. He could lie, of course, but for all he knew one of her friends had seen him driving with another woman in the van. And he wasn't going to lie to his wife. Withhold information, yes, but not lie.

Liz, if that was her name, rabbited on. He should have been rid of her by now, yet there she still sat. She should be miles away from him, with his boot print on her arse, but instead they were headed to his shop. Every extra minute he spent with her increased the chances that someone his wife knew would see them together. Bad enough out on the roads, but if they were seen going into his shop while it was closed...

Soon she fell quiet, maybe out of things to say, or maybe finally aware that he didn't want to talk. They drove in silence. Karl watched the road and tried to pluck up the courage to race to a cop shop before she realised what was going on. Liz spent most of the time staring out the side window with her head on the glass. He figured the talking had helped her forget, which meant the silence was driving it home again. He tried to think of something to ask so she'd talk again. But he discarded subject after subject, and the minutes ticked by. He realised he didn't want to talk, even if it meant leaving her tense and worried. He went back to the road ahead. She stayed with the world slipping by.

After a while, he caught movement as she lifted his business card again. 'So what electronics stuff do you sell? DVD players and things?'

He looked at her for the first time in fifteen minutes. He answered with a simple no, and fell silent again. Minutes ticked by. Liz seemed happy with this, breaking her own silence only once she saw Queen Elizabeth II Olympic Park far off to their left.

'Where are we?'

'Old Ford.'

'Ah. I heard this place was getting a makeover because of the Olympics a few years back.'

'Well, they overlooked the bit we're going to.'

She seemed relaxed, so he figured she might now be open to visiting the police. And when a police station came into view half a minute later, he prayed she wouldn't object. But in his peripheral vision he saw her sit up straight and glare into the side of his head.

She said nothing, though. Looking good. As nervous as a guy topping off a house of cards and praying it didn't tumble down he prepared to make the turn.

And then: 'Don't, please.'

And that was that. As he cruised past the station, he cursed his weak soul.

Sunrise Electronics was nothing but a sign above a large shuttered doorway in a windowless, single-storey building on a tucked-away street. The building was lined with shutters and signs on both sides of the street. The road ended at a high wall covered with faded graffiti and topped with rusted barbed wire. Just the one way in and out.

Karl's place was second from the end, past a place called Fine Ink's and before a joint that sold antiques. He pulled up to the kerb and stopped. Across the road a shutter was rolled up at a place called Computerz. Light washed the street and inside Karl could see shelves of machines and bits and pieces, and a desk at the back. A guy was sitting behind it, putting on a white shirt and suit jacket over his coveralls. There was a pushbike leaning against the exterior wall.

'Wait till this guy's gone,' he said, sinking low in his seat.

Seven minutes later the road was dark, Computerz closed up like all the other places.

They got out and walked to Sunrise Electronics' shuttered door. Karl unlocked it and used a button to raise it three feet. He ducked inside. When Liz didn't immediately follow, he stuck out a hand and waved frantically. She muttered something about expecting him to open the shutter fully, then bent and ducked inside, taking care to make sure she lifted the hem of her dress with one hand and protected her head with the other, or maybe just her expensive hair.

He told her to wait while he moved through the dark and hit a switch that powered a strip light in the ceiling. The room was like the place across the road: just a desk at the back and a few filing cabinets and wall-mounted shelving bloated with stock.

'This is just some workshop,' Liz moaned. 'I can't sleep here.'

'You should have waited a minute, then. The guy driving behind me owned Bedroomworld.' He had saved her, offered to drive to a hotel, and now offered her a roof for the night, and this was his thanks? A wrinkled nose, as if he'd brought her to a pig pen.

'Up in the loft there's a hammock.'

'A what?'

He tugged a string that hung a few inches from the ceiling. A loft hatch flipped open. She made a surprised sound, and then a pleased sound when he lifted a wooden ladder from behind the counter.

He placed the ladder against the open hatch, and she followed him; in a dress, there was no way she was going first. The loft was carpeted and had a window in the sloping roof. Wedged in a corner was a TV/DVD combo, with a PlayStation alongside and a bean bag in front. There was a small coffee table with a kettle, cups and *Ultimate Fighting Championship* DVDs scattered on it. The hammock was strung under the ridgeline of the roof.

She knelt on the carpet and looked around, her head just inches from the roof, and said: 'What's crime like around here? Is it likely to be burgled tonight?'

'You tell me.'

Her look was a puzzled one. She picked up one of the mixed martial arts DVDs. 'A man cave. Is this place for when your wife kicks you out?'

'It's for when North Korea bombs us. So… I'm going home. You make sure—'

'What's all that stuff?' she asked, pointing to the far brick wall where there was a grid-like shoe rack containing electrical gadgetry. On the bottom of the pointing left hand, running from the wrist to the end of her pinky finger, was a tattoo of tiny paw prints.

He got the feeling she was stalling, probably because she didn't want to be left alone. He didn't care. Every minute in this woman's company was one less in Katie's. So, it was time to go. 'Don't worry about all that stuff. And don't touch it. Touch nothing, okay? I'm going home. There's no food, but there's a water bottle next to the TV. The shutter can be unlocked and raised from the inside. I'm back here to open up at eight in the morning. You'll be gone by then, right? And remember, we never met.'

He started to climb down the ladder.

Just his head and shoulders were exposed to her when she said: 'You might be in danger. I don't think you should go home tonight.'

He froze. 'What the hell are you talking about? Why am *I* in danger? They didn't see me.'

But one of them had, or at least his van. His was unmarked and like a thousand white vans that criss-crossed London every day and night. But each had a registration plate for a reason: to be traced to a person and an address. He'd managed to confine this worry to a bit part, but in light of her warning it took the centre stage.

She shrugged. Paused. 'Just be careful.'

'I'm fine,' he said with false boldness. 'Just be gone tomorrow morning. Nice knowing you. And don't answer the phone, okay? We get calls from America, so it might ring early in the morning. I'll turn off the answering machine so you won't be woken. Leave it alone. Leave everything alone. Everything.'

'I'll wait for you. I want you to take me to my friend Danny's house tomorrow.'

His mouth fell open. 'What? There's someone you can go to after all? Why didn't you mention him earlier?'

'I can't go tonight, if that's what you're getting at.'

Exactly what he'd been thinking. An extra half hour out of his life wouldn't have mattered if it had meant getting rid of her. 'Why?'

'Tomorrow. I've explained all this. You can take me there tomorrow.'

He literally roared like a lion in frustration. He knew she wouldn't be convinced, so started down the ladder again. 'When I get back tomorrow, you make sure you're gone. I did my good deed for this year. Be thankful you got any help. I had magnificent news six months back, and I don't think I stopped smiling till you appeared.'

She pulled a scornful face. 'Lucky for some. But I've got nothing to smile about, have I? I need help and you have to help me.'

He jumped the last few feet to the floor. 'Okay,' he said, and it was a blatant lie. He wasn't going to take her home, to this Danny's house or anyplace else. He figured that the morning would give her a fresh outlook and that she'd leave before he returned. But if not, it was a problem for a new day. Right now all he wanted was to go home to a woman he gave a shit about.

He deactivated the answerphone and went for the door. He flicked the light, crossed the dark room, and slid under the shutter. He could see flickering light from the loft: she had turned on the

TV, volume low. For the millionth time he regretted ever having met this woman, then he lowered the shutter, locked it and got into his van.

He hoped he'd seen the last of Liz Smith.

CHAPTER EIGHT

MAC

The ID tag was military chic, unfortunately, so there was no real name, no religious leaning or medical information embossed on it. Just one word: Bosszilla. But it was enough. The detective who found the dog tag knew the word was urban slang for a rampaging, angry superior, Godzilla-like. He was formerly of Operation Trident, now called the Trident Gang Crime Command, which had been set up following a wave of shootings and killings in Lambeth and Brent, and he was well aware of a guy known as Bosszilla: Dave Ramirez.

Grafton hadn't yet been confirmed as one of the dead, but he had a concrete connection to the slaughterhouse and now there was a pretty solid clue that one of his biggest and most notorious rivals had been there. It was enough to put two detectives in a speeding car.

Within fifteen minutes of the find, the two detectives were at an address in Crayford. They knocked and then pushed their way inside past an exhausted-looking and sweaty girl wearing next to nothing. Ramirez's new girlfriend, probably. He was in the bath, and the detectives liked that. They figured it could mean he was washing blood off his skin.

He was a skinny little Latino guy with a bushy moustache that looked like a cartoon version of a disguise. And wide, shocked eyes. A big shot Bosszilla when he had his minions surrounding him, but not alone and naked in a bath, and he knew it. No match for two tall coppers, so he came quietly. He'd been arrested enough times to know that the place to put up a fight was the police station, with a solicitor as a cornerman. Fuckers like Ramirez usually won on points, but no matter how lucky they got, or what weapons they brought to the fight, the cops always got the first strike. And they took pleasure in it now as they yanked him from the bath, slapped on cuffs and spat the word 'murder'.

Mac decided to watch Ramirez's interview on video-feed from another room. He'd investigated Ramirez five years before, when the kid was just nineteen. A murder outside a Chinese takeaway in Kensington, when Mac, a year into DCI status, had headed their murder squad. There had been suspicions that somehow Ramirez had wielded the knife but convinced one of his cronies to take the rap.

DS Gondal and a lanky DC called Cooper conducted the interview. Ramirez hadn't yet been told who he was suspected of murdering. A breach of the rules, sure, but normal rules didn't really apply when dealing with people like Ramirez. They wanted to see how he reacted, and they didn't think he'd be making an official complaint.

What he did was sit in silence and look nervous. Understandable. They'd sourced intel on this guy from the local CID and had been warned that he was cocky and liked to play games during questioning, but that was around coppers he knew: the ones who nicked him for running prostitutes, or peddling heroin, or breaking the legs of people who didn't pay for his protection; charges he always beat. But these were new boys and the stakes were higher.

DS Gondal and DC Cooper made small talk without the tape recorder snooping. Now, backed up by a video camera eyeballing everything, Ramirez had lost his nerves. So, he was one hundred per cent attitude. He hadn't asked for a solicitor yet, and had even admitted why: if his brief got called in, his mum would know it was serious and would hammer him. All three laughed about this. The cops knew Ramirez was trying to get them onside with a bit of larking about, and they pretended to think of him as a regular guy by asking about his hobbies, offering drinks and moaning about the March weather. A nice little party.

And then Mac sent Gondal a text telling him to begin. Gondal started the tape and introduced everyone present. Party over.

'Do you know of a man called Ronald Grafton?'

'Teflon Ron?' Ramirez said, laughing. 'Who doesn't? The guy you assholes can't seem to nail. That fraud thing just gone, fucked you all up on that, didn't he? You had nothing on the Thames suitcase thing, did you?'

And then he stopped laughing. Very abruptly. He looked at each detective and nodded. 'I get it. Oh, man, do I get it. I thought that guy had tried to fuck me over, set me up for some murder. But it's him, isn't it? Teflon Ron, Mr fucking Invincible, has finally been slotted, hasn't he?'

CHAPTER NINE

KARL

You might be in danger. I don't think you should go home tonight.
What a damn thing to say to him. It was bouncing around in his head like a pinball. The desire to return home, get back to Katie and snuggle up was intense, yet he pulled into a bus lay-by and grabbed his mobile off the floor, and booted up the Internet. He had to know more. He typed:

TILE KILN LANE ATTACK

Three months ago a guy walking his Labrador had been accosted and robbed by a low-life hoodie who took the dog's sparkly collar.
Not that.

ELIZABETH SMITH

There was a Liz Smith with a silly blog about her pregnant cats. Another Liz Smith was collecting for a charity parachute jump. Grunge band singer Liz Smith was followed by a plethora of LinkedIn and Facebook Liz Smiths. None of them.
A memory: *his* Liz had mentioned Kensington.

ELIZABETH SMITH KENSINGTON

Christ. There was a Liz Smith, online boot store owner, who was showcasing her gear at the Kensington Shoe Event this month.

ELIZABETH SMITH KENSINGTON PAW PRINT TATTOO

He almost laughed. There was a Liz Smith who ran a kennel called Pawprints, in Kensington Park, Adelaide, Australia, which had been picked up by a newspaper because she had tattooed an advertisement for her business across the whole of her back.

A memory: *his* Liz had called her husband Ron.

ELIZABETH SMITH KENSINGTON PAW PRINT TATTOO
RON

Jackpot. Top of the search results. Online edition of *Home & Fashion* magazine, dated six years ago. The story was titled:

HOLLYWOOD-STYLE WEDDING: THE JOURNEY BEGINS

He clicked it and up came the story, with a photo.

He skimmed the article. Local businessman Ronald Grafton last week married his long-time girlfriend, Elizabeth Smith, at Kensington Palace, at a serious price tag for one afternoon. The lavish outdoor ceremony on the Orangery Lawn had been attended by hundreds, and protected by the police. *Home & Fashion* were the important words here, though, because while the article made a big song and dance about hats and flowers and fancy fabric, it didn't reveal much about the newlyweds.

But there she was, glowing, like an angel, in a white wedding dress. The husband, a good-looking man in his late thirties, was facing her, left arm around her waist, right hand raised and pressed flat against her left hand. Karl saw the paw print tattoo on both their hands, and he understood. A split tattoo, like the broken heart ones he'd seen on some young lovers, with the paw prints denoting the beginning of a long and harmonious journey. Sweet, but only worth one line of text. Geraniums got two.

He impatiently flicked back to the search page, ready to type in a new name:

LIZ GRAFTON

But then he saw the link in second place on the list, and the words:

GANGLORD MARRIES CHILDHOOD SWEETHEART

CHAPTER TEN

MAC

After the pleasant shock of learning that the mighty Ronald Grafton was dead, Ramirez quickly realised why he was sitting where he was, and turned down No-Comment Street. But he didn't yell for a solicitor, so the detectives were still happy. Maybe he was aware that in a murder case police could question a suspect for a day and a half without legal aid if a senior officer authorised it. But he wouldn't know that their superintendent, aware that the tactic was a dog that could bite the owner once a case hit court, had already said, *Don't even ask.*

A pretty gruesome murder, they said. No robbery, this. Revenge. By enemies. Ramirez and Grafton had a long-standing beef, right?

'No comment,' Ramirez shot back.

Tit-for-tat vandalism of one another's property. Violent Braveheart-style clashes between their minions in the streets. Drug zone wars. Then there was that episode with Ramirez's prized restored Cortina, up in flames. Enraged him, surely? Could such a thing be forgiven?

'No comment.'

Question after question about his volatile relationship with Grafton got the same response, altered now and then only by the injection of a swear word. He gave them nothing, but at least that included a request for a solicitor.

Just because he was travelling down No-Comment Street, it didn't mean the detectives couldn't steer the conversation where they wanted. Grafton, as Ramirez had said, was known as Mr Invincible on the streets, and in the media as Teflon Ron, which was a play on the nickname The Teflon Don given to infamous mobster John Gotti because charges never stuck. Most of London's big criminals had these daft names, some they'd picked themselves. Grafton called himself The Boss these days, an inert title he liked because he was trying to project a straight businessman image, and who'd trust someone with a macho tag?

Had Ramirez heard that nickname for Grafton?

'No comment.'

A stretchy name, The Boss. It didn't say much about the man behind it. Bosses could be fair, good, kind, approachable, or completely the opposite. You didn't know which sort you were dealing with if a man was simply The Boss, did you? But Bosszilla, that was different. That painted a certain picture, didn't it? Ever heard that name?

'No comment.'

A few years ago there was a gang of idiots called the GodZillas, in Lewisham, where Ramirez was born. Just kids, runts, fools who thought it would be cool to pretend to be bad boys and collide with other gangs on the streets of London instead of going to school. One chap, now doing twenty for aggravated robbery, was called Rodan, right? Was the youngest of the members called Godzooky?

'No comment,' Ramirez spat over the detectives' laughter.

But the boss, he was Bosszilla, and, according to the Trident files, Bosszilla was a guy called David Ramirez.

'No comment.'

Gondal's phone beeped.

SHOW HIM

He showed Cooper the text and plucked out a plastic bag.

'Found at the murder scene,' he announced, loud and proud.

They noted the puzzlement on Ramirez's face as he scrutinised the dog tag inside. There was no brave attitude now. Just fear.

In the room next door, Mac studied the video closely, looking intently at Ramirez's face.

In that split second No-Comment Street turned onto Lawyer Lane.

'Lawyer? Won't your mum kick your butt for that?' Cooper asked.

Gondal said: 'You're saying this dog tag isn't yours?'

'Lawyer.'

'You're saying that we couldn't find people to say they've seen you wearing this?' Cooper questioned.

'Lawyer.'

Gondal asked: 'You're saying we won't find your DNA on this when the results come back? Or Ronald Grafton's?'

'Get me a damn lawyer.'

They had no choice. The police station duty solicitor had an office upstairs, which was a nice touch to ensure that the arrested didn't wait long for their tax-paid defender to arrive, as long as you got collared before 5 p.m. So, they needed to call a guy in, which meant a wait, and they weren't going to let Ramirez do that on a comfy chair. He got a phone call first, then an hour in a cell. An hour alone in a stone box could feel like a long time.

*

It felt longer for Mac, who found himself experiencing something he hadn't for a long, long time. Worry. He slid by the cell and peeked in, and saw Ramirez pacing. He couldn't read him.

His fears grew worse when Cooper approached with an update. He had called the Crown Prosecution Service, but the government lawyer he reached hadn't been impressed.

The Trident Gang Crime Command had got back to their former colleague with some bad news. They had statements, photos and files on the GodZillas, but all of it old. Nothing more recent than seven years ago. Ramirez had been fifteen when he set it up, but as he aged and upped his reputation and moved to Kensington, he disbanded it in favour of more secret squads, bigger scores, and heavier stuff than street brawls. They had ceased to exist, and Ramirez hadn't been associated with the Bosszilla name in a long time.

According to the CPS, all Ramirez had to do was claim he'd lost the dog tag, and nobody could prove otherwise. Get something meatier, the lawyer had advised. Cooper had even pretended to get cut off so he could call back and talk to another lawyer. A woman this time, with a helpful dislike of gang violence because her sister's friend's son took a wandering turf war bullet. But the same grim outlook. Get something meatier and we'll look at it.

Mac got the feeling he was starting to see their whole case unravel.

CHAPTER ELEVEN

KARL

Ganglord? Karl clicked the link with a shaking hand.

The wedding again but with a different angle to the coverage. *Home & Fashion* had the prim and the elderly to please, but this writer didn't. Here, the cops were not present as security, they were eyeballing the crowd in search of wanted criminals. Many underworld faces had been expected at the wedding of one of Britain's most notorious crime barons.

Karl typed in the name Ronald Grafton, and his worry rose.

Ronald Grafton: bigshot London criminal with ties to organised crime in Spain. His fingers were in every pie unpalatable to the police: prostitution, drugs, fraud, guns, identity theft. Rumoured to be worth £10 million. His nickname was Teflon Ron, and it was quite fitting: five times in the last nine years upholders of law and order had hauled him into court, only to watch him stroll right back out with a shredded prosecution case in his wake. What was then the Serious Organised Crime Agency failed three times to do him for drug smuggling; three years ago, when a former colleague was found in a suitcase floating in a river, he beat a murder charge because the police didn't act upon information about a second suspect; and a year ago he was acquitted of arranging arson attacks on property owned by alleged rival criminals. He was due in court in a few weeks on a charge of fraud. The story was dated two months ago. Nervous, Karl hit the news tab and got a story that was ten hours old.

LOCAL GANGLORD CLEARED OF FRAUD CHARGES

There was a photo: Ron and Liz atop a set of wide stone steps outside a law court. Holding hands, their other arms raised for a crowd of onlookers. Her left hand, his right, with the paw prints denoting the end of a long journey this time. He wore a white suit. She wore the very dress wrapping her body when Karl nearly crushed her in his van.

A neutral piece of reporting this time. It didn't say Ronald Grafton was a businessman wrongly accused, and it didn't say another powerful criminal had beaten the system. It listed facts and handed over to Grafton himself for a quote given to reporters mobbing him like a film star. He said the charges had been absurd, justice had prevailed, now all he wanted to do was go celebrate with his wife and friends – *thanks to all who believed in me, thanks to my loving wife who stood by me at every turn, and* adios.

He couldn't be reached for comment and that evening his Kensington home was dark and silent. He was believed to have flown out of the country to celebrate in one of his Spanish homes with his wife and a couple of close friends.

Oh no he hadn't, Karl thought with a genuine chill on his spine. He'd stayed right here in London, tucked up at some secret hideaway. Maybe the paparazzi couldn't find him, but others knew where he'd gone. The worst possible kind.

Shit.

It explained everything. Why Liz had used her maiden name, and why she had refused to talk about her husband, and most of all why she had refused to go to the cops after their refuge was attacked. High-level criminals had their own code of justice and didn't involve the police in anything, be it a stolen pushbike or attempted slaughter at a remote hideaway home. That was why her husband had ordered her to flee and lay low if ever they got attacked by enemies, of which he must have many.

This was serious, of the deadly kind. Nobody stormed the home of a gangland boss unless they were planning to spill blood, and nobody got where Grafton had if enemies were dealt with by a stern telling-off.

Whatever had happened at the cottage, the decor wasn't going to appeal to *Home & Fashion*.

CHAPTER TWELVE

MAC

Bad news came thick and fast.

First, Ramirez's solicitor arrived with a disk that he said had been delivered to him right outside the station. A hooded man had approached him as he turned into the car park, slapped the disk against his windscreen, and scarpered. Ramirez hadn't explained, so three cops and one solicitor watched the film it contained without knowing what was going to be shown. And once it became apparent, someone quickly hit fast forward to spin through the feature as quickly as possible while the others studied the carpet or their fingernails.

So, Ramirez hadn't phoned his mum, as they'd expected. He'd called one of his boys to bring the video along.

The next piece of bad news: Ramirez's mum had been informed of developments by one of her son's friends, and she'd thundered down to the station to raise hell. She was taken to Ramirez's cell and given five observed minutes, but only after Ramirez promised to placate her and send her on her way, and under no circumstances to discuss the case with her. Clearly someone forgot that this guy was a criminal.

After her five minutes, she got time with the solicitor as she headed for the exit. What was said became clear not long afterwards.

*

The main players grouped in the interview room. Lawyer and client conferred in whispers, like lovers. Ramirez was smug when the lawyer said his client wasn't going to answer questions but would make one statement. Ramirez rolled his shoulders and took a breath, like a guy getting ready for a long and eloquent speech.

'I lost that dog tag. Like years ago. I ain't seen it since. If you found that on Grafton's body, someone's setting me up. You got nothing on me.'

He went on to explain that his mother had admitted she took a whole bunch of her son's stuff and got rid of it. The dog tag, she remembered, had gone into a box that had been stored in the attic. Over the years, all sorts of people had been in that attic: builders, family, friends, even the police. And they'd moved house, so the removal guys also had an opportunity to steal.

And that was that. The interview was paused as the detectives went out for a chat.

*

Mac met them in the hallway. Gondal was angry: he accused the solicitor of coaching the mother and son in how to discredit a major slice of evidence. Cooper, though, liked Mrs Ramirez's input: it backed up his idea that someone out to frame Ramirez could have accessed the dog tag. The two detectives started to argue, but Mac shut them down.

'Let's forget the dog tag. The CPS wasn't interested. It's documented that Ramirez's silly GodZillas gang is defunct. The tag will still make its way into court as padding, but we can't rely on it. So, let's focus on other things. Next step?'

Gondal said they should get the video analysed, just in case there was digital witchcraft involved: anyone planning a triple murder, especially of a man like Grafton, wouldn't just hope for the best. They'd erect a force field.

Cooper disagreed, instead wanting to pursue Ramirez's own theory: the set-up. Guys like Ramirez collected many enemies – 'so let's start looking at who might prosper with him locked in a cell.'

They looked at Mac to see which side of the fence he'd take.

'Send the video for analysis,' he said. 'You never know. Ask him to clarify how to spell his surname. But wake him at four in the morning to do it, just to give him a headache. I'm going home. Call me if anything important pops up.'

Cooper asked: 'You want to apply to hold him for longer?'

They had Ramirez for twenty-four hours before they had to charge or release him, but higher authority could extend that up to ninety-six. Or fourteen days if they could angle towards a terrorism offence, which Gondal made a joke about doing. But Mac told them to hold off until tomorrow, when they knew more, if anything.

That wasn't the end of the bad news.

Before heading home, Mac dropped by the incident room, just to see if the worker ants on the phones and computers had learned anything that would make him groan. Brand new murder case, so the room was bustling with activity, most of the team bleary-eyed because they'd been up all last night on another case and had been woken by the call to arms. On-call detectives knew they could be summoned to a moonlit murder – but they hoped for a daylit discovery. In he walked, and there on the incident board was a printout from a car sales website featuring a dark blue 1999 Volvo V70 estate for £1,200. What the hell?

'Where's this from?' he shouted at the room, his finger stabbing the picture.

A young DC looked up from a file she was studying at her desk, and raised her hand like a kid about to ask for the toilet. In fact, everyone was looking in their direction. A rare outburst from a usually introspective team leader. 'I printed it off. I found it. Someone called it in.'

A helpful member of the public, she explained. A man had seen all the police activity around Tile Kiln Lane and had remembered a suspicious car because it had been driving close to the scene with three men in dark clothing inside. He'd noted the registration and had called in with it. She had interrogated the PNC, the Police National Computer, and discovered that the owner had reported the vehicle stolen four days ago.

Now that she'd explained, she was smiling, perhaps thinking she'd get a compliment – because this was a big lead, right?

'Don't just pin stuff on the board without telling a superior,' Mac roared at her. 'What if I didn't see this for a week?'

She didn't know what to say, but managed: 'I'm sorry. It just came in. Five minutes ago—'

'And what if I'd already had information about this car from another source, but the report said a BMW? I'd be out there looking for a BMW, wouldn't I? While all along you knew it was a Volvo. How much time would that have wasted?'

'I'm sorry I didn't call. You and DS Gondal were busy down-stairs. I was going to say when you came back.' Those watching tried to pretend they were busy minding their own business.

'From now on, all of you, anything important that comes in comes straight to me. Within one minute. Understand?'

A chorus of acknowledgement.

Mac stormed out. Which meant he didn't see the DC, Downey, take a stroll to the kettle. Downey didn't want a drink, though: he wanted to see the details of the car pinned on the board. Back at his seat with a coffee he wasn't going to touch, Downey took out his phone and sent a text to someone very interested in how this investigation was progressing.

CHAPTER THIRTEEN

KARL

Karl arrived at his street twenty minutes later. He checked the time and figured he wasn't much later than he would have been if he'd continued on to the Wilmington job, so there would be no need for a bullshit story to tell his wife. Unless he walked in the door and she straight out accused him of being spotted with a woman in his van.

This was the moment of truth, then. He got out and walked casually to his gate. If bad guys were lying in wait with knives or guns, running for the front door wouldn't help him. Better he got killed out here instead of inside where Katie was.

No gunshot. Nobody jumped out from behind a car. No deadfall was sprung. Of course not – Liz Grafton was letting her paranoia dictate her actions. Karl walked to his front door and unlocked it. He had to use two hands on the key to keep it steady. He looked up and down the street one last time. Once inside, he locked up and set the house alarm, and waited until enough anxiety had sluiced away that Katie wouldn't feel it pulsing off him like an electrical charge. Then he went upstairs to pretend everything was five-star in their world.

Katie was in the bedroom, tucked up in bed with just her head and arms showing. Her long dark hair was splayed on the pillow like black blood from a vicious head wound. She was on her electronic tablet again, probably looking at fireplaces: her new obsession now that they'd bought everything they needed for the back bedroom. He stopped in the doorway. She hadn't seen him yet. He took a breath, cleared his head as best he could, and spoke up.

'Apparently the *British Medical Journal* said athletes live longer lives than the average person by two-point-eight years,' he said, referencing their ongoing joke.

She lowered her tablet and grinned at him. 'That right? Well, Doctor Jane will help by fixing their injuries.'

'Decathlete Gold Medal-winner Michael won't be injured.'

'Maybe Doctor Jane could toss javelins in her free time.'

'Decathlete Michael could read medical books on the tread-mill.'

Her grin widened. She held out her arms for him. Carefully, he laid atop her, bracing himself with his arms so he barely touched her belly. She kissed his nose. 'Any problems tonight?'

He was glad their faces were close because he was certain she would have read the whole damn story in his eyes. He dampened a rising fear that she somehow knew what had happened earlier. Just an inert question, the same asked of husbands by wives all across the city after a working day.

'I cancelled. Too dark to put an alarm in this late. I'll go another time. He won't mind as long as his car isn't nicked tonight.' The lie, as it passed his lips, tasted foul.

But what could he do? The truth was a bad idea. No way was he going to burden her with the possibility of vicious criminals intrud-ing into their lives. End of. He'd get rid of Liz tomorrow and forget her, and Katie need never know. As long as that was the end of it.

She kissed his nose again and said: 'I need water,' which was perfect timing because the pinball of worry was back. Now he had an excuse to go and check out the windows. He kissed her nose right back and headed for the door.

Downstairs again, he flicked off the living room light so he wouldn't be exposed with his face pressed up against the window. Nobody out there. Liz had been wrong. There were no gangsters after him. But what did he expect, a line of bad guys on the street, staring up at him?

Or maybe they didn't know who or where he was. Yet. He pushed that thought from his mind and went back upstairs. At the last second, he veered into the rear bedroom to check that window, slave to a wild idea that intruders were lurking in the back garden. But he didn't reach the window. He stood and looked around. On the bed covers, on the walls, on the shelves, Peppa Pig glared back at him. Michael – or Jane, if Katie got her wish – was three months yet from the world, and already possibly in danger? No, no, no. The worry transformed into anger. His fists clenched by his sides.

'Did you come up?' Katie called. 'Where are you?'

He headed back to the bedroom and produced a Peppa pillow from behind his back like a magician. 'I thought Michael could sleep with Peppa tonight.'

'Oh, Jane says bring, bring, bring.'

He gave her the pillow, and she balanced it on her belly. Karl laid his ear on Peppa's snout. 'Even through this I can feel – ow!' He jerked upright.

With a face as innocent as her unborn child's, Katie said: 'Did you feel a kick?'

'Kick? You slapped me in the head, girl.'

She laughed. 'So didn't. It was Jane, probably telling you she's not happy that you hope she's a boy.'

He climbed over her legs carefully and lay beside her. 'If that was a real kick, Michael's showing us how good he'll be as a decathlete.'

'Did you get my water?'

'Shit.'

He apologised for the language and headed downstairs again. Water came third to another glimpse out the window and a double-check that the front and back doors were locked. For a silly moment he considered staying up all night, in case a group of killers was right now riding his way, weaponed up like a SWAT team. But what could he do, fight them off with a broomstick? Besides, they might come tomorrow night, when he'd be unable to prevent himself dropping off to sleep.

'Besides, she's full of shit,' he said aloud, unable to contain his frustration.

'What?' Katie called down.

'Nothing,' he said when he returned to the bedroom. He handed over the water and undressed, but left his boxer shorts on – to save the ambulance crew some embarrassment, his mind joked. He got into bed, and Katie switched off the bedside lamp. She pulled him close so his chest pressed against her warm back. That was a comfort he needed now it was pitch-black.

'You're cold,' she whispered. 'Oh, I set the Sky Box to record something for you. That cage fighting event you like.'

'Thank you,' he replied. He loved how thoughtful she was, even recording the sports events she couldn't stand herself. 'And you're my big hot water bottle.'

As he lay in bed, he hoped this was all some scam after all. He'd love to get to the shop tomorrow and find Liz and all his stock gone. But then he had a worrying thought: what if her crime boss husband got angry because Karl had dumped Liz to fend on her own? Perhaps he should take her home tomorrow after all? His mind was all over the place.

'Remember you're back early tomorrow to take me for my nails.'

'Yeah. Twelve o'clock. Hair last week and nails tomorrow. You start buying new underwear and I want a paternity test.' That got him a heel kick in the shin.

His mind whirred. He pictured a scene: Grafton and his minions are in the middle of chopping up the guys who stormed their house, and Karl rolls up with Liz as the bin liners of body parts are being loaded into a van. Now he's seen too much.

'I ate your pie, I'm afraid. Cravings.'

'It's okay. Michael needs shot-put muscles.'

The wild thoughts tumbled. He worried that Grafton would *thank* him. He'd seen gangster films before, so he knew you didn't turn down the generosity of the kingpins. And once you'd accepted what they gave you, you were in their pocket. Before he knew it, he'd be asked to make some dodgy delivery, or to hide a suspect package at his house, or to drive three hooded men to a bank and wait outside with the engine running.

'Doctor Jane says night night.'

'Night, Michael.'

Or Grafton thanks him and lets him go, just like that. But the police have the ganglord under surveillance, and now they're very interested in the new player who just shook hands with him. He might get swept up when the cops take everyone down. Or other enemies could be watching, and they might decide Karl was one of Grafton's men and needed carving up.

So, taking her home was out. Hopefully she'd be long gone, giving him no choice at all. But if she was still at the shop, he was going to drag her out into the street and be rid for ever.

'I love you.'

One final scenario played out in his head. Karl rolls up with Liz, but Grafton, instead of being thankful, is suspicious. Accusations of sexual misconduct fly, and the minions fetch another bin bag. Love was a powerful force.

'I love you, too,' he replied.

CHAPTER FOURTEEN

MAC

Mac was driving home when he got a call from DC Cooper. Ramirez was adamant now that he'd been set up, but he'd turned his focus onto the police. His new defence: the cops had been into his attic, and they had taken his dog tag to plant at the scene of Grafton's murder. He was screaming his new theory from his cell like a town crier.

Mac turned his car around. At the station, he haphazardly parked across a disabled spot and, much worse, his superintendent's, and ran up the stairs. Ramirez didn't get off his bunk when his cell door was opened, but he jumped to his feet when Mac walked in.

'Jesus Christ. Of all the wankers. Macintosh, eh?'

'McDevitt. I'm running this case.' He sent away the uniform who'd unlocked the door. Normally not protocol to leave a high-ranking officer alone with a violent criminal, but an aggressive nature didn't equal superhuman powers, and Mac had forearms as thick as the other man's calves.

'I know you,' Ramirez said. 'The takeaway thing way back. I remember you. I knew there was something booky about all this shit. It was your team of cunts back then, when my tag went walkies, and now you're back with a new team of cunts, and my fucking tag is miraculously back. You fuckers planted that dog tag, just like I thought. Shit, man, let's go tell that to my lawyer.'

He stepped forward, meaning to barge past the big cop, who was almost a foot taller. Mac grabbed him around the throat with one hand and pushed him back, hard. Ramirez staggered into his bunk, collapsed across it and banged his head on the wall beyond.

'What the fuck?' he yelled, clutching his skull.

Mac didn't move from the doorway.

'Stop swearing, Mr Ramirez, and stop using stupid gang slang in front of my officers. Now listen. Are you listening?'

'You're done for this, dickhead.' He pulled a hand away to find fingers slick with blood. 'This is your fucking job down the swanny. I should bust your other ear.'

McDevitt ignored the threat. 'Shut your trap and listen to me. Maybe you didn't kill Ronald Grafton, and maybe you did. If you lost your dog tag and someone planted it at the scene to frame you, it will soon come out. If you dropped it while you were cutting him to bits, it will soon come out. Are you still listening?'

Ramirez didn't answer. But that meant the threats stopped, too.

'But you will stop this lark about planted evidence. It muddies the water and gives everyone a headache. Say planted evidence again and I'll spread the word to local hard boys that we're looking closely at you for child molestation. Then I'll have to lie to your bawling mum by saying I'll do everything in my power to find out who strapped her son down and set a wild dog on his balls.'

They faced each other for a time, silent. Then Ramirez said: 'Okay, since we're off the fucking record here, answer me one question. Do you think it was me?'

'You got arrested, Ramirez. That means there was some evidence, and people will remember that. Even if we convict someone else for it, people will still wonder if you did it. They'll fear you. They'll respect you. You'll love it. Bear that in m—'

'Hey. I said do you think it was me?'

'And you slipped here today, right? Accusations of police brutality give everyone headaches, too.'

'Me, yes or fucking no?'

'The truth will out, Mr Ramirez. But let's just say you're an idiot skinny runt wannabe with an ego problem, and no idiot skinny runt wannabe could have done this to Grafton.'

CHAPTER FIFTEEN

MICK

Mick cursed almost all the way home, but mellowed a little when he started to think about Ronald Grafton. Specifically, his eyes. He dumped his bag of Grafton's goodies in the hallway and turned off the light in his son's bedroom. Then he called Brad.

'The police are onto the Volvo,' he snapped. 'Tell me you two put that thing back in the garage, please?'

'Yeah,' Brad said. 'Shit. Wait, if you have to ask that, it means they haven't actually found it.'

'Tell me you sterilised it?'

'We sterilised it. Don't worry. So they haven't physically found it?'

Mick sighed. Pure relief. 'Some interfering and helpful good citizen saw us driving near Grafton's, that's all. Got the reg. Called it in when he saw flashing blue lights around Grafton's place. But if it's sterile, we're okay. No CCTV near that garage.'

'Have we got to move it?'

'We can't. If it's seen on the roads, it's grabbed and whoever's in it. We'll just leave it. No one goes there. If it's sterile, they'll get nothing from it.'

'Okay. So that's not bad news at all, really. What about Ramirez?'

Mick quickly explained.

'Of all the fucking alibis,' Brad said. 'What can you do about it?'

Dave had watched Ramirez and his girlfriend enter the flat and determined that the couple was staying in for the night, so he'd looked good for a weak alibi. Except for the damn video camera. Ramirez's home video had showed him fucking his girlfriend to a live football match on TV. They began at the opening whistle, and Ramirez tried to finish at the final blow, but got there as the players were swapping shirts. Right around the assumed time of death. And it wasn't a pre-recorded or plus-one channel because there was a moment when an elbow caught the TV remote and flicked the channel onto a news show.

'It was to buy time. It bought time.'

'And maybe the arrest will be proof enough for Grafton's men to take revenge.'

There was a pause between the men. Mick turned on the TV because the silent house unnerved him. He still hadn't got used to it.

'Hey, do you remember how Grafton's eyes changed when his head came off? Like his brain was still alive and registering? Is that possible?'

More silence from Brad. Mick wondered if he was reliving earlier events. They hadn't been out of Mick's mind all night.

He wasn't: 'I'm sure you hope so. I don't remember. It's all a blur. Fucking hope it stays that way. So Ramirez is no longer in the frame?'

'Apparently not. But he got a headache.' An idea popped into his own throbbing head. 'Call someone to brick Ramirez's mum's windows. Write a note to make him think Grafton's boys are coming for payback. He'll jump at every sound for the next ten years. Hopefully they'll really come for him.'

'Sure. So, if he's not part of this any more, it doesn't matter if Liz Grafton saw a white face. It doesn't matter what she tells the police, right? So, we don't need to go after her. You should cancel Król.'

That surprised him. Was Brad losing his nerve, or just not thinking straight? 'Her dick husband is dead, Brad. When she learns that, she realises that there's no reason not to tell everything. When a bad guy gets cut down, coppers don't just look at the guy's enemies, Brad. They look at his own people, too. Past and present. In case someone close to him decided to betray him. She'll give names. One of those names will be Brad Smithfield. Maybe she even recognised him just from the eyes.'

The pause of a man weighing up dangerous news. Finally, Brad said: 'That won't stand up in court.'

'Court is okay for you? You're okay with a murder trial? You're okay with the police suspecting you and snooping into your life? I'm surprised. Not something I'm willing to risk.'

'Mick, this isn't about security, it's about revenge.'

Now Mick fell silent for a time. Something Brad had said flashed in his brain: *I'm sure you hope so.* Now he understood: Brad assumed that Mick was only concerned with causing more suffering. Clearly, he was underestimating Grafton's wife's role in all of this. 'Grafton was what he was because of her. Behind every great man stands a great woman, you know?'

Brad said: 'She hasn't got a bad bone in her body, Mick. You think she turned him into a criminal? He hid ninety per cent of what he did from her. She didn't like it. She only settled for his lifestyle because she was there way before he stole his first pound. Creeping normality, that's the term. He was a gangster before she knew it.'

'Give me a child until he is seven and I will show you the man. Heard that one? Maybe she made him exactly who he was. Maybe without her he would have been a priest. Maybe she ran the fucking empire from behind the scenes, new world order-style.'

Brad chuckled again. 'Okay, Mick. Whatever floats your boat.'

Mick's voice raised a notch. 'She was part of him, Brad. They were one together. You've seen that fucking tattoo, haven't you? She's a piece of him, and I want every piece of him dead.' There, he had admitted it. He'd said it out loud. 'I don't even know why

I'm bothering to explain this to you. You need to concentrate on the fact that she could fuck everything up for you. No more bar in Thailand. You can say goodbye to *that* dream.'

'Look, we'll do her, fine, okay. You're right, she could fuck things up for me. I'm in. Just keep your own weird reasons to yourself, okay? Did you call Król?'

Mick didn't want to let it go. He felt he was being mocked. But so what? If Brad didn't understand, it didn't matter. Results mattered. Satisfaction mattered. He took a breath.

'He's on it. Her and the guy who picked her up. Both will cease to be by morning.'

'And then who's next?'

'What?'

Brad sighed. 'Nothing. So I can go back to sleep, then?' he said, and hung up without waiting for an answer.

Mick found sleep impossible. He loaded Facebook Messenger and sent a message to Alize, a girl in Germany he'd been corresponding with for a few months now. She was always quick to reply, no matter how late, but he was too wired to sit and await her response. He wandered the house. He felt burdened and had a load of pent-up energy to get rid of. He took the rubbish out to the wheelie bin, making the loose change in his jacket jingle. When he tossed the coins into Tim's money jar, a large container once bearing boiled sweets, he felt the cogs slicken once more.

Alize got back to him.

Evening, babe. I sold three chairs today. You good?

She crafted and sold bamboo chairs for a living, an art he was planning to have her teach him. He told her he was good, couldn't wait to see her soon, and then stripped and put on a pair of shorts.

A thirty-minute workout, with a photo of Grafton's face stuck on the punchbag, turned placidity into euphoria. A feeling no drug could match. A feeling he hadn't experienced since he turned off the chainsaw, seemingly days ago.

CHAPTER SIXTEEN

IN THE NIGHT

Two of them came during the Devil's Hour. The street was silent and empty, and they rode up on a Beta 300 RR off-road bike. It had been doing eighty miles an hour 1,000 feet away when the engine was killed, and now it coasted silently along the road and turned into an alleyway. Two men in black plastic tracksuits with the hoods up exited, climbed a fence and ran across someone's backyard. Scaling another fence put them in the garden they wanted.

The back door was a sturdy uPVC affair, but it had been compromised by the installation of a cat flap. The smaller of the two men prised away the outer frame with the claw end of a hammer. The inner frame fell away into the kitchen with barely a noise. The hole cut into the door was big enough to let him slip through. The key was in the other side of the door, which meant a few seconds later his partner was able to step through like someone who belonged.

They were seasoned burglars who had good night vision. They crossed a kitchen that had two islands and stools arranged around both without disturbing anything except a cat that shot past them. One man was white, the other dark-skinned. The dark-skinned guy checked the living room while his partner remained at the foot of the stairs. They had learned the hard way that sometimes couples grew apart, where one slept on the sofa downstairs. The dark-skinned guy, still carrying his hammer, returned and gave a thumbs up. All appeared to be good in this couple's relationship.

Both men climbed the stairs. Four doors led off a tiny landing at the top. Two were open. A bathroom and a small bedroom given over to storage. The dark-skinned guy opened one of the others to disclose a second bedroom, neat, and empty – no sex-starved husband sleeping in there. The white guy opened the other door slowly, exposing the main bedroom. The curtains were closed against the moonlight, but the couple in the bed had fallen asleep with a small lamp on the wall above the bed that gave off a soft orange glow. He could see two shapes under the thick quilt. The woman was on her back, mouth open, long dark hair fanned across the pillow, while the guy was on his side and facing away. Bare shoulders suggested both were naked.

They'd already formulated a plan, so they rushed inside quickly, silently. The white guy threw the cover off the male, exposing his nakedness. His half of the quilt fell over his wife. The dark-skinned man leaped on the woman, forcing the quilt over her face. The couple jerked awake at the same time. The woman started to struggle and yell, but he kept his weight on her, smothering her and forcing a gloved hand over her face, using the thick fabric of the quilt to cover her mouth and dull her cries.

The man tried to sit up, shock imprinted all over his sleepy face, but the white man headbutted him right in the nose, then sat astride him holding a shank made from a piece of wood and three four-inch nails jammed into his cheek. His other hand clamped over his mouth. Blood from the guy's nose dribbled down his cheeks like war paint.

'Where's the woman?' the white guy whispered right into his ear. 'Make noise and I bleed you and the wife.'

He released his hand from the man's mouth. The guy's expression was of pain and horror.

'The woman you picked up earlier tonight. Where is she? And what did she say?'

'I don't know what you mean,' the man squealed. 'Please.'

The white burglar twisted the wood back and forth, jamming the nails into the man's face, scraping them against bone. Despite his hand over the man's mouth again, a scream of pain emerged that only dead neighbours wouldn't hear. Blood went everywhere. Two feet away, the dark-skinned man laughed as the woman thrashed beneath him.

'Where's the woman?'

The hand was removed from his mouth. The man snatched a chance to scream for help. The white guy headbutted him again, then stabbed him five times in the same spot on his upper arm, fast, like a piston. Now he didn't care about the guy's screams. He jammed the lethal weapon under the man's chin, right into his throat, and pressed in just shy of hard enough to draw blood.

'Last chance! Where's the fucking woman you picked up tonight?'

CHAPTER SEVENTEEN

MICK

Last night's dream, for once, was different, but no less chilling than the one that had been replaying daily for weeks. Grafton survived the attack, his body parts were reattached in the cottage, and that very same night he walked right on out into a garden full of cheering fans. Weirdly, the worst part was that somehow his suit had managed to avoid getting a single drop of blood on it. Pristine and white, as always.

As a man who craved control, Mick couldn't let even an errant part of his own mind make decisions he didn't like. So he lay there and imagined Grafton once again in that garden, but now his sea of admirers fell silent and parted, and Mick stepped forward to grab the bastard by the neck. He squeezed and the night darkened, and he squeezed and daylight broke over the cottage, and years might have passed before Mick became satisfied.

I'm sure you hope so.

But the vision flickered out when pain took over. He realised he'd been digging his fingers hard into his thigh.

He grabbed his mobile, which said it was six in the morning. He got as far as loading the Internet before he stopped and laughed. His brain must still be waking up because he'd been about to check the news for Grafton's superhuman recovery. Idiot.

He stopped laughing when he realised he'd had no missed calls or texts during the night. No word from Król. He got out of bed and padded naked into the bathroom. In the mirror, his face was tired and angry-looking. He couldn't blame the dream. It was a face he wore a lot these days. He was about to brush his teeth when he caught sight of them. Yellow, getting worse. He hadn't brushed them ten times in the last year, and thought *fuck it* now. What good would it do? Who was he trying to impress?

His jaw was hurting. He'd developed a habit of grinding his teeth, even while asleep. He had a Swan Vestas matchbox full of mints, which helped, and popped a couple into his mouth. Then he went into his son's bedroom, and threw back the covers. 'Wake up, sleepyhead. Breakfast.'

*

He entered the kitchen. A bowl of cornflakes was slid onto the table for Tim. For Mick, it was a fry-up, which was quick and convenient and all he seemed to eat these days, especially when working the streets. He'd stopped caring about cholesterol levels a long time ago. He put the kettle on and moved to the living room. In a corner, out of sight of the window, was a freestanding torso punching bag in realistic pink. It had a rope tied around the badly frayed neck, and a thousand slashes and holes from the knife now sticking out of its shoulder. The ruined picture of Grafton's face had slid off during the night and lay on the floor. He stamped on it, then tore it up and put it in the bin. He should have covered it in tape to preserve it because he didn't have many pictures left, and the hunger would be back time and again.

I'm sure you hope so.

He stepped up to the window. The sight of his neat lawn always made him relax. Even after the dream, even after the lack of contact from Król, it still worked.

Silence, though. Silence had the opposite effect. The house had been silent these past three years, and he'd never become comfortable with it. He put the news on TV while he waited for the kettle, just for noise.

His interest was instantly piqued when he saw police cars behind a cordon and a large warehouse. The news ticker scrolling across the bottom of the screen said:

Police Seize Hoard of Psychedelic Drug 'Buzz' with Street Worth of—

And that was as much as he could bear to see before jabbing a finger hard into the remote to change the channel.

He flicked through channels until he heard canned laughter. An American sitcom. He took a breath to calm himself. He sat on the arm of his sofa and tried to concentrate on the TV. This was what Brad meant: his inability to relax, to do normal things. He got his cup of tea and sat on a sofa cushion, not on the arm. Curled his feet under him and cradled the cup. Just like a normal person. But it felt unnatural. He tried not to think about Król. Tried to concentrate on the TV, but it was no good. He couldn't do it.

Where the fuck was Król?

The sitcom started to wear on him quickly. Everything was too clean, the characters too fresh and neat. And one of them was called Theo, same as the dickhead who used to bully Tim at school. He wanted to smash their buoyant faces, see how perfect they'd be then. Welcome to the fucking real world. He turned off the TV before his brain got the chance to blame the device for what it had just been subjected to. Something else Brad had said he had a habit of doing. Nothing was ever Mick's fault. Maybe it wasn't: nobody knew him these days, certainly not Brad fucking Smithfield. In part, he knew, it was his own fault. He kept his emotions internal as best he could, never talked about himself, his tastes, likes, dislikes, any of that shit. But the one thing he couldn't keep in check was his anger because it was like a disconnected part of him, something out of his control. Everybody in his orbit had witnessed it; he knew it defined him in their eyes. And it was too late to do anything about that.

Brad and Dave often ribbed him about his anger, but what did they know? Dave had a wife, and Brad had a fucking boyfriend. Dave had a mortgage and plans for kids, and Brad had that pathetic dream about opening a bar in Thailand. What future did Mick have to look forward to, apart from more pain? They knew nothing about what it was like to be in Mick's shoes. Most men would have sunk into a whirlpool of despair, while others would have migrated to a monastery in Tibet: you coped how you could. Mick's way was to be, as Brad had put it, angry at the entire world. But it beat shrinking into nothing, or casting aside your entire life for something new. Both were weak responses to life's cruel whip. Plus, it gave him that push needed to go and get what you wanted. Case in point: Grafton.

He finished the tea and dumped the cup in the sink: hard, from a distance, so that the thing made a noise. Mick liked noise because it was the opposite of silence. He liked to slam doors and play his rock music loud, and if the bitch next door banged on his wall to complain, well, he liked shouting right back at her. That certainly made him feel better. In fact, he probably got angrier if she didn't respond.

I'm sure you hope so.

That damn thing in his head couldn't be ignored. And why bother? He couldn't fool himself. Fuck the plan to blame Ramirez and all that scenery. Fuck what Grafton's wife could tell the cops. If Grafton was watching the world above from his fiery pit in Hell, there was only one way to hurt him. And Mick hadn't finished dancing yet.

Where the fuck was Król?

He dressed quickly and slid out a cardboard box from the cupboard under the stairs. It was marked 'Loyalty Box'. Inside, plastic food bags containing his treasures; his favourite items that came in handy to force loyalty from others. The latest addition had gone in last night: Grafton's blood-encrusted wedding ring.

He found the label he needed (date: four months ago; place: Muswell Hill; name: Mohammed Iqbal) and hauled out the bag. He took a photo of the item inside with his phone and carefully placed the bag in the box, the box in the cupboard, the key to the cupboard in his pocket.

At the front door, with the handle in his fist, he paused. He was being too hard on himself. He had a future planned, didn't he? He pulled out his phone, loaded Facebook Messenger, and sent a quick note to Alize:

Morning, Babe. Hope you are well. Can't wait to see you.

He slotted the phone away, already feeling better. 'See you later, Tim,' he called out, then left.

CHAPTER EIGHTEEN

MAC

Mac was halfway to his car when his phone trilled. He expected an update on the triple murder, but Gondal told him about a 'Body in a shed in Longlands. An old dear left her husband fixing his remote control plane late into the night, and he wasn't in bed when she woke up. She found him dead in the shed the next morning, door wide open and a lot of stuff missing. Strangled, she says. I sent Berry and Smith and I'm gonna head over in a mo. You want to spare time off the Grafton case for this one?'

'I'll be right there,' Mac said, and thirty minutes later his car was parked on a patch of gravel outside a corrugated iron shed. He took vinyl gloves from his boot. As he was slipping them on, an old chap exited the structure with a cloth, a small plastic bag and a spray cleaner. He looked nervous.

'What is it, Barry?'

Barry said: 'There was some activity last night. Some cheeky upstarts on motorbikes, those off-road things. Racing about. I chased them off, and I got the registration plate of one. But I was too late to—to…'

He didn't look like he fancied continuing, so Mac took the cleaning supplies and prompted him. A minute later, Mac knelt on grass still damp from last night's rain, churned by tyre tracks everywhere, and saw that Barry had been right. A large crack in the headstone, on the left side, extending down from the top and slicing in half the W in his ex-wife's name.

VVENDY

His phone trilled while he was scraping a week's worth of grime from the headstone, but he ignored it. He returned the call while he was trekking back to the groundkeeper's shed. Gondal told him not to bother attending the Longlands scene because the dead guy hadn't been strangled at all. Barry and Smith suspected a heart attack. Mac hung up, met Barry on the path and returned his cleaning supplies. The groundskeeper apologised again.

'Don't worry about it. Not your fault. I'll order a new stone. See you next Thursday.' They shook hands, but when Barry considered the deed done and tried to pull his back, Mac kept hold and said: 'I should report these silly bikers before they hurt someone next time. Did you say you got a registration?'

CHAPTER NINETEEN

KARL

Karl woke. A good start, since it meant he'd survived the night. But the cold light of day brought a harsh reality. His next thought: police.

Lying in bed, he grabbed his phone and again searched for newsworthy events around the area of Tile Kiln Lane in Bexley. But he closed the Internet before anything could load. He didn't want to know. He didn't care. It wouldn't change what was going to happen in the next few minutes.

He got up, went into the bathroom, and made the call.

And hung up after two nines. Calling the cops would officially stamp him as part of this, whatever 'this' was.

It was only six in the morning, which, he figured, was too early to call the shop. Katie was still asleep on her back. He pressed the covers around her belly to form a hump and imagined a little baby boy in a tent, which lightened his mood a little.

There was no time for a shower. He settled for flattening his wild hair with a wet palm, then slipped on black trousers and a white shirt with Sunrise Electronics stitched on the chest. Katie was starting to stir, so he returned to the bedroom.

'Tea?'

'Of course. Immediately.'

'Soon as Michael's here, I get the pamper treatment.'

'We'll ask Jane if that's okay.'

'*He'll* want his daddy to be pampered.'

'I'm sure *she* will.' She closed her eyes again, and in that moment of being effectively shut out, Karl's worries returned. He kissed his wife's cheek and went downstairs to make tea. But before the tea, he made the call.

It rang.

Get out, he was going to tell Liz Grafton. Go home, or go to the cops, but just go. Not his business. He'd done enough for her. He wanted her gone by the time he got to work.

It rang.

And she had to pretend that they'd never met, he'd remind her. Some other guy had picked her up. She'd never heard of Karl Seabury or Sunrise Electronics.

It rang.

Of course it did: he'd told her not to answer the phone, hadn't he? She was probably at the loft hatch, staring at it.

Maybe not, though. Maybe she had gone, and he'd find a note in her place that said she'd spoken to her husband, all was fine, the attack was a prank, thanks for the ride, see you around.

Katie thumped downstairs. He hung up the phone and moved away from it before she saw him and asked what he was doing. She entered the room wearing a nightgown and a smile, and he smiled back. He remembered the tea and went into the kitchen to make it.

He started to fill the kettle and took a moment to think. He had no choice now but to go to the shop as if it were any normal workday and deal with whatever happened when he got there. He heard Katie enter the kitchen.

'Remember there'll be traffic jams, so don't be back any later than twelve. Nails at one.'

'I'm a white van man, Katie. We invented traffic jams.'

A minute later, tea in hand, she announced that she was going for a bath, pecked his cheek and vanished. His own tea was gulped down before the stairs had stopped creaking. He yelled goodbye around a mouthful of toast and almost pulled the nail out of the wall when he grabbed his keys, so eager was he to get to the shop and erase his worries.

CHAPTER TWENTY

Król

Aleksy Kozaczuk was called Król by those who knew him, a name meaning 'king'. He had run gangs as a teenager in Szczecin, Poland, inspired by his father's tales of Polish criminals making money and earning respect alongside Al Capone and other notable gangsters during America's Prohibition era. It all had to do with some loose family connection to Bugs Moran. Król didn't retain most of what the drunken old fool spouted, but he did like the fact that he was allowed to steal and beat other kids, and his father only reprimanded him if the police got involved. The old fool taught him early that a man without a rich family, a serious talent or massive luck could only strike it rich through crime. He had yearned to set up a new life in America, running guns and girls.

He got to London after the expansion of the European Union in 2004, still eyeing an empire in America, but here he still was more than a decade later. He didn't mind because he was running a gang and sometimes there was a girl he could pimp and now and then he sold a gun. He was tall, skinny, only twenty-eight but had a buzz cut and a face of stubble that was iron grey. It made him look older, but, he felt, meaner. His face was known on the streets. His gang was mostly kids, shorter and stupider, and he liked that they called him their king. Like some Fagin of the modern world, he sent them out to do his robbing so that he could remain untouchable. Of course, theft was in his blood, so he still went on the odd excursion himself.

He lived in a bedsit above a laundrette in Fulham, accessed by an entrance in the side wall and a set of stairs that terminated right at his door. Not exactly the palace he had dreamed of, but paperwork issued by the benevolent British government said he alone owned the keys.

His eyes flickered awake at the sound of the first door being kicked in. His brain oriented itself as footsteps thudded up the stairs. He was sitting up in bed in just his boxer shorts and holding a knife as the inner door was booted open.

'Put that away or I'll store it in your arse,' said the silhouette in the doorway. The intruder yanked on a grimy cord hanging from the ceiling, and a weak bulb cast jaundiced light over the room.

Król recognised his visitor and tossed the knife on a small bookcase beside his bed, on top of which sat his mobile phone and an ashtray heaped with cigarette butts.

'What you doing here?'

There was a cheap plastic clock hanging on the wall beside the door. The intruder yanked it down and skimmed it like a Frisbee, striking Król hard in the chest. 'What time does that say? Is reading the time the same in fucking Poland?'

Król tossed the clock aside after a glance at it – barely past seven in the morning – and rubbed his chest. 'I've had one fucking hour's sleep, Mick. Fuck off.'

Mick strode into the room and stopped at the foot of the bed. 'Same here about the sleep, Król, you piece of shit. Know why? Because I was waiting up for you. You were supposed to call when it got done, remember? Not just piss off home. So, I'm figuring it didn't get done, right?'

'I got burned, man.'

'One of them recognised you?'

Król thrust out his right hand, fingers splayed. 'Nah, I mean I got fucking burned.' Mick stared at the man's fingers, which were red and blistered. 'Some fucking weird electrified security shit on that house in Chiswick. Must have the fucking Crown Jewels in there.'

'That all you learned since you sneaked in my country? That fucking foul language? Which house? So, you didn't get inside?'

'Gave it up, man. You see my fingers? You'll have to go see the guy yourself.'

'Well, that's why I need you again. Get your stolen shit shoes on and let's go.'

Król shifted so he could sit up against the headboard. He lit a cigarette stub plucked from the ashtray and sucked hard on it. 'One hour's sleep, Mick. You listening?'

'I'm listening to you whine, that's all. Let me tell you what else I listened to, Król. Earlier, I heard about some boys in blue being sent to Muswell Hill. Apparently some guy and his wife were attacked in bed. The man got all cut up bad, and now he's in the hospital. Shit, I thought, there's some bad people out there. Not like my man Król, who I sent to ask some questions. Not like Król, who went in there simply to scare someone and find out one little piece of information. Król's smart, and he wouldn't have done anything like that because he knows that someone who's threatened in bed but left unhurt will probably keep his promise to keep quiet about the break-in if he thinks the guys will come back if he talks. Right?'

Król shrugged, finished his butt and grabbed another. 'He was messing with me. But it worked, cos he talked, and I don't think he's your man. Must be the other one.'

Mick strode to where the clock had been tossed, grabbed it and skimmed it again at Król, who complained with expletives when it burst into shards just inches above his head.

'Now that guy has no choice but to talk, you fuckwit, because it's obvious to everyone he got attacked at home. Some nurse called the police. You might get caught for this one, and then you might rat me out.'

Król shook his head. 'Nah, I was playing cards all night with my own pals, and they'll say so. Alibi.'

'Scum like you don't have friends. You're all backstabbing arses who don't even trust each other. And if there's DNA, the word of a bunch of kids who think you're the dog's bollocks won't count for anything. You owe me, so get your Oxfam rags together and let's go.'

And yet again, to be reminded that he owed Mick, Mick brought out the knife. Just a picture on a phone this time, of course, because last time Mick had brought the actual knife, and Król had tried to wrestle it away from him. This time he'd get nowhere near it.

'Clothing, Król. Or a call gets made to Scotland Yard. A concerned member of the community just found a knife close to where that old Asian shopkeeper was stabbed four months ago.'

'You'll never give me that back, so why should I help you?'

'Is that a no, Król?'

It was never a no, was it? Three times recently this arsehole had blackmailed him into doing a job, and each time he'd been promised the knife would be destroyed. And each time it had reared its ugly head again. Król didn't doubt that this process would continue for some time yet, unless he managed to get some dirt on Mick to balance the scales.

Mick said: 'You didn't do the job you were asked to do. Lucky for you I did some research to help you redeem yourself. So, if you want to sleep here tonight instead of a prison cell, get dressed and let's go finish it.'

Just then Mick's phone trilled. Król started to get up as Mick read the text message, but a moment later the big guy rushed forward. Król flopped back onto the bed, hands over his head, protesting, wondering what the hell had been in that text message.

In shock, he watched Mick, instead of attacking him, pluck a couple of novels out of the bookcase.

'For being an arsehole, I'm having these. You can't even read English.'

Król could barely read his native Polish, either, but he was still worried. At what future crime scene might the cops find one of those paperbacks with his prints all over it? What the hell was Mick up to?

CHAPTER TWENTY-ONE

KARL

He was in the van, driving to work, and was watching the mirrors more than the road ahead. Nothing suspicious was reflected at him. Cars followed, but they all turned away eventually. No pedestrians glared at his van as he cruised past. Nobody leaped into the road with a shotgun. Of course not – Liz Grafton was wrong.

So why was he still worrying?

The phone rang. He jerked and caught the brake lightly. Some dick hugging his rear thumped his horn. Withheld number. Karl told himself to relax. The bad guys were hardly likely to phone him, were they?

'Sunrise Electronics.'

'Hey up. I ordered a car alarm, was supposed to be a guy round to install it last night between—'

The Wilmington client that Karl had stood up. Karl hung up, unable to face dealing with him. He was angry at his own paranoia – if people were going to come for him, they would have done it last night. They hadn't – ergo, all was fine. Ergo, Liz had it wrong. He hit the accelerator.

The phone rang again. Katie this time. His foot slipped off the accelerator, and the van started to slow. His eyes latched onto a petrol station whose forecourt he could use to swing the van around if she suddenly said there were men trying to kick in the door.

'What's up?' he said, keeping his voice calm.

'The shed's been broken into,' she said, angry.

It felt like a drip of ice water had just trickled down his spine. But he told himself to think logically: could be pure coincidence. 'Damn idiots. What's been taken?'

'I don't know. It's all junk, isn't it? But it's a right mess. And the lock's busted. I saw it from the kitchen. There's a bag of grass seed been spilled everywhere.'

'Don't worry about it. Just junk. I'll clean the mess. Everything else okay?'

A pause while she calmed. 'Yeah.'

'Let me call you in a minute when I pull over.'

She signed off, and he hit the brake. The same honking idiot behind him butted the horn again. Black Corsa with stupid flame stickers on the bonnet. He turned into the petrol station and pulled up at a pump.

He clicked an application on his phone with a camera icon. His phone could connect to his home desktop computer which managed the house's CCTV recordings. The camera activated whenever the burglar alarm was live, which meant it had been recording all night. He clicked on the file, and the screen filled with a video image of his back garden from a tiny camera hidden in a potted plant on a side fence. The house was on the left, the shed on the right. The image had a bright green hue. Night vision.

He played it in fast forward. The only thing moving was the timestamp, and he prayed it would stay that way. Someone honked behind him. A guy waiting to use the pump. He flicked a glance in the mirror. The Corsa was there again. Karl drove forward and joined four vehicles waiting to exit the forecourt. A young yobbo in a baseball cap bounced out of the Corsa. For a moment Karl stiffened, certain that this young thug had been following him, that he was one of *them*. But his only offence was to flip Karl the bird before grabbing a nozzle to fill his macho ride.

Something blipped on the screen like a subliminal message at 01.18 a.m. Karl felt his heart thud. He rolled the video back and watched at normal speed. A green cat strolled across his garden.

Five drivers waiting to leave the forecourt became four as the head car pulled out and vanished. Karl inched forward with the others. All three were indicating to turn left, but Karl was still unsure which way he should go: left, to the shop, or right, back to Katie?

Onscreen, on his mobile, at 02.13, the kitchen light blinked on. In night vision it was like a nuclear flash and washed out the entire image for eighteen seconds. Probably Katie getting more water.

Four cars became three as a Mondeo spotted a gap and leaped into the road. Karl grabbed the indicator stalk, but didn't move it.

Onscreen, at 03.58 two green men climbed over his green back gate.

'Jesus Christ!'

Shaking with nerves, he watched the two men move left-to-right across the screen, towards the shed. He zoomed in. The men seemed to be wearing one-piece outfits. 'Fuckers,' he hissed as one of the men bust the hasp on the shed and yanked the door open. The door opened towards the camera, so he lost sight of one man as he stepped behind it. The other guy just stood and watched, turning his head to look around from time to time. That guy looked dark-skinned, even as a bright green alien-like figure.

The guy ransacking the shed moved away thirty seconds later and closed the door. Then both scuttled across the grass, and Karl felt a shiver run up his entire body.

Because they didn't head towards the gate. They weren't fleeing the scene with a trowel. They weren't there to rob the shed.

They went to the back door of the house.

Three became two. Karl's van pounced forward, almost striking the back of the car in front. He tried to flick on his right indicator, to race home to Katie, in case these fuckers came again in daylight. She was his priority. She and Michael were the only things he cared about. But the right indicator was already ticking away. He wanted to call her, but couldn't bring himself to end the video. He needed to know what happened next.

One of the burglars put his hand on the back door's handle, then yanked it back quickly, clutching it in obvious pain.

'Electrified, dickheads,' Karl shouted at the phone.

The other guy went to the kitchen window and put his face close, scanning the edges. Karl knew he had seen the metal strip running around the frame. He touched it with a finger, and yanked his hand away fast.

Karl clicked, and the image changed. He had three cameras covering the back of the house. Now he watched the video from the one above the kitchen door. It was the size of a cigarette packet and the colour of the brick it was planted on, invisible in the night. The lens was aimed downwards at an angle, covering just a few feet in front of the door, and it showed the two hooded men in glorious definition. The guy who'd fingered the window was dark-skinned, while the other was a white guy with thick stubble covering most of his face and neck. The white guy scratched his head, momentarily pulling back his hood, and in that moment Karl hit the button to capture a screenshot of the guy's face.

They were talking to each other, one sucking his finger, the other spitting on his own burned digits. They were animated, angry. Karl waited for them to leave, to abandon this target and move on to another. But they didn't. They lurked by the door, talking and pointing. Karl's heart beat faster as he realised what this meant. Normal burglars would have given up by now. But these were not men who had randomly chosen a house and been foiled. They needed to get inside *this* house. *His* house.

They were the men who'd hunted Liz Grafton, and now they had come for the man she had dragged into the cesspool with her.

Another honk from behind. Corsa yob, waiting to leave. Ahead, the way was clear, and probably had been for some time. Karl waited for a gap in traffic and exited fast, which got yet another noisy response from a pissed driver. He turned right. Ten minutes until home. He jabbed Katie's number. They would have to get out of the house. Which meant he would have to tell her. Tell her everything.

He kept the wheel hard right and turned again into the fore-court. This conversation could not be done on the road, despite how eager he was to get home. This time he parked in front of the car wash to avoid blocking the pumps.

*

'Katie. I met a woman last night.'

A line that had destroyed a million marriages, but, strangely, he used it to warm her up for the main event.

A pause, and then, 'Right. Okay.' Suspicion, but not the poisonous kind: he was a joker and certainly not a ladies' man, so she was doubtful that he was about to admit to an affair.

'It's not what you think. It's no one I'm seeing, no one I've done anything with.'

'Karl, what's going on?' Confusion now: she couldn't deny the worry in his tone.

'She was running. Running away—'

Another horn blared. In his mirror, surprise, surprise. The yobbo got out of his car and threw his arms wide like someone at his wits' end.

'Karl, what are you saying? What's going on? Has this got something to do with the shed? You're scaring me now.'

'I picked her up, Katie. She was running from someone…' And now the bombshell: 'The people after her tried to break into the house last night.'

Her next words were smothered by a voice from outside. The yobbo, approaching Karl's van, mouth first. That guy's biggest worry in the world right now was a guy slowing him down, and he was going to thrust that upon a man whose pregnant wife was in danger? No, no, no. Karl flash boiled. He was out of the car before he knew it, and in the next moment everyone on the forecourt stopped and looked.

'FUCK OFF!'

He got back in the van. The yob continued his verbal assault, but he also returned to his ride, and then peeled away, highlighting his disdain with a screech of rubber. Karl rubbed his throbbing throat while Katie asked him what hell was going on.

'Go to your dad's, Katie,' he said. 'Leave now. In case they come back.'

'I'm going nowhere, Karl. Who are you talking about? Who will be back? You tell me what the hell is going on.'

'It's not sa— It might not be safe. If they come back—'

She cut in, her first word yelled in order to ensure that he shut down while she spoke. The remainder was delivered calmly, but with an undercurrent of simmering anger. He'd only heard her this way on a handful of occasions, but knew he had to tread carefully. And do what she asked.

'Who, Karl? Don't you dare just tell me people might come here and I should get out. Don't you do that. You tell me right now what's going on.'

He closed his eyes and told it all. The dark road. The man in the mask. Liz and her gangster husband. And what he'd just watched on CCTV. She didn't interrupt, and when it was over she didn't shout, or hang up the phone.

She said: 'Is that why you were distant last night?'

So he had failed to act naturally. But she hadn't questioned it at the time.

'Is that why you put the house alarm on when you left this morning?'

She would have set it off when she went out to the shed. It was never active while they were indoors.

'Is that why you rushed off so early, to go to this woman?'

Yes. Yes to it all. 'I'm sorry. She wouldn't go to the police. I know now it's because her husband is a criminal and wouldn't want her to. I was going to make her leave. But I'll go straight to your dad's; I'll meet you there, and I'll call the police. I'll send them to the shop, and they can deal with her.'

He thought that would appease her. Prayed it would, in fact, because he could think of no better idea. But it didn't.

'You should have called them last night, Karl. You shouldn't have got involved.'

And as for better ideas: 'I'm not going to my dad's, Karl.'

'Katie, listen to me—'

'No, Karl, you listen to me. I'm not about to flee from my own house just because somebody tried to break into the shed. My own home. If it's a big worry for you, then send the police here.'

'Please, Katie.'

'No, Karl. No way. The police can come here, and we'll talk to them together so I can make sure you tell them everything. But I don't want her in that shop. Can you call her there?'

He explained that he'd told the woman not to answer the phone.

'That was stupid. It was stupid even to leave her there. You should have taken her to a police station. How many thousands of pounds have you got in stock? All of that could be missing. I almost hope it is, because it will teach you not to be such an idiot in the future.'

'I know,' was the only reply he could think of.

'Carry on to the shop and get rid of her, and then come right back here. We'll phone the police afterwards. If that annoys her, so what? She doesn't have to talk to them. But you'll have done the right thing.'

'I don't want you there alone,' Karl replied.

'Karl, it's the middle of the morning. People are on the street. Nobody's coming here. The alarm is still on. Besides, those men trying to break in last night could be a coincidence, you know? They broke into the shed first, didn't they? There's no proof anyone is after you, or this woman. There's only your worrying mind, and because of it she's sitting there in your shop and making us argue.'

'But, Katie, her husband is—'

'Karl, be quiet. I don't care who she is or who her husband is. I care about not having a stranger who might be up to no good sitting in your shop. I don't want her staying there. Throw her out, then come home and we'll call the police together. And don't let her trick you into doing any more favours. Get rid of her, you idiot. I'm not missing my nails because of her.'

She hung up. He sat there with his mind cartwheeling. He couldn't ignore her logic. But he also couldn't ignore that video.

*

He got increasingly wired as the journey progressed, until he was so eager to get it over and done with that he literally leaped out of the van once at the shop and cracked his head as he ducked under the part-risen shutter. The screech of the rising shutter had brought her to the hatch, and there she was, staring down at him. He was glad she hadn't fled in the night because now he could get some answers before he went to the police. A name for the beast in the photo would be nice.

'You okay?' she said.

He rubbed his head, then forgot about the pain and rushed to the ladder. He climbed three steps and thrust out an arm towards her, showing his phone and the photo of the alien-like burglar.

'Who the fuck is this guy?'

He didn't need her words to see that she didn't know. Her eyes showed puzzlement. He wasn't sure whether or not that was good news.

'Why is he green?'

'What is he doing?'

'I don't know him,' she said, still staring at the screen. 'Who is he?'

'That's what I was asking you,' Karl said. He was hit by a sudden fear that the two burglars might also know where he worked and be on their way. He jumped off the ladder and peeked out from under the shutter.

'I meant, why are you showing me some photo?'

'Two knobheads came to my house last night. Tried to break in. Got the shock of their lives. Literally. What do you know about it?'

'My God,' she said. 'It has to be connected. They would have sent them after you.'

He stood and faced her and threw out his arms. 'Well, that's just lovely.'

'I used your phone last night. Tried my husband's mobile, but it's off. The cottage doesn't have one. But as soon as I get hold of him, I'll have him look into these men who came to your house.'

He started pacing. 'This is a goddamn joke, this. Why did you have to jump out in front of *my* bloody van? I told my wife all about it, by the way. So, she knows everything, and she wants me to call the police even if you don't like it.'

She didn't speak.

'Get down from there. Cops, right now. You're going to the police and you're going to tell them men came to my house, looking for you. And you're going to leave me out of it, okay? I don't exist. You slept all night in a damn barn somewhere.'

'How can I tell the police about your house yet leave you out—?'

'Jesus!' he yelled as he realised his error. He started to pace back and forth.

She shook her head. 'No. No police. Not yet. How many more times must I say this? I have to find my husband first, and he will sort out this problem.'

He stopped and glared up at her. 'By killing people, you mean?'

She looked back at him in shock. But guilt was there, too.

'That's right, I know all about your husband, Liz. Teflon Ron. Mr Invincible. Some kind of London ganglord. A bad guy. You were all at that cottage last night to celebrate yet another trial acquittal. And I know that's why you don't want the police in on this. Because he's brainwashed you into believing the police can't be trusted. That's idiotic. Think about what happened last night. Rival gangsters came to hurt him. He could be tied up in a cellar somewhere. He could be dead. And that would put you all on your own. Only the police can help you now.'

The shock and fear of a moment ago were replaced by scorn. Not fear, which he'd tried to elicit in order to make her see sense. Just scorn, big and bright all over her face, as if he'd said something stupid. But, of course, this was Mr Invincible he was talking about. Teflon Ron bested by mere mortals? Impossible! How dare he even suggest that her perfect husband might not be in absolute control of everything in his bubble-wrapped world?

He didn't care. 'Bloody gangsters, Liz. That's the shit you brought crashing down on my head. But now you're going to fix it. Go to the cops or just go home, I don't care. You just get out of here and fix this however you want and leave me out of it.'

'I will, I will. I'm sorry.'

'I told my wife. I wasn't even going to come here after I found out that people tried to break into my house. But she told me to come and make sure you went to the police. That's what you have to do.'

'I will, I will. I'm sorry.'

'She doesn't need grief like this. I shouldn't even be here. I need to get back, so you need to get out of here and find a phone and call the cops. She doesn't need this hassle. These people could come back to my house, and she's there alone, and she's pr—'

'You open yet?' said a voice. Karl whirled to face the shutter, and took a step back as he saw a guy squirming through the three-foot gap. Karl flicked a look behind him, but Liz had vanished.

*

Then the guy was through, and inside, and standing upright, and Karl's heart leaped into his mouth. Today the man just about six feet from him wore a blue tracksuit and a baseball cap, but his face had not changed. Grey stubble, pockmarked skin. He didn't need to check the photo in his hand to know that this was the guy from the night before. One of the men who'd come for him. He hid the hand clutching the phone behind his back.

'I need a computer,' the guy said in an Eastern European accent.

'How did you find me here?' Karl replied before his brain could caution against it.

Luckily, though, the guy thought he was talking about the shop because he said: '*Yellow Pages*, my friend.' His eyes were looking all around. 'You Karl?'

'Karl!' Karl yelled up at the hatch. Then he mounted the ladder and started to climb. Slowly, so he didn't look suspicious. 'Karl, you've got a customer.' It felt like a hollow, childish trick, and he expected a hand to grab his leg, and the man to say, *Nice try*.

Then his torso was through the hatch. His daft little ploy had worked. But that was when Liz appeared and grabbed his shirt to help haul him up. And the guy obviously saw her, because Karl heard a gasp of breath and a thud of feet, and a moment later the ladder was swept from under him. His ribs hit the edge of the hatch, legs swinging free. In order to grab the hatch, he had to drop his phone, or he'd thump down instead. He heard it clatter to the floor. Shit.

'Come here, you cunt,' the intruder said, and grabbed a foot.

Liz yelled. Karl kicked both feet like a drowning man and felt a heel hit something hard. Hopefully his nose. Then his foot was free, and he was scrambling through the hatch with Liz's help.

Together they stared down at the man below. He stared right back, one hand on his ear, his other hand holding a massive knife.

Only it wasn't a knife, Karl realised. It looked like a lawnmower blade, with a sharpened end. From his shed. Karl bit back a horrible image of this guy in his bedroom, standing over him in the dark with that nasty blade at his throat. Or Katie's throat. Or her belly. The picture killed his nerves and anger washed into the void. He'd do anything to protect his wife and his unborn child.

'Oh wow,' the intruder said. 'I know you, darlin'. You're Mr Invincible's missus. And what would my man want with you, eh?'

'What the hell do you want?' Karl yelled.

'Her beside you,' the man said with a leer. He pointed with the blade, as if Karl might not know who he meant.

Beside him, Liz was shaking. 'My husband will kill you for this,' she spat at him.

A flicker of fear, gone the next instant. ''Course he will. Down you come, sweetie, and I promise this will be easier.'

'What do we do, Karl?' Liz moaned.

Karl rushed over to the shoe rack that he'd last night warned Liz to stay away from. He selected one of the items.

'Karl, he's coming up! Do something.'

Karl returned to the hatch. Below them, the intruder set the ladder in place and started to climb.

CHAPTER TWENTY-TWO

MICK

Good news: a twelve-year-old girl went into cardiac arrest and died.

Some organs in the body could survive hours without blood, but not the brain. Measurable brain activity ceased about forty seconds after clinical death, and recovery after three minutes or more was unlikely. Yet there had been reports of people coming back after such time and recounting what they saw while dead, usually the hackneyed bright lights and God. Three minutes. Grafton lay dead for forty minutes before the chainsaw main event. Bad news for Mick.

And then he found a story about a Danish pre-teen who had been resuscitated after sixty-one minutes. She had floated above her own dead body on the operating table, and then she was snatched away by talented surgeons. One hour! By that time, Mick and Grafton had been dancing again. What might Grafton have seen and felt while Mick chopped and scooped and swiped with his Bosch AKE 30?

He was sitting low in the car and watching Sunrise Electronics from the road running past the entrance to the lock-ups. He was wearing a baseball cap pulled low, and had his jacket zipped up high. He put his phone away, and that was when sweet memories were swapped for a bad one: something Król had said on the drive over here. *You're not the only one with evidence of stuff, you know.* Mick had replied: *What's that supposed to mean?* Król had said: *I got webcam, ain't I?*

Some weird shit from Król's foreign mouth, that was all. Just bluster. And it had been left at that. But it was back, having marinated in Mick's maelstrom of a mind, and it wasn't bluster now. Now it was an admission: Król had recorded Mick in the flat at some point. Mick had made five or six visits to Król and had spouted all sorts of things within those walls; if Król had recorded him on webcam at any time, he would have evidence of Mick saying or doing something that Mick didn't want immortalised. Something had to be done about that. But what?

He froze as he caught sight of something. Stark against the pale white clouds clogging the lightening sky, two figures had emerged onto the sloping roof of the building on the left side of the road. Seabury's side. One in shirt and trousers, the other in a dress.

'No fucking way,' he said. He had come here hoping to learn the bitch's location from Seabury, but it had been a long shot because there was no proof the guy had even picked her up. So, the chances that he'd hidden her here, at his shop, were... But even from 300 feet away, he recognised that dress. The bitch had been wearing it for Grafton's final appearance in court.

Mick thumped the steering wheel and laughed. Impossible, implausible, illogical, but real nonetheless: Seabury and the bitch together, right before his eyes, and nary a witness about. He got a whiff of Fate.

The news wasn't all sweet, though, because the pair were escaping across the roof. She'd slipped his clutches once before and was on the verge of doing so again.

Król emerged from the shop, staggering backwards, staring up. He was stupid enough to think they would try to climb down right where they'd escaped. But Mick knew their plan was to drop down into the land beyond the graffiti-covered wall at the end of the road. And sure enough the two figures, moving slowly, started towards the far end of the building, away from Mick.

He wound down his window and screamed at Król: 'Go the way they went! Inside!'

Król turned his head Mick's way, gave a thumbs up, and vanished back inside the shop.

Mick hit the gas. Beside the street containing the lock-ups was a fenced building site, and he looked for a way in. The site was vast and contained stacks of bricks and building materials, but no workers. And no fucking gate. So, Mick waited for a shallow segment of kerb and then turned right, hard, and hit the chain-link fence with enough force to wrench a section from one post and open it like a door. It rasped along the side of his car and snatched his wing mirror.

He twisted the rear-view mirror so that it showed his face. 'Ya fucking dead now,' he yelled, right into his own eyes.

The car bounced where the earth was packed hard from the trundling of heavy machinery, and slipped where the soil was loose and wet from yesterday's rain. He had to slow to a crawl, but even so the wheel struggled in his hands.

Towards two o'clock was the graffitied wall, the two roofs of the long buildings poking above. And the two escaping bastards, right there. He cut towards them.

He had to slew around a dumped mass of concrete pipe sections – if only he could roll one across the bitch and flatten her like dough – and that needed his eyes. When he found the roof again, Seabury and the woman, small at this distance of 300 feet, had already climbed off the end of the building and onto the wall. Below them was a skip full of rubbish, no more than a ten-foot drop. Mick thought it would be too scary for a prim bitch like Liz Grafton, but she amazed him by being the first to leap. He wound down his window as she dropped, hoping to hear a scream as something hard and sharp tore her open.

'Save some for me, bitch,' he yelled into the rear-view.

She vanished into the trash, then resurfaced, apparently unharmed. She started waving at Seabury who paced at the roof's edge.

Mick stared at himself and shouted: 'Just waiting to die, Seabury.'

More movement caught his eye. Król, emerging onto the roof. Mick lost sight of all three of them as he was forced to flick left to pass a shipping container that had been converted into an office.

Once past the office, Mick saw that Seabury had already leaped. He and the bitch were clambering out of the skip. Król was at the edge of the roof and displaying the same damn fear Seabury had shown. Mick glared into his own eyes again.

'Król, you fucki— Jesus!'

He hit the brake, hard. Barely in time. Dried mud was churned into dust beneath the wheels and launched around the car as the vehicle skidded to a halt. Some kind of concrete-lined trench ahead – for sewage or water – blocking his path, whatever the hell it was for. Mick backed up, turned, and powered up again, now driving parallel to the trench. Two hundred feet to his right, the three on foot ran alongside. Seabury and the bitch were making good speed because she had lost her shoes somewhere along the way. Król, although skinny and younger, just couldn't close the distance.

'I'm gonna crush you,' he screamed at his reflection.

Like a fucking scene from a comedy sketch, Seabury and the woman veered to pass a long stack of wooden planks, but Król clearly liked the hurdle analogy and tried to leap it. His foot caught the top, and after that his face caught the ground.

Mick looked away, searched ahead, seeking an end to the concrete trench. But on it ran, for ever. Then he saw a makeshift bridge some way ahead, nothing more than a rusty metal sheet laid across it: constructed for the passage of heavy machinery, which meant his car would have no problem. To get the angle, he turned left, then carved a large semicircle to the right, and came dead-on towards the bridge. Ahead, Seabury and the woman raced past. Król was 130 feet behind them.

'Here we go, fuckers,' Mick bellowed.

The metal bridge held. Rumbled like thunder, but held. On the other side, Mick tugged down hard on the left side of the wheel. Soon he was hot on their tail. A clear run at them now. One hundred and sixty feet to Król, maybe 200 to Seabury and the woman. Nothing beyond them for another 300 feet, until the fence. He would crush them long before they got there.

Król filled the windscreen.

I got webcam, ain't I?

He was stumbling along, giving Mick his back. No meth junkie going cold turkey ever wanted a hit as much as Mick wanted to ram that fool's ass with his Nissan badge and fold him up into a wet red mess between soil and steel. But he skipped alongside at the last minute because he needed to know more about this webcam threat, and he needed an extra pair of hands to deal with dead bodies.

Król slapped the side of the car as it raced by, like a good buddy saying *well done*. Did he think this was a fucking game?

'This is real shit!' Mick roared.

One hundred and thirty feet between the car and the fleeing pair. Ahead of them, Mick saw a torn-up area of concrete and earth, surrounded by traffic cones with yellow tape strung between them. Next to it was a sign:

DANGER HOLE BELOW

The mirror got, 'That's your fucking grave!'

Sixty feet, and then fifteen. They grew in his windscreen as if it was a camera zooming in. He wanted to ram them, but also didn't. Just like with that bastard Grafton before he blasted him into oblivion, Mick wanted to utter some gem of a final line, and give him a deathbed memory. His foot shook on the accelerator as his brain fought itself, both trying and refusing to stamp down hard and send them soaring.

'Fuck it,' he yelled, and crushed the accelerator.

Thirty feet. And then fifteen. And there the choice was taken out of his hands as he realised that the churned area had raised foundations. He stamped the brake and twisted the wheel.

The Almera slewed around, and Seabury and the woman filled his side window, their heads turned to watch him. Just as it seemed he was about to bowl them over, they leaped and cut through the yellow tape like marathon winners, and then the wheels slammed into the raised edge of the foundations and the car stopped dead. The sudden check of momentum sent Mick's right arm and shoulder hard into the door, and his head hard into the part-open window.

As pain and lights flashed through his head, he had a funny thought: *if the window was down, I could have grabbed the bitch.* Instead, he watched Seabury and the woman run across the torn-up concrete. In the centre of the area was a hole surrounded by more cones and tape, like the bullseye on a target. A short way beyond was the perimeter fence, and past that a road, and a thousand escape routes thereafter. But they stopped by the bullseye as if having hit a dead end. Both were panting, exhausted: Seabury more so than the woman, surprisingly. Survivors, like Mick, would have run until there was nothing left in the body, but this pair had given up.

And that suited him just fine.

Mick tried to open his door, but the car was pressed up against the foundations, and it was jammed shut. He scrambled out of the passenger side. But he needn't have panicked because Seabury and the woman were still there. The street was only a hundred or so feet behind them, within shouting distance, but the fence had debris netting and no one would see a thing. They were his for the taking.

Watched by his prey, Mick stepped up onto the smashed raised area. Casually. Calmly. One step, just to say he was here. His eyes were locked on the bitch, and he itched to get at her, but she was the last piece of Grafton to wipe out and he didn't want to rush things.

He realised that this was the first time he'd ever seen her in the flesh, without a window in the way or bodyguards surrounding her. Her skin was dirty, hair a mess, dress tatty, feet shoeless and bloody – but she was a pretty thing. It was pleasing to know that Grafton had lost his most beautiful asset, but also cause for regret: if only he could have stripped her naked and violated her in front of Grafton, that would have topped the cake with a big fat cherry. Revenge would have been sweet. But he would get the next best thing: to wring the blood from her like water from a sponge, and know that Grafton was watching from his place in Hell.

He didn't get to stare for long because she stepped backwards, behind Seabury, using him as a shield.

Król had arrived to spoil a thoughtful moment. 'Got the fuckers,' he said. He tried to step up onto the foundations, but Mick grabbed an arm to pull him back. Said nothing, but Król got the message because he stayed where he was after that. Mick didn't want anyone to ruin this moment.

'We've done nothing. What do you want with us?' Seabury said.

A pleading tone, which Mick liked. But his face wasn't contorted with shock, and Mick didn't like that part at all. Usually that sort of neutral expression was worn by the likes of Mick himself: men who'd faced danger, lived through it, realised that they were tough to put down. Or people with a trick up their sleeve. Seabury didn't strike him as the sort who was accustomed to trouble. He didn't have the scars, or the worry lines, or that look in the eyes that came from constantly facing the edge of the abyss. He was nondescript. Which pointed to the latter: a trick up the sleeve. A little caution wouldn't go amiss. So, he stayed right where he was. For now. Besides, he had an idea: let's see if he could convince Seabury to betray the bitch.

'I'm going to give you a chance I never expected to offer, so you should take it. Turn around, run away, forget all about this morning. I just want her.'

'He can't stop us, so let's just grab them,' Król said. He was almost dancing with anticipation, but Mick's mind was a tranquil lake. No, Seabury could not stop them, but there was no urgency. She could not escape again. You sipped fine wine instead of gulping it.

'Where's my husband, you bastard?' the bitch shouted, poking out her head from behind Seabury's shoulder.

So, she didn't know. The story was in the headlines, but she had missed it. Also realising this, Król started laughing. Mick held up a finger. Król clicked on and locked up, which saved him some pain because Mick would have crushed his head to avoid letting someone else tell her the big news. She needed to hear it from him. But not yet. Not until his eyes were inches from hers, his big, coarse hands around her small, porcelain throat. And not until her mind was already in pieces from the knowledge that the only man in the world working her corner had just abandoned her.

'So here it is, Seabury. Give her up. Don't make me come take her.'

Using the guy's name got the response he wanted: shock. Mick pulled a knife from his pocket and held it up. No words. Just a visual message. In his jacket was a pistol, but for this occasion he preferred the knife, and not just because the sound of a gunshot would roll away across the land.

Now there was fear on the man's face as he said: 'What do you want her for? We've done nothing.'

'Never you mind that, Seabury. Step away, live another day.'

No response. Mick took a single step, and stopped as Seabury yanked something from his pocket. Something that looked like a squat green aerosol can. Mick thought he knew what it was.

'Don't come closer. One more step forward, you'll take a hundred back.'

A bold remark, with, surprisingly, the tone to back it up. And Mick knew why. You needed skill and composure to put down an enemy with a knife or a gun, but even an imbecile could cause serious damage with a—

'Grenade?' Król blurted. 'No way that's a fucking grenade.'

Mick disagreed. He knew the type of shop Seabury ran, and a grenade was a piece of kit that fitted right in there. But there was a vast chasm between being able to wave a grenade about and actually using one.

'Kill four people? I don't think so, Seabury. Karl. This is your last chance to step away.'

The urge to get at her was rising, unstoppable. He wanted to throw her down and smash her apart on the ground. He wanted Grafton, down there in Hell, to stare up and see everything. To try to claw his way to her as Mick's anvil fists ground her up. He imagined the earth as a sheet of glass, Grafton floating just below like a swimmer caught under ice. She was on her front, so their eyes were locked in pain and fear, their scrabbling fingers just inches apart but for ever denied. Mick stared over her shoulder and soaked up Grafton's distress as he broke her open like an Easter egg.

He was grinding his teeth in anticipation. He dragged his eyes away from her and onto Seabury so he could concentrate.

'Think hard, Karl. Step away and go and live your life and forget today. You've got a wife, and a nice job, and you'd be silly to toss all that away. Remember that you're in the shit because of her. So, put that grenade down.'

No response to that. He took a step. It put him just twenty inches closer, still a good distance between them; but it felt like he had moved into their personal space, and Seabury obviously felt it, too, because he waved the grenade.

'This is a momentum device,' Seabury said. 'Explodes in the direction it's moving. I throw it at you, the blast is all yours.'

Brave words, but a flicker in the voice. Clearly Seabury was putting up a front, and that meant he was bluffing. Besides, Mick had never heard of such a device. He took another step forward. One step. Just to prove a point. Just for the fun of the game.

'Let's just stop fucking around and rush them,' Król said.

But that wasn't what Mick wanted. That wasn't a show of power. He wanted to come out top. He wanted to convince Seabury to turn against the woman, even though Seabury knew Mick meant her harm. This was wasting time, yet he wanted to see it through. She'd be his in thirty seconds either way, and thirty seconds he could spare.

'I'll count to three,' he said.

'You can't do this to us,' Liz moaned. 'Where's my husband? He'll kill you for this.'

From behind him, Król said: 'Let's jump them, now.'

Mick ignored him. 'Karl, well done for being the good Samaritan, but now it's time to think about your wife. Your future. Don't fuck it up just because the woman behind you fluttered her eyelashes at you.'

For a moment it looked as if Seabury was considering it. Walking away and forgetting about her. People got hurt every day, wasn't his fault if he couldn't help them all. The guy was, in Mick's opinion, two seconds from making the right choice, and then Król and his big mouth fucked it up.

'Here we come, fuckwits,' he yelled.

Mick turned, pointed his knife right at Król's disgusting face, said: 'Shut the fuck—'

Król threw up a defending arm, turned his face away with a yell. But the action was too much, too overdone for just a pointing knife, and Mick realised the truth a half second before he heard the bang. Loud, monstrous. His arms went up around his head and he dropped onto his knees, expecting a rain of lethal debris to fragment his flesh, a supersonic wave of fiery air to crush his bones. He had turned away from Seabury, and the man had snatched the moment to try a daring escape that was about to kill everyone with shrapnel.

Instead, yellow smoke washed over him. It swallowed the world around him. Not a weapon of murder, then. Just a smoke bomb; although it must have been adapted because they didn't usually create an explosive noise.

Mick stood and turned, but he could see nothing. Król was laughing, and it was the only sound out there. The smoke made Mick cough, but it wasn't vicious on his lungs, so it hadn't been adapted to contain CS gas. Designed only to shock and disorient so the user could escape. Some silly ninja trick by a guy with a shop full of such, and he'd been caught out by it.

Angry, he ran through the smoke towards where Seabury and Liz had been, but stopped after only a few seconds because he had no idea of what he might run into – or he did:

Danger Hole Below

Behind him, Król was shouting again, but laughing also. In the smoke he made out the mouthy Polish bastard's shape, so stepped forward and launched a punch at its head. There was a hard connection, bone on bone, and a raspy grunt as Król crumpled to the ground.

The smoke cleared ninety seconds later, shredded and dispersed by the soft wind. But the grenade had done its job. Mick looked all round, but saw only Król who was clutching his face, moaning about being struck.

Seabury and the bitch had vanished.

CHAPTER TWENTY-THREE

KARL

'Stop, Karl. I can't see.'

'It's fine, just keep going straight.'

'I don't know where straight is. Where are we? Just stop, will you, please?'

'We can't stop. They might come down after us. Come on.'

'No! Stop. Where does this go?'

'Away from those bastards, and that's good.'

'STOP!'

He was far ahead. He stopped in his tracks and turned. In the dark, he could barely make her out. His urge to leave her behind was centre stage, but he knew he couldn't. He had a daft vision of getting out of there and running into her husband, and having to tell him he'd left the man's wife in the dark underground, torn, bloody feet and all.

But they couldn't afford to dawdle. She was moving slowly and carefully because she was unaware of what lay before them.

'We have to get out, and that means moving forward. So, hurry up or I'll leave you here.'

She gasped in shock. He regretted what he'd said and apologised. 'But we have to go. Move faster. You want them to catch us down here?' He turned away. Arms out before him, like a kid playing zombie, he continued to move.

'We're trapped. It's madness to move further – ow!'

Karl stopped as he heard Liz hit the ground with a thump. In the blackness, he moved back, feeling. Found her breast and quickly shifted his hands to her arm, cheeks flushing in the dark. Felt along until he had her hand and lifted her to her feet. He moved away, but kept hold of her hand. Still she wouldn't move.

'It's okay. Come on.'

'My feet,' she moaned.

He remembered: she'd lost her shoes while climbing onto the roof.

He took his off, and felt for her toes. She said nothing as he slipped his shoes onto her feet, tying the laces as tight as he possibly could.

'Come on.'

'What about your feet?' she asked.

'Come on.' Like coaxing a kid. He was getting in some practice. But he wouldn't need it if they never got out of here. He wanted to shout to get her moving. He wanted to damn well drag her. He needed to get back to his family. The men after Liz hadn't had a change of will with the new dawn. If they had decided to visit the shop then there was no reason they wouldn't go back to his house. The thought terrified him.

But he didn't shout at Liz. Instead he mustered all his restraint and said: 'Come on.'

He gave her a gentle tug, and she moved. They walked with careful steps. They got four or five, and something brushed the top of his shoulder. Two seconds later, he heard her cry out again and jerk back, and she almost took his entire arm with her.

'What?' he hissed as he stumbled.

Her grey form dropped to its knees. 'Something hit me.'

He took a step, and the thing that had brushed his shoulder hit him in the cheek and chest. He felt for it: a length of wood poking down from the ceiling.

'We're going back,' she moaned. She got up, arms feeling out before her. Her fingers slipped over his face like giant spiders, then she turned, took a step back the way they came, and fell again, this time forwards. A thud, a grunt of pain. And tears. He saw her throw something from the ground, heard it slap a wall. The brick that had tripped her.

'Where the hell are we?'

'The builders posted a letter to all the shops, warning us about possible subsidence. They were digging up the buildings on this land and found a tunnel.'

With his eyes now fully adjusted to the dark, he saw her face turn to him. He held out a hand. She didn't take it. Just sat there defeated.

'It used to be connected to Victoria Park Station, up north about a mile. Vic Park closed in the forties. The overground lines and station were demolished in the 1960s when they built the East Cross Route.'

Comforted some, she took his outstretched hand.

He bent down, and pressed her hand towards the ground, and closed her fingers around the very thing she had tripped over. A steel rail.

'It's… it's an underground train track?'

'Not the London Underground, either, but a real railway. Something to do with an extension to some line or other. Long disused. I guess they were going to just forget about this underground section, let people in the future find it and wonder what life was like back when humans couldn't teleport everywhere, but the post-Olympics regeneration of this area unearthed it.'

'And we can follow this and… get out?'

'The nearest station was Old Ford, only 500 feet from here, behind us. There's a housing estate there now, though, and the route was filled in years ago. The good news is that this underground section exists all the way to Springfield Station. So, we can go forward. Springfield is also disused, but still there, and there should be a way up. I read that it's close to West Ham Station, which is about two miles. But that will be two miles in the dark.'

'Are you sure there will be a station?'

'I saw plans of the tunnel and stuff. I looked them up once those builders told me about it. It was enough to postpone their building work while they checked it out. I wanted to make sure my shop wasn't going to fall into the ground.'

'So, we just walk straight on? What's ahead of us? What if it's a dead end and we have to go back and they're waiting for us?'

He didn't know how to answer that. The two men hadn't tried to follow them, so maybe that meant they assumed Karl and Liz had fled above ground in the smoke. Surely they wouldn't be lurking up there, waiting. It didn't matter, anyway, because they were not going back. They would find a way out ahead of them somehow.

'This is weird,' Liz said. 'Underground station. Like something from *Tomb Raider*. But what if the station is all bricked up and there's no way out?'

He bit back a sarcastic joke. 'There will be.' He pulled her to her feet, and she came willingly.

'Walk straight and you won't trip.'

'What if a train comes?'

She was making a joke now. To his surprise, he laughed. 'You know trains. Always late. We're fine. Come on. Keep hold of my hand.'

She gripped his hand tightly. Over-tight, which he took to mean she didn't fully trust this plan. Nothing he could do about that because he didn't fully believe in it himself. He took a step, expecting resistance from her. But she came.

'Did you know that second man?' he asked. 'The one in the car? Was he the guy who chased you last night?'

'I don't know. I think he was a different man. The way he moved, and he was bigger. But he was hiding his face, so maybe he thinks we might have recognised him. Did you?'

He shook his head, then realised his error and vocalised his answer. 'But he looked like he was in control. Like, if there's a team, he might be the boss.'

They fell silent for a while. Karl tried not to think about that word he had used: team. The idea of many men after him was terrifying.

They walked between the tracks, taking smaller steps to keep their feet on the sleepers; it made Karl remember doing this as a kid with his friends. Long strolls along the train tracks, where it was peaceful. In Sunday sunshine, not crushing blackness. Something he hoped to do with his own son – or daughter – one day. They walked slowly, for a minute, in silence. By then, his eyes had adjusted to the gloom and he could see arcs and lines of lighter black in the dark. He could see the curve of the roof and the walls. And thin, long lines of grey-black that were the tracks they walked between.

And a fork. The tunnel split like a lizard's tongue. One black hole on the left, and one black hole on the right, and nothing to distinguish between them except the track vanished down the right-hand route. Life and death choices had been made on less, so he chose the track.

But all his mind's eye saw was Katie. He wished he'd gone home. She would be awaiting his call, but his phone was in the shop, a billion miles away, and she would begin to worry soon. He hoped his lack of contact would make her understand the threat they faced and force her out of the house, to her father's place, which surely the men after them didn't know the location of. She would call the police first, hopefully. But there was always a chance that she would remain in the house, waiting for the phone to ring – where the bad guys could be headed right now.

His pace quickened. Her grip tightened again, as if she feared he'd slip away. But then she said something.

'Are you going to tell your wife you touched another woman's breast today?'

He realised she wasn't scared of losing him at all. Maybe she had sensed his growing unease due to his increased pace, and she was trying to shift his attention, to lighten the mood. Even amid her own fear and worry, she was trying to ease his anguish. It didn't, of course, but he stopped and turned to her. Their faces were just inches apart. He wanted to try to ease her pain in return, but no words came.

That was when they heard a noise. Faint. It rolled towards them, and past, and was gone. Karl looked up and over her head, and Liz turned away from him, and they both stared back the way they'd come. The world was black, but way in the distance was a pinprick of light. Like a solitary star in the night sky. Someone had found their entrance.

Someone had entered their world in pursuit.

CHAPTER TWENTY-FOUR

MICK

The collapsed foundations had created a rough and ready ramp into the abyss, with portions of broken concrete forming a handy set of stairs. Mick tried to make his way down slowly, silently, but a wedge-shaped slab of concrete shifted under his weight and took away his legs. Dirt and concrete crumbled down the slope, with Mick sliding behind it on his arse.

Król started laughing from above.

'Shut your trap,' Mick hissed. He looked up. Król was at the edge, on his hands and knees and staring down. Wearing a goofy grin that Mick wanted to widen with his knife. 'Wait in the fucking car.'

Król vanished. Mick got to his feet. The way ahead was pitch-black, but he started jogging anyway. He knew he could trip and smash his nose, might even step out over some great shaft leading a mile down, but he could not dawdle. He had learned about the underground tracks following a quick Google search of this area, but it had taken time, too much time. Seabury and the woman, if they weren't crushed or impaled down here, were far ahead and getting further.

His eyes soon started to adjust to the gloom. He saw walls, and the roof, and under his feet the twin lines of the ancient tracks. He stopped to listen, but heard nothing. No footsteps or voices.

Then he jogged onwards, arms extended before him so they would hit any obstacle ahead before his face did.

His anger started to slip away. This place would make the perfect tomb for the bitch and her saviour. Down here, no chance of a good Samaritan trying to save the day, no matter how loudly she screamed, and he could take his time. Tie them with the string in his pocket, slot his phone on a protrusion in the wall, flashlight illuminating everything, and work at them slowly with his knife. The dark and the cold would heighten their fear. Their cries of pain and his own laughter would probably echo, enhancing the fun. This time, he would record the event, which might go some way to alleviating the irritation that he'd overlooked capturing Grafton's final moments on camera.

Even better: since this place was abandoned, her body would lie undiscovered. There was no further chance to smash up Grafton, but he could repeat and repeat with the bitch. No need for dreams. Every time the urge resurfaced, all he would have to do is drive out here, and there she would be, waiting for him like a lover. He could slice and smash until he was satisfied. Over and over. Again and again.

Soon, he came to a fork in the tunnel.

The tracks went ahead, but to the left was another tunnel shooting off at ten o'clock. Logic told him they'd gone ahead, following the tracks. Most people would. But they could have taken the left fork to trick their pursuer.

'Shit,' he hissed. So far, so close. What to do? He could pick the correct path and be home in an hour, washing their blood off his hands.

But if he chose the wrong route, his prey would escape, and he'd never get another chance to end this.

CHAPTER TWENTY-FIVE

KARL

The shout bounced past them, echoing, as if their assailant had repeated it.

'They'll never find your bodies down here, you know?'

They lay on their fronts, facing back the way they'd come. They lay between the tracks, covered in dirt, feeling the cold seeping into their bones. Karl, at least.

'So your wife is pregnant?' Liz whispered.

'What?' he whispered back. What kind of question was that right now?

'I'm gonna gut you both, right down here, and leave you for the rats.'

The shout sounded no closer than the first, thankfully. Which meant their prayers had been answered: the fork in the tunnel had halted their pursuer out of fear of choosing the wrong route.

'I think you were about to say it before that man came in the shop. How far gone?'

He didn't understand what she was talking about – at first. And then he understood. He had tried—

'Last chance, Seabury. I'll ruin your world or save it. You don't even have to give up. Just knock that bitch out and shout me and you can run and I'll do the rest, and you can live your life.'

—to distract himself to the mood once or twice with a joke, and he figured she was doing something similar now: acting as if everything were normal, pretending that there wasn't a madman down here in the dark with them. So, he went along with it.

'Six months,' he said, voice low, head close to hers.

'What are you having?'

'I want a boy. She wants a girl.'

'You don't know yet? Why not?'

'Seabury, this is your absolute last chance.'

'There's two ways to find out. One is when you hold a new baby in your arms and see him or her in the flesh. The other is to see what basically looks like a chalk rubbing on a screen. You got kids?'

He knew she didn't even before she said so.

'Ron didn't want them. I'm not sure. I like children, but as for my own...'

'He didn't want them entering his lifestyle, eh?'

A slice of verbal Tourette's there. But she didn't seem to take offence.

'No, nothing like that. I don't think he thought he was the settling type. But you have to think of the old people's home, that's what I said to him once.'

'I'm going to make you suffer like you wouldn't believe, Seabury, unless you bring her out right now. No fucking silly gadget's gonna save you down here.'

'The what?' He was finding it hard not to be distracted by the man chasing them. Liz was looking at Karl, but Karl could not ignore the lethal threat just 160 feet from them.

'You have to think about the old people's home. That's where we'll be one day. You don't want to be one of those old ones that gets no visitors. I've seen them before, when I was visiting my father when he was—'

'I see you, bitches. Here I fucking come!'

'Still alive, and I felt sorry for them. They look sad.'

'Like they were thinking, shit, I should have had kids?'

Despite his claim, their pursuer hadn't moved towards them. An idle threat, then. A trick designed to make them break cover.

'Exactly.' Liz spoke too loud, and Karl watched the tunnel carefully, fearing that the man was going to come running at them.

What happened instead was worse.

A flash of light ahead, and in the next instant a cracking sound. It raced past them like a train, impossible to ignore. Liz let out a moan, covered her ears and planted her face in the dirt. Karl put his hands out ahead of him, as if foolishly believing he could stop a bullet that way. If the gunman had been seeking a sliver of movement to latch onto, he'd now got it.

Another gunshot. Another flash, which framed the gunman like a horror-film villain during a burst of lightning. He was aiming right at them.

Then a third gunshot, but this time the gunman was lit in profile, and Karl felt his choking terror abate. The man had fired down the other tunnel this time. He didn't know where they were. He was firing blind, hoping for a lucky hit.

There was silence. Karl reached out and put his hand over Liz's mouth. The gunman was obviously listening, hoping to hear them running, fleeing from the bullets. So, they stayed silent and they stayed put.

A few seconds later, he started shouting again. Loud, fast, a million threats, a billion imaginative scenarios involving suffering and death. But his voice came no closer. This was a chance to put more distance between them.

Karl got up slowly and helped Liz climb to her feet. Their faces close, he stared into her eyes and whispered to her they were going to walk slowly, carefully. But one misstep, one noise, and they would be caught. She nodded her understanding. They turned, giving him their backs. And started walking.

The distance grew. There were no missteps, no noises. There was no sense of forward movement either because they could see nothing ahead. But the gunman's voice began to fade. The darkness condensed behind them, like a series of curtains pulled between pursued and pursuer, and soon his ranting was nothing but a background whisper.

CHAPTER TWENTY-SIX

BRAD

Brad tore off the wrapping paper and shook open a Varsity jacket with a red leather torso and white canvas arms. There was a large B on the breast. He instantly hated it but smiled because Ian was awaiting his reaction.

'Wear it all day. Try it now.'

Brad got it halfway unzipped when his mobile rang. 'Job Centre' popped up.

'Attaboy,' Ian said, leaning close to read the screen. 'Remember to tell them that you're willing to increase your travel distance.'

'I'll take it in the bathroom.'

Ian grabbed his half-finished cigar from the ashtray and flicked a kick at Brad's naked ass as he got off the bed.

'Tell them we'll have your website up and running later today.'

In the bathroom, Brad answered the call from Job Centre--, who he'd been in contact with for the last three months, since his last building site contract expired. The actual centre was in his phonebook, but under Job Centre-, single hyphen. As Ian had proved, at a glance it was hard to tell the difference between one and two hyphens.

'One question of momentous importance,' Mick said, as Brad answered the phone. 'It all hung on Król. It's what we were waiting for. Why didn't you call me about it?' He meant: why hadn't Brad called to find out if Król had found the Grafton woman? Surely the stakes are high enough to warrant him worrying.

Brad said: 'It's all moot now Ramirez is out, so the missus thing is sixes and sevens. It's your thing.'

He meant: Mick was the one worried about Liz Grafton, not Brad. Because with Ramirez no longer in the frame, it didn't matter what she told the cops.

'"My thing"? Like my pet peeve or something?'

'Maybe. So what do you want? Picked who's next yet?'

'You said that before. What's that supposed to mean, Brad?'

'What's next, I meant.'

'Two things. First, I got a job for you. Not that you seem to care, but Król fucked up.'

Brad listened to Mick's story with the door locked and the sink taps running so Ian couldn't hear his replies. When the tale was told, he said: 'Not the best news. But I say let them run.'

'Well, Brad, this is my thing, isn't it? And I say no.'

'Yet you called me, so you think I can do something about it. What?'

Mick explained. 'And it needs to be in thirty seconds' time. Get going.'

'And what else?'

'Ah, yes. The bad news.'

'I thought that was the bad news.'

'Of course not. Sixes and sevens. You had a brick tossed through Ramirez's window, right?'

'Sure. With a note to freak him out. Watch your back, dead man walking. What's that got to do with your guy?'

'It fucking worked a treat, that's what. So much so that Ramirez just called the cops. He's so fucking scared that Grafton's rent-a-lunatics are after him that he wants this case solved quick, before he gets chopped up. Apparently he says it might be a great idea to maybe look at the guys who hit his nightclub—'

'What? Are you telling me we're half a day into this and already the cops—'

'Just calm down. You know there were all sorts of rumours flying around about who might have done it. And rumours that it was a hit on either Grafton or his old rival, Razor Randolph, and plenty of people wanted both of them dead. You haven't forgotten Rocker, have you?'

''Course not, but—'

'But nothing, Brad. So Ramirez is just assuming it's the same guys, back for try number two. He's rehashing old tales. That's all. Just bullshit.'

'But it's not bullshit, is it? Not if my name's been mentioned.'

'Ramirez only mentioned a first name. Brad. A loan shark who worked for Grafton as a leg-breaker.'

'Christ.'

'He might also have said "Nancy-boy leg-breaker",' Mick said, laughing.

'Stop fucking laughing, Mick.'

He did, abruptly. 'Just calm down—'

'There aren't that many gay enforcers called Brad in London, Mick. Jesus.'

That made Mick giggle like a schoolgirl. 'No, there aren't. But relax, okay? Keep your legendary cool. Names are flooding in about who might have done this. You think anyone's going to take a criminal's word as gospel? Wait for the Queen to give you up, and then you can worry. So relax, right? Are you relaxed?'

'And what if Grafton's wife recognised my eyes?'

'What, now you're suddenly worried about her? Let them run, you said. That doesn't sound relaxed, Brad. Try again. Summon it up from deep within. Are you relaxed now?'

'Hell yes,' Brad said with as much sarcasm as he could muster. 'But they'll look into me. Can't afford not to. Then they'll find out I was investigated for that murder a few years back. I'll get the knock on the door at some point, and if Ian—'

'There'll be no door knock for him to answer, Brad. You're just a person of interest based on some claim by a low life, one of a thousand who'd benefit from Grafton in a grave. But you're right, you're a guy with form, and maybe, even if you're innocent, you might go underground if you know the cops are after you. That's an extra headache. So, nobody's going to tell your bloke anything. A pair of guys will probably hang about outside your house, that's all. If you turn up, all they'll do is follow you, see if maybe you go dig up the murder weapon or they can hear you bragging about the killings. Solution: don't turn up for a few days.'

'Why a few days? What can you do to kill this?'

'Nothing. But the plan was always to clear out, right? We bring it forward.'

'Leave the country in a few days? Mick, I can't just hop on a plane. This was supposed to be six months, remember?'

Was Mick's memory bad, or did he just not care? Brad had agreed to hit Grafton, in part, for a share of whatever money they found in the cottage, but mostly because he wouldn't get the chance again. In six months he'd be living in Thailand with Ian, who was transferring to a branch of his company out there. The Ramirez angle, he'd been promised, would muddy the murder investigation long enough to let it go cold. But now the cops were on the cusp of getting Brad's name. And when they learned of his plans to emigrate, their suspicions would increase and they'd lob a spanner in the works. It was all set for six months from now, not a couple of bloody days.

Mick's great plan was: 'So you fly out in a couple of days, and then your bloke goes on the sick for six months.'

Brad cursed. 'Christ, Mick, there's visas to get, a house to sell. Ian's going caravanning with his brother in April. It can't happen, it ain't possible. And even if everything was ready to go, and the sickness thing was possible, I'd have to tell him what's going on, wouldn't I? How's that going to work? He thinks I gave all that crime shit up way back. If he even thought I nicked a Twix from the corner shop, he'd leave me. Now I'm supposed to tell him I'm on the run from the cops for triple murder and we've got to escape the country right now? No, you've got to sort this out.'

'How? The Ramirez plan was good, but now it's out the window and we deal with it. The cops want you, Brad. Like it or not, you don't have six months to sign forms, show people around a house and look at fucking holiday photos of some caravan park.'

'Well, you've got to do something. I can't hide from the cops. And even if Ian never found out I'm on the run, what about the cash? I was supposed to have some magical luck on the horses each week to explain earning ninety grand in six months. I whip out that much dough in a few days' time, he'll know it's nicked. No, Mick. You're supposed to be smarter than everyone else, so prove it. Fucking sort this out.'

Silence, as Mick thought. For a moment he worried that Mick would abandon him because he already had his escape plan ready to go. But he had to trust that their history guaranteed loyalty. Brad was the one who had made everything possible up until this point. Without Brad, Grafton would be walking around still, untouched and untouchable. Mick had to respect that.

'I'm working on a plan,' he said. 'Then that'll just leave the bitch. If she can tell the police who you are, the solution is to make sure she can't tell anyone anything, right? So, go do what I said. You can have Seabury. But you save her for me, right?'

A pause from Brad as he thought about this. There was nothing he could do, so he had to leave it up to Mick. This relaxed him somewhat. 'That tosspot Ramirez really call me a Nancy-boy?'

Mick started laughing again.

CHAPTER TWENTY-SEVEN

KARL

Karl let out a breath, and that was when he realised that he'd been holding it. His chest was heaving as if he'd been running. He heard Liz's ragged breathing a couple of feet away. Saw the shape of her chest rising and falling. Same story. Nervous energy oozing out of both of them.

She stumbled. His anxiety exploded, and he grabbed her, fearful that the noise would bring the gunman pounding down upon them.

'I'm okay,' she said. She struggled out of his grasp, and her black shape bent and sat on one of the rails. He didn't want to stop, was desperate to get out of here and back to Katie, but he sat opposite her, facing her. He knew the gunman was far behind.

'Let's hope a train doesn't come,' she said, repeating her joke from earlier.

'We could do with the light.'

'Nah, you don't want to see my face. Make-up all messy.'

'I think with all this dirt around we probably look like coal miners by now.'

They sat for a few moments. Back down the tunnel, the darkness seemed to pulse and shift. He stared until he was sure the kaleidoscopic swirl didn't camouflage a man crawling towards them.

'What was that thing with the smoke, that grenade thing you threw?'

She was rubbing her hands across her face, trying to remove the grime. His coal miner joke must have set that off.

'The grenade that let off all the smoke? Smoke grenade.'

She laughed. 'Very funny. Where did you get that?'

'Internet. Two hundred quid, up in smoke.'

'Who'd need one of those for personal defence?'

He said: 'People on the run, apparently.'

She laughed. 'I'm guessing that stuff's not legal to sell.'

She was just killing time, talking to make the minutes fly by. Time was not something he could spare, though. He stood. 'No. That's why I had it upstairs.'

He watched her straighten her dress and could tell she was thinking of something else to say. He looked at the way ahead. How far until the station? A mile, or was it thirty feet away? He wanted to get moving.

What she decided upon was: 'How did you meet your wife?'

He sighed. 'Let's go. We can't waste time.'

They started walking again. After a minute, he answered her question.

'Like you. Childhood sweethearts. She was the neighbour's kid. We were the only children on that street. Just friends until she was thirteen, and I was twelve. She wanted to practise kissing, and there was no one else around.'

'So you having a loving wife and a baby on the way. I guess you feel you're a lucky man.'

'I never won the lottery, but never got stabbed to death in a piss-stained alleyway, either. I'm happy with the middle ground.'

More silence. Thirty seconds in, she stumbled over something and he turned, caught her as she crashed into him. In his arms, she said: 'What's your plan?'

He made sure she was balanced, then turned and started walking again. 'Get to a phone. Tell the damn police what happened. And tell my wife she's got to run from our family home because of all this shit.' His anxiety was rising again.

After another minute or so of silence, she said: 'It's morning now. They shouldn't still be after us. Something's wrong. We need to find my husband.'

'I'm going home. You do what you want.' He could feel his anger welling up.

'He might still be tied up at the cottage. Maybe they tied everyone up. We have to go there and release him. Then he can get to work sorting out this problem. You have to take me there.'

Knowing he was so irritated that he would only say something she wouldn't like, he refused to respond. Was the gunman approaching his house right now? Closing in on his wife and child?

'Ron can fix all this. He'll know what to do. But he'll be worried about me. We'll find a taxi and get straight there. They won't still be there, not if they're out chasing us.'

He wanted to believe that Katie would be safe. The gunman and his cronies hadn't gone to the house this morning, had they? They'd chosen the shop. The hunt was for Karl and Liz, after all. Hopefully Katie would be ignored. Safe. Hopefully, when he hadn't called her, she had packed a bag and got out of there.

'Are you listening? I need to get to my husband.'

'Fuck him,' Karl snapped.

'No, fuck you.'

He heard her stop, but he continued walking. Faster now, with bigger steps. If she wanted to stay down here, so be it. But he was going.

He stopped, and turned.

'I'm sorry.'

It hit him then. He had a duty to protect his wife and unborn child any way he could, but that didn't mean he could abandon this woman. The men who had tried to break into his house had failed, hadn't they? Because Katie had slept soundly all night in a warm bed. But they hadn't failed at Liz's house, had they? Because Liz had fled through the woods, pursued by a masked man, and this morning she was lost underground and still had no idea what had happened to the man she loved. He hadn't wanted any of this trouble, but he was in the thick of it now and had a responsibility to help. Anything less would be wrong. If Katie had been lost down here with another man and that guy had refused to help…

But there was something else. Something he hadn't wanted to think about, but now, knowing Katie might be in danger, knowing that their pursuers were not going to give up, it was pushing to the front of his mind.

'I'm sorry. Look, we'll sort this out. We'll call the police and send them to our houses, and we'll get there and make sure everyone's safe. But let's get out of this tunnel first, okay?'

'I don't think you should assume the police will make everything okay.'

Her sentence highlighted exactly what he couldn't stop thinking about. Maybe the cops wouldn't be able to do much. They might fail to get the names of everyone involved, or miss a vital gang member when they took everyone down. All it would take was one bad guy left on the streets with a working pair of legs and Karl's address. Maybe the only person who could totally fix this problem was this woman's husband. Street justice wasn't exactly what Karl wanted, but if it meant an end to the threat against Katie and Michael… And it wouldn't be his fault, would it? All he'd done was save someone's life. What Liz did with her continued existence would not be on his head.

He stopped and waited for her, and, side by side, they stumbled on into the void.

CHAPTER TWENTY-EIGHT

. MICK

Sixty seconds after the call to Brad, Mick's Nissan Almera pulled up outside Karl's shop. Right outside, because nobody was around yet and there were no CCTV cameras about, not even watching the shop specialising in surveillance technology. The road was peaceful, quiet, secretive. But that could change in minutes.

He ran into Sunrise Electronics and found exactly what he'd expected: Król acting like a kid in a sweet shop. There was a large cardboard box in the centre of the room and Król was filling it with items grabbed off shelves.

'What the hell are you doing back here? We need to get away from this place. We need to burn that stolen car. How stupid you are is always a surprise, Król.'

Król ignored him. Electrical items continued to sail through the air and crash into the box.

'These other shops will be open soon. Leave that shit and let's go.'

Król ignored him again. He moved to the ladder, but stopped when his foot stepped on something. He picked it up, took one look and tossed it to Mick.

'That's knackered. You can have it.'

Król climbed the ladder. Mick looked at the item in his hand. A mobile phone with a cracked screen. Mick lit it up and got a surprise.

He was staring at a photo of Król leering close to the camera. Grainy, green. Night vision. Doubtless taken at Seabury's house last night when Król and his crony were trying to break in. A neat idea settled into his head. He put the phone on the floor and kicked it under the counter.

'Get back down here,' he said. He strode to the ladder and grabbed Król's foot, and yanked him right off. Król crashed to the carpet, but the wiry little bastard bounced up in a second. He shoved Mick away, hard. Mick couldn't believe it. He got a bigger shock a second later when Król jerked something out of his jacket. Some kind of knife with no handle. Looked like a lawnmower blade. But it was the look in Król's eyes that concerned Mick more. A look that said he wasn't scared. Not any more.

'Things are a-changing round here, Mick,' he said. He waved the blade. 'Nice, eh? Saw this thing on the floor when I bust in his shed and figured, beats my little home-made shank. Imagine this thing sliding into the guts. You want it in your guts like that shopkeeper? And you don't hold that over me any more. I want that knife back, and some cash for my troubles.'

I got webcam, ain't I?

That explained the determination in the eyes: Król thought he had something on Mick and that he was going to control things from here on. But what?

'And why would I do that?' Mick said, buying time to think.

Król's next words were the biggest shock of all.

'I know that was Mr Invincible's wife. And I saw the news. He's dead, man. Chopped up last night, three of them. And I reckon you did it.'

Mick felt a tightening of his head, as if a steel band around his skull was shrinking. A big problem lay ahead. But it wasn't fear of the blade in Król's hand, and it wasn't fear of the information in Król's little brain.

Król said: 'I ain't taking your shit any more, Mick. Understand? I feed your name to the police, say you did this, and you're fucked. Literally. I know you been missing some action since your missus, and the boys in prison will cosy up to you. I feed it to Grafton's people, and you're fucked there, as well. So, how about the knife, and them two books you took, and, say, two hundred a week, and you throw me some info about nice houses I can slip in to with no problem?'

Mick looked at the blade and remembered the phone, and there was a feeling akin to what you get when a tricky crossword answer clicks into place. Seabury's lawnmower blade, and Seabury's phone with a picture of Król on it. Talk about bloody Fate. He almost laughed aloud. But he kept his face serious and said: 'How about you forget the two hundred and you give me ten per cent of what you make from the houses? I can talk to a guy I know and find some gems.'

As he spoke, Mick walked past Król and to a far wall, and pretended to stare at something on a shelf. Król was between him and the exit.

'Now you're talking my language. But I get the knife back and the books. You ain't setting me up with them.'

'You get the knife and the books back. And I get that nasty blade in your hand. But none of this goes down if the cops find us here. So, can we get going?'

Król picked up the box. It was overflowing, and something slid out to hit the floor. It looked like a simple plug-in air freshener, but here, in this store, was probably some kind of recording device. Mick had bought one for Tim's room when he was twelve, just so he could eavesdrop on what his boy and his new friends were getting up to. This in mind, his anger spiked when Król kicked the item across the floor.

'You can have that, as well.'

Mick started for the door, and, as planned, Król did the same. The damn idiot gave Mick his back as he turned and strode towards the shutter.

He got five steps before it happened, and he only got that many because Mick took two seconds to slip on a pair of vinyl gloves. And pull out his own knife. In haste, he didn't notice his matchbox of mints slip out of his pocket.

The blade did not penetrate the neck cleanly, but caught a glancing blow that carved open one side, releasing a jet of blood. Król dropped the box and stumbled forwards, and Mick staggered back. Król sank to his knees and put a hand to his neck to stem the flow, his fingers arriving there a moment before the blade dropped again. It slid neatly between two fingers without damaging them and sank deep into the flesh beneath.

Mick ducked aside like a boxer avoiding a jab as another gout of blood erupted right at him. Król was screaming again as he face-planted the carpet.

'That Polish for *I got webcam, ain't I?*' Mick asked, laughing.

A moment later Król got to his feet, one hand on his neck, blood washing down his torso.

'Shit,' Mick said. He wasn't worried about an attack, because Król was losing blood fast; he was concerned about getting blood on his clothing if the man rushed at him.

'That's right, bastard,' Król said, grinning. He sprang forward, eyes bearing deadly intent, but stumbled after only two steps. Fell onto his knees and toppled backwards.

'Hurry up now, Król.' Mick hurried to the shutter, bent and stared out, but the street was empty. Behind him, Król was rolling about like a man on fire, but he was gurgling now, and nobody was going to hear that.

'Chop, chop, Król, I need some grub.'

It took eighty more seconds for Król to finally lie still. Mick took his first breath in all that time as Król expelled his last. Just before the eyes glazed over, Mick squatted by him, careful of the blood, and said: 'No one mentions my family, remember? That was the rule. So, when you get to Hell and the Devil asks what happened, you tell him you said the wrong thing to the wrong man, okay? He'll have heard it a billion times.'

It hadn't been fear of the blade in Król's hand, and it hadn't been fear of the information in Król's little brain: the big problem had been what to do when Król was dead. But it wasn't a problem any longer.

Pathologists were good at determining the kind of blade that caused an injury, so Mick took Król's weapon and jabbed it deep into the two knife wounds. He tossed the bloody blade onto Król's body. He stripped off his gloves and pocketed them, and slipped under the shutter. He held his breath again until he was in his car and didn't start to relax until the vehicle was turning off the street. But a few moments later he was calm and smiling and breathing just fine. Yet he was disappointed. Killing Król hadn't produced the buzz he'd expected. Not like last night. Perhaps because he hadn't fantasised about it for months, planning it meticulously. Or maybe because it had been primarily business, not fun.

Whatever. He still had the bitch to come. He pushed Król from his head because there was more business afoot. He made a call to the airline. He'd phoned earlier to change his flight from two weeks to two days away because of the Ramirez situation. And this new development with Król necessitated a more urgent departure. Tomorrow, early. After Seabury and the bitch were over, his new life would begin.

CHAPTER TWENTY-NINE

DAVE

'One question of momentous importance,' Mick said.

Dave's answer to the question was: 'Król is your man, Mick, so he would have called you if he'd found the woman. I figured you'd call me when you knew. I've been waiting for you to phone.'

Silence for a few seconds, as if Mick was sniffing for bullshit. Which it was: Dave didn't care whether or not Król had found the woman. Then he said: 'I hear traffic, Dave, my man. Where are you?'

'Where you sent me at Christ-knows-how-early this morning. I shouldn't be having to do this, Mick. This lark should have been over. But I'm running around like an—'

'Forget it. I doubt the bitch is going there.'

Mick had sent him to Grafton's mum's house in Kensington late last night. In case the bitch woke up this morning and decided to crawl there for sanctuary. A bit of a long shot, since Grafton would surely have arranged for a safe house. But Mick had insisted, and Dave was supposed to have sat there all night in a cold car. Sod that.

'New job for you,' Mick said. 'More important. Get to Król's flat, sharpish. Check for a camera, something like that. Take his computer and the webcam, and then sterilise the place.'

'What's going on? And sterilise it with what? Wet wipes?'

'Up to you. But since the cops will be raining down on that shithole very soon, I'd try to think of a quicker way, if I were you. Let's see if you're a sharp tack. Plus, things have changed a lot and I would again advise you and your wife to think about getting out of this city. Even the country. I'm on a plane out of here first thing tomorrow.'

'I'm thinking about it.' Like hell he was. If Mick and Brad wanted to run away from their lives, so be it. He was going to do what he'd planned all along: use the money stolen from Grafton's slush fund to buy the damn house he lived in. Ninety grand was ten feet from him, hidden in the back of his work van.

'And what about Król? Where the hell is he? What's he doing?'

Mick grinned. 'Król is about to help me nail Seabury and the bitch.' Mick repeated his order and hung up.

Dave slotted his phone away, angry. The slaughterhouse they'd left behind was going to be a treasure trove of clues, or barren as a desert in terms of evidence. The cops would have knocked on his door by now if there was evidence to nail him. They hadn't, so there wasn't. He was free and clear, but that might not be the case if he got further involved in this shit. So, he wasn't going to Król's flat. No damn way.

He noticed his wife was looking at him with raised eyebrows.

'Everything's fine,' he said.

Lucinda watched him for a long moment, as if trying to read his eyes, or even his mind. 'Good. Grab one of those.'

'You got a pound?'

'Didn't that prick Mr Invincible have any coins?' She tossed him a pound coin. As he unlocked a shopping trolley, he watched the Tesco car park for familiar faces, or strange faces scrutinising him. He did it carefully, not wanting to be obvious.

'Stop looking for people coming after you,' Lucinda said as she hauled the trolley out of the shelter and shoved it at him. 'Everything's fine, right? That was why that Mick guy just called:

to say all was fine. And he knows everything. So, no one will be after you, because that wouldn't be fine, would it? But fine it is. He said so, so it must be. All fine and dandy.'

That was why he'd tried to hide his scrutiny of the car park: Lucinda hated his paranoia. He wished he could be like her. She hadn't worried about a single thing since he'd told her they were hitting Grafton. Not even when she'd seen the papers earlier and discovered that a simple robbery had turned into a bloodbath. Then again, she had her own reasons for it –Grafton had almost cost her her dream house a couple of years ago.

They started walking towards the shop. He could hear her breathing getting harsher – she was getting worked up about something. He said nothing.

'Strange that he'd call you just to say everything is fine,' she said a few seconds later. He heard the suspicion in her tone. 'I mean, every other time he's called, there's been a problem and he's called you to sort it out. But not this time, oh no. This time, when none of you know what the next problem could be, he just takes time out to say all is good, when you clearly already believed everything's fine because that was what you said to me last night.'

He still said nothing A few steps later, though, and somewhat sheepishly: 'Mick wanted me to do something for him. I guess we shouldn't risk problems coming along. Perhaps I should do it. To be safe.'

She didn't look at him. 'Something important, probably, yet here you still stand.'

He continued to push the trolley. Then she slapped his hands off and started walking away with it.

'Get your head on straight,' she called over her shoulder. 'Go do this thing before we both get in trouble. Don't come back until everything's fine and it's actually true.'

As he watched her heading towards the supermarket, he vowed this would be the last time he helped Mick. After Król's flat, he was out. He didn't care about the woman running about out there, and he hadn't gone after Grafton for revenge. Water under the bridge as far as he was concerned. He was in this for the money, and what was the point of robbing Grafton if he couldn't enjoy the rewards?

CHAPTER THIRTY

KARL

They walked on in silence. Liz stayed five or six feet behind. At one point Karl tripped over the right-hand track, grazing his ankle, realising that the tunnel was curving to his left. The going was a little slower after that. The next problem announced itself a few minutes later – the sound of rushing water overhead. They didn't see it until they were just a few feet away, where water was leaking from the roof of the tunnel in a great curtain. Liz stopped, refusing to go any further, and he understood her reticence. The waterfall could go on for a whole mile, or the tunnel could slope downwards and be flooded. The roof could be so weak that it fell in on them. What was above them? A sewage pipe, or some rich guy's al fresco swimming pool?

Karl pushed aside his worries and forced his way through the curtain. The water was cold and drenched him in a second, but a second was all that it took to pass through.

Liz darted through after him and stood before him, soaked.

They moved on. Karl kept his eyes and hands ahead, his steps high so he didn't trip on the rail again. His feet were cold and numb. Periodically Liz made a noise at him, and he had to stop and wait. He wanted to tell her not to dawdle, but figured it was probably his own haste that was creating distance between them. So, he said nothing, just waited for her shape to appear by him before he moved on again.

Minutes later, every muscle tensed as he tried to plant a foot on rocky ground. It sank into nothing, and his body started to pitch forward. He let out a shout, unable to stop it as he toppled. But before he could worry about falling into a bottomless hole, he landed on his hands, his arms buckled, and his chest hit hard ground. He scrambled to his feet and to one side, banging hard into brick.

Liz called out, asking him what was wrong. A damn depression, he told her, angry more than hurt.

Then, it was her turn to fall. He cursed, knowing that this was wasting time. He fumbled for her, helped her to her feet. She grabbed his arm, and her hand was wet with warm blood. He rubbed her hands, seeking a gash, but she corrected him: her knee. He bent and wiped her knee with his used-to-be-white shirt, and she thanked him. He grunted an okay and moved on. But she grabbed the back of his shirt, wanting to be led. So, he helped her along.

Down here it was easy to be lulled into a vision of time standing still. But that was not the case. Time was passing, and with each expired minute they had no idea of the safety of the people they loved. He tried not to think about Katie and his unborn son, about how much she might be worrying about him, because down here he could do nothing about it and it would only stop him from focusing on their escape. He told himself she was driving to her father's, and then shut her out.

Liz, of course, would be thinking about her husband. Did she believe he was tied up in the cottage, or did she think he was out there on the streets with an army, looking for her?

And then he tried to put himself in the mind of the gunman and his cohorts. What would be their next move? How many were there, and what sort of connections did they— He stopped. Liz bumped into him. They both became aware of a low rumbling noise.

'What is it?' she asked.

'A train.'

CHAPTER THIRTY-ONE

MICK

Mick missed the days when CCTV cameras were giant boxes on poles and a doddle to avoid. These days minuscule cameras were embedded everywhere, and the police could put together a cinematic series of cuts to show a bad guy strolling around town. So, a high street phone box was out of the question. The only one he knew of without a single camera nearby, which he'd learned about when he visited the nearby charity shop where Tim worked, had already been used to call in the cavalry to Grafton's hideaway cottage, and he couldn't very well use that again. He had a burner phone, already charged, and a pre-paid SIM collecting dust, saved for a rainy day. It was time to use it.

He drove a mile southwest from Sunrise Electronics, changed clothing in the driver's seat, turned off the radio, and made the call. He watched the house. It was a semi-detached property halfway down a residential street. Invisible, inert, just a regular house. Just like the owners. But not for long.

'Hey, is this Bexleyheath Police Station?' he asked in a disguised voice so bad it almost made him laugh. 'Okay, I'm not giving my name, okay, so don't ask. There's a guy called Aleksy, bit of a scumbag. I just saw him enter a shop, a mean look on his face. You got a detective based there called McDevitt, right? Murder squad boss or something.'

As he watched the house, the front door opened and he perked up. A tall woman in a bathrobe exited with a bag of rubbish and walked down the path. He hadn't expected this and scrabbled for his keys.

'I don't need to speak to him. I'm one of his informants, and so's this Aleksy guy. That guy, that Aleksy, he went into some shop on Beverley Drive, in Old Ford. Called Sunrise or something. And – what?'

Mick drove quickly down the street. The woman opened the wheelie bin at the end of the drive and tossed the bag in. Mick's car got within range too late, though, and she turned away, heading back to the house, before he could see her face.

'I saw the guy as I drove past. Think I saw a weapon. You might want to tell McDevitt because I heard he wanted to speak to this Aleksy guy. Been looking for him. That's it.'

He slowed to almost nothing. Knowing it would cause a problem later, Mick lay on his horn. The woman stopped, and turned, and looked. Mick hid his face with the phone, but managed to stare right at her. She watched his car cruise slowly by without any real concern.

'Call me Superman, if you like.'

He hung up. The woman returned to her house and shut the door behind her.

Mick pulled into the kerb 160 feet past the house. The new burner got busted in half and the pieces lobbed down a drain, along with the snapped SIM card. Job done. He switched the radio on and drove by the house again, but didn't spot her at any of the windows.

'See you soon, Mrs Seabury.'

CHAPTER THIRTY-TWO

BRAD

Three hundred feet southwest of West Ham Station, Brad's satnav voice told him he'd arrived at the location. He drove slowly along Banker Avenue, watching his target approach and worrying over new developments. The plan had sounded so good: nail Grafton, blame Ramirez, watch the two crime lords wage war on the streets, then six months down the line he'd elope with Ian. A new country and a new life.

Then Mick had gone too far and killed Grafton, and they'd discovered that his house hadn't contained quite the war chest they'd hoped. Brad remembered a time when Grafton carted at least a million around with him, but the secret stash under the bath had contained only enough to give each man ninety grand.

Not the end of the world, but then Ramirez had spoken Brad's name, and now the police wanted to talk to him. Ian thought Brad was out of the crime game and was actively seeking legit employment back in the construction trade, so that was going to cause tension, even if Mick came up with a plan to clear Brad as a possible suspect. A day in and already two kicks in the teeth. What else might go wrong over the next hundred and fifty days that Brad was forced to remain in the danger zone?

But, as Benjamin Franklin had claimed, there were no gains without pains. So, he told himself to stop moaning. To be a cup half-full guy and get back to the job in hand.

The street was a mix of residential and commercial properties and backed onto Memorial Recreation Ground. Just before the entrance to the park, where the road turned left and became Springfield Road, was a building housing three shops with brick walls painted white and bay windows with black frames and fake antique signs hanging from brackets. Over the fourth doorway hung a small sign saying The Apocalypse. Underneath the white paint above the entrance, Brad could see the faint remains of a relief naming the previous establishment: BAL. So, Mick had been right.

*

There was an intercom with a camera, so he buzzed in. A cockney female voice returned within seconds, telling him they were closed.

'I see that, ma'am.' He flashed his fake warrant card at the camera. Just long enough for someone to see it was police identification, but not to register the name or get a good look at the photo. He regretted donning jeans and the Varsity jacket, but then how was he supposed to know Mick's latest plan would involve pretending to be a cop? 'Detective Sergeant Smith, Metropolitan Police. I need a word with the manager. Inside, if you don't mind.'

She didn't mind at all. She'd been waiting to give her version of the story, and he was buzzed right in.

He walked into a short corridor. Just two doors here: another vault-like iron door in the left wall, shut, and a closed wooden door facing it. Beyond both was a thick black curtain pulled across the corridor, and he quickly peeked through. More doors, only one open, with a toilet inside, so cramped it looked as if you could barely shut the door behind you. Dead ahead, at the end of the corridor, was another curtain, pinned to a length of wood nailed at door height.

The big iron door buzzed. His cue to enter The Apocalypse.

It was a long, thin room. The tables and chairs were wrapped in canvas, as if they'd freshly exited storage. Shelves were loaded with tinned food and dry cereals, all dusty, and water jugs stood against walls with gas masks and biohazard suits hanging above. A large standing menu didn't say menu but 'emergency rations'. Bowls on the bar held military-style ration packs. There was an ancient CRT TV in a corner. Framed posters displayed mushroom clouds, savaged cities and lists for the perfect 'Disaster Supply Kit'. This place was kitted out like a bomb shelter. He got it. Apocalypse. A themed bar.

There were two women behind one of the bar tills fiddling with paperwork. One wore a tight long black skirt and tight white shirt. Brad decided to approach the lady in casual clothing. But first he flicked off the lights using a switch by the door.

'Hey, what are you doing?'

He stopped ten feet away. In the light cast by the fridges, he could still make out their faces, and they his. The name on the warrant card was invented, but he could imagine her sitting with real police and jabbing out his mugshot.

'I'll explain. You the manager?'

She said she was and gave her name, Carla. Owner of that cockney voice, which was an unusual mix with her Chinese appearance. She started to absolve herself of any blame in a bar fight last night, until Brad cut her off.

'This isn't about a fight. I'm investigating a separate crime, and I need your help.'

Carla's cold front thawed instantly. She worked her way around the bar, all smiles, eager to help. And she stood too close, which he didn't like because she got a good look at him. Brad took a step back.

'So what's this about? And why do the lights need to be off?' she asked.

Brad spun her a tale about bank robbers believed to have frequented this bar. Told her he needed to take fingerprints. He spotted a thin door in an end wall. It had a window, though all was black beyond and he swore he could feel a breeze coming from it.

'That lead outside?'

'Sure does. Did you hear about those murders last night? Some country cottage in London. Four dead. The killers raped a woman and took her body away. What do you know?'

Newspaper bullshit, that was what he knew. He repeated his line about fingerprints, then added the portion he wasn't looking forward to: 'I need to be alone when I do it. Body heat affects the chemical. As does heat from lights. I kindly need you both to leave, and I need the lights off.'

The women looked at each other. If either of them was a fan of detective fiction, they'd sniff his bullshit and his guise would come undone.

'Oh, okay. That makes sense, I guess. But can I not help?'

Carla took a little more convincing, locking the till before she left. He was surprised his trick had worked so easily, but work it had. The women were soon gone, and he was alone.

He approached the end door, lit only by the fridge, feeling his adrenaline rising.

CHAPTER THIRTY-THREE

KARL

The rumbling hadn't increased, which meant it wasn't a train coming their way after all. A silly thought made in panic, Karl realised. But the rumbling sound persisted, and they moved onwards slowly, fearful of what might lie ahead.

They turned a corner, and stopped dead at what they saw ahead. Liz grabbed his arm.

'My God, you're right. A train. There must be a way out.'

He didn't share her glee. The train was just an outline in the dark, with nothing to illuminate it. No headlights, no dashboard dials or switches. It sat there dark and dead, and Karl soon realised why. It was a carriage, not a locomotive. Nothing to power it, although he could still hear that soft rumbling coming from somewhere. There were a number of short, cylindrical shapes arranged before it. They'd stumbled across an abandoned carriage, and it blocked their way ahead.

'Oh my god, it's a station. We can get out.'

She released his arm and stumbled ahead. To the left side of the carriage, his eyes made out the edge of the seemingly endless wall on their left, and then a void beside the train. As they inspected their surroundings, Karl realised that the station was nothing but a widening of the tunnel. The platform was simply a stone shelf. No old vending machines, no ticket booth, no turnstiles. The roof was higher; the walls were flat rather than curved. He couldn't see a doorway. He started to lose pace. Something wasn't right here. And the rumbling continued.

'Come on,' she called back, getting further ahead. 'We'll be free soon.'

'Stop,' he shouted. She ignored him.

But Karl's jog became a walk as his eyes started to make out shapes on the platform. Small poles rising up to platforms. Chairs and tables. And some kind of underground chain-link fence, blocking their path.

Seeing it too, Liz halted. He stopped by her side, and she clutched his arm.

'What's going on?' she said, her tone one of dashed hope.

'I heard about this place,' Karl replied, turning away from the fence to inspect the dark shapes before them. Beer barrels, attached by pipes to pumps – the source of the rumbling noise – on the side of the train. 'We're going to get out, Liz. This is Banker Avenue Line train station. It's now an underground bar. The Apocalypse.'

He started walking, but felt resistance on his arm. Liz hadn't budged.

'Why are there no lights?' she said. 'Maybe it used to be a bar and it's abandoned as well.'

He walked on and, although her grip on his arm was lost, he heard her feet on the stones behind him. They threaded their way between empty barrels and stopped just feet from the end of the carriage. There was a set of wooden steps leading to a door. Karl went up and put his face to the glass. He'd already decided that it would be easier to bust the door than to fight past the chain-link fence.

'Fridge lights are on. God, I could do with a beer right now.'

'Is it open? Quick!'

He turned the handle and pushed, and, beautifully, the door swung inwards. Immediately, Liz was up against him, pushing, desperate to get in.

'Liz, Jesus, slow d—' He was halfway to his feet when he heard a series of thumps in the bar, getting closer and closer. In the blackness he couldn't fathom the direction, so he turned to where his back had been facing because that was his vulnerable side, and held up his arms to protect himself.

A moment later a train smashed into him.

Best guess: suspension in the encoding process of his frontal lobe, or however it worked. He'd spent so long immersed in the underground railway that a strange noise in the dark had fired-up a connection to trains. But he was no longer in the tunnel. And it was a disused railway. So, a half second before he was slammed into a wall, logic reassessed what had slammed into him: not a train, but a person.

The proof came in the next instant: 'Going nowhere, arsehole.'

He felt a knee jam into his stomach. As he doubled over in pain, his brain thought, *double-leg takedown*. Just another memory association, but this time a helpful one, based on his love of watching combat sports. You wrapped your arms around the opponent's hips, lifted, twisted, and dumped him hard onto his back. But academic knowledge was a far cry from pulling the moves in reality.

He jerked, but the big mass in his grip didn't move more than an inch off the ground.

He felt something hard ram into his backbone, probably the guy's elbow. A twelve-six elbow strike, highly illegal in combat sports. Pain spread like cracking ice throughout his body, sending his left arm numb. He still couldn't get his breath from the knee strike.

A heavier blow landed, not as sharp this time. Two fists crashing down on his shoulders, accompanied by a grunt of exertion. The next pain was in his forearms, elbows and wrists as he was driven down, hard, onto the floor. He rolled, curling into a ball to protect his cramping stomach from further injury, one arm tucked against his abdomen and the other against his exposed head in case the guy's next tactic was to drive down a boot. Illegal as heck, but the rules weren't in play here.

Instead, he heard pattering footsteps. Then there was the sound of a scuffle, body on body, and a second later a screech of pain.

'Karl!'

A hand hit his head, but just a soft blow. Someone feeling about in the dark. Then it was back, touching his hair, latching onto his collar and pulling him up.

Liz, he realised. The man, nearby, was still yelling. Karl got to his feet, grabbing hold of Liz's hand. He stumbled towards a thin vertical line of light that he hoped was a way out.

CHAPTER THIRTY-FOUR

BRAD

Brad rubbed his sleeves over his eyes to clear the blood running down his face. He saw a thick oblong of light from beyond the open door, and knew he was alone down here.

He got up and rushed through the doorway into the wide stairway he'd come down. As he arrived and cast his gaze upwards, he saw the heavy door at the top swinging shut.

He was soon in the ground-level corridor. He stopped and wiped blood from his eyes again. His vision cleared enough to show him the bar women staring at him from an office dead ahead, both scared by what they had just witnessed. They were the only ones here: Seabury and Grafton's wife must have already made the street.

Carla had a cordless phone in her hand. Brad leaned into the office and slapped it out of her grip.

'No fucking cops,' he yelled, then rushed for the exit.

The street was busy with cars and pedestrians and his hopes of catching Seabury and Liz Grafton fell away. He wiped his eyes again and scanned left and right, but they were gone. Lost in the crowd. People were giving him a wide berth, just as you'd expect of a guy with blood flowing down his face. Another reason to regret the Varsity jacket, because it had white arms, and the blood smeared on both sleeves almost glowed.

But it gave him an idea.

He concentrated on the bloated pavements. Left, in the direction of West Ham Station. Then right, towards Springfield Lane. If a guy dripping blood unnerved the crowds of shoppers keeping to themselves then so would a couple running frantically, blackened by dirt.

But the crowd wasn't parted or scattered, as if avoiding the path of a rampaging tiger. Seabury and the woman had gone. He cleared away the blood from his eyes again, but more immediately trickled from the gashes above his eyebrows. He was lucky his eyes hadn't popped like egg yolks when the woman, after cracking him with a tin of whatever she had found, leaped onto his back like a damn monkey and dug her expensive nails into his face. He scanned the street again. They were nowhere to be seen. But then he noticed something.

Everyone sauntered along without a care, eyes on the pavement or mobiles or shop windows. But Seabury and the woman were dirtied and running and oozing panic, and they would have caused a commotion in the crowd. But there were no pointing fingers or excited chatter.

They hadn't made the street at all. Instinct told him where they had headed.

He turned around and rushed back into the bar. In the corridor, Carla was in the office doorway with her phone in her hand again, so he slapped it out of her grip for a second time as he rushed past. He swatted aside the black curtain. Four doors, three of them shut. Brad was reaching for the first handle when a gut feeling told him they would rather run than hide. They would want distance, not camouflage. So, he ignored the doors and ran to the curtain on the back wall, and tugged it down.

Here, a doorless doorway into a kitchen as narrow as the downstairs bar. Like the train carriage, it had a door at the far end which was open to expose 197 million square miles of hiding places beyond.

As he hurtled through the kitchen, he passed a table with a local newspaper lying next to a pair of hair straighteners. The screaming headline was enough for a two-second pause. Out back was a bare garden, with a gate in the back wall. He rushed through and found himself on a road. No sign of them left or right, and on the other side of the road was a chain-link fence.

The fence was too high to climb, so he focused on a pair of vehicles a hundred feet down the road. A big beast with curtains pulled in the cab so the driver could sleep. It provided the only cover, so Brad ran to it, and along the side, and stopped at the back. The rear doors were wide open to show thieves that there was nothing worth stealing. And that there was nowhere for a fleeing couple to hide. He bent and peered under the vehicle, just in case.

He cursed and wiped his forehead again.

With his phone in his hand and no joy at the prospect of calling Mick with the bad news, he walked down the short corridor between the truck and the fence. He killed the call after one ring. Because this wasn't over yet.

As he walked along the fence, he spotted two concrete posts just two feet apart, like a doorless passageway. If they'd slipped through the gap, they were gone. Beyond the fence: muddy, thick scrubland for 160 feet and then woods.

He pulled his phone out again, but slotted it away almost instantly as he heard something: moving water. He slipped through the gap and, after thirty feet, he was standing before a river at the bottom of steep banks.

And a rickety wooden beam bridge.

A bad sign. If they'd gone across, into the woods, they were gone for good. He cursed and reached into his pocket.

But the call could wait ten seconds. If he told Mick about the bridge, Mick would ask if he'd checked under it. So, he would do that first and then he was out of here.

CHAPTER THIRTY-FIVE

KARL

Yesterday, in the van, he had thrown her across him with ease, but now he had trouble lifting her to her feet. Yesterday: fear and confusion because she didn't know what had happened to her husband. Today: numbing shock because she knew he was dead.

'We have to move, Liz.'

He got her on her feet, unsteady as a day-old fawn. Her eyes were open but he had to lead her, and it was like drawing a large kite against heavy wind. Free arm loose and flapping, feet ungainly, but she came. Dead weight at first, but moving. Her grip on his hand was weak, but there.

They had exited the kitchen and it was behind them for good. But not for Liz. It was where she had seen the newspaper headline

Bexley Cottage Carnage – Three Slaughtered – Cops Confused

And it would exist in HD behind her eyelids for ever. Now, they were under a bridge on wasteland, cramped together, shoulders kissing, heads touching wood. Minutes seemed to have passed. Maybe the guy was out on the street, a mile away and heading the wrong way. Maybe he was still in the cellar, howling like a lunatic in a bedlam. Maybe he had worked out exactly where— The latter of the three, Karl realised, as he heard the slop of feet in mud, dangerously close. He held his breath, and wanted to clamp a hand over Liz's mouth because she was breathing heavily. But she seemed oblivious to his worry. Her knees were up to her chest, forehead bent forward to rest on her forearms, hair all over the place. Still in shock.

Karl froze as, barely six feet to his right, he saw a pair of feet appear on the sloped bank, level with his head. This was it. The guy was going to check under the bridge. He would bend, and look, and smile like it was Christmas. No darkness this time to allow Liz to ambush him. No fight left in Liz anyway. He would kill them both, and slip their bodies into the river's current. It was just seconds away.

'Jesus!' the guy yelled. A slip. He landed on his arse, and now all but his head was visible.

Karl saw a red Varsity jacket with white arms smeared with blood. He put a hand on his chest, an attempt to shield the sound of his thudding heart which he was sure the guy would hear. Beside him, Liz wasn't even looking, oblivious to the world and their final few seconds in it.

He had a horrible thought: she was closest to the guy in the Varsity jacket. He would grab her first, because she was the target, and Karl could escape the other way. The idea made him feel like a weak little boy, and he hated himself for it.

But the guy didn't come any further. Didn't slide five inches lower down the bank, or even lean forward, which was all he needed to do. Instead, he dragged himself to his feet, and turned. One step, then another. Until Karl couldn't see him any more.

Karl let out the breath he'd been holding, slowly, and took an even slower breath back in.

Wood creaked inches above him. The guy was on the bridge. Karl looked up. The gaps between the deck boards were large, an inch or more, and he saw two black shapes above his head: the guy's feet.

Silence. No movement. Was he reconsidering coming down?

'On top of a pile of gold, sure,' the guy said a few seconds later. It took Karl a moment to realise that he was on the phone.

CHAPTER THIRTY-SIX

BRAD

Typical Mick, straight to the point. No *hello*, no *Hi Brad, my old pal*, just: *This is where you tell me they're tied up and waiting for me, right?* So he got Brad's sarcastic response. Then Mick said: 'Pray tell me, how did you fuck this one up?'

He had lied about how she'd escaped the first time because he hadn't wanted to admit that someone half his size had fought him off. He lied again now for the same reason. 'Because someone told me they were underground and sent me on a wild goose chase. They weren't where you said, Mick. Fucking underground train station. I found the bar, but they weren't there.'

'Where are you?'

'The bar. The station. Where you sent me. Where else?'

'They've gotta be there, Brad. I checked maps. That bar blocks the tunnel. It's all collapsed beyond that station. There's no way past.'

'Well, they weren't there. Maybe there's a fork or something they took.'

'There's a fork, sure, but it's a dead end. You took too long, Brad. They must have got out. But don't go worrying your little head about it. I have a plan. I just killed Król.'

That hit Brad like a smack around the head. 'So Król was next. Who's after him? Are you doing this alphabetically? Can't wait until you reach S for Smithfield.'

'Oh, now I get it. You think I'm on some killing rampage? He had surveillance tapes on us, Brad. All three of us. And he was going to spread them around. Well, that just wouldn't do, would it? So, I just killed him in Seabury's shop. But it's part of a great plan. The cottage thing is in all the papers, Brad, and now that you've let her escape again, it's only a matter of time before she knows her guy's dead. Then she goes to the police, her and Seabury together. But first he makes a stop. If you can't find them in the next hour or so, I get to them my way.'

Brad didn't mention the newspaper in the kitchen with its big, glossy picture of her dead husband on the cover. She must have seen it. He focused on something else Mick had said. 'What stop?'

'If I was Seabury, on the run, I'd want to talk to my wife. He probably left home this morning thinking he was going to have a normal day. Now look. So, he'll need to see her again. That's where he'll go before he goes to a cop shop. Home. So, we get to Seabury by getting to his wife. Want to hear my great plan?'

Now Mick was going to put other innocents in the blast zone? Brad knew he wasn't going to like what Mick said next, and what he heard made him shake his head. 'That's nuts, Mick.'

'Yeah? How? Point out a flaw, if you can.'

'It won't stack up to a police investigation, Mick, you know that.'

'Doesn't have to, Brad. Same as Ramirez. It doesn't have to stop the traffic, just detour it. It just has to buy time. Enough time to get me close to Seabury and the bitch.'

'How about the afterwards part, Mick? You can't get away with it.'

'Brad, my friend, you think I care about that? I'll be in Germany. So, don't you worry about me. You'll have your name on a ladyboy bar for the world to trace, but not me. I'll be a ghost. If you want to worry, do it about that fool Dave who thinks he can just live here as normal for the rest of his life. But if you think

I need help get out there and find that pair. You've got an hour or so. Call me.'

He hung up and stared into the trees. An hour? To search the woods? Futile, even if they hadn't already got out the other side and found help. He wasn't going to waste his time.

He slotted the phone away and wiped blood off his face. It had sounded a lot like Mick was saying he didn't care if he got out of this safely. As if getting to Grafton's wife was all that mattered.

It wasn't all that mattered to Brad, though.

CHAPTER THIRTY-SEVEN

KARL

Karl heard Varsity's footsteps leaving but didn't dare move. He looked at Liz. She still had her head resting on her forearms, but she seemed more energised now, as if coming back to reality. Her upper body inflated and deflated with each massive breath she took.

'He's gone,' he whispered. 'But we should wait ten minutes, in case he's still nearby.'

She didn't look up.

'Then we'll get to a phone. We need the police now.' And Katie. Katie first, always. But he wasn't about to say that.

CHAPTER THIRTY-EIGHT

KATIE

Katie promised herself fifteen minutes, and didn't want to panic, so fifteen it was. Exactly. As the second hand hit the ten, she hit redial. Fifteen minutes ago, no answer. Now, no answer again. Karl had been ten minutes away from the shop almost an hour and a half ago. She hung up and looked out of the window in case Karl was pulling up outside. But she wasn't just looking for Karl out there.

She didn't want to admit it to herself, but it was true: Karl had her worried. He should have called by now, or been here, and he hadn't and wasn't. So, against better judgement and her normal optimism, she scanned the street for strange men.

'Karl, you arsehole,' she mumbled into the glass, and then turned away to grab the phone again. She took it upstairs, hardly able to believe what she was about to do. Go upstairs to pack a bag.

In the bedroom, she dialled, one hand clutching the phone, and one hand hauling clothing out of the drawers. She still couldn't believe she was doing this.

'Police, please,' she answered the operator. Suddenly she felt daft. Karl wasn't a missing child, and he hadn't been gone for days. She would tell them what he'd told her, but maybe all they would hear was a wife complaining that her husband had gone to work and she hadn't heard from him for an hour. They might tell her to simply wait. They might tell her not to waste their time.

But she wouldn't get in trouble for a false alarm.

So, when the operator passed her to an emergency control centre, she told her tale. And with that done, she relaxed somewhat. She stopped dragging clothing out of the drawers. She stopped pacing the room. The police were involved now, so everything would be okay. She would wait, and she would do it right here. She would not run from her own house.

CHAPTER THIRTY-NINE

KARL

For a long time they just sat there under the bridge. Waiting felt wrong because he was wracked with worry about Katie, about their little unborn. How was she reacting to the fact that he hadn't called or returned home? What was she doing? Was she panicking? Were the bad men right now making their way to Karl's house to get her? But the part of him that wanted to go running for her was beaten back by a practical voice: Varsity seemed to have gone, but he could still be out there, close, searching. He prayed that the world had stopped while they'd been stuck underground.

His paranoia and urge to run manifested itself in jittery movements, which, he realised, Liz had been aware of when she said: 'Just wait a little longer.' But she didn't look up and her voice was dull. He wondered if she was picturing how things had gone down in the cottage after she'd run. All she had was a pair of words in a newspaper: THREE SLAUGHTERED.

'We need to go. I need to find a phone as quick as possible.'

'I hope she's okay,' Liz said, and then her head came up. Clear streaks through the dirt on her face showed she had been crying. But in those eyes now was a new firmness, as if the tears had sluiced away all sorrow. Maybe a new resolve was developing now that her husband, her protector, was gone.

'She will—' he started, and stopped when he heard a noise. A car engine.

'Liz, wait,' he said as she scrambled quickly out from under the bridge. Before he could grab her and pull her back, he heard a dog bark nearby.

She climbed the bank and vanished. Karl followed, if only because he didn't want to be stuck here if they had to run. Liz was running towards the fence. He noticed that another vehicle had pulled up behind the truck.

He was too late to grab her, and she slipped through the gap, onto the street, and moved towards the new vehicle, a VW Caddy van with 'Anderson Kitchens' written on the side.

There was a guy in paint-smeared utility trousers and a jumper at the open back door. At his feet was a dog that bolted towards Liz as she approached. Karl relaxed as he realised this guy wasn't one of those hunting him, just a nobody bringing his dog to the scrubland for exercise.

What happened next occurred with such speed that Karl found himself caught up in it before he could think. A third vehicle was coming down the road. Liz snatched a ball from the dog's mouth and lobbed it. Hard, high. It sailed over the van and bounced in the middle of the road, and the dog went bounding after it. The driver of the van realised, screamed for the mutt to stop, and chased after it as it ran towards the oncoming third vehicle.

'I can't drive,' Liz said as she snatched open the van's passenger door.

Karl realised her plan right then, because he heard the van's engine still running.

*

Thirty seconds later, they were fleeing in a stolen vehicle. He tackled a number of corners, found the main road, and lost the Caddy in heavy traffic. Only then, as he finally took a breath, did he notice a mobile phone mount on the dashboard. With a mobile phone.

He took deep breaths while the landline rang. He needed to adopt a calm tone when Katie answered so she wouldn't worry. He needed to pretend that all was fine. He had left the shop with Liz, he would say – no mention of psychos chasing them along abandoned subterranean tunnels. He was waiting to call the police, he would say – no mention of hiding under a bridge while killers sniffed out their trail. But he had to insist that she got out of the house. He would get to a nearby supermarket, or somewhere else loaded with people, and arrange to meet her there, and then they'd head to her dad's house in Harrow. There, among his potted plants and sagging bookcases, they would greet the police and end this infernal chapter of their lives.

From an unknown number, but there was a degree of hope in the voice that answered:

'Karl?'

'It's me, baby,' he said, a lump in his throat.

But not just hope, he realised. Distress, too.

'Oh God, Karl, what's going on? They're here, they want you—'

And then her voice went dead, and there was a sound like someone snatching the phone. The mobile made a protest-like series of beeps as his fist tightened around it. The next voice he heard was that of a croaky male, and it said: 'Seabury, you're a hard man to find…'

CHAPTER FORTY

COOPER

DC Cooper was knocking doors for information near Tile Kiln Lane when he got the call from Mac.

'I just got word about an informant of mine,' the DCI said. 'He's up to something. I'm going to go see him, but not alone. You okay there doing the door-to-door?'

Of course not. He'd recently transferred from working robberies in West London under a supervisor who hated him, and this was his chance to impress the new guy holding his career in his hands. And he was trying to make up for his slip: brand new and none the wiser, he'd asked the DCI if he had a family. It had been a month since he'd broken that cardinal rule of the office, but he still gave him funny looks.

So, he took the offer, noted the postcode, and got out of there, leaving an old lady to answer her door to no one.

CHAPTER FORTY-ONE

MICK

At exactly the same time that the old lady was cursing kids for knocking on her door, Mick was feeling as if his heart had stopped. He reached into his pocket for a mint, but the matchbox wasn't there.

He pulled the car to the side of the road, ignoring horns from other drivers, and ran his fingers around the footwell. Not there. He clenched his already-throbbing jaw.

The shop. When he'd pulled out his gloves in order to erase the Król problem, he must have dropped the matchbox of mints. With his DNA all over it. Right there at the crime scene. The one he'd just sent a murder detective to.

Traffic horns played another symphony as Mick slipped back into traffic. He opened the glovebox, just to check his gun was still there. Because he'd need that if the cops got to the scene before him.

CHAPTER FORTY-TWO

COOPER

The postcode from Mac belonged to a shop in Old Ford on a dead-end commercial unit. An electronics/security outlet called Sunrise Electronics. Mac's car wasn't there yet. Cooper pulled in front of a plain white panel van and immediately noted Sunrise's part-risen shutter.

It set off an alarm bell but he knew better than to go in alone. Some of Mac's informants were animals, and he didn't want to get fucked up. But that open shutter was inviting…

No. The brass were obsessive over red tape and those guys were scarier and more dangerous than any criminal out there. So, he was going to sit right here and wait for Mac.

CHAPTER FORTY-THREE

MICK

Mick slowed down as he reached the commercial unit. The pain in his jaw seemed to vanish in a flash. He could be in and out, damning evidence back in his pocket, within half a minute. He shut the glove box – he wouldn't need the gun.

He opened the glove box a second later, though. As he turned into the commercial unit, he saw a car parked behind Seabury's white van.

'Fuck.' The panic and the pain returned with dizzying speed. He was too late.

CHAPTER FORTY-FOUR

COOPER

Mac parked behind Cooper's vehicle and got out.

'How do you want to do this, Boss?' Cooper asked as he shook McDevitt's hand. He hoped he'd done the right thing by waiting for the DCI to turn up, but he couldn't yet tell.

'Just be careful around this guy,' Mac said. 'His nickname's Król, so call him that. Keep your distance. Violent thug. Totally unpredictable.'

They went in, the DCI first, and Król was in there waiting for them. And they kept their distance. But not because he was a violent thug. Because he was dead.

'Know anyone who'd want to do this to him?' Cooper asked.

'Half of London.'

The DCI was looking around the floor: Cooper understood: not seeking evidence, but to avoid looking at his slaughtered informant. Cops often felt at fault when people under their protection got hurt.

'Maybe three-quarters,' Mac continued. 'Call the boys down here. The Yard doesn't pay two mill a year to snitches just to let them get murdered.'

'You want this one?' Cooper said. 'We've already got our hands full. We should pass it to—'

He stopped when Mac gave him a stern look that made Cooper decide he'd second-guessed a superior for the very last time. Ever. He cursed himself for trying to challenge the DCI.

'That's my informant right there. That's my reputation lying dead there if I don't get the bastard responsible.'

Cooper understood but had to bite his tongue. Literally. Operation Nook was only half a day old and looked like it was going to be long and drawn-out. Scope of motive was massive because there were three victims and because of who Grafton had been, and his hardened criminal enemies weren't eager to talk to the police even to help eliminate themselves from the enquiry. Two large roundabouts close to Tile Kiln Lane, as well as a nearby restaurant with a two-for-one deal and a late-night amateur rugby match meant they'd barely scratched the surface when it came to tracing witnesses and vehicles in the vicinity of the crime scene. Grafton's wife was still missing, possibly kidnapped. The post-mortems had been performed but hadn't added much to the story told by the crime scene itself. The crime lab in Abingdon was only just beginning work on what it had been sent, and Grafton's home was still being searched. And then there were two other ongoing murder cases that the team had to deal with. So, Cooper didn't think they could spare the time on this one. Not for a low-life criminal who'd probably had it coming for years.

But he wasn't the boss. McDevitt was. Mac was the guy who could send him on a mundane task in 3 a.m. rain; so, Cooper hauled out his mobile and called the HAT phone.

At the same time, Mac called *his* boss, Superintendent Archer, who ran the four Murder Investigation Teams covering South London. As he dialled, he walked past the body, careful to avoid the blood. He left an abrupt message: 'Just called to a scene, found one of my informants dead, will keep you abreast.'

Both detectives hung up their phones at the same time.

'People work here,' Mac said. 'Make sure nobody's coming.'

It took Cooper just three seconds to walk over to the shutter and check the road. He didn't see Mac pluck something off the floor and slot it into his pocket.

*

The murder squad and the forensics gang were there twenty minutes later, their vehicles clogging the street. While the search team snooped and the pathologist tried to find a place to park, the detectives huddled to solve the riddle. But not Mac. He was outside, listening to music and letting the atmosphere sink into his bones. It was sometimes how he did things.

'Robbery gone wrong,' someone ventured. A known burglar, Król, walks into the shop with a plan to exit with stock he hasn't paid for. The guy manning the counter doesn't like that idea. Król whips out his weapon, a lawnmower blade with a serrated edge and a sharpened point. Counter Guy challenges him. They fight. Król drops dead, and Counter Guy drops everything and runs. The detectives discussed the merits of this theory, and then shut it down when a pair of lady's shoes was found in the attic.

'Extra-marital play,' someone piped up. Counter Guy sneaks a woman into the shop for a little fun. Król, her jilted or tricked other half, turns up to spoil the fun, believing in the old promise of till death do us part. Counter Guy and the woman flee hand-in-hand. The detectives pick at this theory, and then dump it when a mobile phone is found in a dusty gap under the counter.

'Blackmail,' someone announced. No signal, busted in some kind of strike or fall, but it opened up at a swipe, no password needed, onto the last app used, which was a beauty, a real rare-find gem for the detectives. CCTV footage of the dead man and a pal trying to break into a house. High-quality night vision. The video had been paused with the face of the dead man in glorious close-up. So: Król gets wind that a guy has a video of him busting into someone's house, and comes here for a chat. Maybe he appears out of the blue, or maybe Counter Guy has called him in to see if they can do a nice deal to make sure the video doesn't go on YouTube. Either way, it all goes wrong.

By this time, they had a pair of names: Joseph Lewis and Karl Seabury, joint owners of Sunrise Electronics – two guys who needed a visit to help determine which theory was correct.

And then Mac got a call. Seabury's wife had called the police, worried that her husband might be in trouble. Two men had tried to break into the Seabury house last night. Seabury had told his wife a wild tale about why: he rescued a woman last night, hid her at this shop, and was on his way here this morning to talk to her. He believed he might be in danger. Wife tried calling him dozens of times, with no answer. She figured he might be hurt. Called in the cops.

He told the uniforms to leave it to the big boys. He sent two guys to nearby Cubitt Town, where Joseph Lewis lived, and told Cooper to drive him to Seabury's home.

*

They were pulling up some doors away when Mac's mobile rang again.

The name on the screen was 10%. Being a DCI meant that Mac was the guy in charge for most of his working days. But only ninety per cent of the time. This was a call he'd been expecting – and dreading.

Superintendent Archer would know about the Król murder by now, so the conversation would go one of two ways. Archer would start by reiterating the importance of maximum effort in the first few hours of an investigation. He'd remind Mac that one of the dead in the Grafton murder had been a schoolteacher, so the public had to see the police devoting one hundred per cent. And then he'd blab on about stretched resources. All in prelude to: You can't have the Król case. Or worse: he'd start by moaning about the arrest of Ramirez when there was scant evidence. He'd voice his disdain that Mac hadn't attended the Grafton post-mortem, or followed up on this or that lead yet. And then he'd express his understanding of the important bond of trust and loyalty between a detective and his informants. All preamble to: I'm reassigning the Grafton case to another homicide team.

But until Archer said those things, they weren't official. So, Mac declined the call. Nothing was going to stop him now.

'Everything all right?' Cooper said, seeing the intense scrutiny Mac gave his phone.

'Fine. Come on, let's knock the door.'

The woman who answered the door after shutting off the burglar alarm was tall, athletic and in her mid-thirties. She wore a flowing long skirt, a loose blouse and a red puffiness to her eyes. She looked them up and down, pausing at the bandage on Mac's ear, before fixing her eyes on their warrant cards. Mac noticed a bloating to her midsection and realised she was pregnant.

'Metropolitan Police,' Cooper said. 'This is Detective Chief Inspector McDevitt, and I am Detective Constable Cooper. Would you be—?'

'Where's Karl?' she asked.

Katie had expected the police to return from his shop with him. But she couldn't see a police car on the street. Or Karl.

'Can we do this inside?'

Was he at the station, giving a statement? 'I thought he'd be with you—'

'If we could, inside, please?'

Puzzled, she turned and led them into the house. She grabbed her coat from the hallway hook as she went.

In the living room, there were two armchairs and a two-seater sofa. For a reason she couldn't define, Katie didn't want the men to sit together, so she took the sofa. In the middle so nobody could sit next to her. She clutched her coat on her lap.

'So where is he? Did you talk to him? Is he at the police station or something?'

From TV, she knew that detective chief inspectors were the people who ran crime investigations: older, rugged men, like this one; the stars of the TV shows who did the clever thinking and unmasking of villains. A higher rank than detective constables, who were younger and fitter to provide eye candy for the viewers, and more suited to searching rooms and chasing suspects. So, she expected the DCI to sit before her, to show her that he was the guy in charge, and the young DC would stand by him, like a servant, watching an instructor at work. But to her surprise the DC took an armchair, and the DCI remained standing. After that, she didn't know what to expect from this conversation.

The DCI's gaze roamed the room and landed on the largest picture on the wall. She and Karl on their wedding day, standing next to the fancy 1963 Volkswagen Beetle that her father had hired and had painted like Herbie, The Love Bug, because of her childhood love of the movie; a picture she enjoyed pointing out to all visitors, except, for some reason she didn't like the policeman staring at it. She already knew she didn't like this man, although she wasn't sure why yet.

The DC said: 'Is your husband Karl Seabury? Does he live here?'

That only increased her puzzlement. Karl was in the picture, and she had already mentioned his name, and the detectives were here because of her phone call. What were they playing at? 'Haven't you been to his shop? Have you not spoken to him?'

With his back to her, his eyes all over the picture, the DCI said: 'What makes you think we would have?'

'He's at his shop. I told the police that. Have you not been there?'

The DC said: 'You called the police because your husband thinks he might be in danger. Tell us about that, please.'

'No,' she snapped. 'Why are you here? I sent the police to his shop. Did you not get the right message? Where is my husband?'

'Oh, we've been to his shop,' the DCI said, turning to face her finally. The way he said it gave her a sinking feeling. Something wasn't right.

'Is he not there? I don't – don't understand.'

But her sinking feeling said she certainly did. They had been to the shop, and Karl hadn't been there. But where was he? Where had he gone?

'Is he hurt? Tell me. He wasn't at the shop, was he? And he's not answering his phone. What's going on?'

'We hoped you could tell us that,' the creepy DCI said. 'You're right, he's not at his shop. We were hoping you'd know where he is.'

That sinking feeling intensified, joined by a throbbing in her temple. Something had happened, she realised. Something that explained why Karl hadn't answered his phone. Something that necessitated the presence of detectives here instead of uniformed police. 'What's happened? Is my husband hurt?'

The DCI ignored the question and asked: 'Why is your burglar alarm turned on while you're at home?'

'What? That's not important. Why are you here? I know it's not about my call to the police. It's about something that's happened at Karl's shop. Now you two are scaring me, so you'd better tell me what's going on.'

The DCI dropped a hand onto the younger man's shoulder, and they swapped places without a word. He crossed his legs and leaned back, as if this was his own house, the chair his own favourite. She wanted to scream for answers, but something about this man's demeanour made her stay silent. He oozed a bloated confidence that was not just down to his high police rank.

'This woman you say your husband told you he picked up last night. Where was this?'

So, they knew everything. But that only made her understand things less. 'Near Wilmington. Look, what's going on?'

The young DC looked like he'd just been smacked. She didn't like it. Something about Wilmington had clearly made a connection in his brain that shocked him. But what? And why? He looked at his boss, but the DCI didn't take his eyes off her.

Until the DC chipped in and asked: 'Was the woman called Elizabeth Grafton?' That got him a stern glance from his boss.

'I don't know. Liz. He called her Liz.'

'Was the husband Ronald Grafton?'

'I don't know. Look, please, tell me what you think is going on.'

The DCI held up a hand to prevent his subordinate from speaking again, and said: 'We found a dead man in your husband's shop.'

Her heart seemed to judder.

'It's not your husband, don't worry.'

Raw shock subsided as quickly as it had bubbled up, but it was replaced by molten anger. The bastard had paused, deliberately, to frighten her.

'Your husband should be at his shop, but he isn't. Instead, a man is lying dead there. Can we search your house?'

She didn't know what to say, what to think. Karl was missing and there was a dead man at the shop? Who? Why? 'Search for what?' she snapped. 'My husband might be hurt, and you—'

'We don't know until we find it. Can my man here search your shed? We need a warrant if we don't get permission.'

She rubbed her face as it sank in. She could barely think straight. A man dead in the shop. Karl missing.

'We need to do that search. It would be easier if we didn't have to get a warrant.'

Suddenly her brain started to make sense of everything. Karl had been right all along. His worries had been justified. Someone had come for him at the shop this morning. There had been an attack, but Karl had killed the man in self-defence and fled the scene. Police responding to her worried call had arrived at the shop to find a shock. God, why had she doubted him? Why hadn't she read his genuine worry?

'Mrs Seabury?' the DC said. She jerked back to the present and saw the DCI raise a hand to interrupt the younger detective.

'This must be all wrong,' she said. She could feel tears welling up, and she rubbed her eyes before they could escape. She felt so guilty. Karl had been right all along, and she hadn't believed him. Now he was in trouble, and she could have prevented it... somehow. 'I – I can't... do you think my husband killed a man?'

'We know he owns a van and has a Samsung mobile phone. We found both. But does he have access to another vehicle, and does he have another phone?'

She stood up. 'Why? You think he's on the run as a murderer. Now you listen to me. There's no way that—'

'Sit down, please,' the DCI said firmly and with a hard stare. She sat. The DCI rose and sat beside her, and she let him. He surprised her by taking her hand. It was as warm as the tone of his next words.

'Mrs Seabury, your husband is not where you expected him to be. He's missing and he didn't take his vehicle or his phone. We found a weapon that I think came from something we'll find in your shed. On his phone was a picture of the man we found dead in his shop. Now, I understand you believe your husband's story about last night and this morning, but nobody can know anything for sure until we speak to him. It's very important that I speak to Karl to hear his version of events. If he had to run somewhere, to hide, where would he go?'

Somewhat soothed by his kind words, Katie replied: 'Nowhere. I don't know. I would assume he'd come here. Or at least call. Look, he's not a murd—'

'And has he called?'

'No.'

'Mrs Seabury, this is a mess, and you need to trust the good men here. I am the man to help your husband, and you need to understand that. I want killers in prison, not innocent men—'

'I don't know where he is. I know he's not a killer.'

'Don't worry. I believe it's not in his heart. If your husband is innocent, I will do what I can for him. But the evidence is telling us a story, and to get the truth we need to talk to him. He needs to come in. Running doesn't help his case. It's better he finds us before we find him. If he contacts you, you must convince him that he must hand himself in to me.' He handed her his card. 'Do you understand?'

She said nothing, but nodded, looking down at the card in his hand.

'Do you mind if we do that search? We'll be careful.'

She nodded again. He stood, but she grabbed his arm. 'Do you think my Karl did this?'

The eyes staring down at her held a warmth that made her regret her earlier suspicions about this man. 'I'll say again that I believe it's not in his heart. If he's innocent, the truth will come out. Will you tell him to call me, if he contacts you?'

Katie nodded her agreement.

The DCI sent his assistant to search the shed, while he went upstairs. Alone in the silent living room, she sat clutching her coat again, staring at the wedding photo, unable to fully process what was going on. She looked at the phone and willed it to ring. Wherever Karl was, surely he would call her the first chance he got?

The DCI was back a few minutes later to search the kitchen and living room. So, she went upstairs, out of the way.

She went into little Jane's room because it was a place that always calmed her. Except that now it didn't, because she couldn't evade wondering what kind of life little Jane – or little Michael – would have without a father. She couldn't stop imagining their unborn child visiting their father in prison, with bars between them.

She slumped into the seat before Karl's computer desk. There, on the screen, inches from her face, was a CCTV video paused on the image of a man. Night vision, from the garden cameras. The video that the detectives had been talking about.

The timestamp on the video said early morning. Karl must have accessed the video footage from his mobile after she told him about the break-in at the shed. Was this the man they thought Karl had killed? The man who had tried to break into the house last night and who had gone to the shop in search of Karl.

The man Karl had killed in self-defence.

There was a strange mix of emotions making her head feel light. Anger at Karl for bringing all this mess onto their doorstep. Fear of losing him to prison. But relief was there, too, because he was alive, even if he had had to kill a man to guarantee that. Baby Jane or baby Michael would have a father, at least. There would be someone to visit and talk to, which was better than a one-sided conversation with a headstone.

She heard the back door. The DC returning from the shed. Now the two men would talk about what they had found. Katie put her hands on the laptop. She wanted to know what they were going to say, but knew they wouldn't speak their minds in front of her. And she didn't want to go back downstairs anyway. She needed some space.

The screen displayed a feed from a camera in the living room. The tiny device was hidden in a strange painting of a pair of dragons playing chess. Karl had chosen the hiding place because he thought the painting would draw stares and give him a good face shot of anyone who robbed the house. And a lovely cleavage view of your friends, he'd joked. Always the joker. She hoped she'd get to hear him laugh again.

There was a powerful microphone hidden in the ceiling lampshade, and she turned it on, listening to the policemen.

The younger man stood in the centre of the room, talking to his boss's back because the DCI was once again inches from the wedding picture, boring his eyes into it.

'*Lawnmower with a missing blade,*' the DC said. '*The video showed your Król and his accomplice at the shed, so it looks like they took it. Looking very much like your informant went there in search of Seabury when he couldn't get into the house. And Seabury got the better of him.*'

'*Let's not jump to conclusions yet. Finding Seabury is our priority. And Grafton's wife, if indeed it is her.*'

'*You think the wife's hiding anything? Seabury's wife, I mean. She didn't seem right.*'

'*Just shock. I don't think Seabury's called her. Come on, let's search some more before she comes down. You do the kitchen.*'

There was a camera in the kitchen, but Katie didn't care to watch the younger man. She heard a racket as he searched a drawer full of pans, but her attention was on the DCI. His search of the living room was cursory, as if he sought a large item or was already convinced he wouldn't find what he needed. Her unease at having someone root through her belongings was heightened when he found a photo album and leaned against a wall to flick through it. Nothing of importance to their case could be in there, surely, yet he took his sweet time flicking through, and there was a grin on his face throughout.

He snapped it shut when the DC returned from the kitchen, empty-handed. Katie decided it was time to go back downstairs and get rid of the two of them. She took a breath to fortify her nerves and got up.

Seconds from the living room door, she heard a mobile ring and the DCI answer it. She froze, knowing the man would retire to another room for secrecy if she appeared.

Silence for half a minute, and then he bid the caller goodbye and said: 'Henderson just got to Król's flat, and it's a smouldering wreck inside. Fire's burned out, so the exterior is okay. But the inside is gutted. That's the evidence gone, if there was any there.'

'Seabury?' the DC said.

'Let's not guess. Maybe he did it, and maybe it was someone else. Maybe it's not connected at all. Król was not a popular man.'

That final line boosted her confidence. If this 'Król' was unpopular, maybe someone else had followed him to the shop and killed him. Not Karl.

But that still didn't explain why Karl was missing.

The living room phone rang. Karl! She barged into the room. Both men were staring at the phone, but their heads whipped her way as the door smacked open.

'If that's him, you hand me that phone,' the DCI snapped.

She rushed across the room, watched the whole way, and picked it up. She was sure it was going to be a salesman or someone unimportant and bothersome, but then she heard his voice, and her growing anger was washed away by grief and gratitude. 'Oh God, Karl, what's going on? They're here, they just came in, they want you—'

The phone was ripped from her hand. The DCI roughly pushed her aside and slammed the receiver to his ear.

'Seabury,' he said, his voice croaky, 'you're a hard man to find…'

CHAPTER FORTY-FIVE

KARL

'… and I need you to listen carefully to me.'

'Karl, what's going on?' he heard Katie yell. And then a commotion, which he thought was his wife trying to grab the phone and the policeman stopping her.

'This is the police, Mr Seabury. I am Detective Chief Inspector McDevitt, Homicide Command. We need to talk to you.'

His anxiety took a dip, but only slightly. It wasn't one of the killers at his house. But why were the police there? His muscles relaxed as he realised that Katie must have called them. But two seconds later, his world was back aflame: 'This is about a murder at your shop, Seabury, and for your own sake you need to come in.'

He gripped the phone tightly. 'What murder?'

'This isn't going to be done on the phone.' Then his voice went quiet, as if he had removed the receiver from his mouth. He heard something like 'searching the kitchen' spoken to someone else and then the voice was back, loud and clear.

'Seabury, I know it was self-defence. The truth will come out, but you need to come in as quickly as possible.'

The phone came away from his ear. Self-defence. The shop. The detective was talking about one of the men who had chased them. Dead. In his shop. But both guys had been alive and well when they fled. What was going on?

When he put the phone back to his ear, he heard: 'You there, Seabury?'

'I don't know what you're talking about,' Karl replied.

'We know the weapon used was from your shed.'

Karl almost dropped the phone. The lawnmower blade from his own shed. The man had threatened them with it, and now someone was dead by that very weapon. 'This can't be… this isn't…'

'Seabury, listen to me carefully. I will help you. Hand yourself in, immediately.'

'They came to kill me, but we ran, and they were alive. We got away. They were both still alive.'

'You need to hand yourself in, Seabury.'

And in the passage of one moment, Karl went from utter confusion to horrific understanding. Hand yourself in. Self-defence. A weapon from his shed. And: set-up. Someone had killed a man in his shop. Somehow made it look like Karl was the murderer.

'This is… you've got this all wrong. There's more to this than—'

CHAPTER FORTY-SIX

KATIE

CALLER: You think. There's a woman with me?

HOME: I know, Seabury, I know. her name is Elizabeth Grafton. you both need to come in.

CALLER: How do you know?

HOME: Her husband was killed at his hideaway cottage last night. We know that. We know she escaped and you rescued her. We found evidence of that. And your wife told us. She agrees with us that you need to hand yourself in.

CALLER: The people who killed her husband sent two men to my shop. And they sent people to break into my house last night because they thought I had Liz with me.

It was all real, then, Katie realised. Everything Karl had said. Every fear he'd had. If not for the words knitting onto the screen before her very eyes, she wouldn't have believed it.

The DCI had turned away from her, faced the wall, and the DC had herded her into the kitchen doorway, shutting her away so she couldn't hear the conversation. Desperate to know what was being said, she had rushed upstairs, back to the computer. She'd never been so grateful for Karl's career and all the mod-cons that came with it.

The microphones wouldn't pick up Karl's voice, though. But audio capture wasn't the only trick available. Karl had installed transcription software on the phone for business use so clients calling his home could speak their orders or reviews of products and he could email them to the shop.

HOME: Karl, you cannot run. You need to hand yourself in. I will meet you. I will help you.

CALLER: How's my wife doing? She doesn't believe I killed someone, does she? Put her on the phone.

HOME: No, Karl, she doesn't. And I don't, either. And you can't speak to her just yet. I can help you, but not while you're on the run. You need to understand that you cannot run. You cannot flee from this. If you're innocent, we will prove it. But you need to come in. Both of you. You and Liz Grafton. It is very important that I meet you both. Will you meet me, Karl, and end this?

CALLER: And what will happen? There are people after us. On the streets. I don't know how many, or where, or what they look like.

HOME: The safest place for you is in custody, Karl. I will escort you in, take your statement, arrange for your bail, and post men outside your house for protection. The same for Mrs Grafton.

CALLER: So you believe me? You believe that we're hiding from the men who killed her husband? You believe that I haven't hurt anyone?

HOME: I believe you, Seabury. Ronald Grafton had a lot of enemies and they came for him. His wife escaped, and you helped her. We have evidence of all that. You got caught up in this by accident. She talked you out of going to the Police, didn't she?

CALLER: Yes. She wanted to wait until morning. I think she thought her husband would sort it out.

HOME: These are not people who like to involve the police. But we're involved now. No more running. It's not safe for you out there. I want you both to hand yourself in to me. I will arrange to fast-track everything and have a Solicitor waiting at the station, so that this will go as smoothly as possible. And I can arrange for you to see your wife.

CALLER: Okay. which station? And who will be with you?

HOME: I'll come alone. And not a Police station, because it's quicker and easier for you if I record your statement before we book you in. Less time locked in a cell. We need to get you fast-tracked through this so we can get you home quicker. St Dunstan's Church, Stepney. Two hours from now exactly, which will be about twelve-thirty. Make sure Mrs Grafton is with you. Are you okay with that?

CALLER: St Dunstan's, Stepney. twelve-thirty. can you bring my wife? I want to see her before I get locked up in a cage for however long this takes.

HOME: I can bring her along. You can have some time together while I record your statement. Two hours, Seabury.

Let's get this mess cleared up. But it's vital that Elizabeth Grafton is with you, understand?

CALLER: What's your name again?

HOME: I'm DCI McDevitt. But call me Mac, because we're friends now. So you'll be there?

CALLER: Half twelve.

Numb, Katie rushed downstairs. She was not supposed to know what had been said, so knew she had to let the detective tell her. She had to forge ignorance. She walked into the living room, kept the urgency off her face, and said: 'Is he okay?'

The big detective nodded. But said nothing, surprisingly. She prompted him with: 'Is he coming in then?'

'Later today.' He put the phone down, and she noticed a spot of blood on the earpiece from his damaged ear.

She grabbed her coat off the sofa. 'I should come with you to the station.' She was careful to say *station* because she wasn't supposed to know about this St Dunstan's place.

Now he was supposed to say *sure, okay, let's go*. But the response was: 'No, you must stay here. We'll bring you down to the station later.'

That puzzled her. 'Shouldn't I be with him when you take his statement?'

'He'll be allowed visitors, but we need to speak with him before that and get this cleared up. I'll send a car for you when it's time.'

Now she was confused. 'So you're going to meet him at a station? He's going to hand himself into a station? That was what you arranged?'

He gave her a long look, suspicion creeping in. 'A police station is where he needs to be, Mrs Seabury.'

He called for his colleague, who came like a loyal dog, and then they said they were done, thanked her and made to leave. Just like that. Fifteen seconds later, they were walking down the path, and Katie was on the doorstep, watching their backs.

None of this made sense. The detective had lied to her. Why did he want to meet Karl alone?

CHAPTER FORTY-SEVEN

KARL

Karl dropped the phone into his lap. He tried to concentrate on the road as he juggled his options. It would be better for him to meet the detective in charge of the case rather than a bunch of cops inside a police station treating him like a murderer. And Katie would be there, which was what he cared about the most. He needed to see her before he handed himself over because who knew how long it would be before he could hold her again.

In a police station they would process him like a regular criminal, ready to be handed over to the murder squad, not caring whether he was guilty or not. In a cell, awaiting interview, it might be hours. They had all that volume of crime to solve, after all. He might even be put in a mass cell with real criminals. But if he met the detective, they would get straight down to it. The guy would want the real killer, and if Karl was convincing enough, he hoped he might even be released within a couple of hours.

He cursed his stupidity – why had he, as a surveillance expert, never bothered to install CCTV at his own shop? The irony was crushing.

He looked at Liz.

'The police are at my house. One of the men who chased us. He's been murdered. In my shop.'

'Set-up,' she said firmly. 'So that man who chased us is dead. He must have been killed by the one with the gun. He must be the leader.'

'I have to go home,' he said, careful not to mention exactly why. She didn't have a loved one to get back to, and he didn't want to remind her of that.

'Home? I heard you mention something called St Dunstan's. Sounds like a church. You're meeting the police at a church? You think the police will be heading off to the church so you can safely sneak home? That's foolish, Karl. They'll be waiting at the house.'

A harsher tone, almost reprimanding, and it was a surprise. He wanted to argue the point, but he didn't want to upset her. She'd been through enough.

'Why would they do that? I just agreed to come in.'

'In two hours. You think the police are going to wait? They have to assume you might use those hours to run. They will be hunting you. They'll know you might go home.'

'Even if they find out I'm innocent, it won't happen in half an hour, will it? I might be locked up for a week, or a year. I can't wait that long to—' He caught himself in time.

But it didn't matter. She looked at him through bedraggled hair. 'It's fine to mention your wife. I'm glad she's okay. It wouldn't be good if we both lost everything. You ran out on her this morning and want to see her before the police take you in. I understand. You love your wife. I would want the same.'

'I do. I'm sorry about your husband. About how you found out. I don't know what to say to you, Liz. I'm sorry.'

'Just say you'll think about this. If the police capture you before you hand yourself in, they won't believe you ever planned to do so. If you go to the meet, that will be taken into consideration.'

He wasn't surprised, given who her husband was, that she knew how the law worked. Knowledge learned during all the times he got arrested or investigated, no doubt. And he knew she was right. But he didn't care. If he waited, he had no idea when he would see Katie. Certainly not within the next hour. But if he went home, at least there was a chance he could hold her. A sliver of a chance beat no damn chance at all.

'And did you consider that the police might wait with your wife, since you requested that she be at the meeting? Or she might be taken to a police station?'

He said nothing. Of course he hadn't thought of those things. This was uncharted territory for him.

'There might also be other people.'

And that, he realised, was her real concern. She suspected that the bad guys might be waiting back at home for him. 'If that's the case, maybe Katie is in danger. Even more reason to go home.'

She stared at him. Every ounce of meekness seemed to have gone. She flicked her hair out of her face. No more tears, and no sadness in those eyes. She transformed before him. There had been a steady build-up in her tone, and it peaked now.

'I'm not going with you. If that was part of the deal, forget it.'

Said with undeniable conviction. It made it easier for him to respond in kind.

'So, what, you're just going to hide for the rest of your life? Where are you going to go now that—?'

Anger had clouded his brain. He clamped his mouth shut. Too late. He saw the look on her face.

'Now that my husband is *dead*?'

'I didn't mean to—'

'Yes, you did. And yes, he is dead, and I'm alone. Which means the only person I have to look out for is you.'

He laughed. 'Me? What am I, seven? I don't need help. I'm capable of…' He stopped. What had she done to warrant such an attitude? She'd tried to help him, that was all. Tried to convince him of the right thing to do while pushing aside her own fear and grief. He was a selfish dick, he realised. Katie might be scared and alone, but Liz's husband lay cold and stiff in a morgue.

If their roles had been reversed, he would be a blubbering wreck. But Liz wasn't. Her resolve was stronger than his, and that meant her logic might be, too. So, he had to accept that she could be right. The police would expect him to try to go home. They would be watching his house. They would grab him even if they believed he planned to turn himself in. They'd toss him in a cell, and leave him there until the cop called McDevitt came to see him. In a cell, he couldn't comfort Katie.

'At the first sign of trouble near your house, we turn around and run, okay?' she said, surprising him. Had she come around to his way of thinking?

But then he saw the look in her eyes. Pity. It was a dangerous idea but she had seen the determination on his face. She knew that, regardless of the risks, he was going to go through with it, and the only thing she could do was help.

Because now she had become the protector, and he the sorry victim.

CHAPTER FORTY-EIGHT

MAC

'My God,' Cooper said. 'So Liz Grafton wasn't kidnapped at all.'

While Mac sent a text, he said: 'It seems not. But we don't assume anything, okay? Seabury could have killed her, and he could say she ran off again.' Cooper nodded. 'One other thing. From now on, leave the talking to me. You mentioned Ronald Grafton to Seabury's wife.'

Cooper looked puzzled.

'She's worried about her husband. And now she has a name to use on the Internet. She'll find out that Karl's being hunted by killers. A pregnant woman doesn't need that sort of worry.'

'I'm sorry.'

'You're still learning. Pull that surveillance off Seabury's house.'

Cooper said: 'Really? What if he—?'

'He won't come back, Cooper. He's going straight to a police station. I've been around longer than you, and my hunch tells me that. You'll develop one in a few years, and you'll trust it. Heck, even if he did come back, he'd sit tight, hug his wife and call us.'

Mac's phoned pinged. A return text.

'He could be a dangerous man,' Cooper said. 'If he comes back, we should grab—'

'We won't grab him. He's a surveillance expert, Cooper. He'd know we were watching. And then he'd lose trust and carry on running. This guy isn't a hardened killer. What happened with Król was self-defence. He's a scared man. He'll go straight to a station, believe me. Half an hour from now he'll be in custody. Pull the surveillance. It's a waste of manpower.'

Cooper made no move to do so. 'Your informant, is he working for these people? He ever mentioned Ronald Grafton to you?'

'Informants all have secrets. I had no idea. But we're assuming again, aren't we? Leave the fucking thinking to me, okay?'

Cooper, frustrated at being shot down again, opened his mouth to speak, but Mac held up a hand as his phoned pinged once more, and he glanced at the screen.

'I'm sorry I spoke that way to you,' Mac said to Cooper, locking his phone. 'You're a good copper,' he added.

He was putting the phone away when it rang. He was smiling when he removed it from his jacket, thinking it was the same caller as before. But his smile disappeared when he saw the name of the caller. He almost put the phone to his bad ear again, but realised his error just in time. It was still hurting from when he made that mistake earlier.

'Our Nancy-boy leg-breaker is called Brad Smithfield,' Gondal said.

'I know him! I investigated that bastard three years ago.'

But Gondal already knew the background: a guy had been found outside a tower block late one night. Dead by cerebral ischemia: insufficient blood to the brain. Turned out to be a guy affectionately known as Rocker, because he was off his. He was an enforcer employed by an Edinburgh crime figure called Razor Randolph. He'd been investigating a robbery at Grafton's nightclub, in which two masked men had burst in, shot the place up, and fired rounds at Randolph as he and his men sat in a booth with Grafton and his cronies.

The cops had looked at the residents. Brad Smithfield was a career criminal with a plethora of small convictions, one of which had been for choking a guy unconscious. And a stranglehold could cause cerebral ischemia – it was too coincidental. He was visited immediately, and the police thought they had their story: Rocker had information that Smithfield might have been one of the shooters and had decided to pay a visit. Good information, because he was soon dead. The CCTV had been busted in the flats for weeks, and in that area of Erith in Bexley the cops faced a wall of silence when seeking witnesses. A search of Smithfield's flat yielded no evidence. No arrest. No one was ever charged with the killing.

'I bet it was him,' Gondal said. 'The police missed something.'

'I led that investigation,' Mac said. 'He was fully assessed, and interviewed. I missed nothing.'

'I got his address. Nobody home, though. It's owned by a guy called Ian Barker, Smithfield's boyfriend. I've just got hold of his place of work, so—'

'Don't go there,' Mac said. 'We don't want him telling Smithfield that the police are after him. This guy could go underground. Leave the boyfriend out of it. Keep watching the house. But let's not throw everything including the kitchen sink at this guy. Remember his name came from that scumbag Ramirez. Smithfield wasn't the only guy the Scottish mob were after. They had dozens of names. We've got dozens ourselves to check up on. We don't listen to rumours, especially from criminals who might have their own reasons for giving people up.'

He hung up and told Cooper to drive him back to his car. He had a new lead to follow, he told him. It should take him about three hours.

CHAPTER FORTY-NINE

KATIE

Katie rushed upstairs to grab her laptop. A minute later, she was looking at a newspaper website, based on a search of the name the young DC had mentioned: Ronald Grafton. There it was, right before her eyes. Three chopped up in gang war cottage carnage late last night. And one missing woman, Liz Grafton, wife of powerful ganglord, Ronald Grafton. There was a picture of the wife. Katie stared at it and tried to picture Karl with her. Where were they right now? What were they doing?

The DCI, McDevitt, had lied to her about his appointment with Karl, and now she thought she knew why. In a police station, Karl would have his statements recorded with a solicitor present. He would be coached in what to say. But if he met the detective outside, alone, he wouldn't have that security. The detective must be planning to coerce Karl into making some kind of confession. He knew the case against Karl was weak, and wanted him alone and vulnerable so he could be tricked into incriminating himself. Thrown to the wolves like a common criminal.

But there was more. The dead man in the shop was, as DC Cooper had said, the DCI's informant. McDevitt was unhappy that his informant was dead, and he wanted to lash out at Karl because of it. Maybe he would beat Karl at the meeting, then claim he resisted arrest.

Both of these things pointed to the police not believing Karl's story. They thought he was a killer.

There was only one thing worse than seeing her husband thrown in prison for a crime he didn't commit, and that was something she was slowly failing to ignore: Karl might actually be a murderer.

Katie paced because the baby was hurting her back. At least, that was what she told herself. But the pain was pure stress, she knew. She didn't want to believe that Karl had killed a man, but something didn't add up. If Karl had killed someone, even accidentally, even in self-defence, he would have gone immediately to a police station. She knew it. And yet he hadn't. Could that be because of guilt?

It didn't matter. She couldn't let him face the detective alone. She would go to the meeting point, and she would take the police with her. Karl would go into their custody, not the detective's. That man wouldn't get near him until Karl was in a police station.

She grabbed her phone and scoured the Internet, seeking a solicitor. She found one called Miller, Jones & Tuck, on Aldgate High Street. Thirty years' experience, highest level of representation, excellent track record – just some of the lines she read on their homepage. She jabbed the link for the phone number.

That was when it hit her. She was calling solicitors to save her husband. He would sit in a police cell. He would go to court – even if he killed in self-defence, even if the dead man was a criminal.

She started to cry. How old would their baby – Michael, she now hoped it would be a boy because that was what Karl wanted – be when Karl got out of prison? *If.* She had heard about 'whole life tariffs' being given to some criminals, which meant they stayed in prison until they… She could no longer keep the phone to her ear with just one hand. She had to use two.

CHAPTER FIFTY

BRAD

'Repeat: this is a waste of time,' Dave said. Unable to pace in the car, his legs were jumping up and down, fingers drumming on the steering wheel. He looked like a guy missing the buzz of heroin. 'We're sitting here doing nothing but risking arrest.'

Brad didn't look up from his phone. 'Repeat: stop bloody moaning. You'll run out of synovial fluid and then you'll really moan.'

'Whatever.' He looked at Brad's phone, saw that his colleague was scrolling through Varsity jackets for sale and said: 'You could have just bleached the blood out instead of lopping the arms off.'

'And walk round until then looking like I just killed someone?'

'Look at your forehead. People would know the blood was from that. How are you going to find one with a B?'

Remembering, Brad looked down at the emblem on the jacket's breast. 'Shit.'

Dave laughed, then slapped the steering wheel impatiently. 'Why isn't Mick here?'

Brad sighed. 'We're here because he can't be, aren't we?'

'Maybe he ran away to Germany already,' Dave said. 'Maybe for once his brain stopped to think, and he's realised he's made this situation a lot worse by trying to set-up Seabury and the woman. But that's Mick. Shoot first, sod the questions. And he literally did shoot first, didn't he? He's going off the rails a bit, don't you think? I mean more so than normal. Even the Germany thing proves that. Why not a country with no extradition, like Chile?'

That much was true: the man was getting more erratic, and less thorough. Brad put it down to ego. Akin to some undefeated boxer getting sloppy in the ring, Mick was taking more and more risks because he believed he was invincible. Of course, there was a pinch of lunacy, too. But he didn't want to talk about that any longer.

'Maybe he's got a woman over there,' he said. 'I caught him checking out jewellery on his phone one time. He sometimes sends texts with that goofy grin you guys only get when wooing a lady.'

Dave laughed. 'And I thought he'd turned celibate after his ex-wife died.' He abruptly stopped laughing and sighed. 'I shouldn't be here. The plan was to nut Grafton and take his money, and we did that. I got ninety grand. That's the house paid for, so what else do I need? Eh?'

'I don't know,' Brad replied impatiently. He didn't care.

'Nothing, that's what else. So why am I here? What can Grafton's wife tell the cops now that Ramirez is out of the picture? Nothing that comes back on me. All we're doing is risking everything with this foolishness.'

Brad had been waiting for the right moment to drop the bombshell. This wasn't it, but Dave was pissing him off, so he said: 'Ramirez is helping the cops, and he said they should look at the guys who hit The Savannah.'

He felt all nervous movement from Dave cease, turned his head and saw him glaring. 'That's a fucking joke, right?'

Brad needed a piss. He looked on the messy floor for a bottle. 'Funny, eh?'

Dave slapped the dashboard. 'So the cops have our names, that's what you're saying? Well, that's a fucking escalation, isn't it? Jesus Christ.'

'I thought you didn't care? You were worried like an old woman last night, but this morning you said everything was fine. That's what you said.'

'I didn't care. We got away from the scene. No cops kicked in the door at three in the morning. New day, new outlook. But it's fucking different when they've got our names, isn't it? Jesus. My wife will kill me if we lose that house.'

'Don't forget she'll also be a bit down in the dumps if you go in the slammer for thirty years,' Brad said, sarcastically. 'You're not the only one with something to lose here, you know. I've got plans that I don't want to see go down the toilet. I've got a life that I like enough to want to keep.'

Dave rubbed his face and cursed.

Brad said: 'Anyway, the cops don't have *your* name. But don't worry either way. Mick will find a way to deflect the police away from us. Bear in mind they would have looked at people like us anyway, without Ramirez shooting his mouth off. I heard Grafton's lot hit a rival's place earlier, looking for leads. All his enemies will be targets. We're grains of sand in a desert.'

'Mick's head's a mess; so, how's he going to sort it out? He can't think straight. Everything that happened has clearly fucked him up. It explains why he overreacted with Grafton. Then that silliness killing Król just so he could get near Seabury's wife. Now I hear he's talking about watching Gold, Grafton's solicitor. Is he going to kill him, too? And who's gonna be in the cross hairs after that? Ever see that film, *Six Degrees of Separation*?'

'Look, he's just covering all eventualities. It makes sense, if you think about it. They're on the run. Król was going to burn us. Seabury's wife might know where her bloke would hide. And Grafton never took a shit without consulting his lawyer, so maybe his wife thinks that's the guy to go to. She's gotta know by now that her man's dead and the world thinks she's been kidnapped. Some papers even said she's the killer. The cops were always trying to nail Grafton, and she probably believed his bullshit that it was bullying, so a station full of cops is the last place she's going to walk into.'

'What, you agree with all this shit? What's Mick going to resort to if Grafton's wife ends up telling the cops all about us? Bomb London to shift attention? Think you'll kiss the ground he walks on when that happens?'

'That's a bit far-fetched.' *Bomb London.* Brad remembered when Mick had uttered something along those lines. *Unless I burned the whole world, I might miss him and never know it.* A couple of years ago now, and Brad had forgotten all about it. Somewhere along the way Mick had well and truly gone off the rails. With it in mind, he added: 'Anyway, I don't think this is about keeping her silent any lon—'

'"Far-fetched"? What, you mean like overkill? Let me explain overkill, Brad. Overkill is when you shoot a guy dead, and then have a little sit down to get your energy, and then grab a fucking chainsaw to dice him up. Tell me that's the sign of a guy in full control of his grey matter? And we stood by and watched. A quick kill might have got us to the Pearly Gates, but there's a special level of Hell waiting for us now.'

'Hey, as Nietzsche said, all the interesting people are missing from Heaven.' He grabbed an empty plastic Pepsi bottle off the floor. 'I expected as much, to be honest.' He unscrewed the lid, and then unzipped his jeans. 'Maybe the chainsaw was OTT. And he asked me a scary question about life after death. Sort of thing your God-fearing ass would say. But we're not in his position, are we? Who are we to judge? We don't know what it's like after everything he's been through. Maybe I'd have done exactly the same to Grafton if he'd done that to m—'

'Hey, don't piss in that, man. It'll go everywhere. There's a petrol can in the boot.'

Brad tossed the bottle down and grabbed the door release lever.

Dave said: 'I want out. I just wanted the money, and I've got it. I don't owe him anything, so I've got no reason—'

'What are you saying? That I owe him? He got me off a murder charge. He needed us to get to Grafton. It was a business deal. You think I'm doing this as a favour? I'm trying to save my own skin, that's all. Got that? I don't owe anyone anything, okay?'

'Whatever, man. I'm just saying there's no reason for us to be involved. Grafton's dead, so we all got our payback. Payback *and* a paycheque. We should be happy.'

Brad didn't know what to say to that. He knew Dave was right, and he wasn't even sure exactly why he was going along with Mick's plan any longer. Probably because he trusted the guy to keep them safe. He opened the door slowly and got out.

As he stood up he flicked a glance across the road at the Seabury house.

CHAPTER FIFTY-ONE

KARL

The awkward part was Tanter Road because it was a hill, and that meant they couldn't see the dozen police cars and fifty armed cops congregating at the entrance to Karl's street. Karl slowed down and pulled into the side of the road.

Liz wasn't looking ahead, and barely seemed to register that the vehicle had stopped. She was quiet now, eyes facing downward.

The spectrum of her performance was astounding given how docile she was now compared with her actions in stealing the van. Yet again she had displayed a resolve that made him wonder how much influence she had exerted over her husband. How much input did she have into his so-called business?

'Be careful,' she said, still lost in a world behind her eyes.

'I'll go in the back way.'

He pulled into traffic. Ahead, the peak of the hill drew closer. The concrete jungle beyond it sprouted into existence full throttle: houses, lampposts, parked cars. But of the dozen police cars and fifty armed cops he expected... nothing. His street, on the left, was a hundred feet away. The entrance was clear.

An oncoming van, with window installation company livery, turned right, onto Karl's street. At that moment, Karl tugged the wheel to the left, and found himself behind the other vehicle. Just a couple of tradesmen at work. He reeled out some distance between them. Only a handful of cars were close to his house. Apart from Katie's car, the closest was a red BMW, but that was on the other side of the road and sixty feet past. The street looked static, sleepy, but he wasn't—

'Don't be fooled by everything seeming normal,' she said, interrupting his thoughts.

'I know,' he replied, somewhat sharply. He wasn't an idiot. He wasn't about to stop outside his house and stroll to the door. 'We'll turn right at the end and park, and I'll go in down the back alley.'

The cops would use blank cars, of course, because they'd want camouflage. But two could play that game. If the cops didn't leap on Premier Windows man as he drove to install triple glazing, then they wouldn't hassle Mr Anderson en route to lay some tiles. Karl let the distance between them grow.

He noticed a guy standing at the back of the BMW. The Premier Windows van passed his house, and then the parked car, without incident.

He stared at his house. How he'd taken its comfort for granted. What he'd give to be able to flop onto the sofa one more time. He'd eat and sleep on that thing for six straight months if he ever again got the chance.

No movement from inside the house. No sign of Katie. But her car was there. He fought the desire to leap out and rush into his house. Even if cops, or bad guys, swung down from trees and Jack-in-the-boxed out of manholes, he'd get to hold Katie before they dragged him away. And he'd burn that image to his memory for ever.

When the Caddy approached the BMW, Karl noticed a black guy in the driver's seat. The white guy at the back had a petrol can in his hands and his head down, blocked by the open boot hatch.

Then the Caddy was alongside, and slipping past. Karl turned his head and looked at them, struck by panic. Liz was staring, and Karl was staring, and the driver was staring back at them. Just for a second, before he slipped out of view, but long enough. Liz whipped her head away, and he saw her shock and fear. He threw a hand up to cover his face.

Both of them had seen his forehead. Three ragged gashes filled with dried blood. Just like you might get if you tried to kill a man in an underground bar and a woman dug her nails into your face from behind.

Varsity. Here. For them.

They both watched the passenger wing mirror with rising dread. Waiting for the guy to shout, and point, and jump in the car before coming after them – from anonymity to ten o'clock news in a flash.

But Varsity had his back to them. He slammed the boot, and he got in the car – slowly, no haste. And the BMW just sat there.

He hadn't recognised them, Karl realised, breathing a sigh of relief. Perhaps because of the dirty windows of the van, or maybe he just wasn't expecting them to be in Mr Anderson's van.

A damn lucky break. He drove on.

The BMW remained still, waiting for its prey to arrive.

CHAPTER FIFTY-TWO

MICK

Despite his rush, Mick took a moment to put the TV on, to kill the silence of the house and to try to inject some calm into his system. There was a tightness in his chest: he had no loose change for Tim's money box.

With some bullshit morning TV show filling the house with noise instead, Mick threw a few extra items into the large satchel he was taking to Berlin. It would go in the car, along with his son's bag, and the ninety grand liberated from Grafton's house.

A rising urge cut the job in half. From a drawer at the bottom of his wardrobe, he pulled out a bag. From the bag, a pressed linen suit on a hanger, wrapped in cellophane. Grafton's suit. His torso punchbag had no legs, so the trousers wouldn't work, but it could wear the jacket. A decent fit around the chest. From the wardrobe drawer, another bag. Photos this time. He selected a portrait of Grafton with a beaming smile that he would glue to the punchbag's head.

The double was almost complete.

CHAPTER FIFTY-THREE

MAC

A mobile number he didn't know flashed on the caller ID. A female voice he recognised, though. The girl who had messed up his head with the Volvo printout late last night. Tennant was her name. He had meant to apologise to her for his outburst.

Apparently, his warning had sunk deep because she had found out something new and was calling to let him know. He put on a sweet tone, which was easy because of his good mood despite knowing that he probably wasn't going to like what she told him.

'Thanks, DC Tennant. Julie. What or who have you found?'

The second man on the CCTV video from Karl Seabury's phone, that was who. A member of their support staff had popped in to drop off mail for DC Downey and had recognised him. A quick look at the files, and now they knew he was Nikos Avramidis, thirty-one, Greek-born, who did eight months four years ago for assault, and was a known friend of Aleksy Kozaczuk, *aka* Król. But what they didn't know was where he was. No address registered to his name as of last year.

'Well done,' Mac told her. 'Why don't you get out of the office and go find him? Don't approach on your own, mind. Call it in.' A nice little proactive outside job to make her feel like a real detective. Then he thought of something. 'Hang on. This support staff saw the photo? Where?'

She paused. Just a second. But long enough.

'On the board?' he yelled. 'What the hell did I tell you? When did you learn this about Nikos?'

'Half an hour or so ago. I pinned it up, yes. But I tried—'

He cut her off with an insult, and harshly reminded her that he wanted to know everything within one minute. She hung up an unhappy girl.

CHAPTER FIFTY-FOUR

MICK

Bad about Nikos, but no big deal, really. This Nikos, as a friend of Król's, would be similarly of low moral fibre. He wouldn't tell the cops anything. But, just in case, Mick should send someone to remind the guy what happened to snitches in his world.

Then he remembered the Loyalty Box.

He wouldn't need it now, of course, but that didn't mean he could just leave it to be found. It also went into the car, destined for a faraway trash bin. A shame, really, because with its death two dozen nasty bastards who deserved to rot in jail would be protected for ever. The folded suit belonging to Grafton was also tucked beside it, although that item was going to remain with him for a while. It still had a purpose.

In the kitchen, he stood before Tim's filled money boxes. He decided to take only one. Money was easy to replace.

He did a final sweep of the house, just to make sure nothing incriminating was on show. It might be weeks before anyone forced open his door to find out why he was absent from work, but that didn't mean he wanted them to discover the truth immediately. Nothing incriminating, but Tim's cornflakes were still on the kitchen table. He emptied the bowl into the bin. That made him think of the food in the freezer, so he filled a plastic bag with frozen items for the old guy across the road, who he liked.

'See you later, Tim,' he called out, then locked up. He put the bag of frozen goodies on the guy's doorstep and returned to his car. He checked his watch. Good timing. He could get to St Dunstan's in plenty of time to brief his men and scout the area. After Seabury and the bitch were toast, he'd get the fuck out of here early tomorrow morning.

CHAPTER FIFTY-FIVE

MAC

Mac believed there were four types of people in the world, and he met them all in the retirement home that his father, Chris, had called home for nine months. As Mac entered the building, the receptionist gave him a wary look, and the male nurse she was talking to said: 'Yorkshire Ripper admitted to any more killings yet?' Shortly afterwards, he passed a woman who virtually sneered at him.

He noticed a missed call from the same number Tennant had called from. Thirty-seven minutes ago. He almost laughed. He called her back and apologised. She hung up a happy girl. Good deed done for the day.

He found Dad in the garden, playing chess by himself at a table under a bamboo canopy. A big guy, like Mac, with the same granite chin, but his powerful coalman's physique had grown flabby over the years.

'See the guy by the pond?' his dad said as Mac stepped onto the patio.

Mac handed over a couple of detective novels. 'Dad, I have some news,' he said as he sat down.

'Did you see that chap at the pond? He's from Clapham. Here, read this.'

Mac sighed. 'Dad, listen to me. I don't have long. I'm going aw—'

Dad was fumbling in a pocket for something. A sheet of folded paper was thrust out, which Mac took and unfolded. It was a printout of a newspaper story from a website. An old murder. A cold case. Mac sighed again.

People who knew he was a detective made up the four types on the planet. Like the receptionist, some blanked him, as if fearful that he could read their minds and arrest them for some traffic crime or ancient barroom fight. Some cops loved that. Like the nurse chatting to the receptionist, there were those who latched onto him to satisfy their thirst for gossip, and what better subject to natter about around the water cooler than murder and rape? The staff who sneered at him made up the third kind: those who treated him like scum because of some brother or uncle who had been targeted by the police. Worst of all, though, the fourth – amateur sleuths. Because of all the fictional detectives clogging up the bookstores and TV channels, detectives had become real-life superheroes. And every amateur thought he needed their help. Because his son was in the game, Dad had started reading Inspector Morse and Kim Stone and all those other famous characters, and he'd caught that same damn disease.

He pointed past Mac, but he didn't look. 'This is important, Dad—'

'That's John. He's from Clapham. Read it, read it.'

He gave it a quick scan. Some murder in the 1990s in Clapham. Woman's body found in the woods one morning by a dog walker. Run-of the-damn-mill.

'Dad, can we talk? I might not be able to visit for a while.'

'Clapham, you bloody see that? Last night, Mac, he woke up screaming in the night. Screaming he was sorry. You understand?'

Dad had all his marbles, but could turn as single-minded as a dog in heat when something obsessed him. Mac knew his dad wouldn't pay any other subject much attention until after he'd slept it off, but today he couldn't just leave and return after he'd napped.

He knelt on the paving stones so they were eye level. 'Listen to me, Dad. I've got something on. It means I might not be able to visit. Do you understand that?'

'Sure, son, I do. But you'll still be by next week?'

The guy who still followed politics and could argue it with the best of them wasn't understanding. 'No, Dad. This will be a much longer time. I wanted to tell you that I'll phone you when I can. *If* I can.'

Dad jerked his head to one side, staring past. 'Look now, look, you'll get a face-on view.'

So, Mac looked, just to satisfy his father. Some old guy in a wheelchair, grey stubble, big glasses, a bandage on his nose. Feeding the ducks in the pond.

'Did you see?'

And that was that, Mac decided. This was no kind of goodbye. But he wanted to leave his dad with a happy smile.

He said: 'Yes, Dad, I've seen him. We've been watching this place for a few days now, but we never knew who our killer was. Now, thanks to you, we know it's the man in the wheelchair. Well done. But I need you to keep quiet about this.'

'Of course, son. I don't want to jeopardise your investigation. I know you policemen these days are caught up in all the rules and regulations. I'll keep quiet. But is there anything I can do?'

'No, thank you, Dad. This is all thanks to you. You've done your bit already.'

His father smiled as Mac's phone rang. DS Gondal.

'Hey, Gondal. What's up?'

'Good and bad news,' Gondal said, then relayed the bad: DC Shaun Downey, the fool, had just been caught red-handed calling a female journalist with details of Operation Nook, the investigation into the triple murders.

'Christ. And the good?'

'We've found the Volvo.'

Sweet tone: 'Excellent.'

According to Gondal, it was found in a lock-up garage near Danson Park. A local guy, who'd recently set-up CCTV on the abandoned garages because of ongoing vandalism, saw the superintendent's morning press conference and thought he might have spotted the Volvo. Responding uniforms opened a garage up, and there it was. Confirmed. Gondal was en route.

'Touch nothing till I get there,' Mac said. 'I'm coming now.'

He hung up.

'Is that about the case?' his father asked.

Mac shook his head, grabbing the books he'd brought. 'A different case, Dad. I'll pop these in your room.'

*

He moved quickly. Into the building, through the dining area and up the stairs. Two staff stopped him to say his father was outside, and he explained the books. Sixty seconds later he was in his dad's cramped but neat room. At the window, staring down East Lane towards Park View Road. Just across the junction, 500 feet away, he could see the lock-up garages.

And two police cars.

A couple of weeks ago, he'd stood here and stared at the same location, intrigued, before heading over there for a better appraisal. A nice spot, quiet, somewhat remote and accessible from two directions. And no CCTV. Not a place he'd ever imagined would be crawling with cops. His jaw started to throb. His busted ear, too, because the injury might just be his undoing.

As he popped another mint into his mouth, he noticed a drop of Król's blood on the matchbox. One little speck. Enough to send him to prison for the rest of his life, of course, but he'd been lucky.

No, not luck, he corrected himself. None of this had been luck. Luck hadn't put this evidence back in his hands. Luck wasn't going to see him walk right out of this whole mess untouched. Skill, ingenuity and grit would determine the winner, and he had more of each than anyone else.

The guy called Nikos should have already been warned not to talk to the police, and the Volvo should have been completely destroyed, or at least transported out of the area. A pair of fuck-ups, and in the game of murder you didn't get away with that shit. Now he was going to have to go over there for damage limitation. From now on, clear thinking, and no more fucking mistakes.

His mobile pinged. A reply from Alize to the message he'd sent her from the shop that morning.

Hi, Sweetcake. All well? Did u go 2 the Cemetery 2day?

He replied:

I go every Thursday, babe, but I know I shouldn't. Still on for seeing you later this week. Can't wait. XXX

He felt better now that he'd heard from Alize.

He got as far as the stairs, then cursed so loudly that a resident in a nearby room came to her door. He found an alcove and called Gondal back.

Sweet tone: 'I forgot in the heat of the moment. Where's the lock-up garage?'

Maybe Gondal would have assumed he'd got the address elsewhere. Not the point. Still a fucking daft error.

*

'Hey, what, you think I'm blind? If they'd been here, we would have seen them. They're not coming, okay?'

'Fair enough,' he replied on the phone on his way down the stairs. 'Calm down, Brad. Remember that legendary tepid demeanour of yours. It wasn't an accusation. I never believed he'd try to go home, anyway. So now we'll concentrate on the Dunstan thing. Get over there and get ready. Where's Dave?'

'Three feet from me, and just as pissed off that we wasted time sitting here. Listen, have you thought about a plan to get the cops off my back yet? It's gotta happen quick. If Ian finds—'

'Later, Brad. I'm up to my neck. But I'll get a plan. A mother of a plan, just you wait and see. But I've got a job for Dave before we do the Dunstan thing. Put him on. And then I've got to go save all our asses. The damn Volvo's been found. Hundreds of vehicles to check, and it's been found in a day. I knew we should have hung, drawn and quartered that thing. And there's CCTV at the garages now. I'm headed there, maybe into waiting handcuffs. You sure you sterilised it properly?'

'CCTV? Since when?'

'Some old guy must have put it up in the last week, after I scoped the place out.'

'Okay, but it shouldn't even be a problem, should it? We had masks.'

He snorted in derision. 'Masks won't matter if they see the end of that video, Brad.'

Brad cast his mind back, remembered, and said: 'Shit. But you're the damn murder squad leader, you could derail this whole thing.'

'Bullshit, Brad, bullshit. I overlook things, I make a mistake, they pull me off the case and analyse every decision I've made. I've got to be careful. I can't just lie down after the opening bell to throw this fight. I've got to smack my opponent around a bit, go the distance and win on points. I'll deal with the CCTV, but I need to know if you're certain you sterilised the fucking car properly.'

'We'll soon find out, I guess.'

*

On his way out, he kissed his dad's cheek and said he had to rush.

'Go make the world a safe place, Mick.'

As Mick walked past wheelchair John, he pointed two fingers at his own eyes, then the guy's glasses, and told him they were a fine pair of spectacles. Quietly, of course, so his watching Dad didn't hear.

CHAPTER FIFTY-SIX

KARL

Just 1,500 feet east of Karl's home, they parked under a railway bridge near Bow Common Gasworks. Four mechanics in overalls stained with petrol and oil were risking their lives smoking outside the gates of an auto garage on the far side, and other pedestrians were around, but nobody paid them any heed. They could see ahead and behind 500 feet, so would have ample warning if the red BMW found them. Karl called home on the phone he'd found in Anderson's van, but got no answer. Liz waited patiently. If it could be called waiting: since their near-miss back at Karl's street, Liz had been distant, deep in thought. Twiddling her hair, scratching at her knees, staring into space.

When he hung up with no joy from Katie's mobile, either, Liz said: 'She'll be with the cops, so don't worry. If they're going to bring her to the meeting, she'll be in a police station, being questioned, while next door a team of big men prepare for you with a big fishing net.'

He glared at her. The sort of joke he might have made, but it pissed him off to be on the receiving end. At least her spirits had been revived – for the last few minutes he'd felt alone, and hadn't enjoyed it.

'Then we've got no other choice,' he said. 'We have to meet that detective. I'll see Katie that way.'

'Not *we*,' Liz said. 'I have to do this another way.'

'What way?'

'Ron never trusted the police. There were police on his payroll, and no doubt some of his enemies will have police on theirs. I can't take that risk.'

'That's daft. This detective isn't one of the enemy.'

'I don't doubt it. But I'm not just going to hand myself over all alone.'

'So what can you do?' He couldn't hide the anxiety in his voice. He didn't want her to leave him. Not now, during the endgame.

'Use our solicitor. Bartholomew Gold. He's a good man. He'll know how to help us. All of us.'

If he had a client like Ronald Grafton, Karl doubted he was a good man. He didn't say as much, though.

'You should come with me,' she continued. 'I don't like why this detective wants to meet you outside, away from a police station. And don't say it's so he can take your statement without people around making noise. That's the daft part. He'll want to trick you into saying something incriminating without legal representation.'

Karl had already considered this. But he could watch what he said. What he couldn't do was guarantee that he'd get to see Katie and their unborn child any time soon if he just walked into a cop shop and put his hands up. He told Liz as much. She shrugged in response.

'So what will you do?' he asked.

'I'm going to my friend Danny's house. He'll help me. He'll take me to see Mr Gold. I'll walk into a police station with the finest defence lawyer in the country.'

'You'll need a defence lawyer, will you?'

'We both will. We have no idea what's going on. They might think I'm a suspect. And you have no proof that you didn't kill that man in the shop. I'll offer again that you stay with me.'

In answer, he opened his door to get out. But she stopped him.

'You take the van because you're going to be all alone and will need it. I'll keep the phone. Danny will pick me up.'

She got out, and he let her. She shut her door. Turned away, but didn't move. He dropped the passenger window.

'Have a good life, Liz Grafton.'

She turned back. 'Be careful.'

'Never been my thing, as your presence in my life proves.'

He got a smile from her in return. He decided to leave it at that. A nice final image. A genuine smile, which meant he must have done some good in her life. He turned the van onto the road, and drove past her.

In the mirror, he saw that she was watching him leave.

Strangely, he hoped he hadn't seen the last of Liz Smith.

CHAPTER FIFTY-SEVEN

MICK

'I'm busy now, call you later.'

Cooper was also on his mobile. He looked up and said: 'The old guy is coming down.'

Mick replied: 'Why? I don't want him here.'

'He only wants to speak to the head detective. Won't give up the tape otherwise. He's coming down now with the constable.'

'What took so long?'

Cooper asked the question, then said: 'The old guy insisted that the constable watched the CCTV first.'

'Why?' Mick asked, concerned.

'He wanted to give some commentary. The chap wants to be involved.'

If a cop had seen the video, he might recognise him, and that just wouldn't do. Shit. Thinking quick, he said: 'I don't want the constable here. Just members of the investigation team. He can be of better use elsewhere.' Cooper got on it.

They were standing outside a lock-up garage on a patch of grassland backdropped by a playing field, about 160 feet from the main road. Behind them, 100 feet away, were the rear ends of a row of houses, each garden with high hedges that blocked their view of the upstairs windows. And thus any view of the garages.

Exactly the reason he had chosen the place. Yet here they fucking were. It clearly hadn't been enough.

Mick and Cooper were watching the SOCO team milling around the Volvo in the second garage. The warped garage door was up only halfway, as far as the busted contraption would go. Today these guys wore respirators and face shields because they were dealing with a vicious chemical that Dave and Brad had used to sterilise the crime scene.

DC Gondal arrived and was let through the cordon. He almost jogged to his colleagues, which Mick didn't like. His fear that Gondal had news was right on the money.

'I got a couple of neat things on Brad Smithfield,' Gondal said with a grin. 'That Scottish henchman called Rocker, the murder you investigated? Not the only killing Smithfield's name has been tied to. There's another low life with a daft nickname. Robert Dunham, called himself Rapid. Drug dealer specialising in Buzz who got himself whacked in the proverbial dark alley one night just a week after the Rocker fiasco.'

He waited for a response. Mick, feeling the panic rise, could only think of: 'Drug dealers get targeted all the time. Lucrative fodder for underworld taxmen and vigilantes. Give me more.'

'His alibi was perfect: being interviewed by police about the Rocker killing. But shit sticks. Doesn't mean he wasn't involved. And this guy, Rapid, had been known to deal out of Grafton's nightclub.'

'So?'

'So twice, in two different murders and the nightclub robbery, the name Brad Smithfield has appeared as a person of interest. The sweetness is the way it all links to Ronald Grafton.'

'That's not really a link, is it? Dealers operate out of all sorts of nightclubs, and Grafton owned one of the most popular in London. I need more.' More was the last thing he wanted, of course, but he was a cop investigating a triple slaughter and he had to be seen to be doing all he could.

Gondal pulled out a sheet of paper from his pocket. Unfolded it slowly, like a guy playing on the tension to unleash something big. And big it was. Mick found himself staring at a printout from a website called About.me. A single-page user profile, like an online business card.

BRAD SMITHFIELD

was the title. Below, taking up half the page, was a large picture of the man himself in jeans, T-shirt, dusty boots, a battered hard hat and a utility belt, kneeling before the corner of a half-built house, taking time out from laying bricks to grin at the camera.

JOINER, MASON, LANDSCAPER, ELECTRICIAN

said big, bold letters under his name, and below that a button:

BROWSE MY PORTFOLIO

At the bottom was the personal stuff:

HARD WORKER BY DAY AND GENERAL FUN GUY AT NIGHT, BRAD IS KNOWN FOR HIS SENSE OF HUMOUR AND BROAD SHOULDERS, A CHEEKY CHAP WHO...

'Recognise the house?' Gondal said, pointing. And Mick did. His heart sank.

Gondal said: 'So Smithfield worked on Grafton's nice woodland cottage, which meant he knew exactly where it was and what kind of place it was. Maybe he was a long-time employee the cops didn't know about, and maybe he was in the loop enough to know that Grafton would flee there after his advance-fee fraud trial. He was questioned about the death of a dealer working out of Grafton's club. He was suspected of the hit on Grafton's nightclub. He worked on Grafton's house. We need to pull this guy in for a chat. No more playing.'

'Do it,' Mick said, because now he had no choice. He knew Brad had been working on a website in order to find work, but he hadn't expected the damn fool to post a fucking photo of himself at Grafton's country abode.

For now, though, there was a more pressing matter.

A uniformed constable and an old man appeared at the cordon, thirty feet off. Mick turned from them. Out of the corner of his eye, he watched Cooper bring the witness towards him. Thankfully, the cop who could potentially sink Mick was turned away. Mick relaxed.

The old chap was in a tacky suit, something he might have got married in fifty years ago. He didn't look altogether there as he was introduced to the detectives. He was introduced as Alfie Tasker, from number eight, which was the last house on the row behind them. In his hands was a VHS tape.

'You're the boss?'

Mick nodded. 'That's the recording?'

'Secured the perimeter, which is good,' the guy said. 'Have you got guys tracing cars seen in the vicinity last night?'

'We'll get it back to you, if you need it,' Cooper said, with his hand out for the tape.

'What happened to your ear?' Tasker asked, pointing to Mick.

He touched it before he could stop himself. 'What's your camera quality like?' With luck, the guy would admit it was bullshit. With luck, maybe they couldn't distinguish faces.

'Dark, wasn't it? Council wouldn't shell out their own hard-earned, would they? But it's good enough to get these idiot vandals bang to rights. So tell me, what're you going to do about them?'

They'd heard that this chap was annoyed by the constant vandalism of these garages, which needed knocking down anyway.

Thought they could get away with their lark because nobody could see them because of the trees. They caused noise at all hours. Well, the old guy had fixed that problem. Mick glanced at the far end of the block of garages, some forty feet away. There, on the wall, was a tiny camera, aimed this way to watch all the doors. It hadn't fucking been there six days ago when Mick and Brad had come here to assess the place for their needs.

'This is more serious than vandals, Mr Tasker,' Gondal said, annoyed. The old guy had called because of a media release about the murders in which the Volvo had been mentioned. Not vandals.

'I know, I know. But they're the same people, right? Have you dusted for prints?'

'Can we have the tape?' Cooper asked.

The old guy passed it over.

To Mick, Cooper said: 'I know how we can get this hooked up, so we don't have to wait for a transfer to digital.'

They were ready to go back to the station and view it. Which was bad. Mick felt panic rising further. He touched his ear again, and looked at the camera.

The old guy said: 'Smells like drain cleaner.'

Sure was. A bottle of Devil Drain Dasher that Brad and Dave had splashed all over the car. Sodium hydroxide, no friend to forensics guys. But nobody knew that yet, and Mick wasn't about to help them.

'Caustic soda,' the old guy said. 'Good for burning up flesh. Sodium hydroxide, that'll be it. That guy in Mexico who worked for a drug cartel, he used it. Three hundred bodies he got rid of. You got bodies in there?'

Gondal and Cooper grinned at the old guy's fanciful mind, but Mick didn't. No worry, because they'd discover the chemical used pretty soon, and you wouldn't be able to do anything with that information. But still, it wasn't nice to hear an old guy work it out in seconds.

'Thanks for the tape,' Cooper said to the old guy. 'I'll escort you home, if you like.'

But he didn't move.

And then an idea. 'Mr Tasker, you obviously have the ability to watch these tapes, right? Playback. You have a video recorder?' Mick asked.

'I do.'

'Then how about we four go watch this thing right now, at your house?'

Tasker was up for it. Mick knew this guy wanted to be included. Maybe he was a former cop or just a busybody. Mick needed Gondal and Cooper to see it right now, too, because he could control that. He couldn't if they chose to view it later, without him.

All agreed, the four of them headed for Tasker's house. Mick touched his bad ear again, as if he needed a reminder of what was at stake. He needed a plan, quick, or his two colleagues were going to watch a video which showed him with the Volvo. When Gondal and Cooper had joined his team, he'd hoped they were sharp tacks. Now, he hoped for the opposite. Because if they worked this one out, there would be no glory.

'I need something from my car first,' he said.

He slipped the gun out of his glove box and into his pocket.

CHAPTER FIFTY-EIGHT

KATIE

Katie finished packing the bag of items Karl might need while in police custody, and sat staring at it. It seemed so final. She had packed a bag for him a couple of years ago, while he was at work, because they'd had an argument. She remembered packing seven pairs of underwear, holding them in her hands, and throwing two aside, figuring that five days apart would be enough. Then she tossed aside three more. Then she unpacked the bag, and today he still never knew about it.

This time, though, things were out of her hands. So, she took the bag to the car, and beside it put a sandwich wrapped in foil because he must be hungry; a bottle of water; the Smartwatch he'd given her a couple of weeks ago, because it was tiny and maybe he could sneak it into his cell so they could chat by text, even though she knew that was unlikely.

Cell. That thought brought a tear.

Her final task after locking the house and getting into the car was to boot up the satnav E1 0NR. The church was only half a mile southwest of their home. That made her realise that Karl was close. Out there somewhere, a hunted man hiding just minutes from his comfortable home, his wife, his unborn baby.

'I'm coming, Karl,' she said aloud, and started the car.

CHAPTER FIFTY-NINE

BRAD

A taxi dropped Dave and Brad at Western Road Autos. More mechanics in dirty coveralls, but these guys knew Dave. When Dave had been a getaway driver, he used cut and shuts – illegal cars created by welding together the good halves of two written-off vehicles – provided by Western Autos. These days Western was purely legit, although the guys running it were not. And they still offered cut and shuts, albeit for sale only to rally and demolition enthusiasts.

They were there to collect a brown Mercedes Vito panel. Surgery had resulted in the removal of the partition between the cargo space and the cab, which suited them just fine. It could be traced to the garage, so they were to deliver it to a scrapyard once they were finished with it.

Standing outside the vehicle Brad asked: 'Can you make your own way there? Something I want to take care of.'

'There' was the job Mick had given to Dave. He said sure, and got one of the mechanics, an old friend, to give him a lift home to collect his motorbike.

Brad cruised slowly past Ian's house, seeking surveillance. And he found it. No attempt at secrecy, though. There was a patrol car parked near the house with two guys inside. They watched him drive past, and to hide his face he yawned and rubbed his chin.

Around the corner, he called Mick, to urge him to pull the cops from his house and hurry up arranging some kind of plan to erase his name from the investigation. But he didn't get a word out.

'I'm busy now,' Mick answered, 'call you later.' Then he abruptly hung up.

Brad called Ian at work.

'Hey up, Chopper,' Ian answered. It sounded like a gangster's nickname, but Ian had invented it. He thought Brad's snoring sounded like a helicopter. His tone was the happy-to-hear-from-you kind, which was good. It meant the police hadn't been to talk to him.

'Just wanted to say love ya,' Brad said. Ian repeated it, then asked how things were going with the job hunt. Brad replied that things were going well, and they agreed to watch a film tonight over pizza. That call done, worries alleviated, it was time to head to the church.

CHAPTER SIXTY

Dave

Dave didn't have any cop worries as he arrived home. But that was about to change. Instead of collecting his motorbike, he stared at it for a few seconds, ignition key in his hand. Thirty seconds later, he put the key in his pocket, mind made up.

He found Lucinda at the kitchen table, counting the money again. Used twenties. Not a big amount: 4,521 notes, to be exact. She had created equal-sized piles so that the cash filled the table. Then he noticed piles of £10 notes. She had wanted all the notes turned into tens or fives so the mass would be bigger. He had warned her that they couldn't just waltz into a bank and change it. It had to be kept secret. Hell, it was going to be hard enough to try to use it to pay off half their mortgage. That problem still needed working on. Now she'd done this.

'Did you do the church thing already?' she asked, suspicious. Always suspicious. He ignored the question and tapped a pile of tens.

She flicked a hand, like royalty dispatching a beggar. 'Just £500. Nobody's calling the FBI about that. Why are you back? Is it done?'

'I've got some time,' he told her as he grabbed the kettle to make tea. It had been a stressful last evening and this morning, and all he wanted to do now was relax.

'Will it be done when the church thing is done?'

'Yeah. I mean, maybe the odd bit of housekeeping or whatever. Mick wants me to warn some guy not to talk to the cops. But we're good. You want a tea?'

He grabbed a Typhoo teabag. This was real tea, not that flavoured or cold or herbal shit that some people drank.

'"Warn some guy"? What do you mean?'

Milk in the cup first, despite what some said. That way you could choose exactly how full you wanted the cup while getting the correct amount of milk. 'One of the guys Mick sent to that guy's house to find Grafton's wife.'

'You said he was dead. You said you had to go burn his flat down.'

And don't touch the teabag for fifteen seconds. Let the flavour diffuse into the water. 'Yeah. Evidence. There were two guys.'

'And?'

Now he stirred the teabag. Some squashed it against the side of the cup, but that was forcing flavour out, which was just wrong. 'And nothing, really. The cops know someone else was with Król. Mick thinks Król might have told the guy what was going on, and the guy might tell the police when they find him. I doubt it. His kind tell the cops nothing. Hey, you want to watch that comedy at the pictures tonight? It's on at—'

'Shuttup about films a minute. This guy might talk to the cops, so Mick wants you to warn him not to? Why haven't you?'

Twenty seconds of stirring, and the strength was just right. 'It's a waste of time. He won't tell the police anything.'

'But if he does? If he tells them that Mick wanted the house owner and Grafton's wife, that opens up a can of worms, Dave. Might lead to us.'

And no sugar. If you needed sugar, you didn't really like tea. 'I doubt it. Just Mick being – Jesus!'

He jumped as Lucinda appeared beside him and knocked the kettle out of his grip as he was pouring. Boiling water splashed everywhere, including onto his hand.

She spun him around. 'If he gave you a job to do, dickhead, it's because it might ruin everything if you don't do it. Are you stupid?'

Clutching his scalded hand, he opened his mouth to speak, but she got there first.

'Don't even think about arguing with me. You damn idiot. Get out there. Go fuck this guy up before he tells the cops and they come knocking on this door. I'm not going down or losing this house because you're a lazy bastard.'

She slapped his arm to get him moving.

'Get out there and don't come back until it's done.'

CHAPTER SIXTY -ONE

LIZ

A van painted to look like a blue sky turned into the autoyard, so Liz put down her coffee, thanked the man who'd made it for her, and left the reception area. She climbed into the passenger seat without a word and the van backed up. Not until the vehicle was heading southeast along Bow Common Lane did the driver say anything.

'You employed the Rotten Rake, then?'

She saw him looking at her hands, which were in her lap. For the first time since she attacked Brad, she lifted them and peered at her nails. Blood was encrusted underneath and on the tips of her fingers.

'Maybe the Ghastly Gnash, too?'

She was still looking at her nails, and remembering. Not the act of clawing at the man's eyes in the dark train carriage, though. Years earlier, when Ron had shown her the technique. Part joke, given the name of the move, but deadly serious otherwise. Someone had tried to abduct her right out of the hairdresser's and only the early return of her bodyguard had prevented it. After that, Ron taught her self-defence but not your typical kind. No karate moves or jiu-jitsu submissions because, in Ron's world, those things didn't work. In his world, attackers had knives and guns. So, he showed her how to fire a gun. But for the times when a man was close, grabbing her, and a gun was of no use? She was shown how to rake out a man's eyes and bite out a man's throat. Not things she would have ever wanted to be shown, of course, but Ron had insisted. She had prayed it would all be a waste of time.

'I wasn't kidnapped,' she said. 'It was—'

'It was something else,' he finished. 'Enough said. Do you need medical care, and do you need food?'

'Something else, yes. But what? Why wasn't it enough to…' She couldn't finish the sentence as her eyes welled up. She wiped them, then fingered the side of that hand. The paw print tattoo, bringing her some comfort. Danny didn't need to hear the remainder of her unfinished sentence to know what she meant. Why wasn't it enough for these people to do what they had done? Why did they want to harm her, too?

'You're a witness,' he said. 'That's why. They don't want you talking to the police. Soon, hopefully, what you can tell the police won't matter because they'll already know.'

She nodded, understanding his message: once she was no longer a threat neither would they be. But that didn't comfort her right now, with Ron freshly gone and the danger imminent.

He tried to change the subject by asking again if she needed medical aid or food.

But she ignored the question. 'I heard one of them speak. We were at a bridge, hiding. My head was cloudy… I'd just found out about Ron… but I thought… thought I might have heard the voice before. Do you think this is why they want me?'

'Sounds likely. Where did you hear his voice previously?'

She shook her head. 'Maybe I was getting confused. I was in shock.'

She searched his face for something. Recognition. Worry. Understanding. Something that would tell her he knew who might have done this. Because he knew who Ron's enemies were. Had been, she corrected herself, and felt the tears threatening again. But there was nothing in his face except puzzlement, and she figured that was probably good. Somehow.

'I need clothes,' she said.

'I brought you some. And painkillers. And toiletries.'

'Thank you.' She felt a little calmer now.

Danny looked at her, waiting for her to tell him why the killers had targeted Ron. But she had no idea and her silence soon prompted him to veer the conversation.

'You didn't go to number ten. Craig went there to see.'

'I didn't trust the safe house,' she said. 'In case they tortured the information out of Ron. He always said we only should go there together. And I didn't know who the police would visit.'

'As far as I've heard, nobody went to number ten. The camera recorded nothing. The police have been pulling everyone in. Nobody's saying a thing, of course, including about who did this. They've got some ideas, but nobody knew all of Ron's enemies except Ron. And one other person.' He looked at her, and she understood.

Three months before, just after the clock struck midnight. Two days before he got arrested for serious fraud. A candlelit dinner and a swap of New Year resolutions. For her: no more smoking, which she'd achieved, and no more betting on the dogs, which she hadn't. For Ron: no more secrets. She had made a joke (go on, then, tell me how many little Rons are out there?), but hadn't been prepared for what happened next. He had outlined every crime he'd planned, taken part in, was responsible for.

Including murder.

She had listened in stunned silence as her husband exposed dark chasms in a soul that she thought she had well mapped. Four people whose deaths she suspected he was involved with. Three that she had believed were wrongly attributed to him and his gang. And three men that Ron had personally killed with his own hands. Some wives might have fled, but her shock and abhorrence had been overwhelmed by his honesty, and, somehow, she had forgiven him. He promised there would be no more killings. And, to her knowledge, there hadn't been.

'I don't know who could have killed my husband,' she said in response to his unasked question. Even though Ron had confided in her, she was none the wiser.

'Okay,' Danny replied. But he didn't sound that convinced, and his next sentence seemed designed to prompt her: 'Doesn't matter because Ron's boys are out there cracking heads to find out.'

'I don't want that. If my name without his has any sway, you should tell them to stop. What's done is done. There's no need for anyone else to get hurt. It won't rewind time and change last night. You didn't tell them about me, did you?'

She had told him to keep her contacting him a secret.

'I'm long out of the loop, remember. Nobody knows anything. And I'm also in the dark about everything. But I could do with knowing one thing: what's your plan?'

'I'm going to go to the police. I want to talk to Mr Gold first and have him arrange everything. But first, I need your help. To help Karl.'

'The man who helped you?'

She had only briefly mentioned Karl on the phone and didn't want to say much more about him just yet. 'He got me out of trouble and I owe him. I need you to help me. Have you heard of St Dunstan's Church?'

CHAPTER SIXTY-TWO

MICK

It turned out the old guy was a former cop after all. Mid-Anglia Constabulary, 1970–1973. Turned down for detective status, and seemed sour about it. It was as if he was trying to show his skills, proving his worth as a detective, at seventy years of age.

His home was overloaded but neat, as if he were both a hoarder and a clean freak at the same time. A billion vinyl records were set against the wall, so the detectives had to move in single file into the living room. The TV was an old CRT with built-in VHS player on a stand beneath a shelf bearing three ancient rugby trophies and an old black-and-white photo of a woman. Seeing the shelf, and the photo, Mick started to relax a little as a plan formed.

'Can I have a glass of water?' he asked.

He directed his men to take the sofa in front of the TV, even though they wanted to stand. When his water arrived, he placed it on the shelf, and then he sat between his colleagues, their knees touching.

Mick checked the time. Shit. He was due at the church in just forty minutes. He couldn't be late. This thing needed speeding up.

'What you're about to see,' the old chap said as he fiddled with a remote control for the TV, 'is video footage from two different times. I will start the video at 6.44 p.m. yesterday evening.' They let him talk because he wanted to. He probably didn't get many big moments in his life.

The footage was bad, which was good. Shadows were too deep, blacks too black, white parts from the setting sun too bright. But all three detectives, experienced in watching bullshit CCTV footage, barely noticed. Nobody expected a hi-def close-up of a perpetrator's face.

And they also knew they wouldn't get it. The camera was at one end of the row of lock-ups, and the garage was at the other. At 6.44, a car entered the scene from the direction of the main road, its lights off. Too dark to make out, but from the shape it looked like a small hatchback.

'Renault Clio,' Cooper said. 'Curve to the back of rear side window.'

The car stopped, sideways on to the camera, at the end of the path, just past the garages. Both right side doors opened.

'No way. Look, four doors. And that window frame is flat at the bottom. Volkswagen Golf.'

The car was stopped, but nobody got out.

'Headlights are too small,' Mick said. 'Mazda 3.'

He didn't even know why he said it. It was, of course, a Mazda 3. Dave, the car buff, had stolen it a few days before. He cursed himself inwardly.

'Three men,' Gondal said. 'Makes sense.'

The driver was short, slim, and black. They got that from his neck, because all three wore ski masks and gloves. The other passenger and the guy who'd sat behind the driver were taller, both white, one of them with thick shoulders. Dark clothing for all three, nothing distinctive.

'Jesus. This looks promising,' Cooper said.

'Mid-sized guy could be Smithfield,' Gondal said.

It was.

The three men walked past the first garage, coming towards the camera. The black one went down into a squat, and seemed to pick something up off the ground.

'What's he doing?' Gondal asked. All three detectives were leaning forward.

Cooper said: 'Looks like he's fou—'

'—nd a penny.'

'Stop messing about,' Mick said. He grabbed the garage door and lifted. Slowly, because it creaked.

'Find a penny, pick it up,' Dave said, 'and all day you'll have good luck. Don't you reckon we'll need it?'

'Get professional and you don't need luck,' Mick replied. The up-and-over metal door got halfway, then jammed. He couldn't budge it. The door was bent a little across the middle and he understood why: it threatened to bend again now as he pulled, same way he deadlifted at the gym. He shook the door, which was loud, but it came free and screeched its way fully open.

The Volvo lurked within, facing outwards. Untouched for a few days, as they'd expected because none of the garages was used. The three men slipped alongside it, to the back. Dave opened the rear door. Mick nodded at the tools and weapons inside. He hadn't expected Dave to be able to get exactly what he'd asked for, but here it was, right before him. This was going to work, he realised. Revenge, so long in anticipation, was finally taking flesh.

'Well done, Dave,' he said. 'You certainly know what you're do—'

'—ing in there?' Cooper said, looking at Gondal.

'How am I supposed to know what they're doing?'

'Fast forward,' Mick said. Onscreen, the three men had been inside the garage for over a minute. He was on the clock and didn't have six minutes to waste watching a motionless screen. Because he remembered that they had spent seven minutes in the garage, checking the weapons.

Cooper and Gondal yelled at the old guy to rewind the tape when, in double-speed, a car shot out of the garage.

'That's our stolen Volvo,' Cooper said. 'So this is them.'

The killers. Cooper and Gondal got excited, and Mick had to pretend to do the same. But he was far from happy. He glanced at his water, up there on the shelf.

The Volvo turned towards the camera, and the excited detectives leaned forward again, hoping for a close-up of the driver as he passed it. But then the Volvo stopped, and reversed past the parked Mazda, onto a patch of grass made to look like an inkblot by the video quality and high trees that blocked the setting sun.

'All three already inside,' Cooper said as the black guy got out of the Volvo and into the Mazda. He turned right, towards the camera, and then left, into the garage. Fast, neat. Clearly knew how to handle a vehicle.

'I'll see if Smithfield has any friends who resemble this guy,' Gondal said.

The black guy exited the garage and turned to close the door. Got it halfway, but then it moved no more. He tried rocking it, but didn't have the power.

Cooper said, 'Looks like it's jam—'

'—med again.'

Mick got out and approached. 'Get back in the car, you little wimp,' he said, joking. He was not unhappy right now. Not when things were progressing so well. He put his arms on the edge of the door, locked straight, and used all his weight and a rocking motion to try to free the stuck mechanism. He sensed Dave nearby, just watching.

'Dave, piss off into the car.'

Dave started walking back to the Volvo. 'Got some oil. Might need to lubri—'

'—cate the old throat,' Mick said, and stood, and walked towards the TV. He grabbed his drink from the shelf, and took a big gulp. He picked up the photo.

'Your wife died?' he asked.

'Eight years ago,' the old guy replied. 'How did you know?'

The photo. A woman in her prime, probably round about the time the old guy met her, when they were both young, when love was fresh. 'Hunch. Mine died three years ago, although she was my ex-wife by then. Split a year. The job, you see. Clichéd old thing, but the job really was my mistress and it wore her down. But it was amicable, and we still saw each other a lot because of our son. He stayed with me, and I got the house. So, I still sort of miss her some days. I'm sorry for your loss.'

He could almost feel his colleagues' discomfort at this rare show of emotion from their boss. He'd never talked about family since the accident, had banned his social life from being brought up at work. But they said nothing as he replaced the photo and the drink, and slowly walked backwards to his seat.

On the screen, the big guy had stepped back from the garage door. He jumped forward with a powerful kick which freed the jam and shut the door. He stomped back to the Volvo. He got in. The Volvo's headlights blazed on, whitewashing the screen. It turned right, onto the dirt road, and vanished. All told, nine minutes.

'And so we move onto 21.41,' the old guy said. The detectives weren't listening, though. They chatted among themselves about what they had just seen, stopping only when the fast-forwarding video slowed again.

Mick's mind raced. This time he was absent, so had no clue what Dave and Brad had got up to. If one of them had done something that would fuck up everything, well, he was going to find out when it was too late to do anything about it.

But everything was fine. The Volvo returned. It parked while the black guy opened the garage, with no major jamming problem this time. He drove the Mazda out, and the other guy drove the Volvo inside. The black guy entered, and neither returned for eight minutes, which, again, Mick instructed the old guy to fast forward through.

'Must be when they're spraying the chemical around,' Gondal said.

The two walked out, shut the garage door, and got into the Mazda. They vanished. The old guy shut off the video with a claim that he'd watched footage from the rest of the night but the men didn't return.

'You check up on other stolen cars around the same time,' Mick said to Cooper as all three detectives stood. 'I'll take the tape to the station and get it copied for everyone, see if anyone else can spot something we missed.'

He ordered Gondal and Cooper to remain at the garage and oversee the evidence gathering, and then he got the hell out of there.

En route to the meeting with Seabury, he broke the cassette in half, screwed up the tape and found a trash bin to dump it in. That had been a close call. If the detectives had seen the piece of footage Mick had blocked when he stood before the TV to drink the old guy's foul water and spout some shit about his wife, what might they have made of it?

The video showed Mick's hands slip from the garage door as he pushed down hard. Elastic energy in the bending sheet of metal forced it upwards, back into position. The gravitational energy in Mick's thick frame dragged his head downwards. He managed to turn his head, but the thundering connection mashed his ear. He had danced around for two seconds, cursing, clutching his ear, and then angrily kicked shut the garage door. And not so much from pain as embarrassment.

Maybe the detectives wouldn't have thought anything suspicious of Mick's ear and the injury of the masked man on the screen. But it wasn't worth the risk, and it was moot now anyway.

So, he pushed it aside and cast his mind forward to the upcoming meeting.

CHAPTER SIXTY-THREE

KARL

Karl had memorised the basic location of St Dunstan's and was there twenty minutes before he was due to meet the detective. He parked 500 feet away on a side street. He expected the police to be on the lookout for guys sitting in parked cars, so he decided he would walk. First, he checked the back of the Caddy for something to wear, and was rewarded. A hi-vis jacket, which wasn't the ideal outfit because he would stand out. But at least he would not stand out as Karl Seabury. There was also a backpack with a muddied football kit and boots inside. He took that with him, only because the police wouldn't expect him to have a bag. The football boots, though, went onto his throbbing feet. Minus the screw-on studs, they looked like regular training shoes.

He got back in the van and closed his eyes. He wondered where everyone was. Katie – was she at the church, just another 500 feet away, awaiting him with tearful eyes? Liz – was she with her friend yet, or maybe even already in custody? If the latter, how were they treating her? Like a victim who needed compassion, or as a possible suspect in the murder of her husband? He imagined a team of cops surrounding her, oblivious to her grief as they tried to extract information about her dead husband's criminal empire.

And the killers – out there, seeking him, closing in? Or had they fled with their tails between their legs?

Karl took a deep breath, and got out of the van for what might be his last five minutes as a free man.

'Pray when will that be, say the bells of Stepney' was a line from a famous poem that mentioned St Dunstan and All Saints Church. But that was the last thing on his mind as he walked along Stepney Way, heading east. He saw the tall Anglican church past black gates beyond a mini-roundabout, 160 feet away, and slowed down to pause at a bus shelter. He couldn't see much happening at the church, but his view of the grounds either side of the building was restricted. He took a breath and started walking, expecting a swarm of cop cars to target him at any second. Once he got to the roundabout, it would be too late to turn because he would be exposed.

'Here we go,' he said to himself.

*

South of that roundabout, Katie sat in her car a hundred feet from the entrance to the church grounds, and twenty feet in front of a police car. She ignored the activity around her, including a bunch of teenagers shouting at each other in the park to her left, and two police officers talking to them about a report of a man waving a baseball bat around. There was no bat-wielding lunatic, though. Katie had called in the lie in order to get the police to the church. If she had called them about Karl, they would have arrived mob-handed. This way, when she told the two officers who she was and what was going on, nobody would be able to stop her getting to Karl. When she saw a man in a hi-vis jacket and carrying a bag, she tensed. She just knew it was Karl from his walk. It took every milligram of will to prevent herself from running to him.

'Here we go,' she said to herself, then turned and shouted to the policemen in the park.

*

North off that mini-roundabout was Danny's van, parked on a zigzag white line just short of a zebra crossing. Parking here was a big no-no, and many honking cars had let them know this, but from this location the occupants could see McDevitt waiting by the church. In the mirrors, they saw a man in a hi-vis jacket cross the road and enter the church grounds.

'Here we go,' Danny said to Liz.

*

Two hundred and fifty feet east of the van, McDevitt stood by a tree near the church's rear. He saw a man in a hi-vis jacket pass through the single black gateway. Into Mick's world.

'Here we go,' he said into his phone, literally shivering with excitement.

*

East again, 280 feet away, just beyond the perimeter fence, Brad and Dave were sitting in the Mercedes Vito, chosen for its sliding side door. Both men had arrived only minutes earlier, at roughly the same time. Dave's bike was in the cargo space, near Mick's bags.

They didn't even get time to relax before Mick called with the news: Seabury had arrived.

'Here we go,' Brad said to Dave.

*

Karl saw him almost immediately. On the left side of the church as he faced it. Some way back, under a large tree, leaning on it casually. He was in jeans and a black jacket, which Karl hadn't expected from a detective.

But where was Katie? There was a black car in the driveway, but it was empty. And there was a sign in the rear passenger window advertising horse-riding lessons, so he doubted it was the detective's anyway. He wondered where the man's ride was, then figured he might not have one. He might be planning to call a police car. But where was Katie?

Karl stopped at the end of the main driveway. The man raised a hand and rubbed his forehead. Then gave him a thumbs up and waved him over.

'Where's my wife?' Karl shouted.

'In my car. Back this way. I didn't want to park on main roads.'

Karl continued walking. His eyes ran over every tree, bench, nook and cranny, seeking armed cops ready to pounce. But he tried to relax, because by entering the church he'd passed the point of no return. If they were out there, hidden, it was game over already. His best bet was to go quietly.

He stopped thirty feet away. The guy was in the tree's shadow. Big guy, grey buzz cut. There was something familiar about his face, but he couldn't place it.

'Where's the car?'

'Where's Liz Grafton?' the guy asked.

'She didn't want to come. She's going to hand herself in in her own way. She didn't want to do this without help.'

The man looked upset about that. He tried to hide it behind a smile, but the truth was in his eyes. 'That's good. So we need your statement, Karl. Shall we go?' He pointed behind him, deeper into the church grounds, beyond thick trees. Something was wrong here.

'I'm not coming in until my wife's with me.'

'She's waiting. Don't keep a pregnant woman waiting.'

He sounded impatient now, almost angry. Karl didn't move. Something was definitely off. He wished he'd listened to Liz. The detective put a hand into his pocket.

'Let me see your ID.'

The guy pulled a warrant card. It couldn't be scrutinised from this distance, as the guy well knew. But Karl wasn't about to step closer.

When he realised Karl wasn't going to step up to check the ID, he slotted it away and laughed.

Right then, Karl heard the crunch of gravel and turned. A police car had appeared from behind the corner of the church, slowly, like a cruising shark. So, the detective had called in backup after all.

'You lied to...' he said as he turned back, ready to shout at the detective. But the guy was gone.

'Karl!'

Katie's voice. He turned back to the police car. Katie was there with two police officers.

'Stay right there, Karl,' one said, and both quickly made their way towards him.

'Katie, what's going on?' he asked as the cops grabbed him, forced him down onto his front, and cuffed him.

'Karl Seabury, I am arresting you on suspicion of murder—'

Katie pushed past and kissed his head. She was crying. 'Are you hurt, Karl?'

'You do not have to say anything, but it may harm your defence—'

Her hands ran over his face, neck, shoulders. He closed his eyes, overcome with shame.

*

'Oh shit, this went wrong,' Dave said. Brad looked past him, out the driver's window, and saw Mick running across the grass. Alone. And he did not look happy. He slammed into the fence and started to climb.

Brad climbed into the back and opened the sliding door. Mick burst inside, knocking Brad back. Mick's face was pure anger and there was spit on his lips.

'Fucking piece of shit!' he roared as he slammed the door. The spit flew from his lips.

'What happened?' Brad asked as he climbed back into his seat. Mick slapped the metal floor hard three times.

'Drive. Fucking reverse. You should have been parked the other way anyway.'

Dave and Brad looked at him. 'What went wrong?' Dave asked.

'Turn. Back the way you came in. Fucking go.'

'Mick, what's—?'

Mick kicked the back of his seat, hard. 'Fucking go.'

He was clearly in no mood for explanations, so they had no choice but to get moving. Dave Y-turned in the road and headed back towards the gate they'd entered through. Mick kicked his seat again to urge him to go faster. Brad looked around and saw Mick pull out his gun before pulling down his woollen balaclava. Which meant this wasn't over yet.

'Bitch wife of his called the fucking cops. The police got him. They'll go to Carr Street station probably, which means coming east past us. Stop at the end, at the junction.'

'What are you planning, Mick?' Brad asked.

'Balaclavas on unless you want your faces all over the news.'

Brad and Dave looked at each other, panic rising. Dave's foot eased off the accelerator.

Mick slapped the back of his head. 'Faster. To the end.'

'What the fuck, Mick?' Brad said. 'The cops have him? I hope you're not—'

'We are. We fucking are.'

*

Katie managed to convince the police to allow her to sit in the back with Karl as he was transported. He was handcuffed behind his back, which made sitting awkward, but this was a guy who might have killed a man earlier that day, so the two officers were taking no chances. They called the station to report their plan: bringing the suspect in. They also warned her not to touch him, so they sat ten inches apart, which was the most awkward part of all.

Katie didn't speak until the car turned right out of the church grounds.

'I got you help, Karl. A solicitor. As soon as we know where they're taking us, I'm to call him, and he'll come immediately.'

He was overcome with immense embarrassment. Not because of where he sat, but because Katie was with him. Her plan for this afternoon had been to get her nails done, not accompany her husband to jail.

'I'm sorry.'

'Don't think about that just yet. You can do the begging for forgiveness part later. Did you kill that man?'

He couldn't believe she'd asked him. But he understood why. When he said no, the look she gave him was all he could ask for at this moment: belief.

'I don't know what happened. He came after us. Two of them. One is dead, but I don't know what happened.'

She rubbed her face. 'This is a mess. Where is the one who caused all this trouble? That gangster's wife?'

'She didn't come—'

'Abandoned you after what you did for her, eh?'

'No, no. She's planning to hand herself in. But she didn't want to do it like this.'

Katie looked at the policeman, not wanting to give away any more in front of them. 'Look, let's wait until the solicitor arrives. Let's just talk about you. Are you okay?'

He saw the two cops exchange a glance. 'No talking at all,' one said.

Katie leaned her head on Karl's shoulder, but the driver warned her to keep away. When she didn't move, he started to slow the car. So, Katie moved reluctantly. She reached behind him to grab his cuffed hands, to let him know everything was going to be okay.

*

'This is damn madness,' Dave said. 'I don't want any part of this.'

'You'll get part of a prison cell,' Mick shouted at him. 'You fuck this up, you're both going down for twenty. I'll fucking see to it.'

Brad said: 'Mick, he's right. You can't—'

'There!' Mick bellowed, and pointed out of the passenger window.

The Vito was at the junction, poking its nose out. Way down where there was a school and a 20 mph zone, they saw a police car come into view. Four hundred feet away. It took the roundabout and turned in their direction.

Seeing this, Mick clapped both men on the shoulders. 'Right, back up a hundred feet. This is how it goes down…'

*

'It's done,' Danny said from his place sixty feet behind the police car. 'Can we go now?'

'Wait until the station. Think of it as escorting a date home.'

So they drove on, but the station was never going to happen. Just seconds later, a van burst from a side road on the right. Too fast. Intentionally, Danny realised, a moment before the vehicle crossed the westbound lane and struck the patrol car like an anvil. There was a screech of rending metal and shattering glass and the smaller vehicle was shunted to the left as if fired from a slingshot.

'My God!' Liz yelled. 'It's them.'

*

Katie was looking at Karl, and Karl was looking at his knees, so neither of them saw the impact coming. The noise was tremendous, but dulled, as if taking place underwater. It all seemed surreal. He was thrown into his door as the car was whipped aside from under him, like crockery remaining in place as a tablecloth is pulled away.

The next moment, Katie crashed into him. The car was stalled, half on the road and half on the pavement. The driver's side of the front was a convoluted mess of curved and jagged metal, poking into the driver, and he was screaming in pain. The airbags had been shredded. The only flesh Karl could see was the back of his neck, red with blood. Just feet away was the battered front of a larger vehicle.

Katie was beside Karl. She was leaning against her door, clutching her belly and looking at it in fear.

'You okay?' he asked, surprised he'd been able to. He must not be hurt somehow.

She nodded. Unhurt also, which was a miracle. But she was still clutching her belly. When he put his hand there also, it seemed to jolt her out of shock, and she let out a noisy breath of relief.

*

Brad was an experienced man, familiar with blood and violence, and he was able to kick into autopilot to force his mind and body to react and do what needed to be done. But here, listening to the screech of tyres from stopping vehicles and the yells of onlookers, he froze. It had all happened so quickly, too quickly for him to actually think about the consequences. And now they were here, and all bridges were burned behind him, and the only two things he could do were sit numb and think about how they were all fucked now Mick had pushed them a million steps too far.

Mick, though, had entered autopilot mode all too easily. Brad heard the sliding door grate open, and then Mick appeared in his view through the windscreen. Pistol in hand. He yanked open the back door of the police van, and ducked in to yank Seabury out, who fell to his knees on the glass-littered tarmac. Mick then pulled open Brad's door.

'Get him. The fucker's wife's here, too.'

Brad got his arse in gear. He jumped out, grabbed Seabury's handcuff chain and hauled him to his feet, then lifted him and dumped him into the back of the Vito. Brad clambered in after him, in time to see Mick roughly yanking Seabury's wife out of the car.

'Take her.'

Brad got out again and took her arm. She was screaming. He really didn't want to hurt the man's wife, especially when he saw she was pregnant, but they were all in now. Maybe there would be no reason to hurt her, and she could be let go later. For now, though, all loose ends needed tying up.

Mick had gone. He heard another door open.

'I'm fucking driving,' he heard Mick shout. He had gone around to swap places with Dave, and Brad's attention was diverted as he looked through his window to see Mick pulling Dave out of the driver's seat.

Even as he realised his mistake, Seabury was taking full advantage of it.

Brad felt a heavy weight crash into him, and down he went.

'Run, Katie!' Seabury shouted.

Brad tried to stand, but took another blow, a kick in the ribs that bought the Seabury guy another second or two. When the vibrating world calmed, he saw the woman running away down the street.

'Get him back inside, you dickhead,' Mick yelled as Brad saw him bolting in pursuit of the fleeing woman.

'Leave her, Mick, cops coming,' Dave shouted after him.

Dave had hold of Seabury. To reclaim some pride, Brad yanked the guy out of Dave's grip and threw him back inside the van. He got in. Seabury tried to sit up, so Brad grabbed his hair in both hands. The handcuffs meant there was no block to come. So, he took his sweet time pulling back his knee and driving it forward, hard into the guy's face. When he let go of the guy's sweaty hair, Seabury collapsed. His head made a nice dong on the metal floor. Brad slammed the door just as Dave jumped back into the driver's seat.

Dave started the stalled engine.

'Wait for him,' Brad said.

Dave started to reverse and turn the van in the road. 'Fuck that. He can meet us later.'

Brad slapped Dave's shoulder. 'No. Wait.'

*

Seabury's wife lost serious ground every second. Scared, hurt, and holding her fragile belly, she was helpless.

Mick was upon her in seconds.

She whirled and an arm came out defensively. Her hand caught him on the side of the face. Not a painful blow, but his balaclava was whipped away like a magician's cloth.

In that moment, he did something that would haunt his dreams. With his face bared for all to see, he froze with shock. Like a swimmer who'd dived into frigid water, his brain and body locked up.

She tore from his grasp and ran, and he did not follow. Could not. Some way ahead, as he watched but was unable to move, two heroes took her and guided her away, into a shop doorway, and she was lost.

He turned and ran. Back, away. The going was hard, and his heart thumped like never before. Despite the gun still locked in his fist, fear rattled through him. He reached the van and by that time was light-headed. He dragged himself in and slammed the door, and only when it was shut did his breath explode in a noisy rasp.

*

'Think those two cops are okay?'

'Don't give a shit,' Mick said. 'Get him inside while I check this out.'

But Mick did give a shit. Every criminal in the word could drop dead and the world would rejoice, but the guys in the car were cops, and Mick was a cop. Not enough common ground to warrant buying flowers but he hoped both guys were okay.

He paced outside the warehouse as he scoured the Internet for news of his name. Seabury's bitch wife had somehow overheard his plan to meet her husband at the church, and no doubt his face had been captured by onlookers, so there was no chance now of coming out of this one unscathed. But it didn't matter. He would be a ghost soon. Seabury would give up Grafton's bitch in the next few minutes, prompted by a pair of pliers, and then they would go get her. Then he would sterilise his house and he'd be gone. There was no stopping that, but his plane ticket was now a useless scrap of paper because Seabury's wife knew enough to burn him. But that didn't matter, either. There were other ways of getting out of the country. He needed to be at the coast before the news broadcast his face.

The abandoned warehouse had whitewashed windows and gaping holes in the corrugated iron roof where noisy pigeons crowded along the rafters. It was empty apart from a scattering of wooden crates, vast amounts of trash and the remains of components from fairground rides.

Seabury was in a wooden chair in the centre of the littered floor with his hands cuffed behind his back and a second pair of cuffs securing the first to the chair's backrest. When Mick entered, he heard Brad telling Seabury his only way to survive this was to give up the girl, walk away and keep his mouth shut.

'I gave him that choice already and he fucked it up,' Mick said from the doorway, in a deep voice.

He approached Seabury. Dave and Brad stood back. He stood five feet away and folded his arms. The pliers were in his hand, on show, impossible to ignore. He had his cap pulled low, the same one he'd worn when he'd confronted Seabury on the building site.

'Where's my wife?' Seabury asked. His voice didn't sound scared, although his eyes were. Fear overridden by worry for his loved one. They darted everywhere.

'She got away, actually. Lucky girl. Right now she's probably in a hospital, talking to my guys.' He saw the puzzled look on Seabury's face and laughed.

'The police, Seabury, the police.'

Still utter confusion: Seabury hadn't put two and two together yet. Mick made a big show of flicking off his hat.

The transformation on Seabury's face was magical to watch. His eyes grew wide. His jaw quivered. He stumbled over whatever line he tried to speak. Mick liked the idea that Seabury had been half-expecting a miraculous rescue by Detective Chief Inspector McDevitt. It made his little reveal that much more beautiful.

'Don't abandon all hope yet,' Mick said.

He had expected Seabury to latch onto this, but he didn't. Instead, he simply asked 'Why?' and Mick realised he was talking about Grafton. He was angry that a nonentity like this fucker had dared to ask. That he believed he held enough importance to expect an answer.

'Why did I kill that bastard? You don't get the right to ask that.' He wanted to smash him, but he didn't. He took a step back and unzipped his jacket, unbuttoned the top of his shirt.

Seabury looked at the wound, and Mick could see the puzzlement on his face. Mick fingered the old injury. One misshapen right collarbone and a ragged semi-circular scar the size of a baby's fist.

'It's deeper than you think. Even if it wasn't, people have killed for less,' Mick said. He tapped the wound with the pliers. 'I didn't let them fix it. I wanted the scar. A reminder. Kept me motivated. It's all I have, apart from a few fucking routines that would make me look like a raving lunatic but keep me fucking sane, ironically.

'You think it's overkill. You don't understand, of course. You're not meant to. You aren't part of this. You got involved because you wanted to help a woman. And you're still alive right now because I'm giving you a chance to help another woman. Your wife this time. You have no idea how many cops are involved in this. They can get to your wife. The moment I give the order. My nightmare continues, day after day, but yours can end right now. I said don't abandon all hope, right? Because you have a kill switch for this whole sorry fiasco, Seabury. When the shit raining down on you becomes too much, you can go ahead and press that kill switch by telling me where Grafton's bitch wife is—'

'I don't know,' Karl blurted. 'I honestly don't know.' He struggled in the chair, trying to break either it or the handcuffs. He knew it was futile, because the three men would be upon him before he got to his feet. But he tried, anyway, because a drowning man will clutch even at the smallest straw floating within reach. He succeeded in toppling the chair, but the big detective grabbed him before it could crash down. He was set carefully upright once more. He smelled bacon on the guy, which somehow made this whole thing seem even more wrong. It was a reminder that he was human, that he ate, slept, lived a normal life.

The detective stepped back. 'Don't say a word yet. I'll let that one go because you didn't know any better. But not another word, because you only get one chance. A woman is going into that very chair you're in, and you get to pick. Liz Grafton, or Katie Seabury. Do you understand? If you don't tell me where Grafton's bitch is, or you lie about it, I'll send my man to go fetch your wife right now. I'll rip you apart with these pliers and force-feed you to her. Tell me you understand that so we have no confusion.'

Karl nodded. He looked at Varsity, and a short black man he didn't know. Both men looked concerned. They didn't look comfortable with what was happening, which made Karl realise that these two henchmen weren't as unhinged. But he also realised that concern *proved* he was a lunatic. Right then he had no doubt that he would not leave this warehouse alive. And that Katie was in grave danger.

'Good,' the detective said. 'So the only word I want to hear from you is a name. Liz, or Katie. The urge to beg must be great, but you need to bite it back. So, calm down and think. You've got that ability, because there's no pain yet, is there? I'm standing back, and nothing's happened to you yet, the brain isn't going wild with shock. So, use it to think. Think of your wife. And I don't mean think of her lonely without you, bringing up that baby alone. I mean think of her in this chair. You slumped beside her, dead. And her being force-fed little torn-up bits of your flesh. You go ahead and take ten seconds to think.'

Karl flicked his eyes around: at the rusty old shutter, at the high windows and a doorless office at the back where there was a ground-floor window. His brain threw up escape scenarios, but they all depended on his being out of this chair which didn't look likely. And he didn't know where he was. He had been in the dark in the back of a van, unconscious for most of the journey, and they could have driven him anywhere. There might not be a soul around for miles. He might not even be in London.

He realised he'd been wasting time when Mick said: 'Three, two, one,' and stepped forward with the pliers held up.

Karl leaned back, and screamed for help.

A ringing phone froze everyone. Karl raised his hopes as the detective pulled out his mobile and looked at it with a worried frown.

'You get another sixty seconds, Karl. Dave, with me.'

The detective and the black man went into the office. Karl saw him pull out a seat from the table and sit just out of view. He could see the man's feet up on the table. His phone flew into shot and was clumsily caught by the black man.

Karl looked at Varsity, who looked uncomfortable. He knew his eyes were pleading.

'You should just tell the guy what he wants,' Brad said.

'You should tell your boss that you can't get away with this. The police will know everything because my wife will tell them.' A threat, of sorts, but he had the feeling that hurting him was the detective's domain alone. This guy wouldn't lay a finger on him without permission.

Varsity held Karl's look for a moment, then looked at the office, and then at the entrance, the glorious daylight and freedom beyond.

He went to a button on the wall and pressed it, then jogged over to the office. The metal shutter started to lower. It rumbled and rattled and moved slowly, and the square of daylight began to shrink, and with it Karl's hopes of freedom.

Varsity walked into the office and said: 'Hey, we still need to work on a plan to—'

CHAPTER SIXTY-FOUR

MICK

Mick's raised finger and a sneer cut him off. Brad looked on in puzzlement. Mick was watching Dave, and Dave was pacing with Mick's phone to his ear.

Then Dave said: 'Listen carefully. I've got your man's phone. Which means I've got your man. He tried to stick his nose into our business. If you don't want him cut to pieces just like Grafton, then you get fifty grand and leave it at Nelson's Column in one hour.' He hung up.

Brad shut the door and said: 'What the fuck was that?'

'That was some kind of weird twisted shit he got me to do,' Dave said, tossing Mick back his phone.

'My people will suspect I'm involved,' Mick said. 'My detective sergeant just left me a voicemail. Very distraught. Knows I was set to meet Seabury, and then the shit hit the fan. They'll soon suspect I'm involved in the kidnapping. But they're not certain of anything yet, so this will muddy the waters. Maybe now it looks like I was going to bring Seabury in, but the bad guys turned up and took us all hostage. It gives us time. Time to get the bitch, and time to sterilise our houses and run for the hills.'

'Run?' Dave said. 'And burn down a house I just bought? You're joking, right?'

Brad said: 'But what about the plan to get the cops off my back? How can that work now?'

'It can't any more.'

'Jesus. Because you're burned.'

'Wouldn't work even if I wasn't. Because you are.' Mick explained all about the About.me webpage, and the dead dealer, Rapid. 'They don't yet know about your alibi for the night Rapid was killed, but that's just a matter of time. Alerts are going out for you even now. The police are probably talking to your boyfriend right this minute. You are burned, just like me. So, there's no interview, and there's no going home.'

In the shocked silence that followed, Dave said: 'Er, but not me, right? They've got nothing on me.'

'Oh, thanks,' Brad said, which made Mick laugh. But he stopped a moment later when they heard a monstrous crash out in the warehouse.

CHAPTER SIXTY-FIVE

KARL

The shutter's downward rumble increased. It was two feet from clanging shut when Karl realised he was hearing something else.

Engine, he thought.

The shutter burst inward as if a bomb had exploded just outside. With a screeching bang it tore free from its runners and flew into the warehouse, and behind it was a vehicle.

At first he thought it was the van that had smashed into the police car, but it was a different colour. Sky blue, literally. It roared into the warehouse with the shutter folded over its front, held there by force. And it was racing right at him.

He jerked his whole body to the left and tipped the chair, hoping to God that he cleared the vehicle's path. He landed hard on his side and felt the rush of air as the van blew past him, mere feet away. He got a half second glance at the driver: a guy he didn't know but whose face was a mask of joy. Karl knew then this was no bizarre accident.

The van did not slow as it bore down on the office just ten feet away. Beyond the powering vehicle, he saw the door open and Mick standing there, locked in shock. A nanosecond later the van hit the wall right where the office door was and stopped dead with a massive clang from the shutter. The driver had blocked the doorway.

The passenger door crashed open, and Liz leaped out. Karl didn't believe she was real until she bent over him and started yanking at his shoulder to make him stand.

'Tied to it,' he yelled.

She knelt behind him and found the handcuffs.

'Don't back up!' he heard Liz yell to the driver – she had obviously realised that the shutter, pressed against the doorway, was keeping the animals inside.

From this position Karl could see right under the van. He saw a sliver of the doorway. No more than eight inches right at the bottom, but enough to allow the passage of a man. And that was what he saw now: Varsity, down on his front, feeding himself out of the office.

'Back up when I say,' Liz screamed.

'Where's my wife?' Karl asked, feeling his shoulders jerk as she tried to break the chair to free him.

She didn't answer. She stood, and for a moment he thought she was going to give up. Leave him here and flee.

Instead, she raised a bare foot and stomped. Right onto his wrist; it hurt like hell as he heard a snap. A snap like wood. He had been straining to lean forward, and now felt the resistance evaporate. The slat holding him right in place had snapped, and he was free – as free as you could be while still handcuffed and in the presence of killers.

CHAPTER SIXTY-SIX

MICK

At that moment Mick was in the upstairs office, having rushed for the stairs while Brad dropped to his front to crawl under the shutter.

He had heard the initial crash, figured some vehicle had rushed the shutter, and had got as far as the doorway when the shutter slammed the walls either side, forced there hard by the vehicle. The impact was strong enough to crack the doorframe and send a spiderweb of cracks along one wall; dirt and paint flecks from the shutter rained all over him and the booming clang rattled his ears. He knew this was a rescue attempt.

He had rushed up the stairs: the door was locked. Three hard shoulder blows killed the lock. At the far end of the upstairs office was a window that he rushed to. It was simply a sheet of clear plastic, no handle, not designed to open. Mick dislodged a corner with a heavy kick, grabbed the edge and pushed. The whole sheet peeled away like the top of a tin can, nice and neat. He watched it fall and hit the top of the van, eight feet below.

Like something from a cartoon, he stuck his head out in time to see the final inches of a leg slipping inside the open back doors. Then hands reach out to slam the doors. A moment after that, Brad rolled out from underneath. He was halfway to his feet when the van shifted backwards, knocking him over again. Brad rolled aside, barely avoiding the wheels as the van reversed towards the exit. It was halfway there by the time the shutter, with nothing to hold it up, toppled away from the office door with a noise like thunder.

More thunder as Mick's Hi-Point C-9 pistol fired. Half its ten-round magazine gone in seconds. The van swerved left and right. He heard the clang of metal striking metal at high speed, but no tyre popped, the windscreen didn't shatter, and nobody screamed in pain. Three or four direct hits maybe, but all to no good.

The van's engine whined as it J-turned, and he found himself aiming at its blank metal rear. He continued to aim, five shots remaining, but he didn't fire because the bitch was in the back. What he wanted most in the world was to kill that bitch with his bare hands, and the very last thing he wanted was for her to escape. But at least the latter would allow him another chance at the former, and that wouldn't happen if a fluke bullet sprayed her across the interior of the van.

Beyond the gun's sights, he watched the van exit and vanish.

CHAPTER SIXTY-SEVEN

KARL

The van had a single bench seat against each side wall, and Liz and Karl took one each. All windows were curtained, and Karl wondered where the hell he'd been brought. The rough ride made him think: somewhere remote.

'They might go after my wife. I need to get to her,' he called out.

After a series of sharp manoeuvres over rough land, the drive became smooth and the speed dropped. He heard other vehicles. So, not the desolation of the country, then. He moved to the back window as the van took a turn and parted the curtains with his face as his hands were still cuffed. Between two sand-coloured buildings he glimpsed moored yachts and water which vanished as the turn was completed.

'Where the hell are we? Where are we going?' He knew his head was still fuzzy from the wild events of the last hour, but surely they couldn't be at the coast.

'Limehouse,' the driver said. He was a heavyset guy with ginger hair and a ginger beard, heavily muscled shoulders under his T-shirt.

Karl relaxed a little. Limehouse was close to St Dunstan's, so he hadn't blacked out for long. He figured Katie might still be near the crash location.

'Are we going back to the crash?' he asked.

'Don't be silly, pal,' the driver said. Karl figured this was Danny.

'We've got to go back. My wife might still be there, so—'

'She ran away, mate. She's safe. The people who did this got the hell out of there when they lost her. If she's still around there, she's with the police, my friend. They're all over that place by now.'

'She's not safe with the police! That guy was a cop. He was that detective, McDevitt. They can get to her. I need to find out where she is.'

'Calm down, my friend. Yeah, we saw him. He might be a high-ranking cop, but he's shown his face, so he's on the run now and can't get anywhere near her.'

'No, he said there's others—'

'I doubt that, pal. I know enough crooked cops. They steal money from criminals and they hide evidence and stuff, but what they don't do is kill witnesses in custody. So, this guy is probably a cop taking the law into his own hands because Ron beat the system. So, she's fine. We can find your missus later. For now your priority is to get away from this area because they'll throw a net across it. And mine is to get that girl there away from here.'

Liz. He'd forgotten about her for the moment. She sat facing him, but looking down at the floor, hands on her lap, palms up.

'Are you okay?' he asked. And then he realised she wasn't looking at the floor. Her hand. The paw print tattoo. It was now an indelible reminder that her journey had been cut short.

Danny took a quick turn, pulled in somewhere and stopped.

'Lizzy? You hurt?'

Karl knew then that this guy would do anything for her. Including making sure she was safe before he even thought about finding Katie.

She didn't look up when she said: 'This isn't because Ron won his trial. It isn't a police officer taking the law into his own hands.' She wiped her cheek, removing a tear. 'This was an inside job. My husband was betrayed by people he trusted. People who were our friends.'

CHAPTER SIXTY-EIGHT

MICK

Mick moved away from the others to make a call. He spoke for thirty seconds, and then slotted his device away and returned, sitting on the chair Seabury had been handcuffed to.

'What a fucking day so far,' he said, rubbing his face. 'And it's barely lunchtime.'

'So now what?' Dave said. 'This is over, right? That's it.'

'Easy for you to say,' Brad moaned. 'I can't just go home.'

'Well, I'm sorry about that, Brad. But what am I supposed to do, go on the run as well? I've got a wife—'

'And I've got a bloody partner, too. But I—'

'No, it's not over,' Mick cut in. 'They're not safe yet. Didn't you recognise that van?'

'Danny Mall,' Brad said.

'Your old friend.'

'He isn't my friend.'

'Not now, for sure. The bitch had the chance to go to the police, yet she called one of her husband's people. What's that say to you?'

Neither Dave nor Brad had an answer.

'She won't go to the cops yet,' Mick said. 'So, we have time. I think I know the plan. Seabury gave it away. He said she was planning to hand herself in in her own way. Gold. Her husband's solicitor. That's where they're going. It was her plan all along.'

'You mentioned him earlier. But you'd never get there in time.'

For some reason, Mick latched onto Dave's use of the term *you'd*. Not *we'd*. 'I did mention it earlier, and I got a guy I know to watch his office. He went to court and looks like being there all day. I don't think the bitch has contacted him yet. If they're going there, I think her plan is to just turn up on his doorstep. Where we'll be waiting.'

Brad said: 'His office is in the middle of Notting Hill Gate. I can't see them risking exposure on the way there. Besides, he might not go back to the office.'

'Grafton wouldn't be seen dead in a busy high street solicitor's office, sitting next to a car thief in a baseball cap. I think they'll go to his house after hours.'

'I want no part,' Dave said. 'We should cut and run. This revenge thing of yours is getting out of hand, Mick.'

'You're not home and dry, Dave, because there's a man out there who can burn you, too.'

They glared at each other. The realisation sinking in, Dave said: 'You?'

'Me. We're in this till the end. All of us. Look, I don't want to threaten you two. We're friends. But this is a whole new big ass ballgame now. I'm very far from being in a celebratory mood, and we all celebrate together, or we all go down together. But if we do this, and it works, I'll make sure you're both spotless. I need an answer.'

*

A few minutes later, they were driving out of the warehouse grounds. Dave had refused to ride in the Vito, claiming a jaunt on his bike would clear his head, so he was following behind on the Suzuki.

Three minutes after that, both vehicles hit a junction. Green light. The Vito went straight across, heading west, as planned, but the bike stalled and got caught on red. Brad slowed the Vito and looked in his rear-view mirror. He saw the light change to green; and watched the tiny vehicles 500 feet back begin to move again. But Dave's bike swung a fast left at the junction, not west.

Stalling the bike had been a trick. Dave was abandoning them. Cutting them loose. Running. And when Brad looked at Mick, the detective was staring at his own wing mirror. But Mick said nothing.

That was when Brad knew they were about to play a very different ballgame.

CHAPTER SIXTY-NINE

KARL

'His name is Bradley Smithfield. I heard he was some kind of enforcer. I know Ron had people like that. But the Brad I knew was my bodyguard, and a maintenance man. He helped with the house. He fixed my dressing table. He used to give me a lift sometimes.'

She rubbed her face. 'He always seemed like a nice man. I mean, I know what he did for my husband. Threatening people, collecting money. But that wasn't the man I knew. He stopped coming round a few years ago. It was that robbery at our nightclub. Ron's associate suspected some of Ron's men because they knew about the meeting he was having that night. Ron didn't want to look like he was protecting people, so he fired a few of his guys. Bradley and a friend of his, David, I think, were suspected. But I never believed it, and Ron said he wasn't sure who did the robbery. I never saw Bradley after that. I heard he went straight. How could he be involved in this? What did Ron do to make Bradley want to hurt him? Is this revenge for something? For being fired?'

'Don't beat yourself up about it,' Danny said. 'And we don't know anything for sure yet.'

'This is my fault. I should have told you earlier.'

'Fault how?' Karl asked.

'If I'd said something, to both of you, we could have…'

'Not avoided this, if that's what you mean,' Danny said. 'None of this is your fault.'

'How can we go to Ron's solicitor now, though? If a close friend of Ron's can do this, how do we know who we can trust?'

'Gold is on our level,' Danny said. He looked round at her, and in his face Karl saw something that he didn't like. He got the feeling the guy was hiding something.

'I live in Woodford these days,' Danny said, eyes on the road again. 'It's only five miles away. We can eat and clean up. We'll go and work on our plan. And see if we can find out a bit about where your wife is, eh, pal?'

There was something in his tone: Karl knew the man was glad they'd got off the subject of Bradley Smithfield.

CHAPTER SEVENTY

MICK

Brad stopped in a secluded corner of the library car park. Mick stared at the library for a few seconds, trance-like.

'We haven't got all day,' Brad said.

'Tim's still got an overdue book out from there,' Mick said. 'Do libraries still have those amnesty days?'

Brad shook his head in disbelief. 'Mick, we should—'

'Half an hour maximum,' Mick cut in. He kicked his door wide. 'Any longer means I'm in handcuffs: so, get away and have a good life.'

He got out and for a moment stood and thought about how he'd failed himself when Seabury's wife knocked off his mask. The embarrassment was so intense it gave him an instant headache. He got out, crossed a field, and climbed a fence into his backyard. He opened the door and crept into his own house like a burglar.

He checked out the front window. No strange cars. None of his colleagues' cars. The who and why and how of the road traffic collision would still be a source of confusion, so he still had time before someone worked it out. But not much. He got changed: elastic-waisted jeans, a zip fleece and running shoes. All black, of course. Stakeout gear needed to be comfortable. His put his bomber jacket back on and got to work.

He started with the books from his bedroom cabinet. Old paperbacks from the YMCA shop where Tim volunteered. He ripped out page after page and tossed them around like confetti. The clothing was next, hauled from drawers and wardrobes and scattered everywhere.

The fluid came last. Splashed all over. He left the kitchen until last. Five feet from the back door, he grabbed a roll of kitchen towels and pulled a lighter from his pocket.

'Brad Smithfield's alibi for the night Rapid was killed was perfect indeed.'

Mick froze. And slowly turned.

Standing at the back door was DI Gondal.

'He was being interviewed by police about the murder of Rocker,' Gondal continued. 'Just a simple follow-up interview, supposedly at his own house. But I just found out who conducted the interview. DCI Mick McDevitt. And he was all alone with Smithfield for a couple of hours, right around the time Rapid got stabbed in the brain in a stinking alleyway.'

Mick's eyes cast left, to the worktop loaded with money boxes. Eighteen filled sweetie jars that he and Tim had filled together. Just for a moment, he wondered if money could get him out of this one, because he really didn't want to be forced into a different action. He had ninety grand: Gondal would take two years to earn an amount like that.

'Did you put Smithfield up to it? Killing the dealer? Did you just cover it up? Maybe in return for helping him beat the murder of Rocker? You knew that the dealer was selling Buzz, didn't you? Was that why he had to die?'

'Don't say another word about that,' Mick hissed at him.

'Okay. Try this. I thought about what Ramirez's mother had said. About the police going into her attic. I looked into it. Turned out she was talking about when he was suspected of stabbing a guy in Kensington five years ago. You mentioned that investigation.

But you didn't mention that you personally oversaw the search of his house.'

So, he knew. Mick felt his heartbeat increase with the realisation that he wasn't buying passage out of this problem. And then he became aware of the lighter in his hand, and the flammable mess everywhere, and the stench of petrol that was impossible to ignore.

'I was praying I had it wrong, so I dug deeper,' Gondal said. 'I learned that you'd requested a couple of PNC searches. One was this morning. Registration plate for a Suzuki motorbike registered to eighteen-year-old Darren John Crowthorne. An hour after your search, he was riding to college when he was knocked off his bike and then ran over again. Twenty-five-year-old Volkswagen Transporter, but with plates cloned from a five-year-old version of the vehicle.'

But the point of no return was still ahead, and there could still be a way out of this. Mick's brain cycled through options. His jaw started to throb.

'But that's not the scary search,' Gondal continued. 'There was also a PNC search you requested en route to the Grafton murder scene last night. I spoke to the operator you called, and she said DCI McDevitt had spotted a couple of guys racing their vehicles along a street. Basic vehicle search. The results had come back clean. Just a pair of guys comparing dick sizes, no big deal. That's what you said to her. But the names are a big deal. Harold Bond, who was viciously attacked in his home that same night. And Karl Seabury.'

Mick's shoulders relaxed, and he let out a long breath. Gondal took a step forward.

'You have to go in,' Gondal said.

'Why, Manzoor, why?' Mick said, hanging his head.

'Because you lied, Mac. You swore to fairness, integrity, diligence and impartiality. You remember that oath? That badge is a lie. Your life is a lie.'

Mick raised his head, but now laid his eyes upon the ceiling. 'This shouldn't have happened, Manzoor. Shouldn't have happened.'

'But it did, Mac. It did. You chose this path, but part of me understands why. But it ends here.'

Now Mick's eyes dropped to his colleague. 'No, Manzoor, you shouldn't have come here. That shouldn't have happened. I guess I taught you too well.'

Gondal took a step forward, into the kitchen. Into Mick's space, which calmed the waves in his mind. He knew the feeling too well: acceptance of the inevitable.

But Gondal misread it: 'The right choice, Mac. It's over. We'll drive to the station together, but I'll let you walk inside alone. No handcuffs. I'll let you do it that way because, God knows, you've had enough heartache. Old wounds will be opened about—'

'I told you not to bring that up,' Mick said quietly.

'I know, Mac, I know. You returned to work and it was the first thing you said. Nobody is to mention what happened. Nobody is to talk about it. We stick to talking shop. But I think we're past that now. Is all of this because y—'

Gondal stopped as the kitchen roll flew at him. He put a hand up to deflect it, shocked by the attack. In that time, Mick had covered the five feet between them. He landed a hard headbutt, right into the nose, and Gondal dropped straight down onto his knees. Then Mick had the knife in his hand. A big guy with a knife, and an overweight man on his knees was no contest.

Mick grabbed Gondal's hair at the back and pulled him forward, into the blade.

'*I* killed that fucking cunt. For playing a part in it.' Mick dragged Gondal deeper into the kitchen and dropped him. His colleague's blood began to mix with the petrol on the lino. Gondal rolled onto his front, hands clutching his neck as he tried to get his knees under him.

Mick said: 'When you get to Heaven, tell God you said the wrong thing to the wrong man, okay? He'll roll his eyes and wonder why we never learn.'

He picked up the kitchen roll. He stepped into the back doorway.

'By the way, Gondal, here's something else you can take with you. I killed Grafton. There you go. You solved your final case.'

Gondal's fading eyes registered a moment of disbelief. Then the man's movements slowed and stopped, as if his batteries had run out.

Mick lit the kitchen roll aflame, but held it and watched Gondal until the blood pumped no more, until the ragged breathing had stopped. Only when he was sure his long-time partner was beyond the reach of more suffering did he toss the flaming roll.

But at his back fence, ready to climb, he stopped as he felt his heart lurch. He turned, wanting to go back, wanting to drag Gondal out of the burning kitchen, but it was too late. For a moment, he fought back tears, watched black smoke pour out of his doorway, and wished he'd never learned the story of a lucky twelve-year-old Danish girl.

CHAPTER SEVENTY-ONE

KARL

Liz was looking out the back window. At first he thought she was still stressing about Brad Smithfield, but he corrected himself with a mental kick. Her husband was dead, that was what was haunting her. Earlier, under the bridge, he'd seen glimpses of her fortified resolve. But it was gone now. The woman before him was again meek and helpless.

'How did you find me, Liz?' Karl asked.

As she answered, she didn't look away from the outside world. 'We went to the meeting. I wanted to make sure that everything went okay for you with the detective. We followed the police car. And then we followed the van after they took you. Through a window I saw them go into the warehouse office.'

Now she looked at him. 'How is Bradley Smithfield involved in this with a policeman? Why would they work together to kill my husband?'

At that point Danny put the radio on, loud. Probably his effort at deflecting her thoughts. She looked out of the window again. Karl copied, his mind on Katie. As soon as he got to a phone, he would call hospitals and police stations to try to find her.

The van turned down a street lined with terraced houses. The road was slim, made tighter by twin walls of cars parked nose-to-end. Danny barely avoided hitting a neighbour's vehicle as he turned sharply into his driveway.

Karl got out, glad to feel the fresh air. There were people out and about: women talking at gates, kids playing in the road, men fixing cars, just as if it were any old sunny afternoon. He half-expected someone to yell and point, recognising him as a wanted man. But it didn't happen.

He got a shock when the driver's door opened.

Danny was in a wheelchair that took the place of a driver's seat, with braces on his legs that connected to the pedals – no clutch. The vehicle had been converted to allow a disabled guy to pilot it. A mechanical framework around the door was designed to hydraulically lift the wheelchair in and out.

Danny caught him staring. 'Ah, you didn't know. Bet you thought I was a pig for not getting out of the van to help you escape, eh?'

'No, I… er…'

'Don't worry about it.' He set the mechanical framework going. Karl watched as Danny's chair was lifted out of the cab and placed on the ground. He tossed Karl a key. 'Lead on and I'll follow.'

He pegged Danny as one of those self-sufficient guys who abhorred the offer of help. Karl would just offend the guy if he tried to give him a hand getting his wheelchair into the house. So, he stepped up to unlock the door and went inside.

He had expected the house to be modified to accommodate a guy in a wheelchair, but that wasn't the case. It looked like any other house. Maybe it was an ego thing – rather than adapt his surroundings, Danny preferred to push himself and struggle. Or maybe he didn't want visitors to see his house as *different*, that *he* was different. Hell, maybe he believed he'd miraculously wake up one day able to walk. The only concession was the hand grabbers, the sort of tool he had seen street cleaners use to avoiding bending down to retrieve trash. They were everywhere. They were on chairs, on floors, leaning against walls.

Liz said she needed the bathroom and vanished. Danny led Karl into the kitchen, where he proceeded to make tea. He used a grabber to drag the kettle along the worktop, close enough to the edge. There was a lot of overreaching to fill it and to extract mugs from a cupboard. Karl noted that the mugs were in a high cupboard and that Danny pushed the kettle far back along the worktop when finished with it, as if making things hard for himself. He was tempted to help, especially when Danny had trouble hooking a cup, but knew his help would be seen as interference.

They took their teas into the living room to continue their conversation. Again, Karl wanted to help because Danny had trouble wheeling himself. Mug jammed between his legs, he manoeuvred himself slowly to avoid spillage. Karl could hear a shower running upstairs.

Danny caught him looking at a desktop computer in a corner, with a phone nearby. His agitation was unmissable. Danny nodded in that direction. Karl literally ran over to try to find his wife.

CHAPTER SEVENTY-TWO

DAVE

Mick might not be raging around like a psychopath, but he was acting without thinking and that made his actions just as dangerous. The idea to send him to kidnap Seabury's wife, for example. A fucking joke. No way would he have obeyed that order. He would have pretended the girl was out.

Dave's street was lined with semi-detached houses at the end of sloping gardens. A peaceful place, much coveted. Full of old people and respectable couples. He was glad to be home.

He wandered into the living room, and Lucinda sat up sharply. 'What's wrong?' she asked.

Fuck. He had to work on his poker face. He said: 'Nothing,' but knew it was useless. He could feel his clenched jaw, and the sweat on his hands. Sure enough, she got up and asked him what the hell had him worried. He knew there was no point in lying. So he said it. Mick had gone off the rails and he'd quit, got out of there.

'You abandoned him? Did you just run away?'

Sure did, he told her. 'We're done with that. Is there any of that chicken left?'

Earlier, while she was counting the cash again, he'd seen that lovely smile, the one that had drawn him in and made him eventually slip a ring on her finger. Now, as she lifted two handfuls of notes from the bag by her chair and shook them before his face, the expression he saw beyond money was all anger.

'You fucked him over? He'll come for you, you dickhead. I'm not losing this because of your stupidity.'

'He's gone wild. The cops will be after him. No way he can stay out of custody with how mindless he's become. Relax.'

He regretted that final word even as it left his lips.

Lucinda stamped a foot, like a child. 'Relax, you moron? You think he can't fuck us up from jail?'

'He's a bent cop. Cops hate that more than they hate criminals. Even if he gets solitary confinement, they'll pretend to forget to lock his door and let some animals at him. I give him a week in jail, and then he'll be in a grave like his—'

'Go pack a bag,' she cut in. 'We're out of here until this mess is cleaned up.' And she was off, past him, with a barge of her shoulder into his chest.

He rushed up the stairs in pursuit, pleading: calm down, let's think, where would we go, we can't hide away. She grabbed a double handful of his clothing from the wardrobe, tugged it out hard enough to snap the plastic coat hangers. Tossed them at him. 'That'll do you for being stupid.'

He tried to argue, but it did no good. A punch on his arm got him going. He crammed the clothing into a gym bag and took it outside where all was peaceful. This was daft. Mick wouldn't try anything in such a nice area. Hell, he probably wouldn't try anything at all. He had bigger fish to fry.

He threw the bag into their car. Back in the house, he saw Lucinda scooping up the money. She ordered him to grab her clothing and to use the two suitcases in the spare room. All this urgency, and she wanted to pack as if for a month's holiday? He grabbed a double handful of gear from the wardrobe. 'That'll do you for being a bitch.' And he didn't bother with a bag.

He dumped the clothing in the back of the car in a big old mess. Then he heard an engine approaching and scanned the street. A white car with some emblem on the side was cruising down the road. Some tradesman probably. He relaxed. And remembered his bike – parked on the road, where some fool would vandalise it.

As he was wheeling the bike onto the pavement, ready to guide it up the driveway, the van, just thirty feet away, leaped forward with a screech of tyres. Dave turned his head. The vehicle was on the pavement, and you'd need to be pretty stupid to not realise what the plan was here. And to think it didn't involve Mick.

The car hit the bike, forcing it into Dave, sending man and machine bouncing along the road. Dave rolled and stopped and immediately tried to rise, but he was wobbly and his left leg gave way beneath him.

A guy rushed out of the car's passenger side. He wore a balaclava with strands of curly hair poking out from the bottom. Dave didn't recognise him. But just in case there had still been doubt, the knife in the guy's hands cleared away any confusion in Dave's mind. He was done. End of the line. Good night.

The masked man stopped, stabbed and sprinted: two seconds, job done. The car leaped away again like a horse out of the gate, wheels splashing through the blood migrating from Dave's body.

The driver stuck his head out the window as the vehicle roared past him. 'That's for Andy Jones!' he bellowed, louder than the car's engine, and louder than whoever was screaming – Dave's wife, he now knew, because there she was at the door, clutching wads of cash – loud enough for any face that had been drawn to a window.

The realisation set in. Andy Jones. A guy Dave had put in hospital back in the day. Retaliation, the cops would say. What goes around comes around. Just another bad apple getting what he was due. And nothing to do with Mick McDevitt. Little did they know.

His final image before he slipped into another world, or just black oblivion if all that afterlife stuff was bullshit, was of Lucinda pelting towards him, and a swirl of giant snowflakes raining around him. No, not snowflakes, not at all. Money. All that money, blowing down the street because the silly girl had dropped it. A hell to collect.

His last thought: *Good job we didn't change it all into fives.*

CHAPTER SEVENTY-THREE

KARL

One time, when studying electronics at university, Karl and a pal went out for a drink, got drunk, got in a fight with two other guys, and got separated. Karl called hospitals, but they all refused to say whether or not they had his pal as a patient. A safety feature, probably born after some guy who cut someone up got a helpful 'oh yes' from a receptionist and strolled down there with a knife to finish the job. So, he knew he was wasting his time as he called around to try to find Katie. But he did it anyway, and clocked up a big number of polite professionals refusing to give anything away.

He had a list of police stations on Danny's computer screen, too, but he didn't dare risk calling those. At least hospitals didn't trace the calls and wouldn't come to get him with a screaming siren. Besides, he doubted Katie would be in custody. She was a victim, not a perpetrator.

Danny had gone to do something, and when he returned it was to see Karl's shoulders slumped. 'Anyone she could have gone to stay with?' he asked. 'Mum, dad, brother?'

As he said *dad*, Karl was already dialling Peter Davies. Katie's dad was a formidable man, a theatre director and a former drill sergeant, which meant he could still roar like King Kong. Karl was not looking forward to this conversation.

He got an answer machine. For months, Peter had had the same message on his machine: *Not in right now, obviously, so either call Pinnora Playhouse or leave your name and a number and your reason for calling.* But now, the recording Karl got was: *Call my mobile. And only if it's urgent. Back soon. En route to pick someone up.*

Karl had no doubt who that 'someone' was. He called the mobile, and Peter answered quickly.

'Who's this?'

'It's Karl.'

There was the honk of a car horn. Karl imagined the shock of his call almost making Peter crash his car. 'What the hell is going on, Karl? Where are you?'

'Is Katie with you?'

'I just picked her up. Christ, what fun and games, right? Someone tried to kill her. There was a car crash.'

'I know. I was in it. Is she okay?'

'I don't care if you're innocent or guilty, Karl. Get yourself handed in to the police. Before more people get hurt.'

'I am. Soon. But let me speak to Katie.'

'You're not speaking to her. She's asleep in the back. And that's good, seeing as how distraught she is. What the hell is going on, Karl? I'm hearing all this news about three dead people last night, some detective gone missing, another one who's a criminal. No one will tell me anything, and Katie was too full of shock. What have you done, Karl?' His tone was accusing, as if the aforementioned tales of terror were all his doing. Karl Seabury, in league with a bent detective, responsible for murder and mayhem.

'I want to speak to my wife. You don't have all the facts, Peter, and until you do, don't make assumptions, okay? Where's Katie?'

'Katie herself said the police want you, possibly for murder. She claims you're innocent, but a naive wife would say that, wouldn't she?'

'Katie's not naive. I'm innocent and she knows it. Put her on the damn phone, Peter.'

A long pause as Peter considered his options. He decided on: 'I'll get her to call you. But when she gets up on her own. I'm not waking her. Not after this.'

And he hung up. Karl called back, but it went to voicemail. He'd turned off the phone.

'We can't go there yet,' Danny said, as if reading Karl's mind. Karl looked at him in defiance. Danny raised surrendering arms. 'We don't know what that McDevitt guy is doing. If the cops have him, lord knows what he's telling them about you. The police will be watching your wife's dad's house. They're probably following him right now, knowing you'll try to contact your wife. It's safer if you turn up there backed up by a solicitor. You need to just be patient. We all do. We wait for Mr Gold. That's the plan, and if we stick to it, everything will work out okay.'

Karl's glare challenged him. 'My plan for tonight was to cuddle my pregnant wife in front of the TV.'

Liz came downstairs half an hour later, freshly dressed in a pair of tracksuit bottoms and a T-shirt. Although her elegant dress was missing she was finally clean, damp hair in a bun on top of her head. And with red eyes, as if she'd been crying. Karl told her about his earlier chat with Katie, and the plan to hand themselves in to a police station close to her father's house.

Liz had a mobile phone in her hand, which she waved. 'I just spoke to Mr Gold. Bromley is only fifteen miles from here. Twenty-five minute drive.'

'We're going there? He's not coming here? But we're going to Pinner, right?'

She nodded. 'Of course. Mr Gold will take our statements and arrange our surrender. He'll be at home at five o'clock, after court. So, we have three and a half hours to wait.'

'But we go to my wife's dad's house first? *Before* the police. I want to see her for the evening before I do it.'

'Of course.' She actually smiled. Maybe it was relief that all this would finally be over.

'So that's us sorted then,' Danny said. 'We've got a while. Grab a shower, mate. Liz, you must need some food.'

Karl took the hint and left the room. In the preceding half hour, Danny had given him a warning: do not talk about your wife in Liz's presence. She'd lost her husband and shouldn't have someone else's relationship thrust in her face. Karl understood. He understood too that Liz was important to Danny and he wanted to protect her.

He stood under a hot shower for five minutes, needing to refresh his mind. The hot spray felt great, but everything else was wrong. It was wrong to step into another man's bedroom, wrong to wear his clothing, and wrong to use his cutlery.

The food was good, though. Eggs on toast. Three plates on the table, with Danny and Liz waiting for him. Karl was surprised by how fast he attacked the food, and he noticed Liz eating with the same vigour. It reminded him that, bar a slice of toast, he hadn't eaten all day. Even longer for Liz.

Danny used his phone while they ate, and he was the only one who spoke. Liz soaked up the information he imparted without looking away from her meal, as if none of it mattered to her. And it didn't. Rumours of two injured police officers, a woman at the scene being questioned by police, and all of it tied to a heavy police presence at an industrial unit in Old Ford. Nothing about Liz's husband, though: he was shielding her from that.

'Nothing about McDevitt?' Karl said.

'Early doors yet,' Danny said, putting away the phone. 'Let's just eat to get energy for tonight.'

They finished the meal in silence.

CHAPTER SEVENTY-FOUR

MICK

The Vito turned into a car park brimming with small trucks that had Gustafson Foods on their sides. Mick aimed the car towards the road and pointed a finger at a building about a hundred yards away. The curtains were drawn over the large front window and all was dark inside.

The businesses on their side of the street were housed in long structures of glass, metal and plastic, while across the road the buildings looked as if they had been born as homes: two storeys of brick, first-floor bay windows, single wooden front doors. The car parks ran right up to the front doors and windows, as if they had once been gardens. Behind both rows of buildings was agricultural land.

'What now?' Brad asked. The answer was: we wait.

And they did so in silence for half an hour, until Mick said: 'You mentioned Fate the other day, right?' He showed Brad his mobile phone and a Google Earth image of their location, which looked very green from 2,500 feet in the sky. 'Check out this place for a showdown. London's most rural borough, apparently. Fields, peace and quiet, no one around. Perfect. If this isn't a sign of Fate then no such beast exists. This is meant to go our way. Just like before. This'll go down the same way it did with Grafton.'

'You mean she'll run and be picked up on a back road and we'll be hunting another guy all over again? Can't wait.'

Brad felt Mick looking at him intently. He didn't like it. He hadn't liked much today, actually. And it included Mick's refusal to mention Dave. The guy had run out on them, and even Brad, not half as paranoid as Mick, had wondered if his old friend was going to do something stupid, like talk to the cops. But Mick hadn't mentioned him, never mind tried to call, or even asked Brad if he knew what was going on. He had sent a text message to someone on the drive here, but Brad doubted it had been Dave. So, he brought it up.

'Think Dave got lost?'

'No, you saw as well as I did that he bottled it and ran off.'

He sure did, but he wasn't about to agree. He had to protect Dave, so said: 'I thought he might have had something to do, that's all. Thought he'd be here. He might still come.'

'He won't. I know. He's not as loyal as these two.'

These two? Brad repeated in his mind, and then he understood.

Another van was cruising down the road, slowly, like something on the prowl. Brad, looking past Mick and out the passenger window, saw a handsome twenty-something guy with floppy blonde curls at the wheel, staring back. He looked like a surfer right out of a straight-to-video flick and totally fitted the ancient third generation Volkswagen Transporter.

He didn't know this guy. But he now knew who Mick had texted earlier.

The driver got out and, beyond him, Brad saw a passenger, also in a boiler suit. A wide brute of a man. Compact, built for power. A guy designed for busting heads that his baby-faced partner couldn't sweet talk.

Floppy put his face right up to Mick's window, but Mick didn't even look until the guy rapped the glass. He opened his door, forcing the guy to step back, and got out.

'Stay here, Brad.'

The two men walked out of sight, behind the vans. Brad saw the brute glaring at him, like one bodyguard sizing up another. He glared right back. Neither guy backed down, and the game only ended when Mick and Floppy returned. Floppy got into his cheesy T3 with one of Mick's bags. Mick got in and told Brad to get out.

'You're going with these guys on a job. Highly important. After this, I guarantee you'll be free and clear.'

'Who the fuck are this pair? And what job?'

'You'll know them quite well by the time you get to the job. And then you'll know the answer to both your questions.'

'I don't work with guys I don't know, Mick.' He meant he didn't trust them. But to camouflage that he added: 'They could be fuck-ups, and I don't like prison gruel.'

'Fuck-ups they might be.' He looked right into Brad's eyes. 'That's why I need you there, Brad. Make sure it goes smoothly. Look, that young idiot is a guy I keep on the side. He was sixteen when I nabbed him for stealing computers. Let him go scot free, bit like you. Now we help each other, bit like me and you. Except maybe I've got something in the Loyalty Box to keep him motivated. He's handy, but he hasn't got your skills, and his brother there is brainless. I need you on this.'

For six years, ever since he'd made DCI, the Loyalty Box had been Mick's leverage against the army of criminals he had under his spell, like Król, and his weapon against those he desired to stamp down, like Ramirez. Mick had found a jacket with blood on the sleeve, right where Rocker's leaking nose would have gushed if he'd been choked by the wearer. Brad had watched Mick pull it from the laundry basket in the bathroom, just the two of them alone. Their eyes met. In that moment, staring at each other, they had come to a wordless understanding. Brad had said nothing as Mick held aloft the bloody jacket. Mick said nothing as he stuffed the item back into the laundry basket.

With any other man, he would have returned alone for the jacket, to rehome it in the Loyalty Box with other evidence lifted from crime scenes, where it would await the day it was called upon to ruin someone's life. But here, in Brad, he'd sensed such action was not needed. A new, special partnership was being born.

Mick had handed him his card, and he hadn't needed to voice that gesture: We help each other now. Call me if you think of anything I need to know. Then Mick had exited the bathroom and announced to his colleagues that the room was clean, nothing useful found.

Later, Brad called and outright admitted he'd killed the guy. Many suspected that pressure from Razor's men up in Scotland would force Grafton to hand them someone. Grafton had already severed ties and withheld payment from Brad and Dave because they'd failed to kill Randolph. Suspecting that Grafton might try to have him killed to ensure his silence, he had been watching the street below. Had seen a strange car arrive and gone down to meet it. Rocker wanted Brad to accompany him back to Scotland. Brad said no. Rocker insisted. Stalemate – what could be done? A shopkeeper returning home from work found the dead Scotsman's body ten minutes later and hit triple nine.

Brad trusted that Mick would not arrest him after the confession. And there was no arrest. There was only the start of a beautiful relationship between them. Brad had provided Mick with the one thing he'd desperately needed, and for that Mick felt he still needed to protect him. Still owed him.

'And what's the job?' Brad asked.

'Unconnected to this Grafton lark,' Mick said. 'You don't need to know. Loose end I want tying up before I go away, that's all. A guy needs to regret the error of his ways. Look, Brad, it's a big ask, I know. Even for those two, which is why I just paid them twenty grand. I'll give you twenty as well. Twenty extra big ones, and all you have to do is the same shit you've been doing for years. Drive half an hour, kick in a door, shout a bit, break a nose, drive away. If I'm done here, I'll text you where to meet me for the cash.'

It beat doing this, Brad realised. Liz Grafton was Mick's little pet obsession, not his. He didn't really want to go break a stranger's nose. But neither did he really want to do the alternative job. So, he said okay.

He got out, and into the back seat of the T3 via its rear hatch. Some owners would use this contraption as a bus and leave the rows of seats, while others, because it was popular as a weekend adventure ride, turned the interior into a bedsit. This pair of jokers had gone for just the sitting room part. An armchair against each side wall, under the curtained windows, facing each other. The floor was carpeted. Brad ignored the chairs, walked between them with his head bowed, and knelt behind the cabin seats. Floppy gave him a quick look, and a thumbs up, and said: 'Hold tight and don't sing.' The brute turned his head almost 180, and glared again at Brad.

'Let me save you some confusion,' Brad said to him. 'It's you.'

'What the fuck you talking about?' the guy replied, his accent thick Irish.

'You're sizing me up and wondering if me and you got into it who would end up screaming for mummy's help.'

That made Floppy laugh. But it also made the brute face forward.

'Name's Sink,' Floppy said. Also an Irish guy. 'Pleased to meet. This is Guff, my blood. Let's do this.'

CHAPTER SEVENTY-FIVE

KARL

'So, if you don't mind a blunt question—' Karl started, and Danny cut him off.

'Bike crash. No, I don't mind. People wonder. Some people get an IED in Afghanistan story. Those who know I worked for Ronald Grafton think I got done over by him because he kicked me out. That's not true, either. I simply fell off a bike.'

'I did wonder if Liz's husband—'

This time the ringing phone cut Karl short. He almost jumped for it. But it was right by Danny, and he got there first.

'I understand,' Danny said after listening for just a few seconds. Then he hung up. Not Katie, then, but the solicitor. Karl knew it was a delay even before Danny said so.

'Six o'clock. Court stuff.'

Karl was in a state of SAS-like readiness, but it was a drain on his energy. Liz seemed withdrawn, barely aware. Danny was taking it all in his stride, as if he escorted fugitives to jail every day.

'I've got Monopoly,' Danny said.

CHAPTER SEVENTY-SIX

MICK

Last he knew, Theo Timberland worked at a yacht repair unit at Gillingham Marina in Kent, and according to a Google search he was still there. Assistant manager now, at just twenty years of age. Probably that brash attitude of his. The same one that had made him bully Mick's son during primary school. On the map, he drew a line from Ramirez's home to Ramsgate and that line passed nicely by Gillingham. As he'd said to Brad: if this wasn't a sign of Fate, no such beast existed.

His mobile rang. He looked over at the target building, and it was still dark. Still empty. He answered the phone.

'We're here,' Sink said. And then there was a pause.

'Don't make me ask,' Mick said. 'Just talk.' He spotted movement on the darkening road. A mangy dog, snout on the ground, hunting for food or a mate. It was the only life he could see, and it gave the quiet land a surreal ambience, a post-apocalyptic-world sort of feel.

Sink said: 'Semi-detached place. Posh kind of poncy street. Pathway down the side of the house. Lights on in the living room, none upstairs. No sign of anyone. Should we watch a bit or go in now?'

The dog passed before his car, twenty feet away, and his eyes followed.

'How's that memory of yours? Wait for my call, that's what I said. Knock on the door and hide, see if it's him who answers. Just try to make sure there's not a party going on in there. Call when it's done, and just tell me straight out, okay? Don't make me ask. And double-time it back here. But none of that until I give the word. That part is very important.'

He hung up. The dog had vanished.

Decided, then. After the bitch and Seabury were dead, he'd head north ten miles to Ramirez's home, end that bastard, and slip east to Gillingham. He may as well tick another enemy off the list. Once Theo Timberland was well and truly sorry that he'd ever messed with Tim McDevitt, Mick would continue east to Ramsgate where he'd decided he would try to get a trip across the water to Dunkirk or Calais. After that, Germany and a new life.

CHAPTER SEVENTY-SEVEN

KARL

He knew it was the solicitor again, but still flew out of his seat like a pilot who'd thumped the eject button.

Danny answered the phone. An even shorter call this time. Five seconds. 'He'll call us when he's back home,' he told his guests. 'But he thinks about seven o'clock now. Two hours.'

Liz was on Danny's mobile. He wondered if she was looking at news of her husband's murder, but didn't want to ask.

Danny was on his desktop computer, looking at Google Earth. He looked up and said: 'I've found a spot where we can wait. Round the back of Gold's house, over a field. There's an access road, and we can watch Mr Gold's house without being seen. That way we can be there in five minutes when he calls.'

'But it might be hours, right?' Karl said.

Danny looked at him. Long and hard, and Karl knew that his plan, which he'd just come up with, was written all over his face. He had called Katie's dad's house again ten minutes earlier, only to be told she was home now but asleep again, and no, her dad was not about to wake her, not after the ordeal Karl had put her through. So, it was probably pretty obvious what Karl wanted to do.

'When people are on the run, they're expected to head to people they know. Right now, pal, every relative and friend and work colleague you have is an island in shark-infested waters. If you're real lucky, you'll at least get a glimpse of your wife's dad's house before a ton of cops come down on you like a ton of bricks.'

'Why hasn't she called?'

'Asleep, you said.'

He grunted. He hated waiting. But he knew he couldn't call her dad again.

'It's better this way,' Liz said, her first words for half an hour. 'We'll get you to see your wife, don't worry.' Said without even looking up from the phone.

A half-hour trip from here as opposed to a five-minute trek from whatever secret spot Danny had found would mean a twenty-five minute delay in getting to Katie. Karl stood up and looked out of the window. The sky was aflame with red as the sun set. That, more than the ticking clock on the wall, was a reminder that time was pushing on.

'So let's go,' he said.

CHAPTER SEVENTY-EIGHT

MICK

Myriad newbie detective days of stake-outs in cars and empty flats had made Mick a patient man, but this was different. He couldn't relax. He climbed into the cargo area to get one of his bags, and the photo he wanted. Then he got some Sellotape from the glove box and his knife. He coated the back of the photo in tape because he didn't want to ruin it.

Dangling from the keys in the ignition was a micro torch which he turned on so that the beam lit up his knee. He slid the A4 photo beneath.

The little circle of light illuminated the head and shoulders of Ronald Grafton. In his wedding suit and smiling at the camera, because why wouldn't he? He was rich, powerful, invincible, marrying the girl of his dreams.

He shifted his arm to one side and the beam slid across the A4 photo to spotlight Liz Grafton. In her wedding dress and smiling for the camera, because why wouldn't she? She was marrying the rich, powerful and invincible man of her dreams.

Mick slit the photo down the middle, separating the lovers, much as he had torn the couple apart last night. He wrapped tape around the paper Grafton, securing the photo to his thigh. Same with the bitch on the other side. Lots of tape, nice and tight, but none around their heads and shoulders. He swung the torch like a pendulum, lighting up Grafton, then the bitch, Grafton, then the bitch. Helpfully, the curve of his thighs lessened their flat, 2D appearance.

With one hand pressing down on the photo taped to his right thigh, he slit his own leg. One inch, deep enough to let loose blood immediately. It seeped up through the gash in Grafton's paper neck slowly. He raised his leg so the blood ran down Grafton's torso, over his suit. Grafton continued to smile. Throat cut, suit ruined, but still he grinned. Mick ripped the photo off his leg and stuffed it against his mouth like a starving man, and bit the face right off. No more smiling from Grafton.

Then he moved so that the light splashed over the bitch, and picked up the knife again.

CHAPTER SEVENTY-NINE

KATIE

It wasn't often someone woke from a near-death nightmare to find the real world far more frightening. But Katie would have gladly wished for her only problem in the world to be a runaway car with no brakes.

She was in the spare room which her father used for his pottery wheel and storing junk. No indication that it had once been her bedroom except for a small hole in the ceiling where she had poked a crutch at age ten. It brought back memories of the trampoline accident that broke her thigh. She would have gladly accepted a busted leg instead of the reality facing her.

A knocking at the front door. Maybe that was what woke her. She heard her father speaking. Something about a washing machine. And then the door slammed shut. The clock said 6.18 p.m., which meant she had been asleep for only a few hours. But her body ached as if she had been out for half a day.

Movement in her belly erased all negative thoughts. In the dream there had been no pregnancy, so maybe the real world was a better place after all. There was still a chance that Karl could beat the murder charge. If he was still alive.

That got her moving.

Her father heard her on the creaky floorboards and was at the bottom of the stairs by the time she reached the landing. He made a drinking motion, smiling. She made the same forced smile back and gave him a thumbs up.

After a minute's silence at the kitchen table, he said, somewhat deadpan: 'Karl is going to come by the house soon, before he goes to the police.'

Mother, bless her, had always approved of Karl, even when he stepped out of line. Father, though, had retained a neutral air, speaking neither negatively nor positively about him. It meant he never praised him, but neither did he shoot him down. Mother had gone berserk when he passed his driving test at twenty, on his fifth try, and she would have gone berserk about today's situation. But not her father. Karl got his business loan approved. Karl's wanted for murder. Same blank face. She didn't know which reaction she would have preferred.

'He's innocent, Dad.'

He stroked his thick grey beard, thinking of a suitable reply. But she saw the doubt in his eyes, and then he confirmed it with: 'I'm sure your ma would have said the same.'

Was that his way of saying he didn't believe it? She didn't ask. 'Did he sound okay?'

He shrugged. 'I guess. I'm sure he's okay. But are you?'

She patted her belly in answer but father's next line was: 'You should get checked out again about that.'

What a thing to say. Sure, he was concerned, his only grand-child and all, but he should have known how worried she was. The hospital had performed an ultrasound, but that couldn't highlight all possible problems, could it? She had to remind herself that the car crash hadn't caused any harm to her belly, and neither had running from that madman.

'I'll come to the police station with you,' he now said, looking a little ashamed, as if he had realised the error of his words.

She nodded.

'I need to drop something at the theatre,' he said. 'But I'll run you a bath first. Have a good soak. I'll only be an hour. Will you be okay?'

She told him not to fuss over her. To go about his business, because she was going to be fine, didn't need him by her side constantly. He stroked her hand, got up, and pointed at the phone on the wall.

'Karl's waiting for your call.'

CHAPTER EIGHTY

KARL

As Karl was calling Katie's dad's house and getting a dead tone, Danny turned the van into a cul-de-sac in a Bromley housing estate. Karl looked up from Danny's mobile. It seemed they were going to the solicitor's house, not his office. He scrutinised the houses and took a guess, but the van didn't stop. Then they were at the turnaround at the end, and he stared at a detached house that he thought befitted a solicitor's wage and standing, but the van didn't stop. The vehicle mounted the kerb and drove down a path between two houses. There had once been a bollard to thwart cars, but all that remained was a concrete stub. Space was tight, and Danny drove slowly.

As Karl was getting no answer from Peter's mobile, the path delivered them onto a hammerhead turnaround on a wide road that ran straight ahead. There was no street lighting. On the left were commercial businesses, large and lit by lamps, while on the right were smaller buildings, shrouded in gloom, that looked like houses, apart from the fact that each had a tiny car park out front.

As Karl was cursing the same dead tone from the landline, Danny stopped the van and pointed down the road. 'On the right.' He counted: 'Fifteenth place.'

Karl counted. Fifteen was a long way, about 600 feet. There was a single car parked out front. At this angle they couldn't see the front of the building, but there was a pinprick glint of light on the side of the lone car – a reflection from a lit window. It seemed to be the only place that might be occupied.

'This is way out of the way for a solicitor's office or house,' Karl said.

'He likes the peace and quiet,' Liz said.

'And a city office would attract all manner of scum,' Danny said.

That made sense. A man with clients like Ronald Grafton would not want to deal with ASBO breakers and car thieves.

He looked down the left flank of the road and saw what appeared to be an end to the commercial properties because the world turned black.

As if reading his mind, Danny said: 'Where it gets dark, just after the businesses end on the left, there's a food warehouse called Gustafson Foods that's got no lighting on the exterior, so it's the darkest spot here. The best place to hide and watch, so that's where McDevitt will be lurking, if he's here. By coming the way we did, we avoided the entrance to this road, which they'll be watching. If they're there, that is.'

He sounded pretty happy with this turn of events, but the optimism didn't last.

'The problem is they can see the entrance, and they can also see Gold's house. If we drive right up there, they'll spot us long before we get close. There's light on us and none on them, so they'd also see us before we saw them. There's no creeping up.'

'So, we can't get there?' Liz asked.

Danny grinned at them both. 'Think I came all this way without a plan?'

He outlined his idea. Liz was up for it. Karl was dubious because he sensed something like gloom in Danny's voice.

He understood why when Liz touched Danny's arm and said: 'I know you want to do this, Danny, but we'll be fine.'

So her pal was worried that he was sending these two amateurs out there alone. Karl grew extra respect for the man.

'If I honk,' Danny said, 'it means trouble's coming, so run for a galaxy far, far away.'

Liz threw open the door and slipped out. Danny turned off the interior light before it really got a chance to come on.

'Are we not waiting here?' Karl said, worried.

Liz said: 'We'll wait around back, in the fields, so we're closer when he calls.'

Karl paused. He didn't want to go anywhere until he'd spoken to Katie.

As if reading his mind, Liz said: 'We'll call your wife from Mr Gold's phone.'

He nodded.

Danny said: 'Once you're in, call the police, lock the doors and stay there with Gold until they come. I'll wait here and watch until they arrive, then be off. Luck be with.'

'Thanks, Danny,' Karl said to this man who had saved him. A world of supervillains and superheroes, and normal old him in the middle. He'd never felt weaker in his life.

CHAPTER EIGHTY-ONE

BRAD

The junction seemed to be some kind of boundary where council workmen took a lunch break during slum clearance. On the far side was what Sink had called a posh kind of poncy street. Old detached houses with garages and bay windows. On this side were cramped terraced houses with no gardens.

A break on both sides of the terraced street had been used for retail. Nine-to-five joints like hairdressers' and post offices, now closed and dark, faced nocturnal beasts like mini-marts and takeaways alive and bright. Teenagers with nothing to do hung around outside. Sink's T3 lurked on the other side, in the gloom, but no one paid it any heed. Up front of the vehicle, Sink and Guff were playing a card game Brad couldn't work out. But he wasn't watching anyway. He was looking beyond, eyes on the third house on the money side of the street.

Eight minutes ago, Sink had knocked on the door, just like Mick asked. The bay window had prevented Brad from seeing who answered, but according to Sink, who had pretended to be collecting old washing machines, the owner was some old guy getting ready to go out. Now, Brad saw the guy, tall, grey beard, leaving the house and getting into his car. And then Mick called, perfect timing, as if he knew.

'We do it now,' Sink said as he hung up. That puzzled Brad: how was this guy going to 'regret the error of his ways' if he was gone? Was this a house-trashing job? Not Brad's style, and why would it take three to do that anyway? Anxiety crept over him. He didn't like this.

CHAPTER EIGHTY-TWO

MICK

Mick hung up the phone and watched Gold's fat frame, with a big I-love-life grin on his face, as he chatted on his mobile. Mick slapped the steering wheel hard enough to hurt his hand, and immediately regretted it. But not because of the pain: why abuse the vehicle, which had done everything he'd asked of it?

The phone and the ride and that big belly of Gold's were all products of criminal money. Suited, briefcase in hand, phone against his ear, didn't he just look like one of the good defenders of the law? This man who'd kept the wheels of Grafton's criminal empire oiled with blood. Mick gripped the steering wheel and tried to pull it towards him. Planted his feet on the brake and clutch to get the leverage. He leaned back and pulled, angry, and didn't stop until the steering column began to groan. Then he relaxed.

He needed a release for his rage, but why take his anger out on something innocent?

He waited for Gold to get inside the house, then he climbed into the back of the van and opened a toolbox bolted to one wall. The plan had been to await the arrival of Seabury and the bitch, but all main events needed a support act. And he needed to get his blood pumping.

Thirty seconds later, he was scuttling across the road, aimed at Gold's lair. With a hacksaw.

Why unleash his fury on something that didn't feel pain and regret?

CHAPTER EIGHTY-THREE

BRAD

Sink stopped the campervan right across from the target house, other side of the road. Brad scanned the other homes. A metal Neighbourhood Watch sign on a lamppost seemed to glare right at him. But there was no one about and every lit living-room window had the curtains pulled. Brad still wasn't happy about it.

'Too close,' he said.

'Calm down,' Guff said. 'In and out. Are you gonna be the one crying to mummy after all?'

'What are we doing here?' Brad asked, panic rising in his throat.

Both men ignored his question. Then they did something outlandish: played a round of Paper Scissors Stone, and Guff lost. But it was Sink who got out of the van and crossed the road. As he walked, he pulled on a balaclava. Nice and casual, like a guy putting on a woolly hat against the cold.

Then, in the upstairs window of the target house, Brad saw a woman step into view. So, the old man wasn't the target after all. She approached the window and started to pull the curtains. There was a towel slung over her shoulder. Rising dread turned to shock when he recognised the face.

Seabury's wife.

'What's the plan?' Brad asked, trying to sound casual. He moved back, and sat on one of the armchairs. Just to think.

Guff slid between the cabin seats and took the facing chair, their knees almost touching. 'We wait,' he said.

Through a chink in a curtained side window, Brad watched Sink walk casually down the driveway and leap over a tall fence, lithe as a cat. Lithe as a man who'd had lots of practice at breaking into houses. But he also watched Guff because something was afoot here beyond hurting Seabury's wife.

'So what did you do to piss off Mick?' the brother asked from the darkness.

He knew he should have reacted then, right then, as the realisation that Mick had tricked him sank in. But he didn't. He allowed himself a moment of doubt, a moment to think he had it wrong, that Mick wouldn't do this: they were friends; they looked after each other. And in that moment the chance to strike first passed.

By the time Brad had knocked away doubt from his mind, the bruiser had leaped forward with surprising speed for his bulk and grabbed his hair. The other hand pressed something cold and sharp against the side of his neck.

'I guess we just reached "S" in the alphabet,' Brad said.

CHAPTER EIGHTY-FOUR

KARL

Danny hung up. 'We go in the back way, he says. Right now.'

They bid him good luck, and got out. But then the phone rang. It was Katie. Karl scuttled out of earshot to take the call.

'Oh, God, Katie, are you okay? That crash. I tried to call. Your dad—'

'I'm fine. Forget me. Dad unplugged the phone until I was ready. What about you?'

'You got away, thankfully. He didn't hurt you?'

'Nobody hurt me, Karl. This hurts me, though. Are you okay? Where are you?'

It felt like a supreme betrayal to not tell her, but he couldn't. Most of the stuff in his shop was the sort sold to law enforcement. Recording devices hidden in plugs, in business cards, surveillance gear so small it could be planted anywhere in a house. Or on a person.

Was Katie bugged? He was losing his mind.

'I'm going to see a special solicitor,' he said, which seemed like a safe answer. He explained, and she listened, and she didn't shoot him down afterwards. Which seemed like acceptance.

'That's good,' she said. 'I heard things about that police officer. I knew he was... something was wrong. He'll be arrested. Is he part of this?'

'Hell yes,' Karl almost shouted, just in case. For the bugs. He liked to imagine a team of guys in a surveillance van jotting down the name McDevitt.

'He'll be arrested,' she said again. 'You can hand yourself in. I want to meet you there, outside, so I can come in with you.'

'Okay.' The moment the word was out of his mouth, he had to bite back tears. But not because of his wife's affection. Because he needed her, and what kind of a man couldn't face what he was up against without desiring his partner to be with him? The right thing to do, surely, was face this thing alone and keep his pregnant wife away from stress. Or was it? Maybe they should face this problem together? Maybe her stress would be amplified if she was out of the loop.

Hell, he didn't know. He only knew he wanted her there, and she wanted to be there, and there she would be. Even if he said no, probably.

'But not at the station,' he said. 'I don't want to see you with cops all around. We're going to come to your dad's house.'

Silence as she digested this. Would she think it a good idea, or foolish?

'Outside,' she said. 'I'm not sure if my dad would call the police. I'm not sure if the police are watching this house. I'll get out, and meet you nearby, and then we'll go to the police station together.'

'Good.' A good plan indeed. There was nothing he wanted more.

'Oh, and by the way, Mr Karl James Seabury, boy or girl, we are not calling our child Michael.'

That made him laugh. She giggled, too, and he figured this rare moment of levity was the optimum time to shoehorn in: 'Liz is with me.'

Not a beat missed: 'Good, because the police will need her as well.'

He relaxed. 'I love you. I want to hug you.'

'Same, babe. But I probably stink. I'm just going in the bath. For you.' She said it with a hint of cheekiness there that made him miss her more than ever. They'd been apart only hours – he'd spent longer away from her when at work – but it felt like weeks.

The tension flooded away for two hundred seconds. The flirting reminded him of way back when they'd been a week-old couple. Arranging dates with a nervous voice. Unsure of what would happen next. Worried whether it would be the last time they kissed, the last time they saw each other. The world around him vanished, and with it every worry, every bad guy, every cop.

After he hung up, he was ready. He turned to his comrades, and he said: 'Let's go.'

CHAPTER EIGHTY-FIVE

KATIE

Katie sank into the bath, and that was when she heard the noise.

It sounded like the back door shuddering open, and her first thought was that her father had returned quickly. But then she discarded that notion because her father knew the trick with the back door. If it was opened at speed the draught excluder, fixed too low, slid over the lino easily, but if opened slowly it caught and caused the whole door to vibrate loudly enough to hear it throughout the house.

Her father knew about the fault, of course. But Karl didn't!

'Karl?' she shouted down. The faint vibration halted. No answer, but he was probably staying silent in case the police were with her, waiting for him. Maybe even suspecting she was trying to trick him into handcuffs.

She rose slowly from the bath, trying not to make a splash. Even as she did this, she knew it was a futile action because her earlier shouts would have given away the fact that there was someone in the house. And that, right there, was the inescapable truth.

Hearing her shout, Karl would not have remained silent. Her nakedness and delicate condition heightened her fear as she realised what that meant... a stranger was in the house.

She nearly slipped on slick tiles as she stumbled to the towel rail on the wall. Her vision swam, and her head throbbed because

of the heat of the bath. She wrapped herself in a towel, opened
the bathroom door and staggered to the top of the stairs. Out
on the landing it was much cooler, and her head cleared quickly.

The stairs had a bulb at both top and bottom, and she lit up
the one below, leaving herself in darkness. She listened, praying
that she'd been wrong about the sounds she heard.

Too late she realised she should have run for the phone in the
bedroom. Someone appeared at the foot of the stairs. A man in a
boiler suit and a balaclava. He looked up into the darkness, and
she froze. Despite knowing he couldn't see her, she didn't dare
move, couldn't bring herself to. But then the man reached for the
light switch, and she was no longer frozen.

It was a mistake. He did not light her up, but instead turned
off the lower bulb to envelop himself in darkness once again. But
she moved, and he heard it.

His feet thumped the stairs, and she heard an Irish voice
say: 'C'm'ere, darling.' Her fear spiked at the realisation that he
hadn't seen her but clearly knew who to expect. This wasn't some
impatient burglar unwilling to wait for late night. He was here
for her. He had to be one of the men chasing Karl.

She ran into the dark bedroom, turned, threw the door shut.
It bounced right back at her as the hooded man crashed into it,
knocking her into the bed. The moment she landed on her back,
he was right there, right above her. Even in the gloom, she saw
his lascivious eyes behind his balaclava. Hands pinned her arms,
then forced them above her head. He cast her towel aside, and
to cover her naked waist she threw up a leg. Her knee caught the
guy in the balls, and he grunted. It didn't help her cause, though.
He lowered himself onto her, closing the gap so she couldn't strike
again. She felt his clothing against her skin and it sickened her.
His head dropped onto her chest, and she could hear his panting.

'Help!' she yelled, at the top of her voice, giving it all her
lungs had. The neighbours were young people, good ears, and

surely they'd hear and come rushing round. Thirty seconds, she figured. All she had to do was fight this guy off for thirty seconds and she'd be saved.

His knee went between her legs, forcing through and up, until she felt coarse material, very cold, between her legs. She yelled again.

One of his hands released her arm and grabbed her between the legs. Her free hand lashed out, slapping his head. He seemed to barely feel it. In fact, he laughed.

She heard something downstairs. The door again. No vibration this time but a heavy thump, as if someone had slammed it all the way open. Then footsteps on the stairs, just as loud as her attacker's had been.

'You kill that dude, bro?' the guy on top of her said as she saw the black shape of another man framed in the doorway.

The last of her resolve was crushed under a wave of horror as she realised the two men knew each other. She could not defend against two. There was no hope and she felt her muscles relax as her brain gave up the fight.

'Sure did,' the new guy said, then moved forward to help his partner hold her down.

CHAPTER EIGHTY-SIX

SHOWDOWN

Behind the houses was scrubland that terminated at a post and rail fence, with farmland beyond. On the other side of the fence, running parallel, was a gully.

They climbed the fence and walked along it, just their heads visible to anyone who might have been in one of the buildings. They walked slowly because the ground was littered with trash and rocks. Karl led, with Liz bringing up the rear. He was cold and wished he'd selected more than just a T-shirt for the trip. Then again, he hadn't expected to be traipsing around some field. They walked in silence. It didn't take long. Times flies when you're walking into the unknown.

The back of the house had an extension that looked like a kitchen. The light was on and the chimney poured smoke. People sometimes went out and left lights on, but surely not fireplaces burning away. Karl had hoped Gold would be in. Now he wished the guy would pop out of existence. They'd come all this way, but he suddenly had a bad feeling about this house.

To shift his mind off what lay ahead, Karl said: 'Danny said he lost the use of his legs in a bike crash. Is that true?'

In the dark, he saw her chest vibrate. Humour, but the annoyed kind. She said: 'You're wondering if it was actually because of the job he did. Working for my husband. Some kind of gangland thing. Because they all die or end up in prison, right?'

He nodded. 'Understandable, right? Look what we've been through today, Liz.'

'Danny wasn't tortured by a rival gang, he didn't get shot during a bank robbery and a home-made bomb didn't explode while he was fixing it to a prosecution witness's car. It's not like it appears in the movies. Okay?'

He could tell she was sick and tired of people talking about her husband's way of life. Well, he bloody chose it. And she chose him. And Karl had been slap bang in the middle of it today. 'Sorry I asked.'

She mellowed. 'It was a bike crash, Karl. I admit that Danny had a role that he needed to be fit and active for. After the accident Ron booted him out. It didn't go down well with Danny, of course. For his own good, Ron said, but that annoyed Danny. Said it made no sense. But in the end, Ron had to cast aside the caring boss attitude and become mean. He said Danny was no good to him as a cripple. But I'm glad Danny got out. He's my friend.'

It was virtually an admission that it was dangerous to be in Ronald Grafton's orbit, despite her response thirty seconds earlier.

'Now let's talk no more, because we're wasting time.'

He turned his attention to the house again, knowing she was right. A minute wasted here meant a minute longer to get to Katie. 'So what do we do?'

In answer, Liz climbed over the fence and, bent low, scuttled across the scrubland. She stopped at the kitchen window and looked in, eyes and forehead peeking up like some kid noseying on a neighbour. It would have looked funny, except that it proved even Liz was nervous about what they might find at the house. Their pursuers had posted men outside Karl's house: they could have men waiting here too.

Karl shouted a whisper, trying to draw her back until they could formulate a plan. But when she tried the door and it opened, he cursed and followed her.

They stood at the open door, bathed in light, and waited, listening. No sounds. He didn't want to walk inside, even just one step. His instinct was screaming at him not to.

'Through the kitchen door there's a hallway. Three doors and some stairs. A waiting room, a study, and the office. Bedrooms upstairs. Normally he lives in the study with his books and iPad, but if he's waiting for us then he'll be in the office. Second door on the right, just past the stairs.'

Karl forced himself to enter the house. Big, confident steps, although he wasn't sure that they'd look that way to anyone watching. The kitchen floor was carpeted, which helped kill the sound of their footsteps. The door in the far wall was ajar and he put his head through. Slowly. No one chopped it off. As promised, a hallway beyond. Dark, but faint yellow light flickered on the ceiling.

A door in the right-hand wall was wide open. Outwards, just eight feet away, and hinged on the side nearest to him which meant he couldn't see the room it belonged to and, worse, it blocked his view of the entire right side of the hallway. And whoever might be hiding there with a knife. On the left side was a wooden staircase, rising towards him, which meant he could only see the underside of it. Cardboard boxes were neatly stacked underneath. Gold's files, no doubt. There was a door by the foot of the stairs, shut, with a plaque that said:

WAITING ROOM

His two choices were: backtrack and flee into the night, or step out and face what was behind that door.

He scuttled quickly to the door blocking the hallway, leaned close and peeked through the gap. A lamp on a table shed enough light for him to see most of a study. It was empty of life. He shut the door and tried not to convince himself he did it to clear an escape route.

Now the rest of the hallway was exposed. No masked madman. Two more doors: the front door in the far wall, and one at the end of the right-hand wall. The office. The door was open like an invitation. The flickering yellow light, surely from a fireplace, oozed from beyond. The last place to check, because Karl had already decided he wasn't going upstairs. Gold expected them, and if he wasn't waiting down here then something had gone badly wrong. But he could spare three more seconds, make a few more steps, to know for sure. He was tempted to call out for the man, but didn't. Always safer if— He was within two steps of the doorway when he sensed it: the unmistakable feeling of another presence.

*

McDevitt was sitting on the stairs, near the top, where he'd been invisible until right about now. Waiting for his prey to step right into the trap.

Spotting Mick, Karl tensed, ready to grab Liz and run back towards the kitchen. Half the hallway was a blind spot for the gun because of where Mick sat: three steps and he would have no angle to fire at them. It was the very reason they hadn't seen him as they walked the hallway. But he could fire before they took one step.

The gun moved back and forth between Karl and Liz. As if he was unsure of who to shoot first. But the giveaway was that his eyes didn't move from Liz. Karl figured he would shoot him first, to rid himself of the bigger threat.

But Mick didn't fire, and he didn't speak. Karl realised he was awaiting their move. He wanted to see how his trapped rats would react.

So, Karl made a move, hoping to delay what now seemed inevitable. He said: 'We can work this out, Mr McDevitt, sir. There's no need to hurt Elizabeth or me. I just want to go home to my pregnant wife.' A pleading tone, the use of an honorific, and an attempt to humanise Liz and himself, because he'd read about that tactic. All to appease the man.

But Liz, clouded with sudden rage in the presence of her nemesis, wasn't on the same page and cut him right off with: 'You killed my husband, you pathetic animal'.

Karl expected the gunshot and tensed; McDevitt's response was a smile. Her outburst had broadcast her inner anguish, and he was clearly pleased by this. He shook his head slowly.

'His bloody, chopped-up body was the last stop on a route of self-destruction. And his suffering isn't done yet. When I go to Hell, he's got more coming. You'll be there to watch.'

He stood up. While Mick was rising to his feet, Karl hissed *run* and jabbed his arms hard into Liz's back, forcing her forwards. She was propelled along the corridor into Mick's blind spot. He turned and grabbed the doorframe and hauled himself around it. The ploy worked: no gunshot; though Karl did hear footsteps thudding down the stairs as he slammed the door.

Beyond the door: shouting… thudding… still no gunshot.

He was trapped in the room. Some kind of macho thing he'd done there, splitting Liz from him so the lunatic would have to pick one to chase. Liz might escape if she was quick, but Karl had no way out.

He turned to seek another door. What he found was a dead man in a chair. The window was to Karl's left and the desk was facing it so Gold could enjoy a view his clients might never again see; he was turned so that he was facing the door. The desk lamp had been positioned so its meagre light bathed him, illuminating a ragged red slice right through his throat and blood all over him. Beyond him, a fireplace burned with real coals.

A display, Karl realised, feeling his fear and revulsion peak. It was how McDevitt wanted it to go down – Liz and Karl in the doorway, frozen with shock; McDevitt, behind them on the stairs, watching their distress for a few seconds before he announced his presence.

The door started to open. He turned, backed away. In his panic he forgot about the dead guy for a moment and backed right into the man's legs. Liz entered, struggling against a hand clamped in her hair. Mick was right behind her with the gun resting on her shoulder, aiming at Karl. And now he had both of them right where he'd wanted them all along. All Karl had achieved with his macho deed was to save Mick the trouble of herding them into the office.

Mick pushed her hard, right into Karl, slamming them into the dead guy. All three of them fell down: the fat solicitor came out of his chair and slumped on the bloody carpet. Karl and Liz scrambled to their feet and backed up against the far wall, right by the burning fire, with Gold lying near their feet. Mick kicked the door shut, and they saw his shoulders relax, much as a man might do when he'd finally got home after a long day. Their enemy, finally, had what he wanted, nicely packaged up in a box. He gave a laugh, and shook his head – *what-a-day* – and moved to the far side of the desk. He dropped his gun onto the oak.

Their eyes followed the weapon: he'd released it. That was what he wanted, too, because now they couldn't avoid seeing what lay on the desk.

'I got a headache worrying about this,' he said. 'One chance, one dream, and how to live it to its fullest. A headache, I tell you.'

The fingers of one hand slipped over the desk, and settled upon one of the three items.

'Was it about pain and suffering? Or was it about making a statement with ingenuity and gruesomeness? Bones crushed, would that do it for me? A body like a bag of Lego?'

The fingers moved away from the hammer, and touched the second item.

'Skin and flesh sliced up a thousand times, would that do it for me? A body as a piece of kirigami?'

Away from the razor blade slid his fingers, and onto the third item.

'Maybe I would warm up that cold heart of yours instead,' he said as he stroked the fire poker.

Karl tensed. They were only six feet from Mick, who wasn't holding a weapon or looking at them. With luck, he could be across the desk in half a second. It might be their only chance to— He felt Liz grab his hand and squeeze, but not because she was scared. He realised she was anchoring him, preventing him from making a move. He no longer saw Mick as a distracted man open to attack. He saw Mick's proximity, his empty hands, his blind eyes as a test, as a taunt. He was trying to trick them into making a foolish move.

Mick hung his head, eyes on the floor. But Karl's body was locked into inaction by fear as well as by Liz's firm grip. For seconds the scene was frozen: no movement except for the rapid rise and fall of Karl's and Liz's chests.

And then Mick looked up.

'Suicide,' he said. 'Suicide by someone who craves life; surely that kills not just the body but the soul as well, because that's a place my weapons can't reach. I could offer you the hammer and the blade and the poker, but no vital areas, of course. That game is too quick. No hammer to the skull. No blade to the carotid. No burning metal through the eye and into the brain. But suicide is a ticket to Hell, I thought, and I can't have you reunited with him. No way. Not even in a boiling pit in Hades.'

Liz said: 'Hell? You foolish man. Whatever my husband did to a monster like you, you deserved it. He'll be in Heaven, and I'll be right by his side soon. Why don't you just get it over with.'

Karl's legs almost buckled. But the strength quickly returned to them, and with it he did something even more shocking than Liz's softly delivered words. He stepped in front of her.

Mick picked up his gun, and he was smiling. Karl realised his little act of defiance had played right into his hands. With their deaths, Mick's fun ended. So, he was delaying. This was foreplay.

It could provide Karl with an advantage, but his mind was blank as to how to use it to get out alive.

'Step aside, Seabury. If you want it to be quick.'

He moved, but not by choice. Liz thumped him aside.

He stepped in front of her again. Mick's expression didn't change, as if he hadn't noticed, or had something on his mind. '"Whatever",' you said. '"Whatever he did to me." So, you don't know. You don't know because he didn't say, and he didn't say because—'

'I know everything he ever did, you bastard,' Liz yelled, and thumped Karl aside again. This time she even stepped forward so that Mick's gun was only feet away.

'He did nothing to you. He told me everything he ever did. Everything.'

Mick grabbed the collar of his sweater, two-handed, and for a split second the barrel of the gun was pointed right at his chin. Karl prayed the bastard would blow his own head off. He tugged the sweater down to expose the ugly wound on his upper chest.

'He did this to me. He never told you about this, though, did he? And shall I tell you why?' His eyes seemed to become slightly distant, as if his mind was racing back – *a jagged shard of metal, forked, like a lightning bolt, pierces his flesh in two spots, one below and one above the collarbone* – 'Because he was ashamed?' Mick continued.

'No, please don't!' he screams, his right arm outstretched, reaching ahead, but short, too short by inches, or miles, because either way he can't stop this.

The pain in his chest is excruciating, and blood flows. His fingers fall short still.

'Don't, don't, don't!'

His fingers continue forward.

'Please!'

'Because he was ridden with guilt? No, no, no. You want to know why I killed that fucker?'

...a pair of eyes stare blankly back at him, devoid of emotion. He grabs their jacket in desperation, takes a vice-like fistful.

The bolt pushes deeper into his skin. An inch, and then another inch. The pain throbs throughout his chest like an electrical charge.

'Don't, don't, don't!' he moans.

Deeper still. The blood starts to flow, mixing with more blood on the floor. The metal between the jagged forks hits the flesh over his collarbone, and movement is checked.

'Please, T—'

'Fluoxymesterone and imipramine, that's why. Mix them, add a hint of lemon, and you have a psychotropic drug. Cheap, dangerous. It's called Buzz. It's new and popular and your fucking husband sold it through a dealer in his club, a guy called Rapid. It can cause a serious paranoid reaction. It can turn a man into a raving lunatic.'

... there is a massive jerk, all shoulder muscle, and Mick screams as the bolt pushes deeper, bending and then snapping his collarbone, and the prongs force themselves further in, and the blood gushes out of his chest and soaks his clothing.

'Your husband never told you about this.' He drew back his gun arm and slammed the butt of the weapon twice into his wound. 'Because there was nothing to tell. It meant *nothing* to him. Like squashing flies against a car bumper. Not a minute of sleep lost.'

Liz said nothing, and Karl couldn't see her face, but he saw Mick's expression, and the shock written all over it. A happy shock like you'd see on a man hearing against-the-odds cancer remission news. That look was on his face because of the one Karl knew was on hers: belief.

'After all this fannying around, that was all I needed all along,' he said, almost incredulous. 'For you to know that bastard's in Hell.'

He took a deep, satisfied breath, lifted his gun, aimed it right at her face and pulled the trigger.

CHAPTER EIGHTY-SEVEN

DANNY

Danny opened his door again, and closed it again.

He knew it was a bad idea to leave the van, but staying here, doing nothing, made him feel impotent. Action, that was what he needed. He had been threatened with knives and guns. He had taken beatings at the hands of vicious people. And he'd done all that in return. You could take the man out of the fire, but you couldn't take the fire out of the man. And the fire had been reignited the moment he learned that Ron had been killed. Right then he knew heads had to roll. People would have to be put under pressure to give up what they knew, and others would have to be sent a stern message that Ron's death didn't mean his empire was ready to be sliced up like free cake. That was action he wanted in on. And this time Ron couldn't stop him. His legs, though. They might.

He cast his mind back to that day when Ron had forced him to leave. Just a few weeks after the bike crash. Somehow, the man had known. He'd been called into a quiet spot, where nobody could overhear, and hit with a line that changed everything: 'I can't have a man around who's in love with my wife.'

And that was that. No denial, because the boss was never wrong, even when he was. And no argument, because loving a man's wife was a whole lot more than just being attracted to her, and he'd seen what happened to guys who didn't hide the fact that they thought Liz was hot. He remembered a chap behind her in a post office queue. Ron had been waiting outside, and through the window he'd seen the guy's eyes run up and down her body. That was all. Probably as much boredom as physical attraction. No move to chat to her, no step closer to smell her perfume. Just the eyes, up and down, taking her in. He probably would have forgot her within minutes. But Ron had sent a guy to follow him. Now the guy with the roving eyes would remember that day with his last old-man dying breath. So, friends or not, Danny had got off lightly. Liz, of course, never knew a thing about it, having been fed some bullshit about Ron taking Danny out of the game for his own good. Which meant she never learned of Danny's true feelings for h—

Lights hit his wing mirror. He was parked sixty feet from the path out of the cul-de-sac and now watched a vehicle coming along it. It was moving slowly, which was not a good sign, but then again the lane was thin and slow was the order of the day.

The vehicle slipped out of the path and speeded up. It drove past the left side of Danny's van, and he lifted an *A–Z* and lowered his head.

He watched the van drive down the road with two people inside. The street led to a roundabout, and from there the roads went in every direction, so the guys could be going to Scotland, or to Dover to catch a ferry to France. But if he was wrong…

Danny opened his door again, then slammed it. By the time he got his chair out and wheeled himself halfway to Gold's house, it would all be over. And if he drove in pursuit of the van, he would alert the bad guys and lose the element of surprise.

He cursed. Nothing he could do except what he'd promised Liz. So, angry, impotent, lost, Danny lay on the horn.

CHAPTER EIGHTY-EIGHT

KARL

The timing was perfect. A horn, just as Mick fired. Distant, muted, so it wasn't the volume that had made Mick shift his aim a fraction. At a hundred yards, the bullet might have missed Liz by ten feet, but here it ruffled her hair and blasted a hole in the wall two inches from Karl's head. If she'd been a yard closer to Mick, the bullet wouldn't have made the wall. She dropped to her knees in shock, which opened a space for Karl to see the suspicion on Mick's face at the horn. Way out here in the quiet and the dark, all but this place closed for the night, someone had let off a long blast of their horn. Not one of those watch-where-you're-going blasts a thousand motorists did every day. Longer, harder, something to get someone's attention, or give a warning. It had put enough shock and suspicion in Mick's mind to cause the gun to jerk and waste the bullet.

Liz, seething with anger, said: 'That noise means you're in big trouble, McDevitt. Thought we came unprepared, did you?'

He had, and he shouldn't have, that's what Mick's face was saying. He backed off, still aiming the gun. Still watching them, except for a moment when, at the bay window, he turned away to haul open a curtain and peer out. Just one second. Not enough time for Karl to do anything.

But in that second, Karl saw lights beyond the window. Head-lights. A vehicle turning into the car park, towards the house. His hopes flared and died in the same moment, because it had to be Danny out there; what could he do apart from extend their lives for another few seconds before getting killed himself?

Mick let the curtain drop. He stood with his back to it and grinned at them. 'My friends are here,' he said. 'Perhaps it's good we didn't have a quick kill. I couldn't bring myself to touch that bitch, but my friends can have whatever they want from her. You and I will watch, Seabury.'

Not Danny after all. The plan had been to honk the horn if he saw trouble, not honk to announce his arrival.

'Sit down, backs against the wall,' Mick ordered.

Sitting made them more vulnerable, but they had no choice, sitting side by side against the wall behind the desk, with the fallen chair and the dead solicitor in front of them. This close, his lethal throat wound looked much worse. His open eyes seemed to be staring right at their feet, but that, Karl felt, was better than their faces.

'How do you think you'll sell this?' Liz said, her composure on its way back. 'Are you going to be the hero? You find us dead and claim the glory, maybe make superintendent, write your memoirs, play yourself in a film version?'

Mick laughed. 'Not this time. I won't make that mistake again. No bodies. You won't get a funeral. You'll get a yellowing missing persons poster.'

Liz's hand grabbed Karl's for reassurance. They looked at each other, and in her eyes he read strength. That strong new persona of hers, arisen like a phoenix upon news of the death of her husband. She didn't want reassurance: she was giving it.

They heard two doors slam outside. Mick's friends, about to join the party. Karl felt time slipping through his fingers. He shut down an image of Katie and their unborn baby, knowing his fear of losing her would only weaken him.

He heard the front door open. Mick's guys, just seconds away.

And then the office door opened, and the man called Brad Smithfield entered. With him was another person. Karl had a dizzying sensation. He refused to believe his eyes, but it was real. There, with her arm clutched in Brad's fist, was Katie.

'Let her go!' he yelled, and rose to his feet. Mick fired his gun into the air as a warning, but Karl kept rising. Only when the second bullet tore into the wall beside his head, causing plaster and paint chips to sting his face, did he stop. Or rather, Liz stopped him. She still had his hand, and she tugged him down with surprising ease.

He clutched his stinging eye and felt his heart thudding. A foolish move, trying to save Katie like that. Mick would have blasted him into nothingness. Now, because of Liz, he still had a heartbeat.

Then he saw that Mick's gun was aiming at Brad.

Brad was frozen. 'Wow, pal, easy. I'm in your corner, remember.'

The gun tracked back to Karl. But Mick seemed unsure, and the weapon wavered again and settled on a blank wall. Not Karl. Not Brad. Aimed at nothing but equidistant from both men. Half a second from targeting either one. As if he wasn't sure who was the biggest threat.

'Where's the guys?' Mick said, and his tone confirmed it: suspicion. There was something off-kilter between these two. Karl felt his hopes lifting.

Brad said: 'Calm down, Mick. Cops chased them away. I was already in the house. Saw them leg it. Went in and got the wife.' He shook Katie, just to emphasise his point.

'Glad you made it,' Mick said, and again there was doubt in his voice.

But any growing feeling Karl might have had about a broken bond between the two men was dispelled when Brad said: 'So why don't you have a feel of this one, Mick.'

'Don't fucking touch her,' Karl shouted.

Mick just laughed. And the gun shifted to one side. Karl's side.

Mick thought for a moment and then said: 'Give that bitch here.'

Brad took a step forward and thrust Katie towards Mick, who put his hand out to receive her. Karl closed his eyes.

CHAPTER EIGHTY-NINE

KATIE

Katie had struggled under her attacker and watched the second intruder move forward to grab her. Only he hadn't.

Instead he'd grabbed the guy on top of her and yanked him back, and down they'd both gone. Katie heard grunting, thudding, and felt the two men banging into her legs as they rolled and wrestled. She'd lain still, in the dark, unable to move, listening, until finally the noises had stopped and a single human shape had risen and stood before her. There'd been enough light coming through the curtains to allow him to see all her nakedness, but she still hadn't moved. Couldn't. Not even a hand to cover herself.

'Get dressed and come with me,' the guy had said. The new guy. The one who, thus far, had acted as if he was on her side.

He'd turned on the light, and she'd seen that he was wearing a balaclava, same as his colleague, but normal clothes, not a boiler suit. She'd sat up and pulled the blanket around her, and that was when she'd seen the boiler suit guy on her bedroom carpet, eyes wide, blonde hair a mess, blood running from his nose. Dead. She could see these things because he no longer wore a balaclava. The guy standing before her must have taken it from him so she wouldn't see his face. She'd thought it was a good sign: wasn't that what they did in the films, covered their faces if they planned on leaving a captive alive?

'Come with me and you'll be safe,' he'd told her, backing off to the doorway, as if to reassure her.

When she hadn't moved, he'd taken a step closer, and she'd shifted backwards on the bed, and that had made him stop. It had been clear to her, then, that he hadn't wanted to scare her.

He'd stripped off the balaclava, tossed it down. Fear had welled up for a second, but he'd been no one she recognised: a soft face, feminine, although he had three long scratch wounds on his forehead. A face she'd thought she could… trust.

'Who are you?'

'Just get dressed. I'll help you and your husband. Call the cops and I can't do that, and they won't find him, at least not alive. You have a choice. Call them or come with me.' He'd pointed at the bedside phone, but she hadn't moved. Then he'd backed out of the doorway and shut the door. She'd scrambled for the phone.

But she hadn't made the call. She'd thought about what he had said, and about the rogue policeman who had tried to abduct Karl. Other policemen could be involved. This strange man had saved her, but who was he? Some kind of friend, of course, and someone who knew all about what had been going on. Someone who claimed he could take her to him, help them both.

Against her better judgement, she'd moved away from the phone, thrown on clothing, one ear on the door, half-expecting him to burst in, all of it some joke. But the door had stayed shut.

She'd opened the door slowly once dressed, and he'd been there, sitting on the top stair. Just waiting, either for her or the cops. He'd stood, gone down the stairs without a word.

She'd followed, even though her fear radar had been screaming. When she'd got to the top of the stairs and looked down, he'd been there, at the bottom, waiting again. And then he'd moved away.

At the living room doorway, she'd peered round. If this was all some trick, she figured, there would be a surprise for her here, in the living room. But there hadn't been. Just the guy, standing at the kitchen door and waiting for her. He'd vanished again as soon as he'd seen her.

He'd been waiting at the open back door. Moonlight soaked his shoulders and head, but his face had been in shadow. Again, he'd vanished the moment she saw him. She was being led like some dumb animal, she'd realised. No, she'd told herself, he was keeping his distance, that was all.

It had happened again. He'd been at the open back gate just long enough to confirm that she had appeared at the door. When she'd reached the gate, she'd looked out and seen him at the end of the driveway. She'd been reminded of chasing a rainbow as a kid, riding her bike towards the giant arc of colour but never getting any closer.

She'd felt better, then, because she was out where people could see. In fact, there'd been a guy with a dog on the other side of the road, just ambling past. She could have called for help. But she hadn't. Some part of her hadn't wanted to because she trusted the soft-faced man.

When the dog-walker had disappeared behind a white van, she'd seen the stranger inside the vehicle, waiting. She'd gone to it, opened the passenger door and, shocking herself even after coming this far, got inside. As she'd climbed in, she'd seen another guy in the back, slumped on the floor between two armchairs. Dead. It hadn't shocked her but reinforced her belief that the man was there to help. He had killed two men in order to save her, for a reason she didn't yet know.

'Where's Karl?' she'd asked.

Brad had started the engine. He'd known this would have been the point where she would have flown if she'd finally decided to. But she'd just sat there, with no clue that he wasn't taking her to her husband.

'I don't know for sure,' he'd said. 'But I promise I'm here to help you.' He'd handed her a knife. She'd looked at it. She was supposed to have taken it, to know that he'd been offering it as a weapon against him if he'd tried anything. The gesture had seemed to have been enough, though, because she'd shaken her head.

He'd pulled away from the kerb slowly, had given her the option to leap out if she'd suddenly decided she wanted no part of this. She'd stayed in her seat, staring ahead through the windscreen. Doubting herself. Twenty seconds later they'd got up to forty and away from the estate, and Brad had shifted his mind from the woman. She would have baulked by now if planning to, so he had her trust. He'd emptied his mind, because he'd known he could not plan his next move until he'd found out for sure about Dave. He hadn't spoken, and the woman beside him hadn't either, and they'd driven like that, like a married couple comfortable with silence.

If he'd been on the fence about Mick's traitorous intentions tonight, all doubt had vanished when he'd turned onto Dave's street and seen flashing blue lights. Two police cars and an ambulance. It could have been down to a pair of neighbours having a violent confrontation, but he'd known it hadn't been. Dave. Something had happened to Dave. No, Mick. *Mick* had happened to Dave.

He'd turned the van and got the hell out of there before the cops could have seen him. His mind somersaulted. Mick had finally derailed. His plan tonight had been to go out with a bang, regardless of the damage, then escape. Gold and Seabury and Grafton's wife were his enemies and had had to be put down, Brad got that. Brad and Dave had information that could have sunk him, so Brad understood Mick's motivation there, too. Seabury's wife, though… unnecessary. A step too far. Enough to change things. Brad had never intended to take the woman to her husband at all. His plan had been to dump her at a cop shop. Then, though, he'd said: 'I need your help. I'll take you to your husband, but there will be another man there. I need you to play along with me, if you can. I know you're pregnant, but I need something from you. It will be hard, but it's the only way. Let me explain…'

CHAPTER NINETY

MICK

She stumbled forward, unable to stop, and Mick didn't expect her momentum, which amplified her weight. Unprepared for such a heavy impact from a petite woman, he lost his feet. He hit the floor hard, with the woman on top of him.

'Run,' he heard Brad shout.

Catlike, he slipped from under the woman even before her full weight had landed on him. He tried to stand, and took someone's knee right in the face. He fell back, crashing into the bookcase beside the fireplace, and raised the gun and his eyes at the same time. Brad was right there, moving in, a knife in his hand, but the gun changed whatever plan he had and he darted aside as Mick fired.

It gave Mick space. He lunged forward, grabbed Brad around the waist and lifted him up. But Brad crunched his abdominals as his torso went over Mick's shoulder, forcing himself forward fast. Unprepared for the manoeuvre, Mick toppled backwards, falling into the bookcase again, crushing Brad into it.

Mick scrambled away as Brad fell to the ground, and this time it was Mick's knee and Brad's skull that collided. Brad thumped back against the bookcase, and Mick leaned in, grabbed his hair. The pistol was right there on the carpet, so Mick snatched it up with his free hand and swung it, and his head, towards the far wall where his captives were.

'Don't mo—' That was all he got out before he realised he was aiming at nothing. Seabury, Seabury's bitch wife, and Grafton's bitch wife – had seized the moment and darted away like terrified cats.

'Again!' Mick yelled in anger. They had got away yet again, but this time because of his damn dallying about. He yanked on Brad's head, toppling him from his sitting position, dragged him a few feet, and thrust his head into the open fire. Coal jumped and sparked and fell out onto the granite hearth. As he leaped away, screaming in pain, Brad's arm cast over an ornate metal urn holding pokers, spilling them onto the carpet.

Mick stepped back as Brad yelped and clutched his face.

'This, Brad, *this*? After what I did for you?'

'This, Mick, *this*!' Brad yelled back. He swiped at a burning piece of coal on the hearth with his fingers, sending it flying. It went nowhere near Mick. 'After you tried to have me killed. Did you forget?'

Mick had no response to that.

'Dave I could understand, if I had your fucked head.' Brad swiped another dislodged piece of coal. Mick had to jump aside to avoid this one. Brad sat up. 'But I was with you all the way, Mick. You had no reason to think I'd run out on you.'

'Got no reason to think I'll crash on the way home, Brad, but I'm still gonna wear a seatb—'

Brad made to sweep another piece of coal, and Mick reacted by stepping back. Instead Brad grabbed a poker from the spilled urn and launched it. Mick lifted a defensive hand and turned his head, but the poker clipped his busted ear. He yelped, staggered back, brought the gun up but by then Brad was up and moving forward, powering into Mick's legs, driving both men across the room.

Mick pivoted, using Brad's momentum to swing him hard against the wall, hip first. Brad's grip failed, and he collapsed to the carpet, clutching his hip. Mick stepped back, slotted his gun away and snatched up the poker. He cracked it hard against the hand laid on Brad's hip, lacerating the flesh. Brad yelped and clutched the bleeding limb to his chest.

'You'd be long dead in a prison graveyard if not for me, Brad. So, you've got no right to moan that the gift bag is empty.'

'And you'd still need to burn the whole world if not for me.'

That made Mick pause, and Brad saw his chance to crawl towards the doorway in desperate hope. Mick followed him. His eyes sought the next spot to pulverise, decided on the right shoulder so that both arms would be hurt. Brad screamed, but continued to crawl. Out the door, and towards the front doorway. Mick followed.

Brad was halfway across the threshold, halfway into the big wide world, when he raised himself onto his knees. It wouldn't be long before the guy could stand again, and run, so Mick attacked him with a blow across the lower spine. But Brad didn't drop, so Mick helped by kicking him in the ass. Brad sprawled forward onto his belly on the tarmac.

'I won't ever forget!' Mick bellowed. No matter how fast they had run, they'd hear his threat and believe it. He would never forget, and he would never stop, and there would be no place to hide for them ever again. He would emerge from the woodwork when they least expected it.

He raised the poker for another shot, this time a finisher, on the skull. Mick laughed as Brad covered his head with his hands and unleashed a roar of fear.

Only it wasn't a roar, Mick realised. It was the growing sound of an engine. And by the time he had worked this out – half a second after hearing it – it was too late. The speeding van was almost upon him. He jumped back into the doorway a second before the van hit the frame with a thunderous boom and crunch of glass.

Frozen in place, chest heaving, gun raised, and just inches from the crumpled front of the van, Mick laughed as he realised he had been here before. But *this* time something was different. *This* time he was facing no wall of metal.

This time his gun was pointed directly, undeniably, at the guy sitting shocked behind the steering wheel.

'*This* time I see you,' he said, and fired. Four shots. The guy in the van thumped back in his seat four times, and then slumped forward, dead.

CHAPTER NINETY-ONE

KARL

They were hiding behind the solicitor's car, still in the danger zone, but it was the only hiding place unless they wanted to risk running along the street. Katie had been up for that, but both Liz and Karl chose the car when they saw Danny's van, headlights off, cut a sharp and fast curve into the car park. Liz had raised a hand to get his attention, but then Danny had hit the gas, and they could see why: Brad had exited the building with Mick right behind him. Karl had watched with a strange sense of déjà vu as the van slammed hard into the doorway. This time, faster, the van had suffered. There was a great bang, the windscreen blew out, and the entire front of the vehicle crumpled like tinfoil.

'Danny!' Liz cried out when they heard the gunshots.

She tried to rise and run, but this time Karl possessed the anchoring hand. She fought against his grip, but he refused to release her. Katie was crying, asking under her breath, over and over, what was going on.

Then they saw the back doors of the van burst open and Mick was there, holding the gun, aiming out at nothing. He must have climbed inside through the busted windscreen, and smashed his way through the partition between cabin and cargo area.

'One more down and here I come for the rest of you,' Mick screamed into the night, like an over-eager kid playing hide-and-seek.

He jumped down and started running right towards them, but surely he couldn't know where they were hiding?

A moment before they got up and fled in panic, Mick fell. He'd only managed one step, and then he was down, hard. They heard it. They saw his face hit the ground, saw blood from his nose spray across the dark tarmac. Heard his gun scrape across the ground.

Then they saw a hand clutching one of Mick's feet.

Brad was suddenly on Mick's legs, climbing, pulling himself out from under the back of the van. Somehow the entire vehicle had missed him when Danny's van hit the doorway, just like before. Mick tried to turn, but then Brad was astride him, mounting him, and raining down hammer-drill fists. Mick fell away and lay limp, but Brad's fists continued to rise and fall.

Eventually Brad rolled off and crawled to the dropped gun. Both men stood at the same time. Eight feet separated them. Mick's legs were wobbly, and he was covered in blood.

Liz struggled again and this time slipped Karl's anchor.

'Shoot him!' she screamed. She stumbled out from behind the car. 'Shoot him!'

Brad made the mistake of turning to look at her, and that could have been it. Eight feet, one second to close that distance. Game over.

Instead, Mick turned and ran. He was injured, though, and his gait was a messy stumble. But it did its job: distance grew between him and the gun. Brad took a step forward, meaning to pursue, but his leg gave out because of his injured hip and he went down onto one knee, his free hand clutching at his lower spine. The gun continued to track Mick as he stumbled away into the dark. But the gun did not fire.

'Shoot him!' Liz rushed to Brad and tried to grab the gun, but he swatted her away. The gun continued to aim at Mick's back, but the gap between him and the bullet kept growing.

Karl emerged from behind the car and went to Liz, and Katie followed. Six feet behind Brad, they watched the gun and, beyond it, Mick's staggering form, a trick of perspective making the weapon and the man look the same size.

'Shoot that bastard!' Liz screamed.

But the gun did not fire. Beyond it, Mick's shape shrank, and the darkness closed around him, until there was nothing to watch except the inactive gun.

Which continued to stare its single eye at nothing.

*

Violent enforcer, gun in hand, but no longer a threat. They approached him cautiously.

At first, there was a conflict of realities as Brad pointed his gun at them, yet said he was not here to cause any more hurt. Eventually he lowered the gun, although he refused to drop it. He then sat on the kerb and lowered his head. Ready to talk, because he had waited for them.

He'd waited while they had rushed to Danny's van. Liz wanted to remove his body from the van, but it was obvious to Karl it was a no-go: the mechanism designed to extract the chair from the van had been twisted when the vehicle hit the house. Liz tugged at his chair, but failure only increased her woe, and Karl stepped in to pull her away.

'This is no place to leave him,' she cried, but she didn't again try to heave her friend free. She ordered Karl to fetch a cover, and he found a jacket of Danny's in the back. He stepped up to lay it over Danny, but she snatched it in order to perform the task herself. She kissed Danny's cheek, and closed his eyes, just like in the films. She lay the jacket over him, rested her head on his leg and waved Karl away. She wanted to say her goodbyes. He gave her time. When she walked away a few minutes later, she went straight towards Brad.

Liz and Karl stopped eight feet away from him, as if for safety, although it meant nothing while he held the gun. Katie joined them. Karl stepped up, ahead of the women, and said: 'It seems like you want to make amends. The only way would be to give yourself up to the police.'

A firm *no*.

'But I will help you. Closure, I guess. I will tell you what happened last night.'

Karl heard a sharp intake of breath from behind. Liz. 'Let me call the police. You can help clear our names.'

A firm *no*.

'I'll help you though. Closure, like I said.'

He looked up. Liz stepped past Karl and in front of him, into the firing line. He put a warning hand on her shoulder, but she flicked away his fingers.

'He was good to you, Bradley,' she said. '*I* was good to you. Why would you do this? Why would you kill my husband?'

'I broke into his house.'

'I damn well know that, I was there—'

'I attacked you in the clothing shop.'

'That's not an answer, you bastard. Why—?'

'I hunted you down.'

Liz said nothing.

'So why would I lie?' Brad asked.

'What? What are you—?'

'The nightclub shooting, Elizabeth. That's why. I know you don't want to hear this, but this is what I'm going to tell you. Believe it or not. Just ask yourself why I'd lie, after all this.'

Brad said: 'Ron wanted a major rival out of the way and set him up. Me and a guy called Dave, we were meant to shoot the place up, make it look like a robbery, and make sure a man called Razor Randolph got hit. Shot at in the nightclub of a major rival by guys who got past his security. But he survived. How could

Randolph not suspect Grafton? Grafton's only option, apparently, was to give the shooters up. So he did. He betrayed us. He sent us in there, and then he sold us down the river when it didn't work. He put out the word that we were good suspects, to give the impression he was eager to see justice for his good friend and business partner. It was as good as a death sentence.'

Her head said she refused to believe it. Loyal to her husband, Liz snorted with scorn. 'That's not what happened. So, what, you thought you'd been betrayed so went to that dodgy cop for help? What was his reason for wanting revenge? For wanting to slaughter my husband?'

Brad looked at her for a long time. Then he said: 'If Ron didn't tell you—'

She cut in: 'He told me everything, you bastard. *Everything.* I know everything. And he wouldn't have lied. Not to me. There was nothing he did to that cop.'

Calmly, Brad said: 'Then he didn't care enough to remember what he did. It was just another day in the park to him.'

It was exactly what Mick had said.

'And if you don't know,' Brad added, 'it's not my place to tell you.'

'I saw his chest wound,' Karl said.

Brad laughed. 'Yeah, you did. He made sure that fucker didn't heal properly, as a reminder. But that's all I'll say about that.'

She said: 'That man tried to kill you, and you're going to defend—'

'Shut up,' Brad shouted, surprising her into silence. He jumped to his feet. She staggered back, as if physically hit by the shockwave of his yell.

'If you don't know what your husband did to Mick then he was right: it meant nothing to Grafton. Go find out yourselves.'

He paused and then sat on the kerb again. He saw them looking at the gun. A second later it was gone, tucked away. In its place was a mobile phone. His eyes hit the ground again.

'Mick McDevitt wasn't always bad. He started off good. He didn't get knocked off the rails by money or power, unlike your husband.'

'So, what turned him insane?' Katie snarled from the back. Karl grabbed her, terrified that her outburst was going to make the gun and the anger and the violence reappear. But Brad didn't even look up.

'I'm not even sure he turned. Maybe it was in him all along. Nature versus nurture, eh? Maybe it's in us all.'

'You and him got a bigger share,' Katie spat.

Now he looked up, pointing at Liz. 'It was people like your husband who brought it out. Okay? Their ability to walk through the rain without getting wet. And I'm not just talking about murder or fraud, like the trial Ron just beat. People like him, they've got the clout and money to put up a fight, and the government always backs down. That's what changed Mick. The law tied his hands, and it put people like your husband back on the streets. So, Mick didn't respect the law in return. I don't mean he turned corrupt. He wasn't, at first. He didn't fit up innocent people, or take bribes. How Mick put it once: he was bridging the gaps. Overstepping lines to do what was necessary. At least, that's how it started. When he made DCI and got control of investigations, he came up with something he called the Loyalty Box. He kept incriminating evidence to force people to work for him. Some of that evidence was kept in order to take down the bigger fish. He was always working to put bad people away.'

'How commendable,' Liz said, full of scorn.

'Is it really any different to how police informants work? Think of Mick's people as informants who don't get paid. That guy he sent to your shop, for instance. Król. Mick's team searched his flat after an old Asian shopkeeper was stabbed. The knife was right there, but Mick secretly took it. That might seem like a bad move to you because Król didn't go to prison for assault. But in Mick's hands he's given up two killers in the last few months. And he wasn't paid. Two murders solved that wouldn't have been if Mick hadn't held that stabbing over Król. One of those guys, there was no evidence against him for murder, but the Loyalty Box got him for a burglary he had nothing to do with. The bottom line is that the guy is in prison and wouldn't have been if not for Mick.' Nobody looked impressed. Brad tossed his phone. Karl caught it.

'What happens now?' Karl said.

Brad looked at Katie. 'I'm sorry I pushed you into Mick like that, and for tricking you. I know you're pregnant, but there was no other way to get him off guard.' He turned to Karl. 'Start filming, Hitchcock. Show the cops. It's all you'll get. I'll tell you what happened that night. I think you deserve that, daft as that might sound. Whatever. I'll tell it and then I'm out of here.'

'Why are you doing this?' Liz asked.

'You wouldn't get it.'

'Don't act like you know me. You don't. Not any more.'

'*Melius est nomen bonum quam divitae multae,*' Brad said, which puzzled everyone. 'See. You don't know me, either. Now, if you don't want to hear this, start walking.'

Nobody moved.

CHAPTER NINETY-TWO

MICK

Despite the rush to get out of the city, Mick opted to head back to Stepney to collect his car. It had things inside that he needed. He showed his badge to the taxi driver and told him to bill the Metropolitan Police. A few minutes later he was behind the wheel, heading out of London. Despite the rush, he pulled into the side of a desolate road as he spotted something.

The Alsatian, digging its nose into rubbish in the gutter, watched his approach with caution but didn't scarper. It even took his stroke. Not a beaten animal that had escaped a hell of a home, then. Maybe just a stray.

He looked around. He and the dog, the only living things out here with fewer than six legs. Good, but not essential: happening regardless.

'Good boy. What do you weigh, about four stone? Needs must, eh?'

It allowed itself to be led to his car where there was a packet of crisps. He held a crisp high, and the dog reared up to put its forepaws on his waist in order to take the snack.

'Since I've been nice, would you like to help me with something? You'd like to reward my kindness, wouldn't you?'

He got in his car and jabbed the button for the window until it was open six inches. The dog got its head through by turning it sideways. It snatched the next crisp and yanked its head back out to chomp.

'Did you know that a dog called Horand was the first of your kind? I bet you'd like that name.'

The dog stuck its head through to get the next crisp.

'But I'll have to call you Grafton, I'm afraid. Watch my paintwork, won't you?'

The dog took the crisp just as Mick jabbed the window button and raised glass into its throat. Its paws raked the door as it tried to drag its head out. Mick had to use one hand to help the window up because the mechanism wasn't powerful enough to do the job.

He got out the passenger side as the dog struggled. It was still struggling as Mick stopped behind it, with his knife, but its shrieking changed to a low moan, somewhat pleading.

'I promise it won't hurt and will soon be o—' He stopped. The knife slipped from his fingers. 'You're a girl.' He realised that punishing the dog wouldn't satisfy his urge to kill. She wasn't Grafton or some scumbag that deserved to die. He watched Horand struggle for a few more seconds, then got back in the car. He dropped the window.

In his headlights, he watched Horand flee.

CHAPTER NINETY-THREE

MICK

'On the night in question we drove in a stolen Mazda to Bexley, and transferred into a stolen Volvo for the trip to Ronald Grafton's hideaway. We had to wait until he was released after his trial, which we knew he'd win. It was supposed to be a beating and a robbery, because we knew Ron had some rainy-day money stashed. And we were going to drop a piece of jewellery that would make Grafton suspect Ramirez. We went in the back way, through the kitchen. Just sneaked in, three guys in black. I had a knife, Mick had a handgun, and Dave carried a shotgun. We heard voices and laughter. I think they were a little bit drunk. In the living room, there they were: Grafton, and two other people I didn't know. We knew you were upstairs, Liz, when we heard you shout down. Everyone was drinking and talking. Grafton was standing in front of the sofa, while the other two sat there. Laughing and having a great time when we burst in…'

Brad was giving up their secrets for the world on the video that had made its way onto YouTube after some bobby had leaked it from the station. It was the very last thing Mick had expected in a wild week of newspaper headlines. He could hardly believe what his eyes were seeing. But amid the shock… joy. He hadn't thought much about the events prior to Grafton's death, but Brad's words sent his mind sailing back.

He had led the way into the hideaway cottage, handgun pointing ahead. They'd stopped at the living room doorway, listening. Grafton had been centre stage, talking some horseshit or other, and his wife had shouted down. Something Mick couldn't remember, but it had made Grafton groan with embarrassment and the others laugh. That was when Mick had made his move. It was the height of their fun, as laughter echoed. Fast into the living room, behind pointing guns and bellowing voices, for maximum shock – that had been the plan. But he saw a sweeter vision float behind his eyes.

He slipped in, quiet as a mouse, and managed to get right up behind Grafton before his guests even noticed. He jabbed the barrel of the pistol against the back of his neck and actually sighed. A beautiful moment, long, long awaited.

'You forgot our party invites, arsehole,' he said.

The unknown man and woman started moaning, but Dave cocked his shotgun and ended all that. Grafton, hands up, didn't even try to turn around.

'Brad, get his wife,' Mick said.

Brad scuttled past and through a doorway and up the stairs.

Grafton turned. His hands were up but his eyes held no fear, even after they recognised Dave and Mick. In fact, the man had relaxed somewhat, as if he thought he was going to be okay because this was a cop holding a gun on him, not a rival. Cops had to toe a line. Another trial he could walk away from.

He jabbed Grafton in the chin with the gun barrel, knocking him onto the sofa. 'Take a seat.'

All three captives were in a line on the sofa, two of them terrified, but one of them smiling. Especially when Mick took off his mask. 'Ladies and gentlemen,' Grafton announced, 'meet Detective Chief Inspector Michael McDevitt, Metropolitan Police, on his last night as an employed man.'

He was grinning like a man who thought he was in control. Dave was looking nervous: out of the corner of his eye Mick could see the shotgun barrel shivering. Mick had unmasked himself, and there was a chance Grafton could work out who his accomplices were. The comeback would be swift, deadly.

Except it wouldn't. Mick had removed his mask in order to give himself that extra push. Now that Grafton knew who he was, this could no longer be just a scare move. Mick had planned it that way all along.

Nobody moved for a second or two. A frozen scene, neither side wanting to make the next move. Then there was a crash from upstairs, and a shout – 'NO YOU DON'T, YOU BITCH!' – and Grafton tried to stand. Mick pushed him back down with a hand. And then the woman leaned forward, and Mick shifted his aim and fired. Just like that. She sat back nice and neat after that.

Dave grabbed Mick's arm, shouted something like 'STOP', and Mick staggered back. That was the cue for Grafton to shift. Not to do what you might expect of a violent career criminal and fight his attacker, and not to do the doting husband thing and try to help his wife. No, Grafton's purpose and concern was all Ronald Grafton. He was up and running, and the other guy was right behind him, both headed for the back door.

Mick grabbed the shotgun from Dave and followed, fast, calling back: 'Find Brad, kill the wife.' At the living room door, he lifted the shotgun and aimed. The hallway was narrow, and Grafton and the other guy were belting along single file.

He pulled the trigger, still running.

Seconds later he was past the dead body on the floor and through the hallway where he stopped at the kitchen door. Grafton had slipped while trying to turn and now he got up slowly, facing Mick, eyeing the shotgun. The back door was to his left, but he backed off, hands up, until he nudged a wine rack on the wall. Mick stopped just feet away. Grafton's eyes told it all: he knew he wasn't walking away from this.

'I have money,' he pleaded. 'Here. All yours. And I forget about tonight.'

Raising the shotgun to Grafton's face, Mick smiled.

And now, he smiled again as he remembered his final words to his long-time enemy. Good memories. In front of him, on the old coffee table in this grimy flat where he was hiding from the world, was a collection of newspapers he had picked out of bins last night. The story was in every single one. He'd heard it told a dozen ways already, but he was still eager to find out what some of the people connected to him had to say. His good old dad had defended him:

Now listen good, and then piss off from my face or I'll smash that camera over your head. I'll say this once. My son got his world cut apart, and the system let him down. It was the system, the way it hunts the small fish and lets the big players walk around untouched, that's what turned my son. And turned he was, because he was a lovely boy and a fine young man. He was a senior detective, for Christ's sake. He was Flying Squad twenty years ago, back when those guys were all just about crooked. He was clean as a whistle. Okay? So you arseholes ask me if I knew I'd raised a monster? Piss off, okay? The system made the monster, not me. The system let that bastard Ronald Grafton off the hook, literally get away with murder, and my son had just had enough. He did this country a favour, but now it wants him where it failed over and over to put people like Ronald Grafton. This government pays a budget of three billion to the Metropolitan Police each year, and they couldn't get this guy. My son did it off his own back. And for bloody free! He wasn't even on the clock! Bloody unpaid overtime! Let every cop work that way, criminals would go the way of smallpox. God bless my son.

Brad's partner had done the same for his lover:

You've got it all wrong, I'm afraid. I know my Brad, and I know he wouldn't have been involved in this unless he was coerced. Just take a look at the things they're saying this disgraced detective did, and then tell me he wouldn't have blackmailed my Brad and others into doing his bidding? Brad might have been a former criminal, that much is well-documented, but the word to focus on here is former. He put his shameful past behind him. He was a changed man. Believe me, I lived with him for months, I knew him better than anyone, and I'm telling you that Brad, if he did these things, did them because he was forced to. I think the detective threatened to harm me: I would be hurt if Brad didn't help him on this daft and bizarre dark justice mission of his. When you find Brad, ask him. I'll bet that's the truth of it.

But that was because they had been blind to the truth. No so with Dave's wife. Mick hadn't realised that Dave had told his wife everything. Her outlook had made for surprising reading:

You pay for work done, don't you? Hire a painter, he paints, you pay. What happens if you don't pay? You get in trouble. So Ronald Grafton should have expected trouble, shouldn't he? And then he cuts them loose. What did he expect? These weren't painters, were they? Hardened criminals. Ten grand each, and you don't stuff hardened criminals, not my Dave, out of ten grand, not even if you're Ronald Grafton. He's lucky they didn't go straight to Razor Randolph and tell him the score. Hey, Razor, Grafton hired me and a pal to pretend to rob that nightclub, but in reality we were supposed to shoot you dead and make it look like collateral damage. How would that have gone down? Grafton would have been killed a lot sooner. I even told Dave he should do that. I mean, he gets stuffed out of ten grand, and then that bastard Ronald Grafton cuts them loose. He fired, like, ten guys that Razor's people wanted to investigate. Appearances, he says. Can't have guys around that Razor's suspicious of. Got to cut the

*gangrenous flesh, like that sort of thing. That was his reason?
To make it look like he was innocent and trying to help? That's
his damn reason for stuffing my Dave? Appearances? Well, he
should have expected a comeback, shouldn't he? And he got it.
But it was all that copper's idea, you make sure you print that.
That McDevitt. Him and Brad Smithfield, two black peas in a
pod. Dave only went along with it for the cash. For the money
he was owed. And there was no plan to do any killing. You print
that, okay? That cop wanted Grafton dead. Smithfield wanted
Grafton dead. Dave was only after payment. After what he was
owed. It's no different to a painter stealing your wallet because
you didn't pay. He's got that right, hasn't he? I mean, you pay
for work done, don't you?*

She had incriminated herself with this talk, and who knows
what she faced now. She was just a regular woman, not part of the
criminal underworld, not bound by their code of ethics, the *them
and us* attitude to law enforcement. Nikos Avramidis, though, was
a criminal who should have known better, but when journalists
started offering cash for scoops, he oozed out from under a rock
with his mouth far from nailed shut. The reporters had quickly
offered him up to his hunters, but not before they got something
juicy and damning:

*Król just says to me, there's this woman he's gotta find. Says it's
for that cop, the one he's always moaning about. Never really
knew the score with him and that cop. Never said the guy's
name, by the way. I know now it's that weirdo McDevitt. But
one day he's saying the guy's fucked in the head and has evidence
on him. Next minute he's saying the cop's in his pocket. I never
knew what to think. But anyways, this cop wanted a woman
found, and he had the address of someone who'd know, so our
job was to go in at night and beat it out of him.*

And now the story was everywhere. Not much ink for Brad because he was a former underworld enforcer, and guys like that did things like this all the time, so nothing new there. But the newspapers had gone to town on Michael McDevitt, Scotland Yard DCI, believed to be responsible for numerous deaths, and assumed to have fled the country. His life and crimes were offered to the world beneath eye-catching headlines, from 'DEFECTIVE DETECTIVE', to 'ROGUE COP ON KILLING SPREE' and 'OFFICER OF DEATH LOOSE ON STREETS'. Every little threat he'd ever made to another officer or a criminal painted him as evil incarnate. Ramirez, now back on the streets, had been quoted heavily. All of his previous investigations were going under the microscope in a search for injustice.

Thinking about Gondal made his lip tremble. He wished he'd let the man live. Gondal had been a good man, a man dedicated to crime fighting, just like he'd been. He should have respected that common bond. However, it wasn't the fact that Gondal was dead that irked him. He could have tied him up to get him out of the way for a couple of hours – that he hadn't thought of doing such, that he'd acted rashly… it was his own fuzzy thinking that upset him. He was supposed to be better than that.

Strangely, there was no mention of the two goons that he'd sent Brad off with, which meant they were either dead and buried, or alive and keeping silent. He was betting they were gone for ever.

He'd expected people in his orbit to tell the journalists all sorts of daftness, of course. What he hadn't counted on was how many people from his past would jump on the bandwagon. Someone from his school had called a paper to talk about 'KILLER COP'S EVIL STREAK', without, of course, mentioning that all he'd ever done was flushed his head down a toilet for ruining Mick's pencil case. 'KILLER COP'S EX-GIRLFRIEND SUFFERED YEARS OF RAPE AND ABUSE', apparently, which must have happened while he was sleepwalking and she'd chosen never to bring it up. Most infuriating of all, though, some midwife now seventy years old had claimed that she knew 'KILLER COP WAS EVIL BABY' just from the look in his eyes in his mother's arms.

That shallow bullshit was worthy of headlines but where was his highlight reel? Where were the supercop stories? They had him for 'RESPECTED SOLICITOR MURDERED', but there was no ink allocated to the post office robbery he'd single-handedly thwarted while off-duty as a uniformed constable. 'EVIL DETECTIVE SLAUGHTERS DISABLED MAN IN COLD BLOOD' was more headline-worthy than his record of twenty-six killers and eighty-five armed robbers behind bars. Instead of 'PHILANTHROPIST' because he'd organised a 'cops vs criminals' charity football match last year, they called him 'RACIST' because the fellow cop he'd killed had been of Pakistani origin!

Worse than all of that, though, Alize had found out. She hadn't replied to any of his messages in which he'd said he'd be with her soon. He'd agreed to meet her near Berlin where he'd told her he was meeting a guy from the German State Criminal Police Office to discuss a joint venture. Then, three days ago, long after his name had spread across the world, she'd messaged back, right out of the blue.

Missing you, where are you, Sweetcake?

That question had speared his heart.

Eight months of texting since he'd met her online, a hundred phone calls, swapped presents, *and then this!* They would have had a great holiday, and then he would have told her he was staying on in Berlin, and before long he would have moved in with her, and together they would have enjoyed the sweet life, but instead *she fucking did this!* The bitch hadn't even tried to get his version of the story; she had swallowed every word in the papers and run to the police. They were clearly controlling her social media accounts and using her to lead him into a trap.

The only consolation, if it even qualified as one, was that his *be with you soon* claim had his hunters looking overseas. Let them waste manpower hiding in bushes around her home, and let her have sleepless nights as she worried that every noise was the infamous DCI Mick McDevitt, PSYCHO SLEUTH, coming down the fucking chimney.

He was angry, but there was also cause for relief. One vital aspect was missing from every newspaper. The crucial component: the spark that had ignited everything. The event that had instigated his becoming a 'MURDEROUS TOP DETECTIVE' was in there among a plethora of assumptions, but the newshounds and amateur psychologists had missed their chance to solve the case. He was surprised, and a little proud, that Brad hadn't spilled the beans, especially given the prime opportunity he'd had before the video camera.

In other news: in Slade Green, a package had been posted to the parents of a sixteen-year-old girl who had been raped eighteen months ago. Her CitizenCard had been taken by the rapist as a trophy. When it fell through their letterbox, the parents thought the rapist was taunting them, and they handed the card to the police. Scientists quickly found DNA matching a known sexual offender, and yesterday he had been apprehended while sleeping rough with his brother. When Brad's street gossipers had first provided the culprit's name, Seamus Hunt, Mick had been loath to use the man, but over the months the offender had provided the location of three meets at which eight paedophiles had been arrested. Mick had destroyed every other piece of evidence in the Loyalty Box, but he had been unable to allow a child molester to walk free.

Seamus Hunt had so far chosen not to mention 'SLAYBIAN OF THE YARD's' name, so the world didn't know about his involvement in those embarrassing cases. Good.

Finally, he turned his attention to what really mattered.

He typed Karl's name, but got nothing. Liz's name brought up the triple murder and some offshoot stories. Nothing about their involvement in the past few days' activities. Clearly this meant they had not been charged and that their names had been kept out of the papers. Certainly they would have had their lives scrutinised by detectives because they were integral performers in this production: statements checked, pasts unearthed, every coincidence put under the microscope. But, in the end, they had walked through this thing unscathed. Mick burned with anger at that notion: Karl and Liz out there, right now, probably fucking each other and laughing and living their lives as normal, and not giving Detective Chief Inspector Michael McDevitt a second thought.

But gossip wasn't his reason for scouring the newspapers for Liz Grafton. He was after a specific piece of information, and when he found it, it made him sit back in the battered, puke-smelling armchair in shock.

He remembered taking the piss out of Brad for believing that he and his gay lover were destined to be together, but since then a number of occurrences had eaten away at his cynicism. That story in the newspaper finally pushed him from sceptic to believer.

Now he knew why the bitch had escaped his wrath every single time he had her within his grasp. Fate. It was meant to be.

CHAPTER NINETY-FOUR

KARL

Barely twelve miles away, Karl was indeed trying to get on with his life, but he was not sleeping with Liz Grafton. He hadn't seen her since that night. He had asked about her, of course, and knew she was up north somewhere, staying with an old school friend that not even the police had a name for. Still fearing for her life, maybe, or just eager for new surroundings to ease the pain. Karl, though, had stopped worrying about his old enemies. The police had watched his house for the first two days, but since then he'd been a sitting duck. And there had been no attack. Two days ago he'd finally stopped watching the street through a gap in the curtains. McDevitt was gone. He was hiding somewhere in Germany. He was no longer a threat.

New surroundings were something that Katie wanted. They had talked about a long holiday, but didn't have the money just yet. So, they watched TV – never the news – and chatted – never about THAT – and shopped, and cleaned, and tried to return their lives to normal, to reinject the boring, repetitive aspects of life, in order to move on. They were aware that each minute that passed would make acceptance easier. There would be problems, though. Karl couldn't face reopening the shop because a man had died there, and there was tension between he and his business partner because of it. As if it had been Karl's fault. Katie's dad's house was going on the market because Katie couldn't bear to return to it after her ordeal, and Peter was doing a bad job of hiding the fact that he also held Karl at fault. Then there were the headaches. Like a muscle overtrained that aches the next day, his mind had been so seriously assaulted that his head now throbbed constantly. But he got through it by thinking of the muscle analogy: it would heal bigger and stronger.

Katie was in the bath and Karl was in the living room when the phone rang.

'You never did tell me your baby's name.'

It was Liz. He hadn't expected to hear from her again.

'We're going for Alex. We don't know if it's a boy or girl. But that fits both. Alexandra or Alexander.'

'That's nice,' she said.

For a short time they chatted about things inconsequential. Her husband wasn't mentioned, but she did tell him that she was selling 'the businesses' and going back to college to study veterinary medicine, which she had pursued many years ago but given up in order to run two of Grafton's 'enterprises'. Mick McDevitt wasn't mentioned, but she did fleetingly say she was going to be donating serious amounts to charity because 'auditors are sticking their noses in'. She hinted that Britain wouldn't be home for long because there were 'people wanting to muscle in'. He felt bad for her, but couldn't find enough solace to want to continue the conversation. It brought back too many bad memories. And there were niggling doubts that she'd been as innocent as he'd assumed – certainly some newspapers didn't believe Elizabeth Grafton had been nothing but a doting wife love-blind to her husband's crimes. So, there were silences on his end.

She tapered off mid-sentence and said: 'Ronald's funeral is on Saturday. I'd like you to come.'

He paused long enough for her to understand.

'I don't know what good it would do, either,' Liz said. 'But having you there is what my brain's saying is the right thing. Or at least offering you the chance to attend. Up to you.'

He was pretty certain it would turn out to be a bad idea. Maybe the press would be there and would wonder who he was. They might enquire, then poke, then unravel, and before he knew it they'd have the truth, so brilliantly hidden by the police so far. But his brain was telling him he couldn't say no. Liz wanted him to go, so he would go. He couldn't explain why, but he felt he owed her that. It would be a tricky situation because funerals were a time of grief and he felt nothing but abhorrence for Ronald Grafton. But that wasn't what worried him as he ended the call.

The trickiest part of all would be breaking the news to Katie.

CHAPTER NINETY-FIVE

BRAD

Since the target car-shared to and from work and wasn't a social animal, getting to him alone would prove a problem. Luckily, the target had a doctor's appointment at noon the next day.

He saw the car turn into the car park at 11.40 a.m. and find a space near the back where a low wall separated the grounds from those of a Co-op. It backed in, and stopped. He hopped over the wall, yanked open the passenger door and slipped neatly inside, grabbing the back of the driver's head.

Ian broke the kiss after just a second.

'Where the hell have you been, Brad?'

Brad sank low in the seat, watching the road. He'd seen the police watching the house and figured they might have followed Ian. But there was no sign.

'Don't believe what the papers have been saying. Not all of it is true.'

'I know what journalists are like, Brad. And I thought I knew you. Just tell me, is someone dead because of something you did?'

Brad didn't answer and didn't look away from the road. But this time it was because of shame. And his silence gave Ian all the answers he needed.

'I cannot be with a man in prison.'

'They won't catch me.'

'Then I cannot be with a man running from the police.'

'It would be like the early days. Secret meetings.'

'Now is not a time for jokes.'

'You don't know the full story.'

'Maybe you can beat this. But I can't be with a man who lied to me.'

They both watched the road for a few seconds. 'So what happens now?'

Ian said nothing. Brad looked across and saw a mobile in Ian's hands. Using it would end things for ever, he understood.

'Where will you go?' Ian asked.

'You mean where after I leave here?'

Ian didn't answer that. 'I'm supposed to call the police if I hear from you.'

'And is that what you're going to do?'

No answer. But the phone was still in his hands. Brad opened his door and got out. He shut it, but stood there, waiting. After five seconds, nothing happened, so he turned to leave.

The window came down. He stopped, and bent, and they looked at each other.

'You understand my decision, don't you, Brad? There were promises. Jobless and destitute, I don't care. I said that, didn't I? I wanted a good man. I said if you ever went back to that way of life, it was over. Remember?' Ian rolled up his left sleeve to expose a tattoo along the inner forearm.

'I remember. I know I can't win you back. I accept that. But it's not too late for this to still mean something.'

Brad exposed his own inner left forearm, and the same Latin phrase, Proverb 22:1. His return promise.

'Melius est nomen bonum quam divitae multae.'

A good name is more desirable than great riches.

CHAPTER NINETY-SIX

KARL

Karl had seen gangster funerals in films and read about real-life ones in the papers, and this one was nothing like he had expected. Six sleek black limousines followed the hearse which had so many floral tributes hanging off it that it looked like a rolling garden, but the turnout was mediocre. No throngs lined the streets bearing placards with the dead man's face, no shops were shut in tribute, no planes flew overhead with banners. It looked like any other funeral. He put it down to the fact that Ronald Grafton had never achieved high infamy. Many knew his name, but there were many criminals out there and few carved a place in history the way the Kray twins had. He saw no police, either, unless they were undercover.

He had asked Katie if she'd wanted to attend, and she had: for two whole days, right up to the point where they pulled up outside the church.

'I don't want to do this,' she said, which he'd been expecting. He was ready to turn the car around and leave, but she pointed at a greasy spoon across the road and said she would wait there. He said they could forget the funeral. She said he should do this for Liz. He said okay. He kissed her cheek, and stroked her belly, and off she scuttled. He turned his focus to the church.

*

He was on time, but people were already oozing out of the door. Liz must have decided that the service itself was private. Karl stood by his car and scrutinised the mourners. Some of the men who came out of the church were big, mean-looking brutes in suits who shook dozens of hands and were given space wherever they stood or stepped or turned. He assumed these people were other ganglords, maybe rivals who had turned up to pay their respects. They might have been employees, hired muscle mourning the loss of their beloved boss, or just their beloved jobs. Many of the other attendees were ladies attached to those men and a host were children and teenagers. This scene fitted more with the gangland community picture that he'd had in mind, but overall there seemed nothing untoward. It was just a funeral. He wondered how many of the sixty or so present actually wanted to be here. He certainly didn't.

He didn't see Liz.

The burial was elsewhere.

He crossed to the café to fetch Katie.

She was silent for most of the drive to the cemetery and he had a good idea why. She had never quite forgiven Liz for entering their lives and all the damage she brought.

When they arrived at the cemetery, she announced that she would wait in the car.

The crowd was bigger at this venue. At least a hundred, all in black. The sky was overcast, the gravestones were grey, and even the grass in this monochrome world was washed out, all of which added to his depression. Here, further indication of Grafton's criminal status: the gates were manned by shady-looking big guys to keep out intruders. Others lined the perimeter wall at intervals. Karl had a mad moment when he searched the skies for some enemy of Grafton's coming in by parachute.

Finally, he spotted Liz. She was in a black suit dress and had black hair now, dyed to match this dark occasion. It was also cut short, as if she'd opted for practicality rather than appearance. During the burial, she kept her head bowed, dabbing at her eyes now and then. Karl kept back, beside a large mausoleum some 260 feet away, and watched the show. He felt like an intruder.

He couldn't hear anything, and, although the silence was eerie, he preferred that. The things said around the grave wouldn't gel with what he believed about Ronald Grafton. He tried not to look at an open grave near where he stood, lined with wooden planks and tarpaulin, a great mound of dirt next to it. He tried not to wonder which poor bastard was going into that one later today. He pictured a family milling outside the church, waiting for their turn. Busy places, graveyards. People were dying to get in, so went the old joke.

The coffin was lowered. Liz and another woman, facing each other across the hole, tossed in a handful of dirt each. Liz then lowered a small wooden box using a length of rope, tossed the rope in and stepped back.

And then it was done. He wondered why he'd come since he'd been nothing but an observer, and always from a distance. He watched people file away, but Liz broke off and approached him.

'Glad you could come.' She lit a cigarette. Had she started smoking since he'd last seen her?

'I'm sorry,' he said, thinking that was the line to use at a burial. She nodded.

Beyond them, the final few people were vanishing. They were alone except for a mourner off to the left, coming in their direction. Some guy in a suit with an opened umbrella covering most of his head, as if he expected rain to pay its weekly respects to a dead relative. But the grey skies were all bark and no bite.

'The wake is at my house. Both welcome, if you like. I'm guessing your wife felt awkward being here today. I hope she and the baby are okay, by the way.'

As she raised the cigarette to her lips, he noticed a bandage along the underside of her hand where the paw print tattoo was. Or used to be.

She saw his eyes drop to her hand and said: 'Part of the accepting.'

He understood: why pretend the journey wasn't over?

'The wake?' She prompted.

Karl noticed the mourner had veered off a path, and was heading their way. He looked around to make sure he wasn't standing too close to a grave. 'I think I need to get home,' he said. 'Katie and the baby are fine though. Thank you. Are you okay?'

'I'm fine, too. This has been the hardest part. Hopefully life gets easier from here.'

Karl had buried his father five years earlier. He could testify that time was a good healer. But he said nothing. The events of last week had mentally battered and bruised him and he wondered how his wounds would heal over the next five years.

Liz heard the approach of the suited mourner, turned; Karl saw that he was weaving his way past graves just thirty feet away. She sounded like she wanted to wrap things up before the stranger was in their vicinity. 'Well, I should get back. Maybe we'll meet again, Karl Seabury.'

'Maybe, Elizabeth Grafton,' he replied, before he could wonder if she'd reverted to her maiden name. To accept the journey's end.

Liz turned to go. She paused to let the mourner walk across her path, but he didn't. As Karl watched in shock, the mourner stepped across a grave laid with coloured stones, dropped his umbrella, and yanked her, one-handed, into him. He slipped an arm across her chest and his elbow in her throat in a vice-like lock. Even before her scream of shock, Karl recognised the man. The head was shaved and ragged stubble covered his face, but Karl couldn't fail to identify the face that surfaced in his mind a hundred times a day.

Mick McDevitt put a blade to Liz's face and said: 'There's someone I'd like you to meet.'

'Run, Seabury, and I'll gut her right here, and you'll have to live with that.'

He started walking, dragging Liz with him, towards Karl, who backed off, his mind racing. He could scream out, but would that help? The nearest people were over 200 feet away, and even if some of those big guys heard and raced this way, it wouldn't happen immediately, would it? Maybe nobody would see their bodies in the grass at this distance. Just a guy in a suit who'd cried out in distress by the grave of his loved one.

'Stop and turn around,' Mick said. The last thing Karl wanted to do was give this guy his back out here, alone, but his body disobeyed his mind. He stopped, and he turned, and braced for overwhelming pain. But none came. A hand grabbed his shirt collar and he was pushed onwards, and just inches behind was Liz's ragged breathing. The ground levelled out and they hit a path, but didn't follow it. Across, and onto a section of ground where new gravestones poked up, perfectly upright, amid mown grass.

There was an open grave. His fear rose as they moved towards it. There was nobody here. Karl realised McDevitt planned to throw their bodies into that open hole. His eyes searched the ground ahead for a weapon. He'd already decided he was going to make a move, and he even saw it in his mind, like a remembered movie scene: at the edge of the grave, he would grab Mick's hand, clamp it down hard onto his shoulder, and leap over the hole. He'd land on the other side, and Mick and Liz would be yanked into the abyss. From his sunken position, knife or no, Mick wouldn't stand a chance thereafter.

But they were one grave short of the final setting for this blockbuster when Mick pulled him up short. He felt a jerk, and a yell from Liz as she was thrown aside, then a kick to the back of his knees. He landed on his arse, and scrabbled aside, hands thrown up to deflect a blow that never came. As he turned, he saw Mick, just feet away, haul Liz's tiny frame to her feet with ease, and push her hard towards… not the open grave, but the gravestone of its neighbour. She hit it hard, head first, and collapsed onto the grass. He grabbed her hair, that other hand still holding the knife, and ground her face hard into the stone.

'Well, say hello, then,' he said, nice and calm, like a party host introducing two strangers.

Karl understood, right then. Mick had brought them to *this* grave, not the open one. To meet someone after all.

*

The car is on its roof, lying diagonally across a high kerb. It flipped twice, losing a backdoor and the boot lid, and every inch of metal is warped and buckled, like tinfoil scrunched up and then straightened out again. The front end is bent around a tree like lobster claws. The tree and the kerb did the job of compressing the interior of the car into almost nothing.

There is space, though. The passenger door is a twisted mess, the window frame down to barely a slat. But there is space. Mick presses himself up against the smashed side of the car, and a jagged shard of metal, forked, like a lightning bolt, pierces his flesh in two spots, one below and one above the collarbone.

He's already seen that the driver's side is a waste of time. The window is more accessible, but Wendy's head is smashed by the roof, which looks like an inverted mountain range, and her neck bent too far, much too far, and sharp metal has dislocated her jaw so that it is at forty-five degrees. No hope. Dead. He can only hope it happened instantly.

The hundreds of obsessive hours he spent in the gym are now regretted as his thick upper arm fills the gap.

'No, please don't!' he screams, his right arm outstretched, reaching ahead, but short, too short by inches, or miles, because either way he can't stop this.

The pain in his chest is excruciating, and blood flows. His fingers fall short still.

'Don't, don't, don't!'

His fingers continue forward.

'Please!'

Three feet away, a pair of eyes stare blankly back at him, devoid of emotion. He grabs the jacket in desperation, takes a vice-like fistful.

The bolt pushes deeper into his skin. An inch, and then another inch. The pain throbs throughout his chest like an electrical charge.

'Don't, don't, don't!' he moans.

Deeper still. The blood starts to flow, mixing with more blood on the floor. The metal between the jagged forks hits the flesh over his collarbone, and movement is checked.

'Please, Tim!'

And there is a massive jerk, all shoulder muscle, and Mick screams as the bolt pushes deeper, bending and then snapping his collarbone, and the prongs force themselves further in, and the blood gushes out of his chest and soaks his clothing.

But his fingers manage vital extra inches because the bone isn't an obstacle. They slip over ripped, slick flesh. The chest is destroyed, but surgeons can fix that. The heart is still alive. The ribcage is busted open by a great wedge of steel, but the heart is right there, untouched, and it beats still.

'Tim, I promise, okay?' he screams. 'I promise I'll save you.'

His fingers lock onto a rib. He pulls. At first, nothing. Tim is not held by a seatbelt, but his legs are crushed. There's an engine where they should be. He's jammed between the seat and the dashboard. The roof is caught on Tim's head. Compressed from all sides. The biceps contract, and something's got to lose this battle. At first, Mick is pulled closer, and the metal sinking into his chest goes deeper, but there's no more pain than before. His body's got the message – serious shit is happening to you – and there's no need for overkill.

'Come on, you fucking cunt!'

But he pulls again, and this time Tim moves. A trapped arm freed, and now there's space for the torso to shift. His head is tugged back by the roof as his body leans towards Mick, and now he's not looking at his father, but upwards, high into Heaven. Just a few inches of movement, but enough. And just in time. The heart stops beating a moment before his fingers close into a fist that rhythmically thumps the shattered sternum to keep the muscle working.

'There, Tim, there, see, Daddy keeps his promises.'

*

The newspapers had opened up Mick McDevitt's life in an attempt to find out what had turned him into a killer. The last few years had seen an almost fifty per cent rise in stress-related sickness among police officers. Job cuts, overtime bans, and complicated shift patterns, as well as an increasing belief that the public felt let down. If that could make a cop sick, or turn to suicide, then surely it could throw a guy's morals out of whack.

'Routines, that's all I've got left,' Mick said. 'I missed a lot of my son's life because I was hunting people like your fucking husband at all hours. But I always got home, and I always looked after him. If some animal like your man hadn't slaughtered an innocent person, I always tried to make him breakfast if I was there in the morning. If some fucking gangster like Grafton had me out all night, I always made Tim's bed when I came in. And if I got the call that another poor bastard had been cut down by someone like your fucking husband, I always said goodbye when I went out. Except for one night when he went out to celebrate finishing school. It's a full-time job, hunting bastards like Ronald Grafton, and I was in the files, and I didn't hear Tim leave.'

A bike crash as a lowly constable fresh into the Metropolitan Police had been mentioned in the press, too. Frontal lobe trauma could mess up a chap's head. The papers proved it with quotes ripped from medical journals and statements from a plethora of doctors.

'Last thing I said to him: "This is for you". An hour earlier, when I changed some of his loose coins for a £20 note to spend that night. "This is for you." Not "I love you". And then he's gone. And I never got the chance to say that again, did I? The one time I never said it, and it was the most important time of all. Then I get the call from my ex-wife. It's her turn with him. But she's let him go out clubbing. His friends have called her. Tim's taken a drug. A new thing on the streets, very popular. Buzz, it's called. But Tim's not having a buzz, no. He's having a bad reaction. I stand on the street. Waiting. She's bringing him home. I see their car coming down the road, fast. And then Tim… Tim has a bad, bad reaction to the drug. Attacks his mother while she's driving.'

And the car crash deaths of his ex-wife and sixteen-year-old child, the papers made a big deal of that, of course. A good way to screw up a logical head. But McDevitt had been back at work within weeks. A little antisocial, a little more reserved, sleeping less, suffering from headaches and intense muscles spasms. But otherwise unaffected, at least externally. Not like he lost a loving spouse and a baby, that was how some of his more scathing colleagues viewed it. Immune to the heartache of losing loved ones because of his job, said other, more seasoned murder detectives. And no third party was ever blamed. The police never traced the man who sold Timothy McDevitt the drug.

'I searched his room. I tore it apart, looking for more drugs, looking for a clue. But there was nothing. Tim could have got the Buzz off anyone, anytime. None of his friends had seen him buy it. I could have hit out at dealers in that club, but how would I know if I got the right one? I had no one to blame, and there was nothing I could do. Unless I burned the whole world to ashes, I could miss the bastard who sold my boy that filth.'

Staring at the ground, Mick continued. 'But I couldn't sleep at night, tormented by my thoughts. Did I turn my boy to drugs? Did I not see the signs? Was it all my fault for not being at home more, for not keeping him on the right track? Was I the only one to blame all along?'

His eyes refocussed on his prey. And he grinned.

'No, no, no, because one day Brad gave me a name, didn't he? And suddenly the cross hairs shrank. The world was safe. I had a target. Before, I was lost in a maze, but when he gave me that name, a door was opened, and I saw the way out. Just before I put a screwdriver through his brain, the dealer told me two things. He said Tim had told him he'd never taken drugs before. That was good news.'

Quick as a snake, he bent and grabbed Liz's hair again. He jabbed the knife hard into the gravestone an inch from her skin.

'He also gave up your husband. A new name. Others had been involved. Others would have to pay. Tim was in his club that night. Your bastard man was told that Tim was the son of a detective, so he thought it would be funny to overdose him and see what happened. Just for a laugh. So, he sent the dealer across to my son's friends with some freebies. Just for a laugh. And I bet he slept okay that night. Just a tragic accident, not his fault. Just for a fucking laugh. Is he laughing now?'

He twisted her head so she could look at him, but through her wild hair Karl saw that her eyes were screwed shut.

'When I saw the name of the church where you were burying your husband, it all made sense. The very same graveyard where my son is buried. Fate. All along, you wasted your time running and I wasted my time trying to kill you. It was never meant to happen. You were invincible, unlike your husband. Until now. Until Tim was watching.'

'You're insane,' Liz said, barely audible, shaking against the gravestone. 'This is why nobody ever knew you blamed Ron. All this blood, all this… It was just a tragic accident, don't you see that?'

Mick slid the blade of the knife towards her eye. And then he looked into the sky.

'See, Tim. They took your mother from you, and you from me, but I got them, didn't I? And now Daddy's about to keep his last ever promise to you.'

To his right Karl sensed more movement. His eyes flicked that way. Another man, this guy in a baseball cap and a tracksuit. Sixty feet away. Now there were four people on this planet.

Mick dropped the knife and clamped both big hands around Liz's tiny neck and lifted her. Easily. Right off the ground. In two steps he was by the open grave. Karl's eyes went to the knife, there in the grass, just six feet away, but he was frozen in place, unable to will his muscles into action.

'I'll be back for you,' Mick said as he swung her out, over the grave. And then he dropped her, and started to turn, meaning to come for Karl – meaning he would dispatch Karl first so that he could take his time with Liz.

But as she fell, her fingers grabbed his wrist. They slipped away instantly, but there had been enough friction which meant he had to try to take a step sideways to rebalance. But there was nothing to step onto. His foot came down into the abyss, and his arms sought something to grab. But there was nothing to hold onto. He toppled, like a giant oak, and landed hard the far edge of the grave. And then he vanished into the grave with her.

Karl rushed to the open grave and stared down. Liz was on her back with Mick kneeling astride her. He was taking fistfuls of soil, forcing them into her face, but he looked calm, his movements methodical. His demeanour, more than anything else, told Karl that Mick was now a human in shape only.

'Liz,' Karl shouted. That got Mick's attention, as if he'd forgotten about his other enemy. He stood and swiped at Karl, planning to haul him into the pit. But Karl backed off. Mick clambered out of the hole quickly for a big man, and in his hands was a spade. Karl turned, and found himself facing another man.

The guy in the baseball cap. He was right there, running towards them, cap now gone, snatched by the wind. No time to dart aside, so Karl threw up his arms, turned away his head, and got ready for the impact.

He felt a heavy weight brush past, and heard the thud of body hitting body. He turned in time to see the newcomer and Mick hit the ground, roll, and vanish into the grave.

And that was when his brain, delayed and confused, made the connection between the face he had seen and a man in his memory banks. A man he'd hoped never to see again.

Brad.

Two men were in the grave with her, but their focus on each other allowed her to scramble to her feet.

'You gotta help me,' she screamed: the first thing she'd ever said to him. As before, he reached, and grabbed, and pulled. He slid her torso free and she kicked like a drowning woman to get her legs clear, and then she rolled across the grass, crying.

Their chance to flee. But Karl stood tall and stared down, now no longer terrified into inaction. Mick had dropped the spade as Brad thundered into him. There it lay beside the grave. He picked it up and felt a tide turning.

In the grave, Mick was atop Brad, dropping blows hard. Mick rose to his feet and raised a leg to stomp on Brad, and finish this business.

Karl felt the spade suddenly snatched from his hand.

'Has your son returned?'

The question was spoken without anger, as if Liz genuinely wondered. And Karl saw it slashing through Mick's world of rage and cruelty like a rainbow in Hades. He turned, unable not to, his killing blow upon Brad forgotten. Liz's question, the mention of his beloved son, had caused a blip in his bloodlust. He looked up at her. And Karl got the feeling it was exactly what she'd wanted.

In days to come Karl would agree that, after all Mick had done to her, it was perhaps the only way she could find absolute peace.

Her strike landed hard on Mick's shoulder, instantly dislocating it. Mick screamed in pain. And shock.

'Has my Ron returned?' she said, louder, through gritted teeth.

Mick scrambled for the edge of the grave, but the spade fell again and smashed his hand into the dirt. He staggered back with a scream, stumbling over Brad's body. Clutching his shoulder, he stared up.

'Not in front of Tim, you fucking bitch,' he spat.

But even as he was speaking, she prepared to strike again.

'Have you changed a thing with all this blood?' she shouted as she lifted the weapon high in the air and Mick put up his bad arm to block the attack. 'Did Ron's blood bring your son back? Will your blood bring my Ron back?'

She dragged the spade downwards, slicing through the air. The blade landed flat and hard on his bald head with a heavy crack. He staggered, but his momentous willpower, or his unstoppable bloodlust, kept him standing. Blood was pouring down his face. He wiped it away, and stared at it on his hands.

'None of this is changing anything, is it?' she screamed. 'All the spilled blood, it's not enough, is it? It'll never be enough, will it?'

'You'd do this to my son?' he moaned, staring up again, his voice groggy, and loaded with genuine surprise. And fear, Karl understood. Not fear of pain, or even death, but of a son watching a father suffer.

But there was rage, too. It seemed to overcome him in an instant. With an animalistic sneer, Mick scrambled for the grave edge, trying to claw his way out.

She lifted the spade.

'Liz, stop!' Karl shouted. He tried to grab the spade, but too late.

'No matter how much blood we drown our pain in, they won't come back, will they?'

The impact was mammoth, and this time Mick dropped. Liz collapsed to her knees. Karl was kneeling behind her. Brad hauled himself out of the grave and lay panting on the grass. The moment was frozen for a second.

Then Liz uttered a cry and burst into movement. Cursing, crying, she started to sweep soil into the grave. The earth splattered across Mick, but he didn't move.

Karl lunged forward, grabbing her arms. 'Liz, stop.'

She dropped the spade and dropped to her knees. Karl knelt and held her. There was a commotion now: people appearing at the top of the hill, drawn, finally, by the noise. Some started to rush over.

Brad rose to his feet, grabbed the spade from her hands and held it tightly.

Then he turned to face the oncoming people running their way, and stood before them with the spade held like a baseball bat. The crowd quickly stopped advancing. Some backed away, even ran. But some of the bigger men pressed on. Brad stood there in a pose of defiance, ready to fight. But that was not his intention, Karl knew. He was giving the crowd a sight to behold, a lasting image. A tale to tell. Nobody had seen Liz with the spade. The police would find a dead man in the grave and learn of a lunatic who brandished a spade like a weapon, and they would have their story.

Brad let them get close enough to make damned sure nobody got the wrong idea. To make sure they saw his face. Then he dropped the spade, turned, and ran.

His departing shout back, for all to hear, was: 'I'm sorry.'

They would report that, too. A dozen witnesses would claim that the killer had shouted his regret at what he'd done. It would be considered further proof that Brad Smithfield had murdered Mick McDevitt, former cop, former friend, fellow death-dealer.

Karl's statement would say the very same thing. But it would be a lie.

Brad's words, he knew, had been for Liz.

A LETTER FROM JAKE

Dear Reader,

I want to say a huge thank you for choosing to read *The Choice*. If you did enjoy it, and want to keep up-to-date with all my latest releases, just sign up at the following link. Your email address will never be shared, and you can unsubscribe at any time.

www.bookouture.com/jake-cross

Would you stop on a dark road to help someone in trouble?

With *The Choice*, I wanted to create a high-concept thriller that had a simple but compelling premise. Thrillers work most powerfully when the reader can imagine the same thing happening to them, especially if it's because of one, spur-of-the-moment choice. A choice you know you'd make the same way if you were in Karl's position.

I wanted to create tension from simple scenes, without the need for fireworks, and I hope I achieved this. I hope you read this with a shaking hand, laughed at all the right times, and felt for Karl throughout. I hope you wondered if Liz was hiding something but always sided with her. I even hope that you felt a measure of sympathy for Mick McDevitt, enough so that you became eager for his next scene. Maybe some of you even hoped he'd win in the end.

Mostly, though, I hope you have asked yourself the question at the centre of this novel: would you stop on a dark road to help someone in distress?

If in doubt, just remember that, thankfully, creatures like Mick McDevitt are rare.

I hope you loved *The Choice* and if you did I would be very grateful if you could write a review. I'd love to hear what you think, and it makes such a difference helping new readers to discover one of my books for the first time.

I love hearing from my readers – you can get in touch on my Facebook page, through Twitter, Goodreads or my website.

Thanks,
Jake

 jakecrossauthor

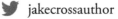 jakecrossauthor

ACKNOWLEDGEMENTS

Thanks go to the entire Bookouture team for basically being fab. Kim, for good advice. Abi, for some choices made and good counsel. Christina, for taking a couch potato of a novel into surgery and delivering the Five-and-a-half Million Dollar Man (bit too arrogant of me to call it the full 'six'). I'm sure none of the above will mind if I give a special shout out to Natalie who remembered some guy's novel she read two years before, took a chance, and made all this possible.

My partner, Jennifer, and the three little ones, who had to put up with a guy sometimes giving more attention to gangsters and crooked cops who didn't exist.

9 781786 814166